Lyn Andrews is one of
selling authors, reachin
paperback bestseller list. Born and brought up in
Liverpool, she is the daughter of a policeman who also
married a policeman. After becoming the mother of
triplets, she took some time off from her writing whilst
she raised her children. Shortlisted for the Romantic
Novelists' Association Award in 1993, she has now
written twenty-seven hugely successful novels. Lyn
Andrews divides her time between Merseyside and
Ireland.

lyn
andrews

*The Sisters
O'Donnell*

headline

First published in 1990 by Corgi Books
an imprint of Transworld Publishers

First published in paperback edition in 2008
by HEADLINE PUBLISHING GROUP

1

ISBN 978 0 7553 4184 9

Typeset in Janson by Avon DataSet Ltd,
Bidford-on-Avon, Warwickshire

Printed and bound in Great Britain by
CPI Group (UK) Ltd, Croydon, CR0 4YY

HEADLINE PUBLISHING GROUP
An Hachette Livre UK Company
338 Euston Road
London NW1 3BH

www.headline.co.uk

In memory of my Great-Grandmother
Mary O'Donnell

Part I

1922

———•❉•———

Chapter One

———◆———

WHEN GINA O'DONNELL LOST her temper, the whole street knew about it. Curtains twitched, doors were inched open and children playing noisily on the cobbles were suddenly struck dumb. Even the marmalade cat that belonged to Ma McCabe pricked up its ears and shifted its overfed carcass to the safety of the potted geraniums on the windowsill.

Gina was possessed of what her mother, Sarah, termed 'the Divil of a temper' and the subject now causing the trouble was the result of a discussion the night before. A discussion conducted in loud whispers between Gina and her two sisters, Mary-Kate and Bridget, in the bedroom they all shared in the house in Anne Street.

Anne Street was a row of twenty-four, early Victorian terraced houses, which had been well maintained, since over the years they had mainly been occupied by artisans. In fact, the girls' father, Patrick O'Donnell, had been a Master Carpenter, like his father before him and, following tradition, both his sons Fergal and Matthew –

3

known to everyone as Matty – had also been apprenticed to that trade.

Collectively the girls were known throughout the small, country town of Clonmel in County Tipperary as 'The Sisters O'Donnell' – a sobriquet bestowed on them by the nuns in the convent school because of their close resemblance to each other. They all had red hair which varied from Mary-Kate's light copper to Gina's fiery Titian and Bridget's dark auburn. They all had hazel eyes and clear, pale complexions. There were some similarities in their characters, too, but not many. The only trait they did all possess was the O'Donnell temper, and even that varied in degrees of volatility, as last night's disagreement had demonstrated.

They were all unanimous in their decision to leave Ireland, but the bone of contention between them was just when they should impart this news to the rest of the family. The night before, Gina had been sitting on the bed vigorously brushing the thick, wavy hair that framed her oval face with its high cheekbones and pointed chin, while Bridget had been neatly folding the navy skirt and white blouse, ready to be worn the following day for work.

At the end of the obligatory one hundred strokes Gina had flung down the hairbrush. 'Will you stop fussing with those clothes and sit down. I want to talk to you!'

'I'm not fussing! I always fold them. You know I like to look my best and Mrs O'Leary is always saying she's never had an assistant who is so neat and tidy and that it reflects, favourably, on the business.' But Bridget had given the skirt a final pat and sat down at the foot of her own bed, tucking her feet under her. She had worked in

O'Leary's Haberdashers on the Main Guard ever since she had left school. 'What do you want to talk about?'

'You know what! Us leaving here. Hasn't it been the most important thing we've had to think about for weeks?' Gina had stared at her sister impatiently, wondering if it had been wise to include her at all. After all, Bridget was not quite twenty, whereas she, at twenty-one, thought of herself as far more 'worldly wise' and Mary-Kate was twenty-two, although that wasn't necessarily an asset. In her opinion Mary-Kate was getting rather staid.

'Hadn't we better wait for Mary-Kate?'

'If we wait for her we might well be up until midnight! I don't know what's got into her lately, she's getting so finicky about stupid household chores.'

'That's not fair, Gina, you know she sees to them so Ma can go to bed earlier and not worry if the kitchen fire has been damped down or the table set for breakfast . . .'

'The way she's carrying on I don't think she really wants to leave at all.'

'She does! When we all decided to go she was just as enthusiastic as you.'

'Will you keep your voice down or everyone will hear you!'

Gina had risen and walked to the window that overlooked the small yard at the back of the house, the view obscured by the cotton lace curtain. 'I think we should tell Ma tomorrow. After all, we've decided to leave so let's get it over with!'

'I thought we'd agreed to wait until the weekend?'

Gina had turned abruptly and frowned. 'What's the matter with you? Have you changed your mind now?'

'No, I haven't! Sure, I'll be sorry to leave Ma and

Matty and even Mrs O'Leary, but I'm not staying here on my own, not the way things are going.'

They had both fallen silent, as Gina stared moodily out of the window seeing nothing, her thoughts elsewhere, and Bridget smoothed out and folded the stockings she would wear next day. She wasn't staying in Clonmel now that Civil War was staring them in the face. She was desperately afraid and both her sisters knew it. Mary-Kate had remarked in her usual, quiet way that anyone who wasn't afraid of the future was a fool.

The last four years had been terrifying and had left their mark on everyone and Bridget couldn't face any more, yet the ties of home and family were strong. She loved her Ma and she was afraid for Matty's safety. She didn't have either Gina's consuming ambition to move on from her job as a Nurses' Aid at the Cottage Hospital, or Mary-Kate's calm, practicality. She was so terrified of the future that when Gina had first suggested they all leave, she had jumped at the chance. And yet, in the rare moments when she could put aside her fears, she realized that she did have her own dreams, her own ambitions.

Bridget had worked for Mrs O'Leary for years, but sometimes she wished she could work in a much bigger shop, one like Cleary's department store in Dublin. She was nearly twenty and had never been in love and all things considered, she reasoned that life was beginning to pass her by. Sitting on the bed, twisting a strand of hair around her finger, she came to the conclusion that perhaps what had just been romantic daydreams, could in fact become reality.

Gina knew exactly what she wanted from life and she intended to get it, by fair means or foul. Of course she loved her Ma, but it had been her Pa who had always held first place in her heart. When he had been killed something had gone out of her life forever. Her eyes had misted as she had thought of him. She'd always been his 'little Gina' his 'wild Irish rose' and he'd have moved heaven and earth for her if she'd asked him to. She firmly believed that he was watching over her from that heaven he was surely in and she had vowed she would make his 'little Gina' someone he would have been proud of. She'd made that vow the day he had been buried and her 'wilfullness' as her Ma called it, had increased since that day.

'Have you been waiting up for me? I was just tidying up.'

Both their thoughts had been interrupted by the appearance of their elder sister.

'I thought you'd decided to stay down there all night!' Gina had muttered, irritably. Whenever she thought about her Pa it always made her miserable and snappy.

Mary-Kate had ignored her and had begun to unpin the coil of light copper hair. 'Gina, draw those curtains. With the lamps lit everyone can see in and it's indecent.'

Gina had jerked the curtains closed, shutting out the last remnants of the April night and the room had been bathed in the mellow light of the two oil lamps.

'Gina wants to tell Ma about us leaving tomorrow.'

Mary-Kate's eyebrows had risen but that had been the only sign of surprise she had displayed. 'Why?'

'Because I think the sooner we tell her the better. Things are going to get worse very soon and I've had enough.'

'Don't you think we all have, especially Ma?'

'You sound just like Bridget. Are you changing your mind, too?'

'Has Bridget?' Mary-Kate asked with a frown.

'No, I haven't! It's just that . . . that I don't like to think of Ma being on her own.'

'She won't be, eejit! She'll have Matty and all her friends.'

'You know what I mean, Gina!'

Mary-Kate had removed her blouse and poured the hot water from the jug she had brought up with her into the china wash bowl. She washed her face and hands, then stared at her reflection in the mirror on the wall as she patted her cheeks dry. She knew exactly what Bridget meant. Since her Pa's death she had drawn even closer to her mother in a way that Gina or Bridget could never fully understand. Maybe it was because she was the eldest daughter. But the face staring back at her had reminded her that that fact was her sole reason for leaving. She was twenty-two and unmarried. Not that there was anything odd in that, she had often told herself resolutely. The men she considered 'eligible' couldn't afford to marry until they were in their middle or late twenties. But all those she had considered were now dead or had fled to America or Australia. The four bloody years of 'The Troubles' had left her with the legacy she feared most: that she would become an Old Maid, destined to look after her mother in old age, and a spinster aunt to her sisters' children. Always available, always dependable, her own wishes and needs ignored.

She was still attractive and her work in the little office at Hearn's Hotel she found not uninteresting, but she wasn't going to suffer the humiliation of those pitying glances, the gossiping and speculation of the married women. Her reason for leaving Ireland was to find a husband and so avoid the fate she dreaded, but was too proud to admit to.

Her eyes had softened. She wanted the love of a good man, she wanted children of her own. Was that too much to ask? She wasn't so old that all the emotions that lay deep in her heart had dried up. Oh, she knew that already some of the girls her sisters were friendly with thought her dull and prim, but she wasn't, not really, not in her heart!

'This time I agree with Gina,' Mary-Kate had said. 'The sooner it's all out in the open the better it will be for Ma. It will give her time to get used to the idea, to try to accept it, even though it will be a shock.' Her love for her mother had made her feel terribly guilty about keeping anything secret from her and there had been times when she had been tempted to confide in Sarah. Only her promise of silence to her sisters had stilled her tongue. Mary-Kate never broke a promise.

'I don't think it's fair at all! It would be better for her if we waited and then told her just the day before, that way she won't have time to brood and worry,' said Bridget.

'I've had my doubts all along about our decision. It's cruel however we tell Ma!' Mary-Kate said.

'Well, there just isn't a "fair" way to do it, so let's get it over and done with!' Gina had begun to wish she had never started this discussion. Why did they have to argue over it? It was typical. It had been her idea and now she wished she hadn't even mentioned it to them in the first place.

As always, Gina was running true to form, Mary-Kate had thought. She was interested only in herself and her own little world. But on this occasion she had to agree with her. 'Then we'll tell her tomorrow, but we'll tell her calmly, Gina. No hysterics or tantrums!'

'Oh, don't be so sanctimonious! Is it my fault I lose my temper more quickly than you two? I can't help it. If everyone were not so perverse then I wouldn't lose it so often!'

'You could learn to control it more. One day it will be the death of you!'

Gina had ignored Mary-Kate's remarks. 'Now that's settled, I'm going to sleep,' she had announced. Mary-Kate had a temper, too, she had thought, although she was more in control of herself these days, but probably that's what came of being older. Even though wild horses wouldn't drag an admission from her, Gina knew her sister was mortally afraid of being 'left on the shelf'. She, herself, viewed the prospect of marriage to any of the young men in Clonmel with abhorrence, but then she had her ambition to sustain her. Mary-Kate was totally uninspired in that respect.

Gina had pulled the quilt up to her chin and closed her eyes, prayers forgotten, to dream of herself as the toast of the musical stage across the Atlantic in America. It was the land of opportunity for those like herself, who were strong and determined enough to take fate in their hands and twist and shape it until they had achieved their goal.

Bridget had lain on her side, staring at a dim shaft of moonlight that had penetrated the crack left between the drawn curtains. She was dreading the look of pain that she knew would haunt her mother's face, yet she felt the cold fingers of fear reach out and touch her heart. She couldn't stay, she just couldn't! She began to say her prayers, counting the decade of the Rosary on her fingers beneath the bedclothes, for she had forgotten where she had left her beads. But between the 'Hail Mary's' her thoughts had begun to stray. They all had to think of themselves now. Once away from all this fear and violence she could concentrate her efforts on following her dreams. She could get a better job and then she was sure she would meet a man who would sweep her off her feet, just as the heroes did in the novels she liked to read.

Only Mary-Kate had taken the trouble to kneel at the side of the bed to pray, the linoleum cold and hard beneath her knees. She had prayed that she was doing the right thing, that her mother would understand and that she wouldn't be too hurt or upset. She had begged forgiveness for the pride that had driven her to this decision, the pride and dignity that the title 'Mrs' would give her. But was it really pride? Wasn't it what God intended women to be – wives and mothers? It was too late to go back, she'd made up her mind and tomorrow . . . well, tomorrow would come soon enough.

So next day, when they were all in the kitchen that served as a dining room as well, and supper was over, Gina had announced their intention to leave Ireland.

Her statement was received first with a shocked silence, then with an outburst of demands and recriminations by Sarah followed by Matty, and despite all Mary-Kate's prior instructions, Gina lost her temper. Her voice

– the shrillness and stridency of which made even the whistle of the train in Prior Park Station pale into insignificance – reverberated along Anne Street.

'I've made up my mind and that's that! I'm going! I don't care what either of you say, I've had enough and nothing will stop me, Ma.'

Mary-Kate slammed down the sash window so hard that the dishes on the dresser rattled. 'Calm down, Gina! You promised there'd be no tantrums. Do you want to be heard all the way down to the Quays?'

'Yes! I don't care if the whole town hears me. I'm sick to death of this place, of this whole country!' she screamed back.

Bridget sat watching them with rising annoyance. Oh, why did Gina always have to explode? 'I thought we were going to discuss this quietly, now with you two yelling at each other it's getting like the Battle of the Widow MacCormack's Cabbage Patch!'

Matty who had been reading the *Clonmel Chronical* flung it down on the table to signify his increasing annoyance.

Sarah stood with her arms folded over her ample bosom. With a mother's intuition she had suspected that something was going on, but she was hurt and angry that they had not discussed it with her instead of just 'announcing' it. From long experience, she also knew that Gina was working herself up into one of her tantrums and she was in no mood to try and humour her out of it, as she could sometimes do. She picked up a large, enamelled jug from the shelf alongside the brown, earthenware sink. It was the only way. Gina wasn't a child who could be dragged screaming and kicking into the yard to have her head held firmly under the cold water pump, but a dousing with cold water was the only effective way of dealing with Gina's temper.

She blamed herself, of course. It was a penance for her 'Sin of Pride' in calling her middle daughter Regina Margaret. Oh, she'd thought it a fine, grand name then, even though Father Maguire had doubted the 'propriety' of it. Sure, wasn't 'Regina Coeli' one of the titles given the Blessed Virgin in the Litany, she had retaliated? Translated from the Latin it meant 'Queen of Heaven' and while to have added the 'coeli' would have been sheer blasphemy, she had stuck to her guns over Regina. And how she'd paid for it. Regina Margaret O'Donnell had turned out to be a holy terror and no mistake!

At the sight of the jug, Mary-Kate, Bridget and even Matty, all edged as far away from their sister as possible.

Gina's eyes narrowed but she held her ground. 'You come near me with that jug, Ma, and I'll go now, this very minute. I swear to heaven I will. I'll walk out of that door and I won't come back – ever!'

'And a fine cut you'd look walking down the street dripping wet,' Matty muttered, sotto voce.

'Then hold your tongue, Miss! Hasn't there been enough arguing and fighting already? And your poor Pa – God rest him – and then our Fergal taken from us only six months ago. It's a short memory you have.'

Gina threw her hands in the air. 'Isn't that what I've been trying to tell you, Ma? I've had enough of the fighting, the killing, the curfews and the raids. And now, when we've got rid of the Black and Tans and the Army, when we've finally got the "Home Rule" that Pa and Fergal died for, don't we just start fighting one another!

I've had enough of Ireland, I'm going to America and I'm going to be "Someone"!'

Matty rose. Now, with both Pa and Fergal gone, he was head of the household. 'The three of you will all stop yelling and we'll sit down and discuss this. Now, sit down!'

Mary-Kate pulled out one of the chairs set around the still cluttered table and sat with resignation. Bridget, already sitting, cast her gaze first towards her mother and then Gina. Gina remained standing, her manner openly mutinous.

'I said sit down!' For a moment Matty thought she was going to defy him and he wondered just what he would do if she did. Then she yanked the chair out, its legs scraping on the floor. She finally sat with a very bad grace, tossing her hair back defiantly as she always did when thwarted.

'You, too, Ma. We'll discuss this as a family should.'

'Some family!' Gina muttered. Families were supposed to support one another, to stick together. But all the families she knew spent most of their time fighting and feuding, and recently theirs had been no exception.

Sarah looked around at what had once been a united, happy family and wondered sadly what had gone so terribly wrong. Then she sighed. What had gone wrong was 'The Troubles'. They'd had a good life before that. She and Pat had been respected citizens of Clonmel. They'd never been short of money. True, they'd never had money for real luxuries, not with five children to bring up. But she'd always managed to save some small amount each year. Now she was glad she'd been so frugal and prudent. With both Pat and Fergal dead she would need that money.

She could never think about Pat without an ache in her heart. He'd never been involved in any trouble, he went out of his way to avoid it. Going 'out of his way' he'd been caught in the crossfire between the 'Tans' and the Tipperary Brigade on the night the Boys had stormed the Barracks. The grief of that tragedy had turned Fergal to vengeful anger and nothing she had done or said had stopped him from joining a Flying Column. He'd only lasted six months before he'd been killed in an ambush and she'd seen him laid beside his Pa. A pain tore at her heart. Oh, the waste! There was no sense in violence and still it wasn't over! The worst kind of war loomed ahead. Already father and son were at each others throats. She certainly didn't blame Gina for wanting to leave Ireland.

Matty interrupted her thoughts. 'So, you want to go to America?'

'Yes!'

'What for, apart from running from what looks like an inevitable Civil War, and for that I don't blame you?'

'What is there for us here? Who knows how long all this trouble will go on? I want a chance to make something of my life.' Gina was trying desperately to keep calm.

'And I do, too, Ma! I like working for Mrs O'Leary but I'm never going to manage the shop or have one of my own and I don't want to end up marrying some cottier, have a dozen children and look fifty when I'm twenty-eight!'

'It was good enough for me, Miss!'

'Oh, things were different then, Ma, and besides Pa

had a good trade. Women don't have to . . .' Bridget's forehead puckered into a frown as she searched for the right word . . . 'conform! That's it, conform! Women have careers now!'

'Not in Ireland they don't.' Gina stated caustically. 'This country is about fifty years behind everyone else! When I wanted my hair cut in that new "bob" didn't Celia Delaney come rushing up here to tell you and then didn't you absolutely forbid me to have it cut? And that's just for a beginning. I want to be stylish, I want to be "in vogue".' She'd read that in a magazine but didn't really know what it meant.

Sarah sighed again. Pat would have known what to have done. He had always known how to deal with Gina. But Pat was lying in St Mary's churchyard, and so she looked for guidance from Matty.

'So you all want to go, do you?' Matty asked. 'You've all made up your minds?'

All three nodded.

'And what will you two do? We all know what Gina wants, as well as being "in vogue", whatever that means!'

'Aye, riding to Hell on the Divil's back as fast as she can!'

'Ma, it's not that bad!' Matty interrupted. 'She's got a good voice and not everyone can be utterly depraved and . . .'

'Oh, I know she's got the voice. The clearest soprano in the whole of this county since she was twelve. Didn't the Archbishop of Waterford and Lismore himself say that when she sang "Veni Sancte Spiritus" at the Confirmation Service?'

'And I sang at that soiree Mrs Butler-Power had and

at the "Musicale Interlude" at Kilsheelan Castle! Count de la Poer especially asked Father Maguire for me, you know he did! And how many Saturday mornings have I had off work to sing at weddings? So many that even Matron has said I should make a career of it!'

Matty continued undeterred. 'And how do you two intend to support yourselves, because you'll have to, there's no money to spare here?'

Bridget was undaunted. 'We'll find work. There'll be bigger shops, bigger hotels, bigger hospitals.'

'I'm not working in any hospital,' Gina cried. 'I've had enough of hospitals to last me a lifetime. I'm going into the Theatre and I'm going to be a success!'

'And what about you, Mary-Kate? I thought you liked working at Hearn's, and you're well thought of there.' With an effort Sarah stopped herself from showing the pain of losing her eldest daughter whom she had thought of as being more 'settled' and a comfort to her in the dark days ahead.

'I've had enough of being at everyone's beck and call and they pay me buttons, you know that, Ma. I can get a better job and send money home.' Mary-Kate refused to meet her mother's eyes but her reply was quietly emphatic.

Sarah was no fool and she knew her daughter inside out. She had watched Mary-Kate's cheeks flush and her eyes become hard whenever people spoke of Kitty Cassidy. Poor Kitty who hadn't even gone 'walking out' with a young man, through no fault of her own. Someone had to look after her old, widowed mother and Kitty was to be admired for devoting her life to that task, everyone said so. But whenever Kitty's name was mentioned she had seen the change in her daughter's attitude. Mary-Kate had her pride and if she wanted a husband so badly that she was prepared to cross the ocean to fulfil that desire, she wouldn't stand in her way no matter how much it would hurt to lose her. No one would accuse her of keeping Mary-Kate at home like the Widow Cassidy had kept poor Kitty.

Matty faced Gina again. 'And what about Michael Feehey? I thought you two had an understanding?'

She laughed derisively. 'Michael Feehey! Michael Feehey and me!'

'You weren't scorning him a month ago, were you?' Sarah interrupted. 'Then it was "Michael this and Michael that"!'

'I've never given him any encouragement,' Gina snapped. 'And I've no intention of ending up the wife of a butcher.'

'There's half a dozen girls in Clonmel who would be only too delighted to be serving alongside such a husband! Isn't Feehey's the biggest and best butchers in the town and haven't they their own house – bought and paid for?'

'And they're welcome to it.' Gina glowered. She'd had what she had thought of as a brief flirtation with the only son of the town's most prosperous butcher, but she had dismissed him after a while, feeling he was dull and predictable, like every other young man she knew.

'Well, you're not going to America and that's final!' Matty announced firmly.

At this statement Gina erupted again, jumping to her feet and knocking her chair over. 'I'm twenty-one, Matty O'Donnell, just three years younger than you, and I'll not have you telling me where I can and where I can't go!' she yelled.

'Sit down and use your brain, if you have one, which I doubt!' he yelled back, also rising to his feet.

Sarah got up and reached for her coat. 'I've had enough of this altogether! There's nothing else for it, I'm going for Father Maguire.'

At the mention of the parish priest's name and the look of grim determination on their mother's face, both Gina and Matty fell silent.

It was Mary-Kate who reached out and pulled at the sleeve of Gina's blouse, willing her to sit down. When the presence of the parish priest was required at a house things must be desperate indeed and the whole street would know all about it in a few minutes. The rest of the town would find out before the night was out. 'Is it a spectacle you want to make of us all!' she hissed.

With her lips tightly compressed but her eyes still snapping fire, Gina slowly picked up her chair and sat down. When she set her heart and mind on something she could be immovable and she was determined to find fame and fortune.

Matron's remarks, uttered with sarcasm, had sown the seeds in her mind. The 'Musicale Interlude' at Kilsheelan Castle had nurtured them. She'd been terrified that night, though she would never admit it, for everyone of importance in the South Riding of Tipperary had been there, right up to the Lord Provost of the County. But she'd managed to appear calm and even a little vivacious and her rendering of 'The Last Rose of Summer' and 'My Wild Irish Rose', her special favourite as it always reminded her of her Pa, had been well received. Both the

Count himself and the Lord Provost had complimented her on her voice and composure.

It had been on the way home – driven in the Count's own motor car to the very door – that she had felt the first real stirrings of ambition. If she could impress them, she could surely captivate an audience of lesser mortals? That thought had had a powerful effect on her. She had leaned back against the real leather upholstery and closed her eyes. Why shouldn't she try? Why shouldn't she live like them? Why shouldn't she have a motor car? It was an intoxicating revelation. It had been then that the seed had really borne fruit and nothing was going to stop her – ever!

'Matty, please?' Bridget murmured, a hand on his arm.

Matty resumed his seat.

Sarah hung the coat back on its peg behind the door.

The room fell silent, the only noise the low hissing of the peat fire in the hearth.

Bridget broke the silence. 'And why not America?'

'Because it's too far away and we don't know anyone there. No one at all! If I were coming with you, that would be different, but three young girls alone . . . you have to go to someone we can trust.'

'Holy Mother of God, would you listen to him! Isn't he just the pompous one. It's *nineteen* twenty-two, not *eighteen* twenty-two, Matty O'Donnell!'

Matty ignored Gina's outburst. 'You can go to Liverpool.'

'Liverpool!' they all chorused scornfully.

Suddenly Sarah smiled. Oh, Matty was a smart one. Liverpool was not too far away should disaster befall them, despite Gina's optimism, and of course Maura and Bart would have them. Who better to keep her eye on them than her own sister and her husband, even though she and Maura had never been close.

'Your Aunt Maura will have you and there's plenty of work there,' Matty continued.

No one spoke, they were all trying to digest this statement.

Finally Bridget spoke. 'Isn't she the one that came over for Patsy Ryan's wedding?'

Matty nodded.

'And a great lump of an idle piece she looked, too!'

'That's enough of that, Bridget O'Donnell! A fine way to talk about family. Downright disrespectful it is. She's a fine woman.'

'So, it's agreed then?' Matty queried.

One by one they nodded. Gina was the last, the movement of her head just perceptible. She wasn't stupid. If she continued to harp on about going to America she might never get out of Ireland at all, and wasn't it from Liverpool that all the ships sailed to New York? Liverpool would suit her – to start with.

Bridget began to clear the dishes from the table. She stacked the plates in the sink, smiling. She'd find a job in one of the big stores and then maybe she'd settle down, if the right man came along.

Sarah squared her shoulders resolutely. 'I'll write to your Aunt Maura now and then the matter will be settled altogether. Not that I want you to go and I'm hurt and angry that you have just sprung this on me, but we won't be going into all that now. I'll miss you, all of you, but maybe you're well out of it.'

Mary-Kate reached out and took her mother's hand. 'Ma, we won't give you any cause to worry and if things get very bad here, well . . . you could come over to us.'

Gina smiled, magnanimous now she had achieved some measure of success. 'Oh, Ma, don't you think we'll miss you, too? We'll write every week and one day . . .' she looked over Sarah's head, seeing before her in a dazzling future the realization of all her dreams '. . . one day I'll come back and you'll be so proud of me because everyone will have heard of me! I'll be rich and famous. I'll buy you a grand house and . . .'

'Aye, and pigs might fly!' Matty interrupted. She wasn't the first and she certainly wouldn't be the last to leave Ireland thinking she could conquer the world with a pretty face, a bewitching smile and a clear soprano voice.

Chapter Two

THE LETTER WAS DULY written and sent and everyone awaited the reply with varying degrees of apprehension. It came a week later. Sure, Maura would love to have them, that she would. From what she remembered they were nicely-mannered, quiet girls and would Sarah just let her know when she should expect them? The bit about them being 'quiet' caused a somewhat caustic remark from Matty, which had almost resulted in another row.

With Pat and Fergal dead and the girls going away, Sarah had decided to move back to her old home. Both her parents were long dead and her bachelor brother, Richard, was finding it more and more difficult to keep the small farm going. He would find Matty's help a blessing and Matty was quite happy to go. In the long term, Sarah thought, it would ensure that the land stayed in the family and the house, too. In the short term, it might just keep Matty out of trouble with the warring factions until the new Irish Free State had sorted itself out. She had sacrificed her husband and one son, she wasn't about to lose another if she could help it!

Bridget was arranging strips of narrow satin ribbon of different colours that were rolled on stiff reels made of heavy card. She had spread the ends of them in a fan shape on the top of the glass showcase which stood in front of the shelves holding the bolts of cotton prints, striped ticking, calico, woollen tweeds and chintz.

'You've a good eye for colour, Bridget. That's very effective, one colour to match or contrast with each roll of cloth; very imaginative. Ah, it's sorry I am to be losing you.'

Bridget looked up. She liked her employer. Mrs O'Leary could be very brisk and business-like when the need arose, but she was pleasant and knew all her customers by name and noted all their purchases in a series of notebooks for reference.

'I'll be sorry to go,' Bridget answered, with real regret in her voice. 'You've been very good to me and taught me so much.'

'Heaven alone knows where I'm going to get someone I can trust and who has some taste and can be tactful with the most perverse of customers.'

Bridget began to feel uneasy and guilty. Mrs O'Leary would have to train someone else if she wanted to take time off from the business, as she frequently did these days. 'It's not that I'm dissatisfied, nothing like that at all!' she tried to explain.

'Oh, I can understand, Bridget. I hear they have some very elegant shops in Liverpool and it's only natural that you want to get ahead. I was like that myself at your age.

When I first came here this place was like an undertaker's parlour! Everything was drab and dowdy and shoddy, and you know I won't have shoddy goods in my shop! So don't you be feeling guilty now, even though I'll have to scour the whole county for a decent girl . . .'

Her words only made Bridget feel worse. 'The real reason why I'm going, Mrs O'Leary, is that . . . that I'm afraid. We lost Pa and then Fergal and I couldn't stand it if Matty were killed too.' She rearranged a piece of ribbon. 'And when I hear the sound of a cart rattling over the cobbles at night or a horse being galloped along the street, I start shaking all over and I can't stop! I keep remembering the raids and the Crossley tenders rumbling through the night while we sat and waited. And it will be worse this time, unless the Republicans give up, and they won't, Matty says. So I suppose I'm trying to run away from my fear.'

Mrs O'Leary frowned. She held the views of many of her generation. They had suffered enough over the last years, and now that the Irish Free State had come into being she thought the die-hards should be content and lay down their arms. What everyone wanted now was to live in peace. There had been too many men killed already without neighbour killing neighbour. She understood how the girl felt; they would all bear the hidden scars for years to come. She patted Bridget's hand.

'Don't you go worrying over it now, and as a farewell gift you can choose anything you like from the stock – within reason of course!'

Bridget bit her lip. If only things were different, she would stay on, she really would. Oh, how she longed for the days of her childhood when there had been peace. When Pa had taken them down to the banks of the Suir on summer evenings and they had watched the fish rising in the slow-moving water. He would point out the dragonflies skimming the surface, the rays of the setting sun turning their wings emerald green and vivid blue. It had been years since they had wandered along the tow path beside the river, where once the heavy horses had pulled the barges from Clonmel to Carrick-on-Suir. Now it was a dangerous place, you never knew who was lurking in the tall pines on the Gurteen bank or in the overgrown churchyard of the ruins of Saint Sillan's church beside the river at Kilsheelan.

The shop bell tinkled and Bridget looked up, pushing away the memories and smiling automatically.

'Don't forget what I said now, Bridget, anything within reason! Isn't it grand for the time of year, Mrs Butler-Power? Bridget will be only too pleased to serve you, I have to nip out for half an hour. A bit of business you understand.'

Mrs Butler-Power smiled frostily at Bridget. A bit of business was it? It didn't fool her, more like afternoon tea with Joseph Ryan, the solicitor, and him a widower of only three months. The whole town was talking about it. 'I hear you're leaving us, Bridget?' she asked, curiously.

'Yes, ma'am, I'm going to Liverpool with my sisters.'

The woman gave her a more genuine smile. That would put paid to Mrs O'Leary's little 'bits of business'. 'Good luck to you, dear, there's not much here for ambitious young things. Now, what was it I wanted? I've a head like a sieve lately.'

*

After Mass the following week they all stood on the steps of St Mary's, Irishtown, the district just beyond the west gate of the old town walls.

It had been a hectic week. Everything was packed up at the house in Anne Street, indeed some of the furniture had already gone to the farmhouse outside the village of Kilsheelan, just a few miles up the road from Clonmel. The girls were to travel to Dublin the following day by train and from there board the ferry to Liverpool.

It was a beautiful April day. The sort of mild spring day that makes everything look fresh and newly washed. There were a few cirrus clouds scattered high in the pale blue sky and shafts of sunlight picked out the golden clumps of daffodils dotted around the churchyard.

They all wore their best clothes and all three knew they were the object of many admiring and speculative glances. By choosing their outfits with care and by using the odd piece of ribbon here, the carefully placed brooch there, they always managed to achieve a slightly more stylish appearance than even Mrs Butler-Power, who had: 'a crock of gold and no more dress sense than a Dublin kitchen maid', as Bridget described her.

Gina wore a heather-coloured suit, the jacket of which reached below her slender hips. The straight skirt ended six inches above her ankles, showing the one pair of greatly treasured silk stockings she owned and black shoes with hour-glass heels and a strap over the instep. Her hair was tucked up under a toque hat of soft velour, to the front of which she had pinned a small bunch of artificial violets, purchased at Mrs O'Leary's. The shade of the hat almost matched the suit. Almost, but not quite, and the fact irritated her. Then she shrugged. Who would even notice anyway?

Bridget's coat had been a plainly cut, russet wool until she had painstakingly edged the collar, cuffs and pockets with some black velvet ribbon she'd bought cost price from work. The cream blouse, the carefully ironed flounces of which frothed at her throat, made her skin appear flawlessly pale. She wore a large-brimmed, black felt hat, adorned with the tail feathers of a cock pheasant, begged from Mr Feehey the elder.

As Mary-Kate's hair was a paler shade than her sisters, blue was one of her favourite colours. Her coat-dress, bought especially for Patsy Ryan's wedding, had been refurbished by covering the lapels and cuffs with some black, crushed velvet, unpicked from an old and very outdated dress of Sarah's. She wore a matching blue hat, one side of which had been pinned up with her mother's jet mourning brooch, and she was very pleased with the whole effect. It made her look younger and quite elegant, so Gina had assured her.

As the church emptied, people stood in the warm sunshine in small groups, chatting. Some of the younger men and a few of the the older ones, too, were already sloping off in the direction of the nearest bar. Their retreat duly noted by the sharp eyes of Father Maguire as he stood bidding 'Good day and the Lord go with you!' to his parishioners. As the O'Donnell family stood on the top step of the portico, the priest turned to them and tutted.

'So, Clonmel is losing the three of you and tomorrow, too?'

'Father, I've made a dozen novenas but nothing will keep them here!'

'Maybe it's for the best, Sarah. We live in troubled times, God help us.'

'We're moving back to Kilsheelan, Father, did I tell you?'

'Aye, you did that. A good move, Sarah. Sensible. Altogether sensible.' He inclined his head in Matty's direction. 'So you'll be under the pastoral care of Father Hyland at St Mary's, then, but I'll expect you back here, every now and then.'

The three girls had begun to walk slowly down the steps. To their right a group of young men stood talking. Gina glanced at them from beneath her lashes to see what effect their presence and the news of their departure was having.

'So, you're off to Liverpool to make your fortunes, then?' one called.

'And what's it to do with you, at all, Michael Feehey?' Gina tried to sound cold. It only made the group smile.

'Nothing! Nothing at all! I suppose you'll be back to visit us when you're rich and famous?'

There was no missing the note of sarcasm in his voice. Once, when she had tried to impress him, in what she now termed a 'fit of sheer stupidity', she had told him of her ambitions. Now he was openly making fun of her.

'And when you're famous, I expect we'll all have to pay to even talk to you?' Dinny Magee had a shock of unruly, carroty hair and a laugh like the braying of a disgruntled donkey. 'And I suppose you're takin' the other two to be your Lady's Maids?' He laughed. It was infectious. The whole group was openly smirking. Some of the lingering congregation turned towards them and Father Maguire frowned. He'd have no rows outside his church and them all a bare five minutes out of Mass!

Gina's temper began to rise. She straightened her shoulders and drew herself up into what she hoped was a dignified posture and glared at them all.

Before she had time to deliver a cutting reply, Michael laughed. 'Gather round and listen now! The Sisters O'Donnell are leaving Clonmel, isn't that a grand thing altogether? And isn't it a fine Music Hall act they'll make? Ladies and Gentlemen, we present, for your entertainment, "The Sisters O'Donnell!" ' And with the flourish of a handkerchief, he swept them an exaggerated bow. The older men stiffened. Blood feuds had started with less provocation than this.

Gina was shaking so hard she had to fight to stop herself storming down the steps and slapping the smirk off that mocking, impudent face, right there and then in front of everyone, Father Maguire included. She caught a movement from the corner of her eye as Matty moved down the steps towards the group, but it was Mary-Kate who stepped in front of her. Mary-Kate whose eyes flashed as dangerously as her own.

'Well, since you've taken it on yourself to tell the whole neighbourhood, Michael Feehey, yes we are leaving and it's because we don't want to end up married to the likes of eejits like you that we are going!'

A cutting laugh rang out behind her. 'Marry him! I'd sooner live in a bohreen with the pigs he sells than marry the likes of him!'

Gina's derision had its effect. Michael's laughter faded and he stood glaring at her. As she was still on the steps and therefore in a more elevated position than him and most of the others, she turned her head slowly, her gaze sweeping over them all.

'The "Sisters O'Donnell" *are* leaving and we *will* be back and we *will* be rich or famous or even both, so we'll be saying our Goodbyes now, and there won't be any need for you all to traipse over to Prior Park Station in the morning!' And with that she walked down the remaining steps with Bridget on her right and Mary-Kate on her left.

The little groups parted to let them through while Sarah followed, nodding her acquaintance to those in the crowd.

Once out of earshot Bridget gave an irritated little snort. 'You've done it now, all right! We can't come back even if we wanted to.'

Gina patted her hat purposefully. 'Oh, I'll come back and just as I promised. Rich and famous and Michael Feehey will eat his words!'

It cost five shillings for a private cabin or 'berth' on the overnight ferry from Dublin to Liverpool. A fact that caused an instant disagreement. A disagreement instigated by Gina who had, as Mary-Kate declared witheringly, got more and more 'above herself' ever since they'd left Clonmel.

They were queuing to buy their tickets in the large shed that served as an office, in company with what looked like half the population of Dublin, as Bridget tersely put it.

'That train journey was desperate! I'm tired, hungry and I must look a fright. At least if we have a cabin we'll get a decent night's sleep and we can have a good wash.'

'Ever since we left you've done nothing but moan and complain. We're not going First Class and we're not wasting five whole shillings on a cabin when we'll be quite comfortable in the Saloon,' Bridget snapped. They were *all* tired and hungry.

'Comfortable! Comfortable, with this lot and with half the men on board drinking the bar dry and probably fighting! You call that "comfort", and what's more, if it's rough, everyone will be sick!'

'We agreed, Gina. It was good of Ma to give us twenty-five shillings, you know she can't afford it, and five shillings for a cabin is just a pure waste, besides being daylight robbery. We haven't got money to burn. We can just about pay for seats in the Saloon out of our own money, and keep Ma's for later.' Mary-Kate's common sense was usually the deciding factor when such arguments sprang up. So they paid the standard fare and struggled with their bags up the gangway of the *Connaught*.

The Saloon comprised of a room that covered most of the space between the deck and the cargo hold. It was furnished with wooden, bench-type seats, set in double rows with passageways between them, but around the sides the seating was a little more comfortable, due to the superstructure forming a back to the benches. However, there was nothing remotely luxurious about the Saloon and little thought had been given to the comfort of passengers paying Steerage fare.

It was already filling up, but with her characteristic single-mindedness, Gina headed straight for a corner that was still empty. Ignoring all the curses and comments as she shoved her way through the crowd, she plumped herself down on the seat, dumping her valise at her feet. The other two sat either side of her.

The train journey from home had been interminably slow and tedious and darkness had fallen when they had finally arrived in Dublin. There hadn't even been time to see any of the 'sights'. Never having been to the capital before, this omission had increased Gina's irritability, until Mary-Kate had reminded her that they were leaving a City devastated by four years of war and that the 'sights' would only be shattered buildings and piles of rubble. And had she forgotten already that even the General Post Office in O'Connell Street was still a burnt-out shell? Her words had brought a sigh of relief from Bridget, who had no wish to be reminded of the horrors.

They had eaten the sandwiches and soda bread Sarah had given them, neatly parcelled in a piece of slightly damp, clean cloth to keep them fresh, and now they were all hungry and thirsty.

'We should have saved the soda bread.'

'Didn't I say just that, but no, it was you who insisted on eating it, Gina!'

Bridget jumped edgily as the loud blast of the *Connaught*'s siren announced their departure from Dublin. 'They must sell something to eat. They sell drinks, after all. I'll go and see.'

As she disappeared into the crowd, Mary-Kate picked up her bag and put it on the seat beside her, in case anyone should think it vacant. The room was crowded with people now. All with a single purpose, to escape from the growing violence. They were weary of years of war, afraid to lose yet more husbands, fathers and sons, for there were many families amongst them that consisted of just women and children. Children already fractious and confused.

'We'll get no sleep tonight! Would you just listen to the noise out of them already.'

'Gina, will you stop harping on! We've got to give Aunt Maura fifteen shillings for our keep until we get a job, and the rest we'll need for expenses.' Mary-Kate's exhaustion had begun to take its toll on her nerves. 'So the sooner we get work the better. You have still got the address?'

'Don't I know it from memory! Eighteen, Lancaster Street, Walton. It's just before you get to the Hospital, by Rice Lane Police Station.'

Mary-Kate nodded, satisfied, then reached out to remove her bag as Bridget approached.

'I've got us a bottle of lemonade each. They don't have food at all and look who I found!' Bridget was clutching three small bottles and one glass, while behind her stood a girl of her own age. 'It's Bernie O'Hagan, don't you remember her? We were in the same class?'

Forgetting her intended complaints about the lack of food, Gina looked closely at the girl. Oh, she remembered Bernadette O'Hagan all right. Who could forget the O'Hagans? Little better than tinkers they were, living in a broken-down cottage near the old House of Industry on the road to Cahir. As far as she could remember, Bernie was the only one who ever went to school at all. She had hordes of sisters and brothers and cousins, all with runny noses – winter and summer – bare feet, grubby faces and tattered clothes. She'd heard her Ma say that none of the girls had any drawers even and wasn't that a sin altogether?

Bernie certainly looked different now, Gina thought, taking in the fashionable, but rather gaudy, deep purple coat, the black cloche hat and gloves to match. Gloves! She almost laughed aloud. Bernie O'Hagan with gloves! Instead she sniffed depreciatingly. On closer scrutiny the coat was of a very cheap material and the gloves were only cotton. Obviously the whole lot hadn't come from the likes of Grafton Street in Dublin.

Bridget handed out the bottles. 'If we push up a bit she can sit beside me.'

'Couldn't the barman count? There's only one glass. Are we expected to drink it out of the bottle?' Gina retorted, grudgingly moving an inch or two further along the seat.

'He said he could only spare us one and would we please take it back when we've finished with it as he has to account for them all.'

'What does he think we are? Thieves or tinkers?'

Bridget jabbed her in the ribs with her elbow.

'Fancy you being on the same boat, then, Bernie,' Mary-Kate intervened. 'Come to think of it, I've not seen you in town for ages.'

Bernie smiled and deliberately smoothed the backs of the gloves. 'Oh, I'd had enough of that lot, so I up an' left and went to Dublin.'

'I don't blame you. I don't know how you all fitted in to that house. What have you been doing in Dublin, then?' Bridget was openly curious to find out what miracle had been wrought on her former classmate.

'At the start I went into service, as a kitchen maid, but I soon left there, that I did! It was worse than home. Then I got a job in a shop.'

'What kind of a shop?' Gina cut in. As far as she could remember Bernie O'Hagan couldn't even add up two and two and get four.

'A grocers, but I didn't stay there either. Holy Mary! I couldn't stand them old shawlies complainin' about how I'd overcharged them or underweighed their ha'penny worth of tea.'

She didn't seem to have stuck anywhere for long, Gina thought, sipping the warmish lemonade and trying to look disinterested.

'Then I worked in a hotel. Well, it was more a sort of boardin' house-cum-bar really.'

That sounded more her style, Gina thought. 'One down by the Liffey, on the Quays, I suppose?' she asked, sweetly sarcastic.

Again Bridget jabbed her.

'Bridget, will you keep still or you'll have this all down the front of me!'

'It was, too, and that's where I met my Archie.'

'Who's he?' Bridget asked. Gina wasn't the only one who had noticed the cheap finery.

'We're "walkin' out", and that's why I'm off to Glasgow. My Archie's goin' to get me a job there.'

'Then wouldn't it have been quicker to have gone from Belfast?'

Bernie seemed to ponder Mary-Kate's question, then she nodded. 'I suppose it would, but Archie said I might as well see Liverpool and a bit of England. He gave me the money. "See a wee bit o' the country, Hen, but dinna be too lang about it."' She tried to imitate the Glaswegian accent and failed. No one noticed.

Despite feigned disinterest, Gina found herself being drawn into the conversation. 'And what does he do, this Archie?'

'He works in engineering, what else would anyone do in Glasgow?'

'I'm sure I wouldn't be knowing, not being interested in such things. I intend to go into the theatre.'

'Oh, and are you all goin' into "the theatre" then?' Bernie made it sound the most degrading of professions.

'No, only Gina. She's the one with the talent. Don't you remember she always sang when anyone important came to school – and she's even sung at Kilsheelan Castle!'

Bernie chose to ignore this. 'So what will you do, Bridget?'

'I want to work in one of the big stores, selling furs or hats or model gowns. But I don't just want a job, I want a career.' That sounded more impressive than going into 'the theatre', and Bernie was looking at her admiringly. 'We're going to stay with Ma's sister and her husband,' Bridget added.

'What about you, Mary-Kate?'

Mary-Kate was so tired she was having difficulty keeping her eyes open, and the heat and tobacco smoke weren't helping. Also she was thinking how unfair life was when the likes of Bernie O'Hagan, who was younger than her, could be walking out with a man who was obviously not short of money. Although the fact did encourage her, helping to dispel some of her unhappiness and guilt. 'I'll try for office work, but at the moment I'm so tired I can't think straight. We've been travelling since ten o'clock this morning.'

Bernie looked incredulous. Office work! Why, you had to have all kinds of examinations and a letter from the Holy Ghost Himself to get that kind of work, and as far as she knew Mary-Kate O'Donnell had neither. 'And how will you be after getting work like that?' She was openly sceptical.

Gina was instantly on the offensive. 'She worked in the office at Hearn's Hotel, which is Clonmel's most respectable hotel – a proper hotel in case you've forgotten, but then you probably wouldn't know about things like that, being up in Dublin.'

With that subject dismissed and Bernie put firmly in her place, Gina handed the now empty bottles back to her sister, along with the glass. 'Will you take these back, Bridget, please? I feel as though I could sleep for a week.'

Bernie got to her feet as Bridget rose. 'Come on, I'll buy you a drink, Bridget. A *real* drink and we'll catch up on all the gossip, it seems there's a lot I've missed out on.'

Gina glared up at her sister. None of them had ever been over the doorstep of a pub and no alcohol had ever passed their lips, except a hot toddy when they had a heavy cold. Ma would skin Bridget alive if she found out she was consorting – and worse – drinking, with the likes of Bernie O'Hagan. She was a bold piece if ever there was one and Gina could well imagine the sort of man this Archie was! 'She doesn't drink. None of us do, it's common!' she snapped.

Bernie laughed. 'Well now, we're all in the "common"

38

Saloon, aren't we? Come on, Bridget, one sherry won't hurt. I was thinking, if you get fed up with Liverpool, why not come up to Glasgow? My Archie says the shops on Sauchiehall Street are as good as those in London.' And with that she caught Bridget's arm and steered her through the throng.

'Did you hear that? Did you? Bold as brass, she is! You should have listened to me, Mary-Kate! It would have been worth five shillings to have avoided being in the same room as that . . . that . . . tinker's trollop!'

Her words fell on deaf ears. Mary-Kate was asleep, her head drooping on her chest, her feet resting on her valise.

Gina tutted in annoyance, then tried to find a comfortable position to rest her head against the hard, steel superstructure. She might as well try to get some sleep herself. If Bridget wanted to stay up all night that was her affair and if she had a headache in the morning, then it would be her own fault, she wasn't going to lose any sleep over it. Despite the noise, which was gradually diminishing as people tried to settle down, she fell into a deep sleep.

The *Connaught* passed the Bar Light in the dim, grey dawn of the late April day. Those passengers on deck were denied the views of the distant Welsh coastline by the low, hazy cloud, but the coastline of Southport, Formby and Crosby was just visible.

They had all slept fitfully, their positions cramped. Their slumber disturbed when numbed limbs were moved and circulation restored with the accompanying pins and needles. It had been a calm crossing, but the consumption of too much alcohol by certain passengers resulted in many ashen faces and bloodshot eyes as people started to stir. Fortunately, there had only been one small fracas, the culprits having been quickly hauled away by the burly members of the deck crew.

The stench of the stale odours of tobacco, beer, whisky and sweat caused Mary-Kate to screw up her face as she rubbed the sleep from her eyes. Gina's head had been resting on her shoulder and the movement awakened her sister.

'Have we arrived?' Gina mumbled.

'No, but I can't stand the smell in here, I'm going up on deck. Even if it's cold and damp it'll be better than this stink!' She got to her feet, stretched and then placing her hands in the small of her back, straightened up. She felt stiff, dirty and hungry.

With a groan of complaint Gina also got up. 'I feel as though I've been wedged in a cupboard all night. You on one side and Bridget on the other and that damned Bernie O'Hagan snoring like a pig!'

'Should we wake Bridget?'

'No. Leave her alone! Up half the night and drinking, too! I hope she has the mother and father of all hangovers!'

'Oh, Gina, don't be so cruel. I don't condone it, but there's no need to be so nasty.'

They were threading their way between people still asleep on the floor in the passageways, heading for the staircase that led up on deck.

'The sooner we get off this . . . this floating pig-pen the better. And the sooner we see the back of "that" one the better, too! If Bridget has any ideas about asking her to come with us, she can just forget them. Aunt Maura isn't going to be falling about with delight when she sets eyes on us, the state we're in, without having "that" one tagging along, too!'

They turned their coat collars up and tried to pull the garments closer to them, for the air was damp and chilly. It was also fresh and tangy with salt.

'It's only just dawn!' Gina complained.

'We're supposed to arrive at seven o'clock and it can't be far off that now.'

They both gripped the rail and looked towards the shoreline. Watery sunlight was just beginning to penetrate the clouds, its rays catching the murky, grey water and turning the top of the bow wave silver-gilt. Gina shielded her eyes and peered into the distance, and at the sight of the faint outlines of the docks, the shipping and the buildings her heart gave a tiny leap. Of course, it wasn't the skyline of Manhattan, but she'd taken the first real step in what she knew was going to be a brilliant career. She'd left Ireland and ahead of her lay one of the biggest cities in England; one of the busiest ports in the whole of the British Isles. This was just the beginning!

The shafts of sunlight were stronger and brighter now, picking out the unmistakable landmark of the twin towers of the Liver Buildings atop of which the two Liver Birds looked out across the River Mersey. Gina felt a surge of anticipation and she felt warmer. The next time she made this crossing it would be in style. Five shillings would be a paltry amount to her then. She'd need porters to carry all her baggage and the passengers would feel honoured to have made the crossing to Dublin on the same boat as the famous Miss Gina O'Donnell.

Mary-Kate watched the waterfront drawing closer with mixed feelings. She tried to shrug off her darker thoughts. She just had to put the old life behind her now. She hadn't known what to expect of Liverpool, but she'd never envisaged a sight like this. The fine buildings, the streets of houses that seemed to spread out for miles and miles and all the ships! She'd never seen so many ships; she'd never imagined that some of them could be so big! For the first time she felt her heart quicken with excitement. This fine, grand city was so . . . alive! She looked at her sister. Gina must feel the way she did for she was smiling and there were dancing lights in her eyes. But there was something else as well.

'You look pleased with yourself?'

'Just think, Mary-Kate, this is really the beginning of a whole new life for us all! Doesn't it look fine and isn't it big?'.

Mary-Kate didn't answer.

'What's the matter, don't you like the look of it? You're not home-sick already, are you?'

'No, and it looks a wonderful place, it's just that I don't have the grand notions you have.'

Gina laughed. 'Make sure your husband is rich, Mary-Kate. Then sit back and be a Lady for the rest of your life! You're the one who is so sensible, make sure he's got plenty of money.'

'Don't be so cold and calculating, there are other things besides money.'

'You have to be hard if you want to get on in life, I've learned that much. I know what I want and I'm going to get it.'

The expression on Gina's face was one Mary-Kate

knew of old. 'You're up to something, I know you are?'

'And just what would I be "up" to?'

'You don't intend staying in Liverpool, do you? Tell me the truth now?'

'No, I don't!'

'You promised!'

'No, I didn't! I didn't say a word when Matty said, "It's all settled then".'

'But you nodded, it's the same thing. What will you tell Aunt Maura? What will you tell Ma? I won't have you worrying her!'

'Nothing.' Despite her ambition, Gina did have a practical streak. 'I can't go anywhere just yet can I? I'll have to get a job and earn some money first, even if it's only for my fare and when the time comes, I'll tell Ma myself – you're not my keeper, I'm twenty-one!'

'Your fare to where?'

'America, of course! Look.' She pointed to the massive bulk of an ocean-going liner tied up in dock. 'The next boat I sail on will be one of those and bound for New York!'

'Then you'll have to find yourself someone like my Archie to pay the fare. It costs a fortune to sail on one of those.'

They both spun around to find a dishevelled Bridget standing behind them with Bernie at her side.

'I won't need any man to keep me, Bernadette O'Hagan, I'll earn my own money and make my own way in the world!'

Bernie laughed derisively. 'Oh, will you now?

Everyone needs someone to give them a bit of a hand up now and then, even you, Gina O'Donnell!'

Gina turned away. She wasn't going to lower herself by having a public argument with the likes of this bold piece. They were drawing near the Princes Landing Stage and the deck was crowded. She looked at Bridget. 'You look awful, can't you tidy yourself up. You look as though you've slept in a ditch all night.'

'I've got a headache.'

'Serves you right!'

Mary-Kate intervened. 'Oh, for heaven's sake stop it, you two. We all look like tin . . . terrible! There must be somewhere we can tidy up a bit before going to Aunt Maura's.'

A woman standing on the other side of them craned her head forward. 'There's the Ladies Waitin' Room at Exchange Station, luv. Yer can gerra wash an' tidy up there for a penny.'

Mary-Kate turned to her. 'Thank you, where's Exchange Station?'

'When yer gerroff, walk up the floatin' roadway an gerra tram. One that's got Walton or Anfield or Everton on the front, an' ask the Conductor ter put yer off at Exchange. Yer can't miss it, a great big, mucky, black buildin' it is.'

'How much will the tram cost?' Mary-Kate asked.

'A ha'penny, seein' as 'ow yer only goin' a few stops. Come over ter work? I've been over ter see me sister in Dublin, she's been took bad again an' I don't wonder! Molly, I says, why don't yer cum 'ome what with all this fightin', and she ain't never been the same since 'er lad were killed.'

'I'm sorry for your trouble,' Mary-Kate replied.

'Is the road really floating on water?' Gina was intrigued.

'Oh, aye, but yer don't really notice it. Except when the tide's out an' then it's that steep I 'ave ter stop 'alf way up, ter get me breath. The whole Landin' Stage is floatin'.' Being a native Liverpudlian and having a captive audience, she wasn't about to let them escape without pointing out some of the marvels of her city.

'All of it? Won't it sink with all these people on it?'

The woman laughed. 'Don't be daft! This owld tub is only little beside the liners an' they tie up 'ere. It's been 'ere as long as anyone can remember an' it 'asn't sunk yet. There's the Overhead Railway, too. The "Docker's Umbrella" we calls it.'

'Overhead?' Bridget echoed.

'Aye, up in the air it is, runs all the way along the docks an' the goods trains runs under it. Yer'll be able ter see it better soon, when we get closer, like. Comin' over ter work?' She repeated the question.

'Yes.' Mary-Kate answered before Gina could make any remarks about her intended aspirations.

'Got someone ter stay with?'

'Yes. Our Aunt, who lives in Lancaster Street, Walton. Do you know it?'

'Oh, it's quite posh round there. Not as posh as Aintree or West Derby, but nice. Meself, I live in Athol Street, near the docks. We 'aven't got much but we all muck in an' 'elp each other, if yer know what I mean.' She shifted the weight of her bundle to her other hip. 'I'll be glad ter gerr 'ome. I'm that tired me eyes is fightin' for the one corner!'

Gina cast a supercilious glance at Bernie. 'We're not all going to Walton. She's going to Glasgow.'

The woman pulled a face. 'I 'ear it's a shockin' rough place that. People always fightin' an' murderin' each other, an' not only on Saturday nights, either!'

'I've heard that there's not much to choose between Liverpool and Glasgow!' Bernie retaliated. 'Didn't all the police go on strike a few years back and they had to bring in the Army? My Archie said there were tanks in the streets and soldiers to stop the lootin' and even a Navy gunboat!' she finished, triumphantly.

The woman glowered at her. 'Oh, she'll do well in Glasgow, she will! Right little 'ardclock, ain't she?' She had no wish to recall the riots or the fact that there had been tanks on the plateau in front of St George's Hall, or that the dreadnought *Valiant* and two destroyers had stood out in the river, men and guns at the ready if needed. She turned to Gina and smiled. 'Take no notice of 'er, yer'll do well in Liverpool. I'm off now ter gerra place near where they put up the gangway. It's a shockin' crush ter gerrof. Good Luck an' tarrah, then!'

Mary-Kate purposefully straightened her hat and turned down the collar of her coat. 'We'll go straight to this Exchange Station and tidy up, then we can get the tram. She said it would have Walton on the front, didn't she?'

'Is no one coming to meet you then?' Bernie put in.

'Why should they? Uncle Bart will have his work to go to and you can't expect people to get up at the crack of dawn to come all the way down here, just so we can all go back again on the tram. You never did have any common sense, even when you were at school, which

46

wasn't often!' Gina's tone was cutting. If she never saw Bernie O'Hagan again it would be too soon.

Bernie gave Bridget a scrap of paper.

'What's that?' Gina demanded.

'My address in Glasgow, not that it's got anything to do with you!'

Bridget thanked her and put it in her coat pocket. She had no intention of ever going to Glasgow and she wished she hadn't had the sherry Bernie had bought last night. At the time it had seemed harmless and as her fears had subsided they had laughed and giggled about childhood memories at the school of Saints Peter and Paul. Now she felt awful, but to admit it would only bring about another tirade from Gina and she just couldn't stand that. Her head was thudding. She wished she hadn't been quite so friendly towards Bernie, after all they had only been in the same class. Even then her Ma had forbidden her to sit within three feet of Bernie, after having been up to see Mother Superior in a rare fit of anger, when she had come home with nits. She could almost feel the scraping of the fine-toothed metal comb over her scalp and smell the noxious odour of paraffin and lye soap, her Ma's remedy for head lice. No, they had never been close friends. The O'Hagans just didn't have close friends, only relations.

The bump as the side of the ferry came into contact with the Landing Stage threw Bridget off balance and she felt dizzy and sick. She glanced at her sisters. Mary-Kate looked pale and tired but, strangely, Gina didn't look tired at all. There was a gleam in her eye and the corners of her mouth were tilted in a smile. She'd caught the end of Gina's conversation, but she felt too ill to even think about its implications. As the crowd surged forward en masse, carrying her with them, she thought she'd always remember the day she arrived in Liverpool. She swore then that she'd never touch another drink in her life.

Chapter Three

———◆———

LANCASTER STREET WAS NOT quite as 'posh' as they had been led to believe. True it was in a fairly quiet area and the houses in the street were all neat-looking. Their steps were donkey-stoned, knockers and letter-boxes were polished and the curtains were clean and crisp. All except number eighteen that was. There was a dilapidated look about number eighteen. The paint on the door was dirty, the knocker dull and pitted, the lace curtains at the window sagged untidily and were grey in comparison to those of the adjoining houses. Their discomfort was increased by all the curtains they had noticed twitching as they had walked down the street and stopped outside the house.

'Didn't I say she looked like a great, idle lump?' Bridget remarked glumly as Gina rapped loudly on the door.

Aunt Maura greeted them warmly with loud exclamations as to how they'd grown and didn't they look grand and weren't they all so smartly turned out, as she ushered them into the dark, narrow hall. The smell that drifted from the kitchen at the back made Bridget feel ill

49

again. It was a mixture of stale tobacco, wet washing and rancid fat. The kitchen, as they crowded in, seemed far smaller and more sparsely furnished than the one at home. There was linoleum on the floor, but it was cracked and so dirty that it was impossible to see what colour it had been. Mary-Kate quickly took in the range, heaped with ashes, that obviously hadn't been cleaned out for weeks, and Aunt Maura's dirty, faded, cross-over pinafore that looked as though it had not seen soap and water for almost as long as the range had been without black-leading.

To their surprise, Uncle Bart was sitting in a battered chair close to the fire. He was a thin, weasel-faced man with wispy hair and a thin, tobacco-stained moustache. In his right hand, the lighted end towards his palm, he held a cigarette. Five Woodbines in their green paper packet with its tracery of yellow honeysuckle, rested with a box of matches on the arm of the chair. His collarless shirt was grubby and stained.

'We thought you'd be at work, Uncle Bart,' Mary-Kate said flatly, but with a note of disapproval in her voice.

'Oh, the poor man is a martyr to his back, he's been on the "Panel" for months, haven't you, Bart?'

He nodded before coughing, then spitting the phlegm into the fire.

Gina shuddered and curled her lip with distaste while Bridget turned her head away, feeling nausea rising in her throat.

Mary-Kate stared at him hard until he looked away. 'You should see a doctor with that cough and you should use a handkerchief. That's a disgusting habit and it spreads disease!'

'Doesn't she sound just like her Ma, Bart? If I closed my eyes I would swear it was our Sarah speakin'!' Maura interrupted jokily. She had decided she didn't like Mary-Kate; she was just like her Ma whom she had no time for – which was why she had been happy to leave Clonmel all those years ago.

Bart didn't answer.

'Come on now, I'll show you your room, you must be fair worn out. Then we'll have a cup of tea and something to eat.' Maura went out into the hall and they all followed. As she set foot on the first, uncarpeted stair she turned. 'Do you have the fifteen shillings your Ma sent?'

'Yes, why?' Mary-Kate challenged.

'I'll just have to nip down to Rice Lane for some bacon, that's all, for your breakfast. We're a bit short today. Bart's "Panel" money can't be had until tomorrow.'

Mary-Kate opened her bag and drew out half-a-crown. 'This should do for now, we'll sort everything out later . . . when we've unpacked.'

There was no mistaking the annoyance in her tone and Maura took the money without a word.

Mary-Kate was seething. Panel money or not, Uncle Bart didn't seem to go without his Woodbines or his pint of stout, judging by the stains on his shirt and the dirty glass, half-hidden by the side of his chair.

In the back bedroom which had been allotted to them, they stood in silence until Aunt Maura had gone back downstairs, the boards creaking beneath her weight. After the rigours of the journey and the effects of the hangover, Bridget felt like breaking down and crying.

'I feel so ill and now . . . this! I almost wish we hadn't come at all.'

'Oh, shut up! Just wait until I write and tell Ma about this!'

'And what good will that do any of us, Gina? She'll send Matty over to drag us all back!'

'Do we have to stay here?' Bridget pleaded.

'We've no choice. It was the only reason they both let us come at all and we've no jobs and less than twenty-two shillings between us.'

'Do you always have to be so practical? Sometimes, Mary-Kate, I could scream at you, that I could!'

'Oh, don't you start, Gina, or I'll slap you, so help me I will!'

Gina sat down gingerly on the faded patchwork quilt that covered the one double bed, with its old, rusted bedstead and lumpy mattress. She fingered the quilt with distaste. 'And I suppose we've all got to share this one bed?'

Mary-Kate had taken off her hat and coat. 'If she thinks she's getting fifteen shillings for this . . . this hovel, she's mistaken! And when Uncle Bart draws his Panel money – whatever that is – he can buy a single bed and I'll go with him if I have to, but until then we'll have to make the best of it. First things first, we'll clean up this room. Gina, take your coat off and find an old dress.'

'I didn't bring any,' came the bitter reply.

'Then you'll have to get that one dirty. Get your sleeves rolled up, she must have soap and water . . .'

'Our privy at home was cleaner than this,' Bridget said with a sob in her voice.

'Oh, God! What must the privy be like?' Gina groaned.

Gina had never been any good in situations like this,

Mary-Kate thought grimly. 'I'll go down and see her and, if necessary, I'll threaten her with telegraphing Ma to come over and see the state of the place for herself!'

'And you can tell her that all she's going to get out of us is five shillings and we'll buy our own food and cook it, too, when she's cleaned up that kitchen. Don't they have a Public Health Board or something? How does she get away with it, surely the landlord must get complaints from the neighbours? Every other house looked spotless. Oh, this is a fine start this is!' Gina paced up and down the room, still fuming.

Bridget had begun to cry softly as Mary-Kate left the room. 'Oh, Gina, what are we going to do? I feel so sick . . .'

Gina sat down beside her and put her arm around her. 'Oh, come on now, hush! We'll manage. Haven't Mary-Kate and I always taken care of things? Hush now, Mary-Kate and I will clean it up, we'll sort it out.' She patted Bridget's shaking shoulders with more confidence than she felt. But there was no going back, her pride wouldn't let her even think about it. She could hear raised voices from below and she stood up. 'I think I'd better go down. Mary-Kate sounds as though she's getting the worst of it.'

As she opened the kitchen door, Gina quickly took in the scene. Uncle Bart was still sitting in his chair but he was scowling blackly. Aunt Maura, her hands on her hips, her face an ugly shade of puce, stood confronting a white-faced, tight-lipped Mary-Kate.

'She's told you then?'

'Fifteen shillings your Ma said we was to have for keeping you!' Uncle Bart growled.

'And five is all you're going to get and be thankful for

that! Now we both intend to turn this house upside down. It's worse than a pigsty and is probably hopping with fleas.'

Aunt Maura took a step towards her. 'This is my house! Mine, do you hear me!'

'The whole street can hear you I don't wonder. You're a disgrace to the family, Aunt Maura,' Gina flung back at her.

Maura lunged at her, but Gina side-stepped neatly. 'You lay a finger on me and I'll telegraph Ma and Matty and see what they have to say!'

'Oh, you as well. I've just had that from her!' Maura yelled.

'If we're going to stay here, and you should be thankful we haven't walked out and reported you to the Public Health Office, then we're going to have to come to some agreement. You can provide the soap and bleach and cloths and we'll do the work. And if either of you touch a single thing belonging to us, then I'll be straight down to the Police Station or bring the Priest down here to see how you live.' Mary-Kate's controlled iciness had far more effect than Gina's heated insults.

Aunt Maura backed off and tried a different approach. 'Where am I going to get the money from? Bart's not fit to work. It's not our fault, things cost money,' she whined.

'He doesn't look that bad to me!' Gina snapped. 'There must be something he can do. He needn't think we're all going to work to keep him in beer and cigarettes!'

'Hard-faced little bitch!' Bart snarled, getting to his feet with an agility that belied his affliction.

'Well, you can get out of that chair quick enough when you want to,' Gina scoffed. 'Bad back my foot! You should be reported to the head of this "Panel" for malingering and obtaining money under false pretences. Holy Mother! What have we come to!'

Uncle Bart went pale and sat down suddenly, staring shiftily at Gina.

'Just where is the nearest church and who is the parish priest?' Mary-Kate demanded.

They looked at one another and Aunt Maura ran her tongue over her bottom lip.

Gina turned, her hand on the door latch. 'I'll go and knock next door and ask.'

'It's Father Morley at Saint Francis de Salles, Hale Road,' her aunt muttered.

Gina smiled to herself. They'd won that round. Things could only get better, but she didn't trust the pair of them and knew there would be other rows.

Mary-Kate had followed Aunt Maura into a tiny, dark scullery that led off the kitchen. Ignoring the clutter of dirty dishes and pans, she instructed her aunt to fill the biggest pans she had and heat them on the fire while she searched for soap, rags and a scrubbing brush. Eventually, Mary-Kate found a brush with worn-down bristles under the sink. Her aunt was muttering under her breath but she ignored her. Obviously Gina's threat of informing the mysterious 'Panel' about Uncle Bart's non-existent ailment had had more effect than Gina had realized.

They would start by stripping off that bed, then they could air the mattress by hanging it over the windowsill and then she'd scrub the floor while Gina washed the bed linen. Aunt Maura could make some effort with that kitchen and get a meal cooked. If Bridget felt up to it she could clean the window and wash out the wardrobe and chest of drawers. The sooner they all got jobs in Liverpool the better, she thought grimly, but Aunt Maura, Uncle Bart and number eighteen, Lancaster Street were obstacles they would soon sort out.

For the first time in nearly a week, Mary-Kate had the house to herself. Uncle Bart had gone off to the offices of the Panel to produce the obligatory proof of his afflictions and collect whatever money they decided the said afflictions were worth. Aunt Maura had gone to the shops with instructions to buy decent food for a change and not put it 'on the slate'. This means of obtaining credit had been discovered when Gina had gone into the Maypole Dairy at the top of Rice Lane when they had run short of milk. She had been told in no uncertain terms that until the bill was paid and the 'slate' wiped clean, the occupants of eighteen, Lancaster Street were not welcome in that establishment. That and the stew comprised of fatty, gristly meat and green-tinged potatoes that had been set before them had been the cause of yet another argument. Mary-Kate sighed at the memory.

This morning Bridget had gone into Liverpool to try for a position in one of the smart shops, and Gina had taken herself off to the Rotunda Lyric Theatre at the junction of Scotland Road and Boundary Road and Everton Valley.

On her expeditions to familiarize herself with the area, Mary-Kate had noticed the Dunlop Rubber Company, situated just past Walton Hospital on the other side of the road, next door to the Black Horse public house. She had enquired at the gate if the factory had offices and on hearing that they did, she had made up her mind to go and try for a job there. It was within walking distance and that would cut out travelling expenses. It would also provide her with the opportunity of going home at lunch time to keep an eye on her disreputable relatives. She was rather reluctant to try the larger city offices, since her work at Hearn's hadn't exactly been of a highly taxing nature and the large shipping and banking companies might demand qualifications and experience she didn't have.

Mary-Kate looked around the kitchen to make sure everything was tidy. It had taken them four full days to clean the house from top to bottom, but as the furnishings were old and shabby, it still looked drab and seedy and they had received no thanks from Aunt Maura and only muttered curses about 'interfering, bossy little upstarts' from Uncle Bart. However, she could see he was beginning to fear Gina's vituperative tongue and explosive temper.

She had checked her appearance in the mirror that hung above the mantel and was just about to put on her hat when the sharp, tinny sound of the door knocker echoed through the house. 'And it's about time too. She's been gone hours, and she's probably spent half the morning whining to her cronies about her "hard-faced nieces",' Mary-Kate muttered as she went to the door. She pulled it open, ready to inform her aunt that she was going out but that she wouldn't be long and that there was a line of washing out in the yard that was ready to come in and be folded.

'Oh, so someone's finally at home! Who are you?'

She was startled and took a step backwards. On the doorstep was a middle-aged man of medium height and build with cold grey eyes beneath bushy eyebrows, and a pursed, disapproving mouth under a clipped, grey moustache. He was well dressed in a dark suit, clean white shirt with a starched, winged collar and charcoal grey necktie. Across his waistcoat was a heavy gold watch-chain.

'I beg your pardon?'

'I said who are you?'

Mary-Kate collected herself. 'Miss O'Donnell, Miss Mary-Kate O'Donnell, and who, sir, are you?'

At the calm, precise yet lilting tone he removed his hat. 'Mr Vannin. Mr Lewis Vannin.'

'Should I know you?'

'I own this house, Miss O'Donnell. I'm the landlord. Is Mrs Milligan in?'

'No. No, she's not.' Understanding was beginning to dawn on her as to why Aunt Maura had stayed out so long and an unpleasant suspicion had begun to form in her mind.

'Then I'll wait.'

As he clasped his hands behind his back with his feet, in highly polished boots, planted firmly apart, Mr Vannin was the epitome of stern disapproval. In fact he reminded her of Father Maguire when confronting a wayward parishioner. Out of the corner of her eye Mary-Kate saw the curtains of number sixteen twitch.

'Then you'd better come in, Mr Vannin, we can't have you standing on the doorstep of your own house, now can we? Mrs Milligan shouldn't be long, she's been gone hours. Was she expecting you, then?'

'Very likely.'

And likely that's why she's stayed out, Mary-Kate thought. 'Have you called before?' she asked as she ushered him in.

'No, but my collector has and he can never get an answer.'

Oh, she'd have a few choice words to say to her aunt when she finally showed her face, that she would! Gina wasn't the only one with an explosive temper.

'I'm afraid you will have to wait in the kitchen, the parlour is empty, except for an old table.' Mary-Kate was acutely embarrassed. A gentleman of his obvious standing would have been shown into a clean and decently furnished parlour at home, not a shabby kitchen.

'I've had complaints, from some of my other tenants,' Mr Vannin said, coolly.

'I'm sure you have. I'd complain, too, living next door to this . . . !' She flung out her hands, expressively, her cheeks flushed, her eyes bright with suppressed anger.

Mr Vannin remained standing, but he did let her take his hat.

'Are you related to Mrs Milligan?'

'Unfortunately, yes. She's my aunt. My mother's sister. My two sisters and I are staying with her – for the moment,' she added, wondering if their presence was a breach of any tenancy agreement. To forestall any awkward questions, she turned and faced him squarely. 'How much does she owe you, Mr Vannin, and how long has it been owing?'

From the inside pocket of his jacket the landlord took out a small notebook and opened it. 'Four weeks' rent. At seven and sixpence a week, that's . . .'

'Thirty shillings,' Mary-Kate rapped out. She wasn't having him think she was an ignoramus straight from the bogs.

'You have a quick brain, Miss O'Donnell.'

'I work with figures and books.'

'Indeed?'

She opened her bag and took out her purse. 'I can pay you a pound off the arrears now, and I'll make sure that you get the rest of the money by the end of next week.' She held out the coins and he took them.

'And how do I know that you won't all have "flitted" by then?'

Her cheeks felt as though they were on fire and her eyes blazed. Oh, just wait until she got her hands on those two. 'You have my word on it and I never break a promise! Never! I will bring the money so you won't have the inconvenience of having to come here again. If you will just give me the address of your home or office?'

There was something about her manner and the conviction in her voice that made him believe her. She was an attractive young woman, too, and she looked so incongruous in that small, dingy room in her neat, grey two-piece and white blouse with the cameo brooch at the neck. Added to which, she was very obviously furious. He noted the light copper hair, coiled tidily but becomingly on the top of her head. He had also noticed the small, black felt hat on the table beside the black gloves and handbag. They were not expensive, but they were decent. She was clearly a cut above her relations who caused him so much trouble. She looked totally out of place, but he had to admire her spirit.

'Very well, Miss O'Donnell. I live at number three, Walton Park, or you can drop the money into my office. I have a haulage business, my yard and office is on the corner of Parkinson Road. I'm there most days, when I don't have to go out collecting the rents my employee finds it impossible to recover!'

'You've made your point, Mr Vannin. It won't happen again, you have my word on that, too, not as long as I live here!' She handed him back his hat and walked towards the door.

'And do you intend to stay here long?'

'I don't know. That depends on . . . circumstances.'

As Mary-Kate opened the front door, it was of small comfort that Bridget had washed down all the paintwork, polished up the knocker and whitened the step. 'I've given my word, you'll have your money by the end of next week. Good day to you.'

Lewis Vannin raised his hat politely before turning away and she shut the door quickly and leaned against it. Oh, the humiliation . . . the utter degradation! In future she'd make sure that either she or Gina went with Uncle Bart to collect his 'Panel' money, so that half of it wouldn't be missing by the time he got home and the rent would get paid. Now she'd have to make sure she got a job and quickly, they'd all have to, for they had almost no money left. She'd go over to Dunlop's now and when she got back she'd deal with Aunt Maura and Uncle Bart!

Bridget had walked the length of Bold Street mingling with the smartly-dressed men and women, noting how many cars – many of them with chauffeurs – were parked at the kerbside. This was a far cry from the Main Guard and O'Leary's and her courage was beginning to fail. She tried to think how Gina would approach the situation. Gina would exude confidence, she wouldn't hesitate at all. She would march straight through the doors and demand to see the manager or manageress as the case might be. She wouldn't be standing like a half-wit outside number seventy-six, Bold Street, staring miserably at the plain blind with 'De Jong et Cie – Modes Parisiennes' printed on it, that obscured the view inside.

Bridget turned away and walked towards the Church Street end past Orchard's, Sloan's and the wrought-iron façade of Cripps Son & Company. She had almost reached the bottom of the street and panic was overtaking her. 'Now just you take a grip of yourself, Bridget O'Donnell, and don't be such an eejit!' she scolded herself. That's what Gina would say. 'You want a career and you haven't come all this way to end up working in Woolworths.' She felt a little better, a little braver, as she caught sight of herself in the window of a large establishment that declared 'Gladys Drinkwater' to be the proprietress. Bridget was wearing the same outfit she'd worn to Mass on their last Sunday in Clonmel and although the cut and cloth of her coat was far inferior to that of the outfits in the window, she drew comfort and courage that she didn't look too dowdy and that her black gloves – part of her farewell gift from Mrs O'Leary – were of fine, soft leather.

She took a deep breath. She had to start somewhere and it might as well be here. She stepped forward and the door was magically opened for her by a liveried doorman.

'May I be of assistance, madam?'

'Thank you, could you direct me to . . . to Miss Drinkwater's office, please?'

'It's on the second floor, up the central staircase and to the right.'

She thanked him and walked in the direction he had pointed out. Her feet sank into the deep pile of the carpet and as she ascended the staircase her knees felt weak. She had noticed the coolness in his voice as soon as she had spoken. She passed tasteful displays of evening bags, long evening gloves, plumed and jewelled hair ornaments in glass cases. She stopped to admire an evening gown of ice-blue, crystal satin decorated with pearls and bugle beads. She'd never seen anything so exquisite and she dreaded to even think how much it cost. From the corner of her eye she could see a sales assistant bearing down on her and she had to stop herself from turning and racing for the stairs. As the girl spoke she made a desperate attempt to stay calm.

'Is there anything I can show you, madam?'

'Only the way to Miss Drinkwater's office, if you please.'

The girl looked taken aback. 'Is Miss Drinkwater expecting you?'

'Yes!' she lied, feeling sick, aware that every item of clothing she wore was being noted and assessed for cut and cost.

'Would you follow me, please? Who shall I say it is? I don't think I've seen you before, if you don't mind me saying so.'

'Miss O'Donnell,' she answered, hoping the girl hadn't noticed the tremor in her voice. A middle-aged woman, swathed in furs, was being attended to by two assistants both older than either herself or the girl she was following. So engrossed were they that they didn't even turn in her direction.

The girl rapped smartly on a panelled door and on hearing the response from within, opened it. 'A Miss O'Donnell to see you, Miss Drinkwater. She assures me she has an appointment.'

Bridget had no time to think just how easy it had been to gain access to the woman who obviously dressed the wealthy of Liverpool, and had done so for many years. She found herself in a small room, lined with shelves that held manila folders, swatches of materials, ribbons and braids. Behind the desk in the middle of it all sat Miss Drinkwater, a thin woman in a plain black dress with crisp white collar and cuffs, a pince-nez perched at the end of her long, aquiline nose. Bridget's courage deserted her entirely. She began to clench and unclench her hands. She shifted her weight from her right foot to her left and then plucked at the ruffles of her blouse.

'I have no appointments for today, Miss O'Donnell, so obviously you have made some sort of mistake.'

'I . . . well, no, not really . . .'

Miss Drinkwater rose impatiently and removed her glasses. 'Then what may I do for you?'

Now that she was here she had to try, at least she had to try.

'I would very much like to work here, Miss Drinkwater. I do have experience. I already know about ordering and invoices and my previous employer said I had taste and was imaginative.' Bridget delved into her bag to find the letter Mrs O'Leary had given her. 'And I have a good reference.'

Miss Drinkwater took the letter without a word and read it, then folding it, she handed it back to her. 'It's a very good reference, Miss O'Donnell, but a small haberdashery establishment in Ireland is not quite the same as this . . .' She gestured with one hand, and to Bridget that gesture was far more eloquent than any words. But she must press on, she must. 'Oh, no, of course not, I understand that, that I do! But I don't just want a job, I want a career. I hope that one day I can be . . . like you!' It all came out in a rush and not at all the way she had wanted it to sound.

The thin lips twitched in a half-smile. 'I'm sure one day you will be. Believe me, it takes quite a lot of nerve to walk in here, off the street, or should I say off the boat, and ask to be considered for employment in an establishment like this! You'll go far, Miss O'Donnell, but not here, I'm afraid.'

'Why? Mrs O'Leary said . . .'

'I'm not doubting this Mrs O'Leary, but I will tell you this for your own good and to save you a great deal of disappointment. There is no emporium of any distinction in this City that would employ you with that accent and without the years of experience all my girls have. Do you realize that most of them have spent nearly half their lives working their way up from the sewing room? They start at fourteen as apprentices and if they prove capable and diligent, then they will be promoted to a bodice hand, a coat hand or a finisher. It takes years, Miss O'Donnell. If I were you I would try some of the smaller, less exclusive shops.'

Bridget's eyes were bright with unshed tears. She felt gauche and small and she smarted with humiliation, although Miss Drinkwater's tone had not been cutting or sarcastic, in fact she had been most civil. 'I . . . I had such grand hopes . . . I didn't come all this way to work in a small, poky shop!'

'I'm sure you didn't, but take my advice, you'll have to start at the bottom, try somewhere smaller. Now, I'm very busy . . .'

Bridget turned away.

'Oh, on your way out would you send Miss Frazer in to see me? The young lady who showed you in?' Miss Drinkwater added, seeing the query in Bridget's eyes.

She didn't even think about the carpet as she ran down the staircase and she couldn't see the doorman clearly for her tears. She'd never get another chance like that, not to see someone like Miss Gladys Drinkwater without an appointment. Oblivious to the disdainful looks and the exclamations of 'Well, really!' Bridget pushed past everyone in the street with her head bent. At the top of Bold Street the gardens of Saint Luke's church beckoned invitingly, a haven of quiet away from all these people. She went in and sat down on a bench.

'Somewhere smaller. Less exclusive. Start at the bottom. With that accent . . .' The words buzzed in her head. She just wasn't 'genteel' enough for them, that was the real reason. She couldn't help her accent and until now she had never thought about it, let alone considered it a burden. She felt so miserable and humiliated and hurt that she couldn't try anywhere else – not today. She wanted to go home. Not to that house in Lancaster Street, but home to her Ma and Mrs O'Leary. But at home there was trouble; the fighting had already begun.

Bridget wiped her eyes with one of the lace-edged

handkerchiefs, her other gift from her former employer. She'd always admired them and Ma had said they were a wise choice, for you could always tell a lady by her gloves and linen. That thought made her feel worse. She wasn't a lady and she never would be; all she wanted to do was to serve such 'Ladies' and now . . . she jerked up her chin. Oh, she couldn't go back to that awful house and see the look on Aunt Maura's face or have to listen to her acid comments about, 'The higher they go, the harder they fall!' She wouldn't tell them. She'd say she'd had some offers and was considering them. Tucking the handkerchief back in her bag she rose and walked towards the gates.

Chapter Four

THE SIGN MARKED 'STAGE DOOR' was so grimy that it was difficult to read the letters at all. The entrance was in an alleyway behind the theatre which was dark even in daylight. The cobbles were dirty and slippery with rubbish. Gina had found it only after walking around the theatre twice and finally asking two women who were studying the names on the poster at the front doors.

She hammered loudly on the scarred, wooden door with its peeling paint, the word 'Private' just discernible under the dirt. Finally, it was opened by an old man in shirtsleeves, a greasy waistcoat and old trousers that looked as though they had originally been intended for someone much larger.

'I've come to see someone about an audition.'

'What "audition"?'

'The old fool,' Gina muttered impatiently. 'You have heard of auditions, I suppose?'

He thrust his face closer, peering up at her with watery eyes. She stepped back, wrinkling her nose.

Obviously soap and water didn't mix with him very often.

'I've been in this business years, girl. I know what an audition is!'

'Right, now we've got that sorted out perhaps you could tell me who I have to see?'

'Won't be no one 'ere until ternight.' He made to close the door but he hadn't reckoned on Gina's determination. With a quick swipe she jerked the door back and it crashed against the inside wall.

''Ere, what the 'ell's yer game! I'll 'ave the scuffer on yer!'

'Who is it I have to see and exactly what time will they be here?'

'They pleases themselves.'

'A fine way to run a theatre!'

'An' what d'yer know about runnin' a theatre? Just gor off the boat by the sound of yer. What d'yer do?'

'I sing,' Gina answered coldly, ignoring his remarks. She wasn't going to lower herself by arguing with him, he was probably only some sort of caretaker.

'Doesn't everyone?'

Her temper began to rise. 'Just give me the name of the manager or whoever it is that runs this place, if it's not too much trouble?'

'Joe Donnelly's the fella yer want.'

'You're taking my name in vain again, Harry! Well, who've we got here then?'

Gina turned abruptly and found herself looking down at a swarthy, dark-haired man dressed in a light-grey checked suit. She disliked him instantly, from the shiny black hair, plastered down with some sickly-smelling oil, to the black boots that protruded from beneath the loud, chequered trousers. 'Mr Donnelly?'

He tucked his thumbs in the pockets of his waistcoat and looked her up and down. 'Who are you?'

'Miss Gina O'Donnell.'

'She's cum for an audition, she sings,' Harry interrupted.

'Does she then?'

Gina glared at the old man. Did they think she was deaf or stupid? 'Yes, I sing. I can also speak up for myself, thank you.'

'Then you'd better come into the office, miss . . .'

'O'Donnell,' she repeated shortly as she followed him down the corridor and into a small room. The furnishings were shabby and the carpet threadbare and the whole room reeked of stale cigar smoke. There were some framed photos on the walls and old posters which she scrutinized quickly. There weren't many names she recognized.

'I've never heard of you before – been working the Halls long?'

'No.'

'Didn't think so. What kind of an act do you do?'

'I told you, I sing.'

'No novelty numbers?'

'What?'

'Novelties – specialities?'

He was looking her up and down again in that way that made her skin crawl. He made her feel as though she were a brood mare at the Tipperary Horse Fair. 'Do you mean do I stand on my head and juggle half a dozen oranges and sing at the same time?' she snapped sarcastically.

'Something like that.'

'I sing "Society" songs for people who appreciate decent music!'

'Well, we don't get a lot of that sort in here, luv. The customers want entertainment, amusement. They don't want to think they're in church! This is a Music Hall not Covent Garden bloody Opera!'

'And how do you know I can't entertain until you've heard me?'

'I don't, but I know I'm wasting my time by just looking at you. Straight off the boat, never trodden the boards in your life I'll bet. If I had a pound for every girl that's come badgering me for a job, I'd be a bloody millionaire!'

He stepped towards her and laid a hand on her arm. 'Look, luv, I know what I'm talking about. The days of Marie Lloyd are gone – more's the pity – so the competition is harder and you're an outsider. Most of the acts started out when they were just kids, their whole families have been in the business for donkey's years! Get yourself a novelty act, something different, then maybe someone will give you a start.'

She flung off his arm. There was something repugnant about him. 'I'll thank you to keep your hands to yourself and your advice, too!' She laughed derisively. 'Sure, what would a third-rate, jumped up little weasel like you know about anything refined.'

He walked to the door and opened it. 'Show her out, Harry, she's just another bloody prima donna!' he called.

Gina stormed past him. 'I'll find my own way out and I'll have you know that I wouldn't be caught dead appearing in this . . . this flea-pit.'

His laughter followed her down the corridor and she slammed the door behind her so hard that it shook the frame. Oh, the sheer cheek and arrogance of the man. Who did he think he was? Some common little, rat-faced manager of a third-rate Music Hall!

It wasn't until she found herself back on the street in front of the theatre that she realized that she had failed in her first attempt to even get an audition. That realization shocked her into immobility. She had been so sure of herself, so determined, and now she had ruined everything. 'Damn!' she muttered. 'Damn him!' But she knew that it had been partly her own fault that she had missed her chance. My temper! My damned temper! she thought furiously.

She'd had it all planned how she would go home and triumphantly announce that she had been engaged to appear at the Rotunda Theatre. How she would have savoured the expression on Maura's face, and now . . .

As she walked across towards the tram stop it began to rain and she felt utterly dejected and miserable. It was bad enough that she had to go back and tell her sisters! A piece of paper blown by the wind had become entangled around her feet and irritably she bent down to pull it away. The words suddenly caught her attention as she smoothed it out.

THE HIPPODROME THEATRE
TALENT NIGHT. FRIDAY NIGHT
COME ALONG AND SEE THE STARS
OF TOMORROW!

A Talent Night! She'd heard of them, most theatres had them. They had them in Dublin. They were popular for it was a chance for all hopeful artists to appear before a live audience and often to go on to greater things. And they were a free evening's entertainment for the theatre concerned. She folded the paper and shoved it into her bag and began to smile as a tram appeared through the drizzle. The smile had reached her eyes and they began to sparkle. This time there wouldn't be any insulting little upstarts like Joe Donnelly and this time she just 'knew' she would win and then . . .

The clanking of the tram and the ''Urry up there, girl, if yer gettin' on!' from the conductor interrupted her daydream and she jumped lightly on to the platform with a new spring in her step.

By the time she reached Lancaster Street her thoughts were in a whirl and despite the rain she walked jauntily down the street. Heedless of the havoc the dampness was causing to her hat and the dirty splashes down the front of her coat.

It was Bridget who opened the door to her and at the sight of her sister's face and the sound of raised voices within, her smile died.

'What's the matter now?'

'They haven't paid the rent. The landlord's been round and I haven't got a job . . .'

'That makes two of us then!' she muttered grimly as she followed Bridget into the kitchen.

At their appearance the shouting stopped. Gina quickly took in Mary-Kate's pursed lips and dangerously narrowed eyes. Maura's pale puce complexion and flaccid mouth and Uncle Bart's sly, cunning expression. 'I hear the landlord's been?'

Maura, with the back-up of Bart, hadn't been doing too badly. She'd been holding her own against Mary-Kate but with Gina's appearance she knew any advantage she had had was gone. By the Saints! She'd never met anyone with such a temper and the tongue of a viper that this one had! She changed her tactics. 'Is it my fault he always sends his tallyman when we're out? Is it my fault that I have to dip into the rent every now and then for food?' she complained.

'Every now and then! Your hand's never out of that biscuit tin! How much do you owe?'

'A month's rent.' It was Mary-Kate who answered her. 'And what's more, he's managed to spend half of this week's "Panel" money on the way home!'

'I owed some people some money,' Bart muttered.

'Oh, that's just fine that is. You owe money to nearly everyone from here to Walton Vale and back. We can't go into a shop without facing demands for money that you owe.' After her abortive attempt to be accepted into her chosen profession, Gina let fly with a vengeance. She pointed a stabbing finger at Uncle Bart who shrank further into the depths of his chair. 'First thing in the morning you can get out and take your bad back down to the Labour Exchange and find a job. And if you don't, then I'm going straight down to the Police Station at the end of the road to tell them all about you.'

'Ah, you wouldn't be doing anything like that to your own uncle, Gina, would you? Sure, we didn't mean to get into this mess, did we Bart? Gina, you wouldn't see your poor uncle in jail and your poor aunt thrown into the street, would you?' Maura was snivelling.

'Yes, I would!' she yelled.

'Gina, that's enough! I've paid Mr Vannin part of the back rent and I've got a job in the office at Dunlop's, I start tomorrow. But she's right about you, Uncle Bart, there's not a thing wrong with your back!'

'Oh, he'll try, Mary-Kate, that he will! He'll try, won't you Bart?' Maura whined. He nodded. 'If we all pull together we'll all get along together just fine. Will I be makin' us all a pot of tea?'

'Yes, please Aunt and I'll take the biscuit tin and we'll sort out the finances – such as they are. Uncle Bart!' Mary-Kate held out her hand in front of her Uncle. Without looking at her he rummaged in his pocket and produced a handful of coins. Maura handed over the old biscuit tin and Mary-Kate took it, along with the coins. 'Is that all? We've put everything we had in, so must you.'

'I haven't a penny to me name now!' he said peevishly, then as she turned away he shot her a quick, venomous glance and uttered, sotto voce, 'I'll make you sorry you ever came here, you see if I don't. I'll get even!'

Upstairs Gina threw her hat on the chest of drawers and plumped herself down wearily on the bed. 'This is a fine state of affairs. Matty should have listened to me – you all should have listened to me – we couldn't be worse off in America!'

'Don't you start again, Gina, I've had enough for one day. First I had Mr Vannin on the doorstep, then I almost had to get down and beg for that job at Dunlop's, and then when I got home I had those two to confront. Anyway, how did you get on?'

'Oh, wonderful! I wouldn't perform there if they paid me a hundred pounds a week.'

'They turned you down.'

'They didn't get the chance,' she retorted, but she knew Mary-Kate saw through her blustering pretence. 'What about you, Bridget?'

'They did turn me down. I've never been so humiliated . . . so hurt. The woman I saw said that with my accent no decent shop would employ me. Did you ever hear the like? No one has ever said anything so nasty before.'

'Oh, take no notice. Half the population of this city are Irish,' Mary-Kate soothed.

'And half the population of Liverpool don't have careers either!'

Mary-Kate sat down beside Bridget and took the lid off the biscuit tin and dropped Uncle Bart's coins in it. 'I gave Mr Vannin a pound and promised he'd have the rest by the end of next week. I have to work a week "in hand" and so we've got less than two shillings left of the money Ma gave us. So, with the six shillings and twopence from Uncle Bart we've only got about eight shillings, and that won't go far.'

'There's a talent contest at the Hippodrome Theatre on Friday and I'm entering it,' Gina offered.

'Good luck, but even if you win that won't pay the rent.'

'Did I say it would? Uncle Bart can earn something. I meant what I said, if he doesn't go out and get a job – any job – I'm off to the police.'

Bridget sniffed then dashed away the tears on her cheeks with the back of her hand. Things just seemed to be getting worse.

'Oh, don't you start weeping and wailing,' Gina snapped.

'Can we all just quieten down, this is getting us nowhere. We've all had a rotten day, but flying at each other isn't going to help at all. You'll both have to get jobs soon. I made some enquiries and there are jobs available at Dunlop's. They're in the factory, but the pay is good, much higher than in many shops.'

Gina jumped up from the bed. 'In a factory! A factory! You expect us to work in a place like that?'

'You've got a choice, Gina, Walton Hospital or Dunlop's. And so have you Bridget, the factory or slicing bacon at the co-operative store on the corner of Long Lane. Look, it probably won't be for long, there won't be any travelling expenses and we can come home for lunch. You can still both make plans for the future, but in the meantime we have to eat and I gave my promise that the rent would be paid.'

'Oh, it's grand for you, isn't it? You'll be sitting in a nice, clean office all day while we're sweating in a smelly, dirty rubber factory making wellington boots or whatever they make there! And what's Ma going to say when she hears? We'd have been better off staying at home.'

'She won't say anything because we're not going to tell her. For one thing just think how Michael Feehey and his cronies would laugh if it ever got out, and for another Ma has enough to worry about. There's real trouble in Dublin.'

Still smarting from the humiliation of having to choose between hospital drudgery and factory drudgery, Gina couldn't have cared less what was going on in Dublin. 'When hasn't there been trouble in Dublin? Isn't that why we came here in the first place?'

'Have we had a letter?' Bridget asked, still tearful.

Mary-Kate drew the envelope from her bag and pulled out a sheet of writing paper and read aloud:

My Dear Girls,

Everyone here is fine. Matty is enjoying working with your Uncle Richard, who is glad of the help and I am grateful that it keeps Matty busy from morning to night, so he's no energy to go to any political meetings. The news from Dublin is bad, but you've probably heard that already. The Republicans have taken over the Four Courts and are refusing to give up. Sure, Father Maguire says it can only end in disaster for them, but enough of that.

Mrs Feehey asks to be remembered to you all, especially Gina, and she wishes you hadn't gone as you were a "steadying influence" on Michael (although I would have thought it the other way around), for he's done nothing but argue with his father and uncles. He says that Michael Collins and de Valera have "sold out" and she can see nothing but trouble ahead.

Mrs O'Leary has a new assistant, a nice young thing, but she's come all the way from Cahir. Herself wishes you had stayed, Bridget, and hopes you are doing well and if you have the time, would you write and let her know all the latest fashions in the grand shop you work in, so she can keep up with the times here. She always had a good head for business.

Give my love to your Aunt Maura and Uncle Bart and I hope you're not causing them any worry. Don't forget to say your Rosary every night that it might not be too late to stop any more trouble over here. God Bless you all and may the Holy Virgin watch over you.
Your loving mother,
Sarah

At the part dealing with Mrs O'Leary and her requests, Bridget had started crying again. Oh, why had she ever left? Surely if her Ma and all the other women she knew could face the future, she could have done, too. She was just a coward. She'd always shut up or given in for the sake of peace, even as a child.

'Oh, be quiet, Bridget. Every time something goes wrong you start wailing like the Banshee. Will you grow up!'

'Will you stop yelling at her, Gina. What good is it doing? We've got to be practical about things.'

'Practical! Practical! Practical! That's all I hear from you. I've never been so sick of a word in my life, Mary-Kate O'Donnell! It's no wonder you never had the boys lining up to take you out, you're too much of a kill-joy with your damned "Practical" ways.'

'Don't swear! And I have no intention of getting drawn into a screaming match with you. Now what are the pair of you going to do?'

Inwardly, Mary-Kate was seething, stung by Gina's barbs. She wasn't a kill-joy and she couldn't help her serious nature. Where would they all be now if it hadn't been for her common sense? Out on the street, hungry and completely penniless, most likely.

The shuffling and creaking on the stairs silenced them as Aunt Maura lumbered in with a battered tin tray on which were set three cups and saucers, none of which matched, the teapot covered by a knitted cosy that was scorched from being placed too near the fire, and a white milk jug with so many hairline cracks that it looked like the result of a badly put together jigsaw puzzle.

'You needn't have brought it up, aunt, we'd have come down, but thank you anyway.'

Maura glanced sideways at Mary-Kate, thinking she was being sarcastic. She wasn't. 'Your Uncle Bart and I have been thinking and talking and we've come up with a plan.'

'Really?'

'He knows this man who might give him a job.'

'Doing what?'

'Cleaning windows. Of course, Bart can't climb ladders, but he can do the downstairs ones.' She didn't tell them that he still intended to claim his Panel money and that the job was just a bit of moonlighting.

'People around here clean their own windows,' Gina pointed out.

'Not everyone. Them that lives in the big houses in Walton Park and Yew Tree Road and Rawcliffe Road pay to have them done.'

'And this man will take Uncle Bart in with him?'

Maura shuffled uneasily. 'He will that.'

'It's not a very reliable job. You can't clean windows in the rain,' Gina stated tersely. 'Why can't he work on the docks or in any of the factories on the Dock Road?'

'It would kill him!'

'A hard day's work would kill him anyway!'

'It's the fumes, his bronchials wouldn't stand them fumes, and I swear that's the truth of it.'

'If he didn't smoke so much he might have less trouble with his "bronchials",' Gina shot back with venom.

Maura glowered at all three of them before leaving.

They waited until they heard her lumbering tread on the stairs before anyone spoke.

'Pour out the tea, Bridget, there's a good girl, my head is thumping. You two will have to make up your minds about work now.'

Bridget poured out the tea, her shoulders sagging dejectedly. 'What else can we do? We need the money quickly and it might not be too bad, and I can still keep trying the smaller shops.'

'At least you've got some sense. What about you, Gina?'

'Oh, I suppose so, but I don't intend to stay there a single day longer than I have to. And if either of you ever tell anyone back home, and I mean anyone . . . I'll kill you!' Oh, she'd win this talent contest and then she'd be out of Lancaster Street like a flash and she didn't care where to. Anywhere would be better than here!

Only Mary-Kate was happy in her work. Both Bridget and Gina hated it right from the minute they walked through the gates. A circumstance that made them both all the more determined to find other employment and quickly.

Each night after she unwound the turban that covered her head, and brushed her hair until it shone like glowing copper, Gina counted the days to the talent contest. She hadn't mentioned it to anyone except her sisters, but as she scrutinized her reflection in the mirror, she often felt a stab of despair. Would she ever realize that dream of sailing to New York on a luxury liner? Would she ever become a 'star'? At such times she would shut her eyes and will away the doubts. You had to get out and grab every opportunity – no matter how small. Why, even the noise in the rolling shop where she and Bridget worked was useful. It gave her the chance to practise her choice of song for the all-important Talent Contest. At first she had begun by just humming the tune, then, when she realized that no one could hear her above the din, she sang as loudly as she could to her heart's content.

The choice of song had been her decision, but the clothes she would wear had been the subject of many joint consultations in the bedroom. Outfit after outfit had been tried and rejected for one reason or another. Fortunately, they were all of the same slender build so it was possible to combine their wardrobes, although Gina, being a few inches taller than the other two, often had to let down hems.

'I think my pale green looks best. You can pin this bunch of yellow silk roses to the shoulder and put your hair up and thread a green ribbon through it,' Bridget had suggested.

'Um, I think you're right,' Gina had mused, smoothing down the bias-cut folds of eau-de-nil crêpe. 'But I'm having my hair cut so I won't need any ribbon.'

'Your hair is one of your greatest assets and besides, I

don't think these new hairstyles are very feminine at all.'

'Don't be so old-fashioned, Bridget! They look wonderful with the right clothes. Maybe I can pin a piece of green ribbon around my head, like this.' She pulled the ribbon across her forehead and tied it at the back.

'And if we pin a flower to the left side, like this . . .' Bridget attached a small artificial rose, then pulled Gina's curls back and tucked them up, trying to imitate the lines of the 'bob'. 'That looks very smart.'

'Mavis, that girl who works on the machine next to mine, says she is a whizz with a pair of scissors and she'll cut my hair if I want her to. She's done her sister's and I've seen it and it won't cost me anything.'

'Oh, Gina, aren't you terrified? Getting up on a real stage and singing in front of all those people?'

Gina tossed her head. 'Don't be an eejit, Bridget! Isn't this what I've always wanted? And, didn't I sing at Kilsheelan Castle without turning so much as a single hair?' She refused to dwell on the memory of how terrified she'd been that night, nor would she admit that she was indeed having 'nerves' about her forthcoming performance.

'Will there be other singers?'

'I suppose so. Lots of people go in for these contests.'

'And what will you do if you win?'

'*If* I win? I'm going to win!'

'Don't count your chickens before they're hatched,' Mary-Kate interrupted. 'You'd better give me that dress, the hem needs letting down and pressing and I'd think very carefully about letting this Mavis cut your hair. She might make a mess of it and then what will you do?'

Gina raised her eyes to the ceiling. Why couldn't

Mary-Kate see that she was becoming a stick-in-the-mud? She'd be rooted here in this awful house forever, unless she met someone at work, which was highly unlikely as the only men she worked with were a couple of ageing clerks. The men who worked in the factory were far beneath what her sister termed 'suitable'. If she didn't start to go out and mix with people of her own age, she'd soon find she was old before her time and would probably end up an old maid in Liverpool instead of in Clonmel.

'Isn't it tomorrow you said you'd take the rest of the rent money?'

'Yes.'

'Will we have enough? None of us gets paid until next week?'

'No, and with this week's rent we'll owe seventeen and sixpence.'

Gina stopped fiddling with her hair. 'And where are we going to get that from? We'll need what's left in the biscuit tin to survive on, unless we all starve until pay day.'

Mary-Kate began to unfasten the gold chain around her neck, from which hung a small, gold crucifix.

'Oh, no, you don't! We haven't sunk so low that we've got to pawn your gold cross,' Gina cried.

'What else can we do? Aunt Maura hasn't got anything worth pawning, I've looked! I'll get it back when I get paid, lots of people do it.'

'We're not "lots of people"! It's the one thing that Ma was so proud of, that she's never had to pawn anything in her life. I'll not let you, Mary-Kate!'

'What else is there?'

'We can all ask for a sub on our wages. They'll give it you, Mavis told me. If we each have five shillings that would be . . .'

'Fifteen shillings. It's still not enough.'

'Oh, I could just kill that little rat! I hate him! Surely he must have some money, he's been out every day? I'm going down to see him, he's frightened of me!' And with that Gina wrenched open the door and ran downstairs, her stockinged feet making no noise.

'Do you think he'll have any?' Bridget ventured.

Mary-Kate shrugged. 'At least he's trying.'

'As long as the weather is fine. Wait until it rains and then we'll have all the complaints about the back and the "bronchials".'

The voices below became more strident and then they heard Gina screaming at the top of her voice.

'Oh, dear God, now what?' Mary-Kate exclaimed.

They both rushed down the stairs and burst into the kitchen together. Gina was so livid she was almost dancing with temper.

'I caught them! I caught them red-handed! Look. Just look at that.' She pointed to a pile of coins on the table.

Bridget and Mary-Kate looked at each other, mystified.

'He's been moonlighting! No wonder he's quite happy to go cleaning windows, he's still drawing his Panel money! And we've virtually been living on bread and dripping and you were all set to pawn your cross and chain. You sneaking little, good-for-nothing thief! Give me that money.'

Before anyone could stop her, Gina had swept the coins off the table.

'You give that back, he earned it!' Maura yelled.

'Prove it! Go on, prove it! We'll all go down to the Police Station together so he can swear he earned over two pounds cleaning windows.'

Maura sat down as Gina stormed out of the room followed by Bridget.

'If this happens again, Aunt,' Mary-Kate said stonily, 'I won't be responsible for Gina and I won't try to stop her. I never thought anyone could sink so low. You both deserve to go to jail, but Confession will do this time and you can be sure that Father Morley will hear of this.'

Uncle Bart got to his feet, his face twisted in an ugly sneer. 'I don't care about any bloody priest and you'll be sorry for this . . . all of you!'

'God forgive you! But I don't think I will, and I'm not afraid of your threats.' But as she slammed the door behind her Mary-Kate wondered if Gina hadn't pushed him too far. Desperate men do desperate things. Then she shrugged. At least the rent would be paid and they would all eat and she wouldn't have to pawn anything and come pay day, they could settle a few more debts.

Chapter Five

━━━◆◆◆━━━

MARY-KATE WAS SURPRISED to find how near Walton Park was. She had hurried out of the works entrance and down Rice Lane, calling into the haulage yard on the corner of Parkinson Road. The man in the office there had told her that she had just missed 'the Boss', he'd gone home for lunch.

She was out of breath when she turned into the wide road, lined with trees just bursting into leaf. The houses were big and fairly new, some were four storeys high. Flights of steps led up to the front doors. She would have preferred to have paid the rent to him in his office, being acutely aware that it was not quite the thing to call at his home as a debtor. Mary-Kate looked up the steps to the solid, varnished front door with its gleaming brass knocker in the shape of a lion's head, and decided that it would be better to go around the back to the tradesman's entrance. Before she had time to turn away the door opened and a woman stood on the step.

'Are you Miss O'Donnell?' she called.

Mary-Kate nodded.

'Then you're to come in.' She held the door open. 'Mr Vannin's just come in himself, he saw you through the library window.'

She followed the woman – who by her dress was obviously a servant – into a wide hallway.

'He'll be out in a minute. Wait there.' And with that instruction the woman disappeared along the corridor and through a door at the end.

Mary-Kate looked around. Mr Vannin obviously wasn't short of money, judging by the fine quality of the mahogany hall-stand and the framed prints and the large gilt-framed mirror. Yet there was something lacking about the place and she just couldn't put her finger on it.

'Miss O'Donnell, I'm sorry to keep you waiting. Would you come in?'

She turned, catching sight of him in the doorway of the library. 'Thank you. I did call at the yard but they said you'd just left.'

She walked forward and placed an envelope on the top of the leather-topped desk, littered with papers. 'There's the rest of the money, just as I promised, and from now on the rent will be paid promptly. If you will just tell me when your man calls, I'll make sure someone is in.' She spoke quietly and confidently, aware that he was watching her closely. It was a relief to be out of his debt. That fact restored much of her pride and took away some of the indignity of their last meeting. 'Now, if you'll excuse me, I have to get back to work.'

'Ah, yes, you have obtained a job with the Dunlop Rubber Company.'

She looked at him, openly surprised. Just how did he know that?

The Sisters O'Donnell

'Yes, I work in the office.'

'And your sisters work in the factory.'

'Temporarily, until they can obtain better positions. We needed some money quickly. My aunt and uncle seemed to be in debt to the whole neighbourhood, but no doubt you know that as well!' Mary-Kate could feel her cheeks growing hot.

'Miss O'Donnell, I have a proposition to make you. Would you be interested in doing a little extra work, in the evenings perhaps?'

'And what kind of work would that be?'

'Exactly what you are doing now. The business is growing and Johnson, my clerk, is getting on and can't cope with the extra work. I had thought of taking on someone else as well, but then it occurred to me that a young lady of your obvious abilities could help out.'

'I don't want your charity, thank you. We'll manage quite well!'

'I'm not offering charity. I'm not a charitable man, I'm a business man. I'll pay the same rate as you are paid during the day.'

She stared at him in silence, not knowing what to say. The extra money would be useful, just as long as it wasn't a sense of pity that motivated him. But as she stared at him she thought pity wasn't one of his more obvious traits. 'Wouldn't your wife think it rather strange for a young woman to be coming here during the evenings?'

'I'm a widower.'

'Oh, I'm sorry.'

'There would be nothing improper about the arrangements. I'm often out during the evenings and Mrs

Rickard, my housekeeper, will be here. Will you think about it?'

'Yes. Yes, I'll think about it, if I may. Now I really must go or Mr Chapman will be extremely cross and besides, I hate to be late.'

Mr Vannin opened the door and ushered her into the hall. 'When may I expect your decision?'

'Will Saturday be all right? Shall I call into the office?'

'Saturday will be fine and, please, call here after lunch. I never work on Saturday afternoons.'

As she hurried down the road Mary-Kate pondered the experience. Why on earth should he ask her to work for him? He could have hired a young clerk who'd be only too willing to pore over the long columns of figures and ruin his eyesight for a pittance each week. Why ask her? He was a strange man. Obviously well off, obviously very practical, but now she knew what it was that was missing in that house. It had no mistress to give it that special individuality. There was no feminine touch. No vases of flowers, no fragrances of lavender or roses. She wondered if he had any children. If he did, they were probably grown up for he must be at least fifty. By the time she reached the works entrance she had made up her mind that she would accept his offer.

They all got off the number seventeen tram outside 'Gregson's Well' public house on the corner of Cobden Street. Facing them was the Hippodrome Theatre on West Derby Road. It was a fine evening and the doors of the pub were open and raucous laughter issued from within.

'I just hope none of that lot will be in the audience!'

Gina stated as they crossed the road. Already she was feeling nervous and edgy.

Bridget had spent nearly an hour sewing the floral spray to the shoulder of the dress and then arranging the ribbon headband around her newly, and successfully, cropped hair, and both her sisters had assured her that she looked as elegant and attractive as any of the women who shopped at Cripps or Sloan's or Miss Drinkwater's.

There was already quite a throng outside the theatre and they had to push their way through to the doors, where Gina explained that she was a contestant. The doorman gave her directions as to where she would find the dressing rooms, told her to hand her music in to the stage manager, and then told the others to buy their tickets in the foyer. With a quick hug each and a whispered 'Good Luck' they left her to find her way backstage.

It was nothing like what she had expected. It was dingy and cold and badly lit. After she had given her music to the stage manager, Gina made her way towards the dressing rooms. They were little more than large cupboards with a mirror and a couple of hooks on the wall and were already crowded. But she pushed her way into one, took off her coat and hung it on top of the other garments.

'Where do you leave your handbag?' she asked a girl who was dressed in a red satin hobble skirt and a black taffeta, low-cut top trimmed with red bows, who was applying rouge to her already ruddy cheeks.

'You should 'ave left it with yer fella, luv, if yer can trust 'im. This lot will pinch anythin' that's not nailed down! You 'aven't done this before 'ave you?'

'No.'

'Oh, take it with yer then.' The girl peered into the mirror, pouting her lips into a cupid's bow. 'What do yer do?'

'Sing.'

'Me, too. What's yer name?'

'Gina. Regina O'Donnell.'

'I mean yer real name?'

'It is my real name!'

'Oh, I thought it was yer stage name. Regina! Never 'eard of that before.'

The discordant sound of a band tuning up wafted along the corridor, along with the cry of 'Get your numbers please, Ladies and Gents! Numbers! Numbers!'

There was instant pandemonium as everyone tried to get out of the room simultaneously and Gina found herself trapped in a corner with an elbow in her face and someone's foot treading heavily on hers. Her hair would be ruined and she would look a fright before she even started! Lashing out wildly, she managed to free herself, earning a few curses in the process. The girl in the red satin and black taffeta was elbowing her way ruthlessly back through the crowd, clutching a piece of stiff white card.

'I gorrit! Nine. Me lucky number. 'Aven't yer got yours yet? Gerra move on or yer'll be last an' that's as bad as bein' first! If yer first they forget about yer and if yer last they're fed up by then!'

By the time Gina had pushed through the crowd she had no option but to accept the last piece of card with the number seventeen on it.

The girl sucked in her breath. 'Ah, now that's a real shame.'

'Seventeen is my lucky number!' Gina rejoined dogmatically. 'I'm Irish and isn't the seventeenth of March Saint Patrick's Day, so for me it's good luck! And, like you said, by the time they get to me they'll have forgotten the early acts and I'll make sure they don't get fed up with me!'

The girl pulled a wry face at her before disappearing along the corridor.

Gina wasn't as confident as she had sounded. She sat down on a three-legged stool that comprised the only furniture in the room and patted her hair. She looked pale; she should have borrowed some rouge. With all those lights on her she might look like a corpse. She got out her lipstick and dotted two spots on each cheek then rubbed it in, leaning closer to the mirror to observe the effect. Then she retouched her lips and fiddled with the corsage. Would it have looked better on the other shoulder? Was the flower attached to the headband a little over decorative? Butterflies were dancing maniacally in her stomach.

She got up and began to pace up and down, but as the room was so small that didn't help. She could hear the bursts of cheering and clapping that came from the end of the corridor, but where was everyone? No one had come back to the dressing room yet, was there somewhere else you had to wait? Oh, this was the worst part, this terrible waiting with your stomach in knots and your hands shaking, the palms damp and sticky. If she didn't do something she would lose her nerve completely and run out.

With her bag held tightly under her arm she walked along the corridor, clasping the piece of card with her number on it. She didn't even know how they judged who was to be the winner! Ahead of her the subterranean gloom of the tunnel opened into a wide space where small groups of people stood in silence. So that's where they were, waiting and watching the progress of the competition.

It was cold in the wings and it smelled musty. Pieces of painted wood, depicting various scenes, stood propped against the far wall. A few tables and chairs were half covered by grubby dustsheets, as were other indistinguishable objects. Gina craned her head forward. Now she could see the stage. A brilliantly lit expanse of infinite vastness. The act now performing was a troupe of acrobats, got up as gypsies, and she watched their twisting, tumbling and somersaulting antics with mounting panic.

'Yer on next, luv!'

The girl in red was standing beside her.

Now that the time had arrived, nausea swept over her and she clapped a hand to her mouth.

'Oh, gerron with it! It's not that bad, yer'll ger over it. 'Ere, give us yer bag, I'll mind it.'

The acrobats pushed past her and she heard her name and number announced. She stood rooted to the spot, she couldn't move!

'Miss Gina O'Donnell!' The voice out there thundered again.

'Go on. Move yerself!'

Suddenly she was out on the stage. The lights were blinding and she couldn't see anyone at all, but she could hear them. She wanted to die, she wished the ground would open and swallow her.

'Will you get on with it then, or is it struck dumb ye are?' someone shouted from somewhere high above her. It was a voice thick with the brogue – a man's voice and she remembered her Pa.

Gina stepped forward. Struck dumb she certainly wasn't! She walked to the front of the stage and nodded to the conductor. Dimly she could see the faces of the people occupying the first row of seats. The band had to compete with the restless and rather noisy audience and she realized that if she were waiting for quiet she would wait all night.

She had a little difficulty at first, then her voice gathered strength and she felt the blood coursing through her veins. This was what she wanted. This was the fulfilment of a hundred dreams. Tonight she would win! Her name would be on the programme as a 'new star'. Her clear, vibrant voice rose above the diminishing noise. They were listening to her! To her! She went into the second verse exultantly. Her expression animated, her eyes sparkling.

'For the beauty of your love,
I will bless the Heavens above,
My sweet, my wild Irish rose.'

The last haunting notes hung in the air for a second and then the whole theatre was silent. Then came the applause. It was clamorous. They were applauding her! She could have laughed and cried at the same time. Oh, it was so wonderful. Her heart was racing madly, her eyes and cheeks bright with excitement. She dropped a deep curtsey, then blew them a kiss and flung her arms wide as though to embrace them all. Oh, seventeen *was* her lucky number! 'God Bless you, Saint Patrick!' she whispered.

As she walked back into the wings she stumbled, her eyes still dazzled by the lights on stage.

'I know "break a leg" is the usual good luck message, but there's no need to take it literally.'

She couldn't see the man, but his grip was strong and his voice was warm and humorous.

'Thanks. I'm still so dazzled and . . .'

'I know, it's like wine, isn't it? Sweet and heady.'

She still couldn't see him clearly, but he was tall and quite well built, that much she could discern. 'What happens now?'

'They announce the winner.'

She turned back towards the stage. It must be her! It had to be, they had loved her, they were still clapping and shouting!

A man in an evening suit had stepped into the centre of the stage and was shouting something. She took a step forward, but a strong hand held her back. As she turned to shake it off, the girl in red shoved her bag into her hands.

'It's me! It's me! I told yer nine was me lucky number!'

The figures around her moved like ghosts and merged into an obscure mass. Surely, surely it couldn't be . . . ? There must be some mistake? Not her, that painted, overdressed, common . . . it must be a mistake. Again Gina felt sick, but this time with despair.

Everyone was drifting away, some with heads down, others trying to laugh and joke. She turned away. Her throat felt dry and raw.

'Miss O'Donnell!'

She stopped, wondering if she had heard her name or was that just another part of this whole nightmare?

'Miss O'Donnell? Don't go, I want to talk to you.'

She turned her head. She still couldn't see him clearly. 'What is there to talk about?'

'You.'

'Me? I didn't win, it's her in the red skirt you want.'

'No thanks. I see a dozen like her every day.'

'Who are you anyway?'

He stepped into the light and now she could see him clearly. He was tall and broad shouldered. His hair was dark, as were his eyes – eyes that were smiling at her. He was immaculately dressed in an evening suit and the stiff, white shirt and bow tie made his skin look even swarthier. He smiled, revealing strong, white teeth. He was a strikingly handsome man. Dazed as she was, that fact registered in her mind.

'I'm Edward Vinetti. I'm a theatrical agent.'

'Oh.' She was too numb to think of anything else to say.

'Don't be disappointed, you do have talent.'

Feelings were beginning to return. 'But not enough to win.'

'Look around you. What do you see? A small provincial theatre with run of the mill acts.'

'So?'

He looked down at her. She was beautiful, with those large hazel eyes, clear skin and that flaming hair, set off by the green crêpe dress, and she did have talent, he wasn't just flattering her. A talent he wasn't prepared to see ruined. 'How old are you?'

Disappointment was now a dull ache. Her eyes had a

hard glint in them. She'd heard of men like him. 'I'm twenty-one, why?'

'Is this your first public appearance?'

Her chin jerked up. If he took her for a simple fool then she'd soon put him straight on that matter. 'No! I've sung in public before! I've even sung at a Castle!'

'In Ireland?' There was just a faint hint of laughter in his voice.

'Yes! And if you've quite finished with this . . . this inquisition, I'm going home. My sisters are waiting for me.'

'You have sisters? Are they as talented and as beautiful?'

She heard Michael Feehey's mocking voice: '*The Sisters O'Donnell are leaving Clonmel!*' 'Get out of my way!'

'I see you've got the temper that goes with the hair.'

She pushed past him but he caught her arm again.

'Will you just listen to me, Miss Gina O'Donnell?'

'No! And if you don't let go of me I'll scream blue murder, so I will!'

'Do you want to waste your time in places like this? Do you? The Music Hall is finished! The Stage Musical is the thing of the future, or Musical Comedy as some call it, and eventually it will be the Cinema Musical. Anyone who makes it to the top won't just be seen by a few hundred people in small places like this, but by thousands right across the country and in America, too! Now, will you listen to me?'

'I've been warned about men like you, Mr Vinetti! Do you think I'm some ignorant little fool straight off the boat who'll believe everything you tell her? Well, I'm not, so you can take your fancy promises and . . .'

'I get the gist of your meaning and I don't think you're a fool – far from it! I think you've got brains behind that pretty face. Brains and ambition and talent. I'm not what you think I am, I am a theatrical agent – a respected one – and I occasionally come North to look for girls like you . . .'

'Oh, I bet you do! Let go of me!'

'You see, you've forgotten all about losing this second-rate contest already, haven't you?'

She had. She'd completely forgotten it.

'And that's what a true professional does. Forgets the bad breaks and looks forward. I think you've got the guts to keep on looking forward, but I could be wrong. So, you're free to go, to whine and moan and give up. See!' He released her.

She took a few steps forward then stopped. What if he was speaking the truth? What if she turned down this chance? She turned back. 'I've never been a coward. That's something you can't be when you've been through four years of war and besides, I promised someone I'd make him proud of me!'

'Just my luck, you're married?' he joked.

'No. It was my father. He . . . he was killed.'

Vinetti continued to gaze at her steadily and quite suddenly she felt she could trust him. It was as though she'd known him all her life.

'You were his "Wild Irish Rose"?' he asked, softly, without a trace of mockery.

Gina nodded.

'Then I'm offering you a contract, Miss Gina O'Donnell, will you come to London?'

'When?'

'Just as soon as you are ready.'

Even though she was overwhelmed by the opulence of the Adelphi Hotel, Bridget could not be persuaded to have even a small glass of wine, remembering the Dublin to Liverpool ferry and the way she had felt that morning. The sheer luxury and grandeur that surrounded her were intoxicating enough and this Mr Vinetti was the most handsome and charming man she'd ever met.

Mary-Kate was not so overwhelmed and viewed Gina's mentor with suspicion. She sipped the sweet white wine slowly. 'So you want Gina to go to London? You think she has the talent for these "Stage Musicals"?'

'I do. Believe me Mary-Kate – may I call you that? Believe me, I understand your reticence and I respect you for it. You wouldn't think much of your sister if you let her go chasing off to London with a complete stranger without being concerned, now would you?'

'And where will she live? And what will she live on?'

'You sound just like Ma!' Gina interrupted. She had intended to ask these questions herself. After all it was her life, her decision, not Mary-Kate's.

'She'll live in what are known in the business as "digs", lodgings, and she'll have to work – hard.'

'As I happen to be the person concerned here, I'd thank you both not to talk about me as if I weren't even here!'

Vinetti smiled at Mary-Kate. 'And you're worrying

about her? With that temper I'd worry about anyone who crossed her!'

Gina opened her mouth, then closed it. Her temper had already lost her one opportunity.

'I'll find you work, in the smaller theatres. The "Empire" chain probably, they still draw audiences.'

'I thought you said music halls were finished?'

'Oh, they're not quite dead. You'll have to learn your trade and there's no better way of doing it than working the halls, and you'll have to learn to dance and take singing lessons between . . .'

'I don't need anyone to teach me how to sing.'

He smiled a little sardonically. She had a lot to learn and he could foresee some right royal rows ahead, but she was a challenge and one he would enjoy. 'There she goes again!'

'You'll have your work cut out, Mr Vinetti, you might be getting more than you bargained for,' Mary-Kate murmured.

Gina glared at her sister.

'Call me Edward, please. Do we have to be so formal?'

At last Mary-Kate smiled. 'It's her life, Edward.'

'Well, thank you! Now we've got that fact established, can we finish our supper? I'm going to London with Edward and there's an end to the matter.'

Mary-Kate toyed with the meringue on her plate. 'Vinetti? Where do you come from, Edward?'

Again Gina glared at her. Oh, would she never let matters rest? She was like a dog with a bone.

'Here. Liverpool.'

Gina almost choked. 'Liverpool?'

'What's wrong with Liverpool? This city produces a lot of talent.'

'Nothing. I like Liverpool,' Mary-Kate announced while Gina was getting her breath back.

'My Grandfather was an Italian but he married an Irish girl. I was born here and I was brought up in the theatre. Although my grandmother looked after me in the early years while my parents went on tour around the country, later I went with them. But then I realized that if you wanted to get on, London was the place to be. But I still regard this as my home. So you see, I'm not some kind of foreign gigolo! And now, if we've all finished, I'll get you a cab. Knowing this place so well, I don't want you molested on your way home.'

Although she liked him and he had dispelled some of her initial fears, Mary-Kate was still just a little suspicious. Cautious, she told herself, she was just being cautious. After all, it was she who would have to explain all this to Ma. 'Edward, may I have a word with you before we go?'

'Of course.'

'Gina, perhaps you and Bridget would like to freshen up?'

Gina had been on the point of demanding an explanation from Mary-Kate about what she viewed as yet another instance of interference, but her curiosity got the better of her. The hotel was so palatial that she couldn't resist the chance to see what lay behind the doors discretely marked 'Powder Room'. So with Bridget at her side she made her way across the richly decorated and carpeted foyer. 'We might as well see what some of the place looks like. We'll probably never get the chance again and Mary-Kate is only going to fuss and fret about me, asking more stupid questions that I'd sooner not hear,' she stated as she turned the gold-plated door handle.

Edward led Mary-Kate to a velvet-covered sofa set in an alcove flanked with small palms and potted shrubs.

'Come on, Mary-Kate, you're not happy about something, are you?'

'No, I'm not. I don't want to sound ungracious or appear over suspicious, but obviously I do care about Gina and I feel responsible for both of them and I'm going to have to write and explain to Ma and you do hear such dreadful things . . .'

'You still don't trust me, do you? Not fully? I can understand that. I'll give you both my card and the address of Gina's digs. They won't be palatial – they never are, believe me, but if there's one person in this business that you can trust, it's Mrs Rose Weston. She'll be Gina's landlady and believe me she is a person to be reckoned with. She'll stand no nonsense from anyone! A very formidable lady indeed and either you or your mother are free to write to her, if you wish. As for me,' he shrugged, 'what else can I tell you? I believe Gina will go far and I will look after her as best I can. I know the "right" people and the "wrong" ones, too. And by the time she's finished working, rehearsing and practising, she'll have no energy for anything else. I'm a hard taskmaster. But you know Gina far better than I do . . .'

'Indeed I do, and I know what she's like when she's set on something or someone!'

'I have a very strict rule Mary-Kate, I never mix business with pleasure. It only leads to trouble. To me, Gina is an investment and I look after my business investments – you'll have to take my word on that.' He took out a printed card and a pen and wrote an address on the back of the card, then handed it to her. 'Here's Mrs Weston's address in Bloomsbury. Put it in your bag before Gina sees it for I've a feeling that she might not be too happy about our little discussion.'

Mary-Kate took the card and smiled at him, feeling much easier in her mind. She did like him and now she felt she could trust him. With Mrs Weston's address safely in her bag, should she ever need it, she rose as her sisters crossed the foyer towards them.

'I think your cab is waiting. Here is my card and the name and address of your landlady. As soon as you arrive, telephone me and I'll come to the station for you,' Edward instructed her.

Gina nodded. She wanted to pinch herself to make sure it wasn't all a dream.

'Don't worry, Mary-Kate,' Edward said, smiling gently. 'She'll be just fine. I hope we meet again.'

She shook the extended hand. 'Thank you, Edward, for . . . everything.'

'Goodbye, Bridget.'

'Goodbye, Mr . . . Edward.' She liked him, too. Gina was so lucky. She wished she had someone like him to take an interest in her, to buy her expensive suppers and take her to places like the Adelphi, where even the toilets had marble floors, gold taps on the washbasins and soft, pale pink towels and pink perfumed soap in small, square tablets. But Gina didn't seem to think he was anything special, just someone to help her in her career.

'Aren't you going to say anything? You've sat there like two tailor's dummies ever since we left the hotel.' Gina was just bursting with excitement. Couldn't they see that this was the most wonderful thing that had ever happened to her?

'There's nothing much left to say, is there?' Mary-Kate said dryly.

'What are you going to tell Ma?' Bridget asked.

'Nothing. I want to surprise her. I'll write and tell her when I get my first real break.'

'Oh, that'll surprise her all right. It will give her a heart attack!'

'Oh, why can't you be happy for me? You're jealous, that's what you are.'

'Don't be ridiculous, Gina. I am happy for you but I am worried about you, too. You hear such terrible things . . .'

'You're off again! You're middle-aged and staid, Mary-Kate and you're only twenty-two. I can take care of myself. If I didn't trust him I wouldn't go. I'm not a complete eejit! And it won't be all wining and dining. You heard him, it will be hard work and there are no guarantees that I'll become a star. But he did say I had talent and ambition and guts.'

'You've always had all that and I'm happy for you, Gina, but . . .'

'Well then, no more buts. I have my own life to lead. You think about yourself for a change!'

Mary-Kate closed her eyes. She supposed Gina was right. Perhaps she did worry too much; was she becoming old before her time? When Gina had appeared on that stage looking so vital and beautiful and utterly composed and confident, and when her voice had soared over the buzz of the crowd, she had felt so proud of her, and when her song had ended she had stood up, like Bridget, and clapped until her hands were stinging. She had suffered the same sense of numbing shock when that awful girl with the painted face and flashy clothes had been announced as the winner. She cared what happened to Gina just as much as she cared what happened to Bridget. But in worrying about them, was she losing her youth? Out of the two of them she had less cause to worry about Gina – she could take care of herself. She leaned her head against the back of the seat feeling tired and still a little confused.

Bridget had said nothing at all, she was too wrapped up in her own thoughts. Gina was leaving them, there would be just herself and Mary-Kate in that awful house and just her in that awful factory. Gina had got what she wanted, while she . . . she had to find another job! It was all right for Gina, accents weren't noticeable when you sang.

She hadn't been able to get Miss Drinkwater's remarks out of her mind. There were some nice shops along County Road, and even Walton Vale, perhaps she should try them. She simply couldn't bear that factory without Gina. Unlike Mary-Kate, she had liked Edward Vinetti from the start. Of course, he was quite a bit older than even Mary-Kate, but he was so handsome, so charming and he had treated her as though she were just as important as Gina. He had taken her arm as she had alighted from the cab, made sure she had everything she wanted, and then had shaken her hand and smiled that wonderful smile. Mary-Kate had asked him all those pointed questions because she was worried about Gina, but even Mary-Kate liked him.

Another thought struck her. Mary-Kate was going to do some work for Mr Vannin. That would mean she would be alone with her aunt and uncle. The thought made her shudder. She was wary of Uncle Bart, although he said little to her. It was the way she caught him looking at her when he thought no one was watching. There was a sly, crafty look in his eyes, as though he wanted to lash out at her but was afraid to. She knew he was afraid of both Mary-Kate and Gina, and he was also very much under Aunt Maura's thumb, but with Gina gone and Mary-Kate out, she would make sure Aunt Maura never left the house without her.

Chapter Six

———◆———

GINA LEFT THE FOLLOWING week and as they hugged and kissed her on the station, both girls felt miserable. Gina herself had tears in her eyes, but she dashed them away. Oh, it was goodbye to that boring, smelly, dirty job and goodbye to Lancaster Street and Maùra and Bart. She had Edward's card in her bag and lodgings in Bloomsbury. As she walked down the platform she turned back and waved, then, looking upwards at the soot-blackened arches of the glass-domed roof of Lime Street Station, she smiled. And it was goodbye to Liverpool, too. During her short stay she hadn't liked the city much. Oh, there were fine buildings and pleasant parks but there was also dirt and squalor and poverty on a scale she had never seen before and never wanted to see again. It would be hard work but now she was on her way!

'I'll write! I promise!' she called, but her voice was lost in the piercing whistle and outrush of steam that announced the train's departure.

Bridget and Mary-Kate stood and waved until the train had completely disappeared.

'Do we have to go back straight away?'

Mary-Kate looked at the pale, tearful face and smiled. 'No, let's go and treat ourselves. We'll have tea and scones at Lyon's in Clayton Square, then, if you like, we'll go window shopping.'

Bridget brightened up as they walked out into the sunlight.

'Do you think she'll be all right?'

'Don't be an eejit, you know our Gina, she can look after herself and I don't think Edward Vinetti will be quite so taken with her after she's lost her temper a few times. Although I think he may just be the right person to handle her.'

Over the tea and scones Mary-Kate studied her sister. Bridget had been quiet and withdrawn ever since the night of the talent contest. She was probably worrying about Gina, too. Oh, there you go again, she thought, fussing like an old mother hen! 'Are you feeling all right, Bridget? You look very pale and you've not been your usual bright self for days?'

Bridget stirred her tea slowly, wondering if she should tell her sister of her dread of being left alone with Uncle Bart. It would sound stupid. He was such an insignificant little runt of a man and besides, Mary-Kate had enough to worry about. She was doing two jobs and virtually running the house as Aunt Maura, if let, quickly slipped back into her slovenly ways and wasn't above appropriating a few shillings when she thought she could get away with it. 'I'm just grand, truly. It's that place. I hate the job!'

'Then we'll have to do something about it, won't we? Maybe Mr Vannin knows someone who has a shop; he seems to know everyone.'

'No, don't go asking him, you've enough to do. I'll go along County Road next Saturday afternoon.'

'I'd try Frosts, it looks nice without being over-priced. In fact Mrs Rickard, Mr Vannin's housekeeper, told me that they are very reasonable and that a Miss Kay, I think she said, was a very pleasant woman. Ask for her. I'll feel happier myself when you're out of that place. I think Aunt Maura is right about the fumes, you've not been looking at all well, Bridget.'

'Are you going to Mr Vannin's tonight?'

'Yes, it will take my mind off . . . other things.' Mary-Kate sipped her tea. She enjoyed going to the big house in Walton Park more than she would admit. It was so quiet and peaceful. The rooms were large and airy and clean and there wasn't a shoddy or worn piece of furniture anywhere. Of course, she had only seen the hall, library and the small adjoining study where she worked and she often wondered what the other rooms were like, but she would never presume to take even the smallest peek. She had also realized that Lewis Vannin was on his way to becoming a wealthy man. He had had the foresight to invest his money in more property and more wagons, he was even toying with the idea of a motorized lorry.

He was very deferential in his attitude towards her, never once had he overstepped the bounds of propriety. Conversation was restricted to business, although he sometimes enquired after her sisters, but never her aunt and uncle.

She had learned from Mrs Rickard that the 'missus' had only died two years ago and that he did have children. Two daughters. The elder one, Elizabeth, was

married and a right madam she was too, with a face that
would stop a clock and eyes in the back of her head and
God help anyone who dared to call her Bessie or Lizzie.
She insisted on her full title, Mrs Elizabeth Winskill.
Obviously Mrs Rickard disliked her intensely and she
didn't have much time for 'that old skinflint', as she called
her employer.

'He's as hard as a cargo of Irish confetti! Sorry, luv, I
didn't mean to offend,' had been her comments.

Mary-Kate had smiled and then laughed when she
found out that 'Irish confetti' was a cargo of stone
chippings. She liked the native Liverpudlians and their
wry sense of humour. But she had tended to agree with
the housekeeper when she had learnt that the other
daughter was only ten years old and had been packed off
to a convent boarding school. 'So she doesn't get under
his feet. He's no time for her at all, poor little thing! She
was heart-broken over her Ma, she loved her Ma did
Ellen. Course it would have been different if he'd had a
son, never forgave the Missus for that!' Mrs Rickard had
continued.

'But that wasn't her fault.' she had protested.

'Try tellin' him that. Three she bore and three she
buried, God rest her! He's a hard man, Mary-Kate. Hard
and cold,' she had finished.

'Drink up your tea, Bridget or we'll have no time to
look at the shops,' Mary-Kate urged, dragging her
thoughts back to the present.

They had been late getting back and Mary-Kate had to
dash off straight away to work, leaving Bridget and
Maura to make the supper. After the meal was finished

Maura got up and went into the hall, returning with her coat and a navy blue felt hat with a green ribbon around the crown.

'Have you been shopping then, aunt? It suits you.' Bridget felt bound to make some complimentary remark.

'Aye, got it down Paddy's Market for a tanner. I can't afford ter go to them shops you buy things from!'

'I haven't bought anything since I've been here.'

'No, but the other one bought enough for the three of you!'

She meant Gina and Bridget bit her lip. She was missing Gina already. 'Are you going out?'

'I am that.'

'Is Uncle Bart going too?'

Maura snorted, then tilted the hat at an angle over one eye. 'He is not. Me and some of the girls are havin' a night out on our own, just for a change.'

Bridget gripped the edge of the table tightly as the nameless dread crept over her. 'Can I come too?'

'No you can't! Sure, we don't want the likes of you lookin' down your nose at us and with those ears of yours flappin' and takin' everythin' in. Didn't you say you'd some mendin' to do and that you were goin' to write to your Ma?'

'Please let me come with you? I hate being on my own and with Mary-Kate at work . . .'

'Has the Divil addled your brain or what? Your Uncle Bart will be in and there's nothin' in this house worth stealin' and doesn't everyone know it! When your Uncle Bart comes in, tell him not to wait up for me.'

'Where is he?'

'He'll be havin' a quick bevvy in the Black Horse after

his work. He's entitled to that, isn't he?' Maura snapped.

Bridget began to clear away the dishes. 'Will I put his supper between two plates on the hob?' Her question fell on empty air. Maura had already gone.

Bridget had made three attempts at a letter to her Ma, trying to be cheerful and optimistic and not mention Gina, and the table was littered with screwed up pieces of paper. She didn't hear Uncle Bart come in. She looked up and he was standing in the doorway. It was another trait he had that made her uncomfortable. She got up. 'I'll get your supper. Aunt Maura has gone out with some friends. She said not to wait up for her.' Bridget put the hot plate down on the table.

'Where's the other one?'

'She's out, working for Mr Vannin.' She went into the tiny scullery and began to scour the pans, hoping he would remain in the kitchen. It would be hours before Mary-Kate got back.

'It's all dried up. I'm not eatin' that swill!' His voice came from behind her.

She turned her head. 'You should get home on time, shouldn't you and not stay out drinking, then it wouldn't be ruined.' She tried to sound as sharp as Gina.

'You're just the same as the other two, aren't yer? An 'ardfaced, interferin' little bitch an' with a mouth like a parish oven!'

She felt his hands on her shoulders and she tried to wrench herself free but the room was too small and she was wedged between him and the stone sink. His face was close to hers and she could smell the beer on his breath.

'Well, Bart Milligan's 'ad enough of the lot of yer! I'll teach yer to 'ave a bit of respect!'

His hand caught her across the mouth, snapping her head back and she felt the salty taste of blood in her mouth. She screamed as she tried to claw at his face. She'd never realized he was so strong. She heard him yelp and curse and then he grabbed her by the front of her blouse. The thin cotton ripped. The screams died in her throat as she saw the expression in his eyes. If he touched her she would faint. She would be sick . . . her fingers searched frantically over the wooden draining board until they closed over the object she had been seeking. The bread knife. It shook in her hand but she managed to thrust it between herself and him. 'If you touch me, I'll kill you . . . I swear I will!'

He backed away from her, his eyes riveted on the wavering blade. 'Put that down now, Bridget! I didn't mean it, it was only a bit of fun.'

She lunged at him. 'Fun!' Already her mouth was swollen and the word was slurred. 'Get out of my way!'

He shrank back against the wall as she stepped past him, the knife still between them, his eyes still following the blade.

Once in the kitchen she slumped into a chair, feeling dizzy and faint, but she had to get upstairs, away from him! She could lock the door and keep the knife with her. She got to her feet, swaying for an instant, then ran out and up the stairs.

'If yer tell them anythin' I'll say you threw yourself at me, an' don't think your Aunt Maura won't believe me, either. She 'ates yer all!' he yelled up the stairs after her.

Bridget slammed the door and locked it and then

threw herself on the bed, the knife still in her hand. She was shivering yet her head felt as though it were on fire. She pulled the edges of her blouse together. He was the most repulsive man she had ever met and she hated him! She had to get away from him; she couldn't stand living under the same roof, never knowing when . . . He had sworn he would get even with Mary-Kate and now she knew what form his revenge would take. He knew she didn't have the same temperament as either of her sisters. He knew she was afraid of him. He would find other opportunities to torment and even attack her and she couldn't live with that constant fear!

She got up and went to the washstand. Her hair was tangled, her eyes like those of a frightened animal and her lip swollen and tender. She poured some cold water from the jug and washed her face. She would never feel safe ever again in this house; she'd have to go. She brushed her hair and took off the torn blouse, stuffing it in the mending basket, then she took a clean one from the chest of drawers. As soon as Mary-Kate came in she'd tell her and they'd both leave. Mary-Kate would find somewhere else. She sat down abruptly on the bed as another traumatic thought occurred to her. Mary-Kate would send her home!

She was so confused and frightened that she began to cry noisily. She wanted to go home, but how could she? For a start she would have to travel through Dublin and from all accounts there was a full-scale battle under way there as the Free State Army tried to flush out the rebels in the Four Courts. And then when she got home, what would she find? The nightmare of 'The Troubles' descended again. The terror that reduced her to a jibbering idiot who screamed and jumped at every sound. The sight of her Pa's broken body when they had brought him home, and Fergal . . . No, she couldn't face all that again! And Maura did hate her, she would believe Bart, if Bridget tried to accuse him! Oh, Gina had been right, they should have gone to America, they shouldn't have come here. She hated the place. They should have gone anywhere but here.

Round and round her aching head the thoughts and her dilemma hammered. She was trapped, there was no way out, nowhere she could go, no one to whom she could turn . . . she didn't even have any friends; the girls she worked with called her 'Miss Mouse' because she was quiet and didn't mix. Friends! The word was like a bell pealing through the fog that clogged her mind. Bernie! Bernie O'Hagan!

Bridget pulled out her coat from the wardrobe, searching the pockets, praying she hadn't lost the now so precious scrap of grubby paper. No, it was still there, screwed up in a ball in one corner. She laid it on the windowsill and smoothed it out. She could just make out the words. 'Warwick Street, Glasgow'. She straightened up. If Bernie could get a job in Glasgow surely she could, and what had Bernie said about the shops on that street with a strange name? They were as fine as those in London. And accents wouldn't matter, for everyone had an accent in Scotland!

· She counted the money in her purse, grateful she'd been paid that morning. She had more than enough for her fare and some over to give Bernie for her keep. She felt a little calmer, but her courage was still shaky. It was a big step to take, to go to a strange city alone. She tried to pull herself together. She couldn't stay here and she wouldn't go home, so there was nothing else for it! She felt somehow older. If Gina could do it then so could she! She'd have to leave a note for Mary-Kate and she hoped she would forgive her and not worry too much. At least she could tell her the reason why. She could tell her about Bart, then she would understand.

Half an hour later her valise was packed and the note written. Bridget propped it up against the jug on the washstand so Mary-Kate would see it. Then, with a last look around the room, she opened the door and walked down the stairs without a backward glance and slammed the door behind her.

As she went up the steps of number three, Walton Park, Mary-Kate saw that the front door was open. She was late, but she hoped Mrs Rickard had left the door ajar for her so that Mr Vannin wouldn't notice her slipping in. As she pushed it open she noticed that every door leading off the hall was wide open and from the back of the house came the faint sound of raised voices. What on earth was going on? Usually everything was so quiet and orderly. Even the morning mail lay unopened on the hallstand.

'Miss O'Donnell, would you come in here please!'

She turned to see Lewis Vannin in the doorway of what looked like the front parlour. She followed him into the room, but there was no time to take in the furnishings or the quality of the furniture, she followed his gaze to the sofa on which sat a young girl with soft grey eyes and long, light-brown ringlets. The child stared at her defiantly.

'You find me in a very awkward situation! This is my daughter, Ellen.'

'Hello, Ellen.'

The child ignored her.

'Have the manners to speak when you're spoken to!'

The child muttered something that passed for a greeting.

'Mr Vannin, what is going on here? Where is Mrs Rickard and why was the front door open?'

'Mrs Rickard has left. Gone! And all because of this . . .' he pointed to the girl . . . 'baggage!'

'Don't you think we should discuss this somewhere else?' Mary-Kate had never seen him so angry and she had never heard him raise his voice before; he was almost shouting. Without thinking, she walked towards the door and he followed. He turned to the child. 'You stay there and don't move until I send for you!'

Mary-Kate crossed the hall and went into the library and shut the door behind them. 'I know it's none of my business, but if it will help, will you tell me what has happened?'

He stood before the empty fire grate, his hands behind his back. 'My daughter has been expelled from the convent for stealing. Stealing! She has no need to steal, I provide her with everything she needs. And as if that isn't bad enough, Mrs Rickard takes the opportunity to tell me that I'm a hard, cruel man and that it's all my own fault. My fault! I told her to pack her bags and get out. I'll not stand for such impertinence. I've put up with that woman for too long and that little baggage could always twist her around her little finger. I've yet to deal with her!'

118

Well, this was certainly a revelation, Mary-Kate thought. How wrong she had been when she had supposed that this was a quiet, well-run household. 'So, what do you intend to do? Are your maid and handyman here, or have they been sacked, too?'

'Dick and Annie are still here. At least they know which side their bread's buttered on.'

'Then they will have to cope until you can find yourself a new housekeeper, won't they?'

He cleared his throat, obviously embarrassed. 'I was wondering Miss O'Donnell if . . . well if you would consider taking the position? There'll be no trouble with the child, I'll attend to her! You will have a free hand with the running of the house and I will pay you ten shillings a week more than I paid that woman. Will you consider it?'

She stared at him in dumbfounded silence.

'Well, will you consider it?' he barked.

'I don't think I can, Mr Vannin. I have my younger sister to think about, I don't want to leave her on her own with my aunt and uncle. I'm sure you will understand that.'

'Of course I can, but a man in my position must have a reliable housekeeper!'

'And I'm sure there are plenty of . . .'

'I don't have the time to go chasing around. Will you just consider the offer? If it's the child . . .'

'No, it's got nothing to do with Ellen!' Mary-Kate interrupted. Why did he insist on calling her 'the child'?

'You could go home each night, you needn't live in, if that's what's causing the problem.'

'I've never kept house before, not a house like this, with servants.'

119

He began to pace up and down. 'You are the most capable young woman I have ever met. You are efficient and honest and practical and I will be paying you a good wage.'

He was interrupted by a loud knock on the door which then opened slowly to reveal Ellen standing on the threshold.

'I want to go to the bathroom.' The grey eyes were still mutinous as she stared up at her father, but Mary-Kate noticed the slight tremble of the lower lip. Before he had time to denounce his daughter again she turned to him.

'I'll consider it. I'll let you know in the morning, after Mass. You go to the Blessed Sacrament church, don't you?' She turned to the child. 'Go on up to the bathroom, Ellen, and then ask Annie to help you with your things.'

Lewis Vannin opened his mouth to remonstrate but thought better of it. Damn all women he thought, but at least she had some sense in her head and nothing seemed to ruffle her.

'I don't think there's much point in trying to do any work tonight, do you, Mr Vannin. So, I'll leave you. I'll give you my answer tomorrow. Goodnight.'

Mary-Kate walked home very slowly, thinking over the situation until she had finally made up her mind. The sight of that rebellious little face had touched her deeply. She would insist on remaining with Maura and Bart, to make sure Bridget was all right, and she would also insist on a day off every week.

What a strange day it had been. Sometimes there were days like that when all kinds of things happened and then there were others – far more frequent – when nothing happened at all, except the same dull things. She wondered how Bridget would take the news and that thought caused her concern. Bridget on her own was no match for those two conniving, bullying reprobates. She'd have to get something sorted out with Bridget.

As she opened the door and walked into the hall she realized that the house was unusually silent. She took off her coat and hat and hung them on the pegs behind the door. There was a strange atmosphere, something was not quite right, she could sense it. Oh, she was just being over-imaginative. She shook herself and went into the kitchen. Uncle Bart was sitting in his chair, the *Echo* that he was reading hiding most of his face.

'Has Aunt Maura gone out?' Mary-Kate asked evenly.

He rustled the paper as if in irritation. 'So what if she 'as?'

'Where's Bridget?'

Again he shook the paper, but she noticed that he seemed rather pale and was refusing to meet her eyes. In fact he looked even more shifty than usual.

'Well?'

''Ow the 'ell should I know where she is? Always comin' and goin' the lot of you. Get no bloody peace in me own 'ome.'

She could see she wasn't going to get a civil word out of him so, after bidding him 'goodnight', she closed the door behind her, none too gently.

As soon as she opened the bedroom door she saw the note. She read it and then sank down on the bed. Oh, Bridget! Bridget! Why hadn't she told her of her fear of Uncle Bart? But why hadn't she noticed it herself? He'd sworn to 'get even', but worrying about Gina had blinded her to what was under her very nose. Now she realized the reason for the strange atmosphere and Uncle Bart's shiftiness and evasive answers. Oh, poor, poor Bridget! She must have been in a desperate state, totally distraught; unable to stay, but terrified of the thought of returning to Ireland. She'd failed Bridget and Bridget wasn't like Gina who was well able to look after herself. But to go chasing off to Glasgow to find Bernie O'Hagan, of all people!

Mary-Kate covered her face with her hands. What should she do? Go to the police? Try to follow her and bring her back? She didn't even know where Bernie lived and Glasgow was a big place. And if she found her what then? She couldn't bring her back here and Bridget wouldn't go back to Ireland. She was even more terrified of war than she was of Bart. Mary-Kate looked at the note again and a tear dropped onto the page. 'He said if I told Aunt Maura he would say I'd led him on and she'd believe him, you know she would,' she read. And she would too; there was ill-concealed hatred between them all. Oh, why hadn't she seen this coming? They had all come here with such high hopes and now . . . At least Gina had what she wanted. All she could do about Bridget was hope and pray that she would write and let her know she was safe and where exactly she was. The Lord above knew how she was going to break this to Ma. Perhaps she should start by writing to Gina.

She looked around the room that only a few days ago had been filled with their laughter and bickering. Well, she wasn't staying here either! Lewis Vannin would have his answer and she'd live in. When Maura and Bart got behind with the rent again – which they were bound to do and soon – she would take the utmost pleasure in seeing them turned out on to the street, and first thing Monday morning she would inform the Panel of Bart's fraudulent conduct at their expense. Oh, she'd take great delight in watching the bailiffs go into number eighteen, Lancaster Street!

Chapter Seven

BRIDGET STOOD ON THE corner of Bedford Street and Warwick Street peering at the scrap of paper in her hand. Bernie hadn't given her the number of the house, but then there didn't seem to be any houses, only these large, closely packed buildings, the like of which she'd never seen before. It was dark and the jaundiced glow of the gas lamp made the street look sinister and ominous.

It had been a long journey and she'd had to change trains three times, but she'd kept her spirits up by spinning a web of daydreams. She had envisaged a Utopia encompassing all her desires, but all these romantic figments of imagination had been shattered as the tram crossed the Victoria Bridge spanning the oily waters of the Clyde and rumbled on into the Gorbals. She hadn't known what to expect, but she hadn't been prepared for anything like this! The three-storeyed, soot-blackened, decaying buildings flanked either side of the street. In between them were some small shops, little more than ramshackle sheds, and old stables, all of which were boarded up. Beneath her feet the paving stones were uneven, broken and littered with rubbish and small pools of filthy, stagnant water oozed between the cracks.

Bridget walked on slowly, her valise becoming heavier with every step she took. She'd have to ask someone. There were a few people about. Some youths loitering across the street, half in shadow, and a couple of urchins who reminded her of Bernie's younger brothers with their tattered, dirty jumpers, cut-down trousers and bare feet.

'Do you know where Bernie O'Hagan lives?'

They stared at her, looked at each other, then shook their heads.

'But we'll carry your bag for ye, Missus, if ye'll gi' us a penny?' the bigger of the two said.

'Away with the pair o' ye, or I'll tell your Faether ye're beggin' again!'

She turned around and found herself looking up into the face of a very tall, well-built young man. She took a step backwards, clutching her bag tightly. She'd not heard him come up behind her.

'I'm no' going to rob you! Are you looking for someone? I've not seen you around here before?'

'I'm . . . I'm looking for a friend, Bernadette O'Hagan, can you tell me where she lives?'

A broad smile spread across his face. 'Why didn't you say you were looking for Bernie?'

Relief gave her courage. 'Can you just tell me which one of these buildings she lives in?'

'I can do better than that. I'll take you. I was on my way to Archie's anyway. Can I take your bag?'

'No, thank you. I can manage it. I've dragged it on and off trains all the way from Liverpool.'

He shrugged his broad shoulders and began to walk down the road.

She fell into step beside him, trying to concentrate on avoiding stepping into the worst of the filth that fouled the pavement. They walked in silence, but she cast surreptitious glances at him from time to time. He reminded her of Edward Vinetti, except that he was younger and much taller and his eyes were blue and the clothes he wore were of a poor quality. She did notice that his shirt was clean and although his jacket and trousers didn't match, they, too, were clean and decent enough. He had pushed the cloth cap to the back of his head and shoved his hands into the pockets of his trousers, as if to reassure her that he wasn't about to snatch her bag and run.

'Bernie never mentioned she was expecting a friend.'

'She doesn't know I'm here, but she told me if I got fed up with Liverpool to come up to Glasgow.'

'What's your name?' He had already guessed that she had run away from something or someone and she didn't look as though she was used to living in neighbourhoods like the Gorbals. Her clothes alone told him that much, quite apart from the glazed, disbelieving look in her eyes. She was an attractive lassie, but a timid, scared one, too.

'Bridget. Bridget O'Donnell.'

'I'm Andrew MacDonald. My mates call me "big Andy MacDonald".'

She could see why. He must be about six-foot-three she surmised and he was handsome with that dark, curling hair, blue eyes and strong chiselled features. He walked with the air of a man who feared nothing and was totally at ease in this squalid environment.

'Here we are, follow me and mind your step!'

He turned into what looked like a narrow opening in the wall and she followed. Instantly the stench hit her.

'It's the ash-pit in the court at the back. You'll get used to it,' he said stoically, hearing the gasp behind him.

Her eyes gradually adjusted to the weak light of a guttering, open gas jet and she could discern a narrow stone staircase. Andrew MacDonald was already half way up it. The steps themselves were worn and cracked. The walls were a dirty, greyish-yellow, their plaster surface was pitted and in parts completely missing, revealing the bare brickwork. There was no bannister rail and she had to keep her balance by pressing her hand against the wall.

'Here, give me that bag or you'll fall down and break your neck!'

She made no protest as he took the bag from her, since it enabled her to cover her nose and mouth with her hand. The smell was overpowering and she tried to breathe only through her mouth. As they turned on a narrow landing he pointed to a door.

'That's the lavatory, it's a flush one, but they hardly ever work or the soil pipe gets blocked.'

'They have an inside privy?' She was slightly embarrassed by his forthright statement and amazed that such a luxury could exist in this decaying building.

'Aye, one for every three flats, but more often than not it's every six flats as they never work. Watch where you're putting your feet!'

She didn't reply. If she thought about the implications of his words she would be physically sick. He'd stopped and was hammering on a door.

Bernie opened it, dressed in a cheap print dress, her

hair screwed up in curling papers. 'Oh, it's you! Well, he's takin' me out tonight, Andy MacDonald, so you'll have to go to your bloody political meeting on your own.' Then she saw the figure standing beside him and her eyes widened. 'Holy Mother of God! Bridget O'Donnell!'

'I found her wandering up and down the street looking for this place.'

'Bridget! Sure, I never expected to see you again.'

'Are you no' going to ask the lassie in, seein' as how she's come all the way from Liverpool?'

With a gentle push Bridget was propelled into the room and Andrew followed, placing her bag down on the floor.

Bernie shut the door as a second young man appeared in the room.

'I thought I heard you, Andy. Who's this?'

'This is Bridget, she's a friend of mine from back home. This is Archie.'

Bridget nodded to the stocky young man with light, sandy-coloured hair and pale blue eyes. He smiled back. 'Nice to see you, Bridget.'

'I told her to come up here any time she got fed up with Liverpool.'

Archie nodded.

'Are you coming to the Workers' Circle then, man?'

Archie's gaze flitted from his friend's face to that of Bernie and finally Bridget.

'Oh, go on then the pair of you! But you're takin' me out tomorrow night, Archie Dalrymple, that you are!'

His face cracked in a broad grin. 'It's a promise, hen. I'll just get my coat and we'll be away. Come on, Andy, before she changes her mind.' And grabbing his jacket he kissed Bernie on the cheek, nodded to Bridget and followed Andy MacDonald, who was already half way out of the door.

Bridget looked around. It reminded her of Aunt Maura's kitchen on the morning they had arrived at Lancaster Street and she felt exactly the same sense of despair, compounded with weariness and disillusionment. The tears welled up and trickled down her cheeks.

'So you've up and left them, then? Come on, sit down and tell me all about it. Sure, I couldn't put up with those two for long meself.'

Bridget broke down and between sobs told her the whole story. When she'd finished, Bernie got up and pushed the kettle back on the hob.

'Blow your nose. God above! Every time I see you you're in a desperate state about something. I'll make us a cup of tea. The place is a bit of a mess, but beggars can't be choosers! It'll be a bit of a crush, you'll have to share with me and Eileen. She'll tidy up when she gets in.'

'Who's Eileen?' Bridget sniffed, feeling a bit calmer now.

Bernie lit a cigarette and threw the match in the general direction of the range. 'Archie's sister. You don't think I'm "living in sin" with him, do you? God, we'd be lynched! It may not be much of a neighbourhood but they still have some standards.' Bernie clattered around and then set two mugs of steaming hot tea down on the table and resumed her seat. 'If you've come here with all those fancy notions then you're in for a shock! It's out of the frying pan, into the fire! Oh, your accent won't matter much here, but your religion will.'

'Why?'

'Sure the place is full of Orangemen! "Billys" they call themselves, so if anyone asks you if you're a "Billy" or a "Dan" tell them you're a heathen or a Jew – there's enough of them here – I do! Though why they call us "Dans" I wouldn't be knowin'!' Bernie stubbed out the cigarette in an old, cracked saucer already full of dog-ends. 'The trouble is they don't tell you what they are first!'

It was getting worse. It was totally incomprehensible that she should have to deny her religion. First she had been humiliated because of her accent, now it seemed the same applied to her religion. Tears were threatening again.

Bernie looked at her steadily. 'The trouble with you, Bridget O'Donnell, is that you've always had those two to take your side and look after you. Sure, there was no one in our class that would say "Boo" to you because of your Gina and her desperate temper. But you've left them. You're on your own now. You've got to grow up, Bridget, because I can't look after you, I'm too busy lookin' after meself! Holy Mother! You're nearly twenty and you're cryin' and sobbin' like a six year old. Get a grip of yourself and grow up. I never had any of the things you had, so I don't miss them, but you've got to learn to do without all that. You'll have to stand up for yourself and you'll have to learn to grab what you want, fight for it and hang on to it. Expect nothin' and you'll not be disappointed me Ma always said and she's right. Mind you, you've made a good start.'

'How?'

'Big Andy MacDonald, that's how. Isn't he the most handsome man around and aren't half the girls in the

Gorbals after him and tryin' to get him to "stamp their card"! And doesn't he pick you up off the street and bring you here, and carryin' your bag, too.'

'I didn't think about him like that . . . What's "stamp their card"?'

Bernie looked at her incredulously. 'God, but you're an innocent! Get them pregnant so he'll have to marry them.'

Bridget stared back, just as incredulous, a blush spreading over her cheeks. 'But that's . . . it's a Mortal Sin!'

'Tell that to them! It's the only way some of them will ever get wedded. Archie sleeps there.' She pointed to a curtained alcove next to the range, as if reading Bridget's mind. Eileen and me share the bedroom.' She finished her tea. 'Bring your bag and we'll get you unpacked and tomorrow you can come with me to McFarlane's garment factory. They'll take you on, they're always mad busy this time of year. Don't go pullin' such a face, it's a job! I know it's not Copeland and Lye on Sauchiehall Street, but you've got to start somewhere.'

'I've got some money, Bernie, I can pay for my keep,' Bridget opened her purse and passed the coins over.

'I'll take this for now but when we get paid, we'll sort things out properly. I'll not have you sayin' I'm robbin' you blind.'

'Where does Archie work?'

'Dixon's Blazes, the big iron foundry. You must have seen its chimney belching out smoke and flames, you can see it for miles. Andy works there, too, most of the time. Sometimes they're laid off and then they have to go on the "Broo", the Unemployment.'

Bridget picked up her bag but before she could move

into the other room the door opened and a girl of about fifteen came in. She had the same sandy hair and pale blue eyes as Archie, but she was painfully thin. Her hair, scraped back into a loose plait, looked damp and her face shone as though it had been scrubbed. Under her arm was a rolled up towel.

'Oh, you're back then.'

'Who's she?'

'Bridget, and she's stayin' with us. She's a friend of mine and before you start, Archie knows! Po face little bitch,' Bernie muttered before going into the bedroom.

Bridget smiled at the girl before turning to follow Bernie. Eileen turned mutely away.

Together they unpacked the bag with Bernie exclaiming how 'grand' her things were and then bemoaning the fact that they were totally unsuitable and would soon get dirty and probably ruined and wasn't that a sin altogether? To Bridget's surprise the room, although small, was clean and neat. The bedlinen was clean but on closer inspection was much darned and mended. The rag rug on the otherwise bare floor added the only touch of colour to the uniform drabness. The old, scarred chest was dusted and a cheap brush and comb were laid neatly side by side, on one half of the top.

'That's *her* half,' Bernie informed her, as Bridget put her brush and hair clips beside them.

'She drives me mad, that she does! Always scrubbin' and dustin' and tidyin' up and it's a pure waste of time around here!'

As if to emphasize that statement, the distinct rattling of dishes came from the kitchen. '"A right dour little lassie" Archie calls her, takes after her Ma, he says.'

Bridget felt sorry for the girl. 'Where is her Ma?'

'Dead and her Pa, too.'

'Where's she been?'

'For a bath, she goes every Sunday. Waste of good money, it is. Sixpence a week!' Bernie stopped covertly admiring Bridget's cream blouse. 'I know what we'll do. There's nothing better than a good soak when you're worn out, why don't we go down to the Baths?'

'Won't they be back soon?'

Bernie laughed. 'Those two? They'll be hours setting the world to rights and don't they do it every night, too, but it's not made much difference that I can see. Come on, I'll get a towel and some soap.'

The thought of a hot bath was so tempting that Bridget forgot about her plight momentarily. She took her own towel and wrapped her soap in it and went into the kitchen. The table had been cleared of dishes, the hearth had been swept and Eileen's towel was hanging over the back of a chair that had been set in front of the range.

As they went down the staircase and back into the street, the grim scene that confronted Bridget brought down the cloud of depression to settle over her again.

'You don't seem to like Eileen, why.'

'She doesn't approve of me. She thinks I'm not good enough for her Archie. You'd think he was a plaster saint, that you would, the way she goes on about him. She called me a slut, did you ever hear the like? I told her a few home truths, I can tell you, and Archie told her he'd not have her calling me names like that and he wouldn't have us fighting like cat and dog either, so now she hardly ever speaks to me at all. Not that I care. My Archie's the only one I care about. He's the only person who has ever cared about me – really cared, I mean.'

They lapsed into silence and Bridget could see both Bernie's and Eileen's points of view. Bernie – in some people's estimation – was a slut, but it wasn't her fault. Not with the home she'd had and the way she'd been brought up. Dragged up, more like. Obviously Eileen had had a better upbringing and having undertaken the running of the home, she wouldn't take kindly to Bernie just walking in and taking over. Bridget hoped her arrival and inclusion in the household wouldn't make matters worse.

'Are you sure I'll get a job?'

'They're always busy in the spring. Everyone knows that!'

'But surely there are plenty of local girls wanting jobs?'

Bernie frowned and cast a quick, appraising look in her direction. 'I told you they're busy, but . . . well, you could be laid off in a few weeks, then taken back on again when business picks up. It's "last in, first out" but at least you'll have a few weeks' work, that's better than nothing, isn't it?'

'Yes, but maybe I can get a job in one of the big stores after a while, when I'm settled?'

'Jobs like that don't grow on trees, Bridget O'Donnell and I don't know of anyone who lives around here and works in Sauchiehall Street. You just be thankful if MacFarlane's do take you on.'

Bernie was right. When she'd fled Liverpool she hadn't really given her future much thought, she'd only had one thing on her mind, to get away from Uncle Bart and find Bernie. Well, she'd found Bernie and she should be thankful, but her thoughts returned to her new surroundings.

'Surely it's not all like this, the whole city?' she asked as they walked the short distance to Bedford Street where the Gorbals Baths were situated.

'Don't be an eejit, of course it's not! On the other side of the river there're plenty of nice areas and there are really grand houses up at Newton Mearns.'

Bridget thought about Clonmel on summer evenings. The air had been calm and clear and sweet-smelling, the houses and shops unblemished by soot and dirt. Of course there was poverty; there were families like Bernie's, but even they didn't live like this in a world of noise and dirt, the very air rank and noxious. This was poverty and squalor on a scale she had never thought possible. She was jolted out of her sober reverie by Bernie's announcement that they'd arrived, and looking up she wondered how such an ornate and imposing building, with its scrolls and cornices and stained-glass windows, could exist in such a wasteland.

She followed Bernie through the door marked 'Ladies' and along a corridor of coloured and moulded tiling that opened out into a large room partitioned into small cubicles. A hefty woman, reddened arms below the rolled-up sleeves of her uniform, came towards them.

'Have you both the money?'

'That we have! Here, sixpence each.'

The woman took the money and led them towards two cubicles in each of which were a stoneware slipper bath, a wooden stool and a wooden platform raised off the cement floor. From the pocket of her smock-like garment she extracted a spanner and turned two bolts set into the wall at the head of the bath. Obviously they didn't trust you to have taps and even the two brushes – a long-handled back brush and a hand brush – were attached to the wall by brass chains and had 'Corporation of Glasgow' burned into their backs. The bath was half full and the attendant reversed the ritual with the spanner, tested the water with her hand and then shut the door with the parting instruction of, 'No longer than fifteen minutes!'

Standing on the wooden platform, Bridget stripped off her clothes and placed them neatly on the wooden stool. Then she stepped into the hot water and easing herself down, let it lap over her. The warmth made her drowsy and she began to relax, slowly going over the events of the last hours in her mind. Bernie was right. She'd always had Gina and Mary-Kate to take care of her, but now she was alone. When she thought about it she realized what a whining little fool she must have sounded. 'Expect nothing and you'll not be disappointed.' Well, she wasn't going to live by that maxim. From now on she'd take a grip of herself, as Bernie put it. No more blubbering like a baby, no more moaning. She couldn't go on being afraid of everything for the rest of her life. She'd have to grow up. If she was going to stay here she'd have to stand on her own two feet and grab what she wanted and hang on to it!

Bridget was taken on at MacFarlane's on the understanding that she would be a 'temporary seasonal worker' and that when the spring rush was over she would be laid off. But, she was told, if her work and time-keeping proved satisfactory, she might be taken back on again. That was the way the system worked, Robbie Frazer, the under manager, told her. She could take it or leave it. She took it, but by six o'clock on the first day the firm resolve with which she'd left the baths on her first night, had gone. Her head was aching, her back and shoulders were aching and she'd never been so exhausted, not even after a day at Dunlop's. MacFarlane's was a nightmare of heat, noise and frenetic activity. The room where she worked was like a huge barn with rows of sewing machines set in double banks facing each other, the motorized belt that drove them, running on wheels slung from the ceiling. In the middle of the rows of machines was a shallow, wooden trough. The work was 'piece work' which accounted for the frenzied activity. Each worker relying on the others to keep the line going; stoppages or slowness resulted in a loss of pay for everyone.

At first Bridget couldn't keep up with the others and there had been curses and black looks cast in her direction. She'd tried to ignore them, remembering Bernie's warnings issued on their walk to the factory. Accidents often happened. The most common being the machine needle piercing the tip of the finger and often breaking, leaving half embedded in the nail. One girl had once had her hair caught and but for the prompt action of one of the pressers who had cut her free, she would undoubtedly have been seriously maimed.

As the day wore on Bridget became more proficient, forcing the material under the drumming head of the needle, her head bent, shoulders hunched, her eyes burning and smarting from the effort of concentrating on the straightness of the seam.

'Now that wasn't so bad, was it? And you'll get faster and the more you do the more you earn!' Bernie comforted her at the end of their shift.

'I feel terrible.'

Bernie was also tired and stiff. 'Oh, for God's sake, Bridget, stop moaning. Didn't I tell you to grow up.'

'I'm trying,' she replied, gritting her teeth. 'But it's not easy.'

'What is? All you've been used to is O'Leary's and that's not work.'

In the light of the day she had just put in, Bridget silently agreed with her.

They arrived home to find the table set and the smell of cooking issuing from a pan on the range.

Bernie sank into a chair. 'Eileen, put the kettle on, we're done in.'

The girl didn't answer but continued stirring the pan.

'I'll do it,' Bridget offered wearily, placing the kettle on the hob, but she received no look or word of thanks.

'It's going to be a grand evening, if I can find the energy maybe Archie and me will go for a walk later.'

'Our Archie'll be too tired.'

'Who asked you? He'll do as he pleases!'

Eileen slammed two plates on the table and ladled out a watery stew.

'Aren't you going to have any, Eileen?' Bridget asked.

'I've already eaten.'

They ate in silence and afterwards the girl cleared the dishes and washed them. Bernie had gone into the bedroom to 'perk myself up' as she put it, and although the only thing she wanted to do was to lie down and sleep, Bridget knew she had to write to Mary-Kate. From her bag she took a small notepad and an envelope and placed them on the table.

For the first time Eileen's pale eyes held a spark of interest. 'What are you doing?'

'I'm writing to my sister in Liverpool, she doesn't know where I am and she'll be worried to death.' She paused. 'Eileen, I don't want you to think that I'm going to be a burden on you. I don't want you to think I'm another stranger coming into your home and expecting to be waited on. I don't mind helping in the house, I'm used to it. I always helped at home. I'm used to shopping and cooking, cleaning, sewing and ironing. If I'm going to live here, then I'll expect to do my share of the work, too, and pay my share of the expenses.'

Eileen didn't reply and so Bridget began to write, telling Mary-Kate that she was living with Bernie and that she had a job and that she was not to worry about her, then she realized the girl was standing beside her, watching her. She looked up.

'Where do you work Eileen?'

'At Feinstein's Bakery. I scrub out.'

'Can you read and write?'

Eileen shook her head slowly. 'Not very well. I had to look after my Mammy, I didna go to school often.'

'Would you like me to teach you?' It seemed a small gesture of thanks.

The ghost of a smile crossed Eileen's pale, thin face. 'Would you?'

Bridget nodded. 'But not tonight, I'm too tired.'

'Don't you go fillin' her head with all kinds of nonsense, Bridget O'Donnell!'

They both turned. Bernie had changed into a print dress and had brushed her hair.

'What harm is there in it?'

'She'll go gettin' grand notions, like you, that's what and no good will come of it either!'

The look Eileen directed at Bernie was one of pure venom, but at the sound of boots on the landing she immediately went to the range and poured the remainder of the stew on to a plate and from somewhere she produced half a loaf of bread.

'Aren't you the little sneak then! You never said they'd given you any bread.'

'It's for our Archie.'

The appearance of Archie, followed by Andy MacDonald, cut short the imminent argument and Eileen set the meal on the table for him.

'I thought we'd go for a stroll, it's a grand evening,' Bernie put in, glaring at Andy. 'But obviously you've planned something else!'

'Bridget is going to teach me to read an' write, our Archie.' Eileen announced.

'Is she now. That's good of her.' Andy sat, uninvited, beside Bridget and his presence made her uneasy. 'Who are you writing to, or is it a secret?'

He smiled at her and she hastily signed the letter, folded the sheet and put it in the envelope, sealing it firmly.

'There's nothing secretive about it at all. I'm writing to my sister.'

'Have you a stamp?' he asked.

'I have. I bought some at the station.'

'Then if you like, I'll walk you to the nearest postbox.'

She looked at him, uncertain what to say or do. She was tired and she didn't feel in the mood to be sociable, but the offer was tempting. The letter would have to be posted.

'We'll all go!' Bernie chimed in. 'Archie, finish up your meal and tidy yourself up. We'll go to the Suspension Bridge; you get a good view from there.'

Bernie had settled the matter and so Bridget rose, excusing herself while she brushed her hair and changed her blouse and to her surprise she found she didn't feel quite as tired as before.

They posted the letter and walked along Carlton Place towards the Suspension Bridge and the Custom House Quay on the opposite bank of the Clyde. After a while Bernie and Archie dropped behind a little and Bridget made no attempt to slow her steps, they obviously wanted to talk. She felt a little awkward as Andy MacDonald walked beside her, pointing out the Civic Buildings in the distance.

'You don't say much, do you?'

'It's all so new and strange to me. I come from a small country town.'

'You lived in Liverpool, that's a city.'

'I wasn't there very long.'

'Don't you like cities then?'

'I don't really know. I suppose I'll get used to it, but I didn't expect all the dirt and poverty.'

'Don't they have dirt and poverty in Ireland? Bernie tells a different tale.'

'Of course they do, but I suppose I was more fortunate than Bernie.'

She'd noticed the glances they had attracted, or rather he had attracted, mainly from the girls they passed and she thought about Bernie's words. He was handsome and he was taking an interest in her. But was that just because he was Archie's friend and she was Bernie's?

'A lot depends on what you expect to gain from life in a city,' he deliberated. 'What did you leave Ireland for, Bridget? Bernie left because of Archie.'

'I didn't leave because of a man. I wanted a better job and I couldn't stand any more violence.'

'You've come to the wrong place to escape that, this is a violent city – parts of it are anyway!'

She looked up at him and her expression reminded him of a picture he'd seen of a frightened roe deer. She was shy and quiet and he felt protective towards her. 'Oh, don't worry, I'll look after you, if you like.'

'What does that mean?' she heard herself say bluntly.

'You're a pretty lassie, Bridget, but you need someone to look out for you.'

'I hardly know you.'

'This isn't Ireland and what's to stop you getting to know me?'

'I don't want you thinking I'm fast.'

'I don't think you're fast, not compared with the girls around here anyway. There's a dance at the Locarno on Saturday night, it's nothing fancy, but would you like to go?'

'With you?'

'Yes, unless you intend going on your own?'

'Will Bernie and Archie be going?'

'Who knows? Can't you go anywhere without Bernie?' he mocked, gently.

'I don't know.' She liked him, he was easy to talk to and he was very handsome and after all she'd been through why shouldn't she have a little fun. She smiled. 'All right and thank you for inviting me.'

'We can go for a drink first, if you like, to get to know each other.'

'I'd like that, but I don't drink – not anything alcoholic anyway.'

He laughed. 'Have you signed the pledge?'

'No, I haven't. I just don't like it, that's all.'

'Oh, I see you have got spirit. You're not everything you appear to be, Bridget O'Donnell!'

'You hardly know me, so how do you know what I'm really like?'

'I don't, but I intend to find out!'

She smiled. She really did like him and when he held his hand out to help her down the steps at the bottom of the bridge's ramp, she took it without hesitation.

Chapter Eight

M<small>ARY-KATE SORTED THROUGH THE</small> mail, placing the ones marked 'L.R.Vannin, Esq' on the hallstand, then she uttered a prayer of thanks as she recognized Bridget's handwriting. The postmark was Gorbals, Glasgow. It was addressed to eighteen, Lancaster Street, but that had been crossed out and three, Walton Park written in untidy, sprawling letters above it. Thank God Maura had forwarded it. As she tucked the envelope into her pocket she thought what a strange, foreign-sounding name it was. Gorbals. She'd make sure Annie was clearing up after breakfast, then she'd read it before going shopping.

She'd not regretted her decision to take over as housekeeper and she'd left her aunt and uncle under no illusions as to what would happen to them if they so much as missed one week's rent.

Lewis Vannin's house was bigger than she had imagined it to be and there was plenty of work, for she still helped with the office work in the evenings, but she had her own room, large, bright, clean and nicely furnished. She'd found her employer to be a man of few words who adhered to a strict routine, but she respected him and was grateful to him and endeavoured to maintain the high standards he insisted on. She found she could handle the servants quite well; neither of them lived in and Dick only came for a few hours each day, the rest of the time he was employed in the haulage yard.

Mary-Kate had only come into conflict with Lewis Vannin once and that had been over Ellen. She'd caught the child in the hall one night as she was about to retire. Only a dim light burned on the landing and as she had closed the kitchen door a movement in the semi-darkness had caught her attention.

'Ellen, is that you?' she'd asked, softly.

There had been no reply.

'Ellen, I know you're there. Do I have to switch on the main light?'

The little girl had stepped out of the shadows. She had her hat and coat on and was clutching an old Gladstone bag.

'Where are you going?'

The question had been met with silence and a sullen expression.

She'd taken her by the arm and led her to the foot of the stairs, then, placing her hands on her shoulders, she'd gently pushed her down on to the bottom stair. She'd sat down beside her.

'You're running away, aren't you?'

'Yes.'

'Why? Do you hate your home that much?'

'No.'

'Then why?'

'Because . . . I'm not telling you. You don't care either.'

'How do you know that?'

'You don't. No one does.'

'You're wrong. I do care.'

The child hadn't answered or even turned her head.

'I know what it's like Ellen, to lose someone you love very much. I lost my father and my brother. I loved them both and they were killed, shot dead.'

'Who killed them?'

'Soldiers.'

There had been a short silence. 'I'm going away because . . . because he's sending me away to another hateful school!'

Mary-Kate had almost been able to feel the misery trapped in the small body beside her. 'He's only trying to do the best for you, give you a good education.'

'No, he's not, he doesn't want me here! He doesn't want me at all!' Her voice had risen louder and had echoed through the quiet house.

The library door had opened, throwing a beam of light across the hall, catching them both in its glow.

'What's the matter?'

She had risen slowly and Ellen had tried to hide herself behind her.

'What is that child doing up at this hour and dressed like that?'

She had been in a terrible dilemma. She wanted to speak out for Ellen, but that had been Mrs Rickard's downfall and she couldn't afford to lose her job. 'Could I speak to you, sir?'

His gaze moved from his daughter to herself and she had quailed.

'Go upstairs, Ellen,' she'd instructed, quietly. The child had stared at her hard for a few seconds, her expression almost identical to her father's, but before she turned Mary-Kate had caught a fleeting, pleading glance in the grey eyes.

Mr Vannin had closed the door behind her and she'd stood in silence, her hands clasped in front of her, until he'd sat down at his desk again.

'She said she was running away because you are sending her to another school,' Mary-Kate said as firmly as she could.

'Did she?'

'She doesn't want to go.'

'Miss O'Donnell, what I do with my daughter is my affair. Mrs Rickard found that out to her cost!'

'I'm aware of that, sir. I know my place.'

'But?'

Oh, dare she go on? she had wondered frantically. 'But she is desperately unhappy. I told her you were only thinking of her education, but she seems to think you don't . . .'

'Don't what?'

'You don't want her at all.'

He had continued to stare at her and she had dropped her eyes. He hadn't spoken and she'd felt fear rising. Had she said too much? At last he broke the silence.

'That is nonsense!'

'I tried to tell her that. I told her that I knew how miserable she felt.'

'Did you? And do you?'

She'd raised her head. 'Yes, I do. I lost my father and

my elder brother, they were killed. My brother was only twenty-five.'

There was pain and heartache in the clear, hazel eyes, although her manner was calm and dutiful. There was no trace of the aggressive, blustering of his former housekeeper, and yet he felt her very calmness to be an accusation. He'd thought about Mrs Rickard's acid comments, after his initial anger had passed. True, he hadn't given her accusations much credence, but strangely they had hurt. Whenever he looked at Molly's photograph he felt a stirring of guilt.

'And what opinion do you hold of me?'

'It's not my place to have opinions.'

'But you do, don't you?'

She had bitten back the words.

'Speak freely, Miss O'Donnell, please.'

She wasn't going to be drawn on that account. 'I think perhaps if Ellen went to a day school she'd be happier,' she had ventured.

There had been another long, heavy silence before he had said, 'I will consider it. Goodnight, Miss O'Donnell,' and she had been dismissed.

She'd found Ellen crouched on the landing, peering between the spindles of the bannister rail like a small, caged animal, and the sight had tugged sharply at her heart. 'Were you listening?'

Ellen had nodded.

'It's very rude to eavesdrop. I told you to go upstairs.'

'I am upstairs!' had been the whispered retort.

'Ellen, you are far too bold for your own good. It won't do you any good with your father or me, and probably no one else either. No one likes an insolent child. Would you like people to speak so nastily to you? Of course you wouldn't, so stop it. "Do as you would be done by," my Ma always taught me.'

The sullen expression had vanished and the bottom lip had trembled.

'Now go to bed. I'll come and tuck you in and hear you say your prayers. At least your father's considering my suggestion and if I were you I wouldn't be rude or objectionable towards him, not if you want to stay here!'

Mary-Kate had escorted her to the door of her room but, before she went in, Ellen had turned to her. 'I'm too big to be tucked in, that's for babies and I can say my prayers, too!'

'Very well, but make sure you ask God to look after your pa, Ellen. I'm sure that's what your ma would want you to do.'

She had been rewarded by a nod and a muttered 'Thank you' before Ellen had closed her door.

The following day, Lewis Vannin called Mary-Kate into the library and told her that he was arranging for Ellen to go to a day school convent in Crosby.

Annie was scouring the pans as Mary-Kate entered, but she looked up and smiled. 'Could you add some scouring powder to the list, Miss O'Donnell, I've just used the last?'

Mary-Kate nodded and sat down at the table, drawing the letter from her pocket.

'Is that a letter from home?'

'No, it's from my sister in Glasgow.' She ripped open the envelope.

24 Warwick St
Gorbals
Glasgow

Dear Mary-Kate,

I am writing to tell you not to worry about me, I'm living with Bernie and Archie and Archie's sister, Eileen. It's not a house as we know them. They're called tenements: one big building on three storeys with a set of rooms for each family. But Eileen works very hard at keeping it nice and clean. I have a job, too, in a garment factory and the money is good. It's not what I want and I've told Bernie just that, but it's a start and I'm sure I'll get a better job soon. Accents don't matter here, everyone has one. I can't even understand some of the people I work with, so mine can't be that bad.

I can't write to Ma, I just don't know how to explain everything, so could you do it? I know it's really very wrong of me to even ask you. Bernie says I have to grow up, but how can I explain about Uncle Bart without putting you in an awkward position? Please forgive me? I promise to write again next week. Give my love to Gina when you write to her. God Bless you.

Your loving sister,
Bridget

Mary-Kate folded the letter up, not knowing whether it was a relief or not. At least Bridget seemed to be all right, but how was she going to tell Ma she had gone to live with Bernie O'Hagan? The sound of the doorbell interrupted her deliberations. She rose, wondering who would be calling at this time in the morning.

On the doorstep stood a nun, the starched white wings of her veil contrasting sharply with the red-tinged cheeks of the thin face. Beside her stood Ellen, her face a pale, sickly colour.

'Ellen, what's the matter? Come in, please, Sister.'

They both stepped into the hall and Ellen moved a pace closer to Mary-Kate.

'I have brought her home and I demand to see her father!'

'Mr Vannin is at his work. What's wrong?'

An exercise book was thrust into her hand.

'This is what's wrong – amongst other things!'

Mary-Kate opened it. Instead of the rows of neat handwriting, there was a crudely drawn figure of a man with pins sticking out of him and underneath in large, black letters were the words '*I hate my father and I wish he were in hell*'.

'Oh, Ellen, you didn't do this, did you?'

The child refused to look at her. 'Sister, would you like to come in here? Ellen, please go up to your room.' Shocked though she was, Mary-Kate maintained her calm façade as she ushered the nun into the front parlour and motioned her to sit down.

'I won't say I'm not shocked, I am, but, Sister, the child is very disturbed. She was very close to her late mother I believe and children sometimes do strange things . . .'

'I would call that more than "strange" Miss . . . ?'

'O'Donnell,' she supplied.

'I'd call it downright evil and Mother Superior is of the same opinion! The child shows no respect for anyone, she's insolent and slovenly and that' – she pointed to the exercise book – 'that is the work of the Devil himself!'

Mary-Kate had been taught by nuns and had grown up with respect and affection for most of them, except for one. Sister Augustina had had a temper that matched Gina's, an intolerant and vindictive nature and her Ma had said she should never have 'taken the veil' in the first place. This one reminded Mary-Kate of Sister Augustina. 'Surely you're not suggesting that she's "possessed", that's utterly ridiculous! They abolished the Inquisition years ago and they've even stopped witch-hunting, or at least I thought they had, Sister . . . ?'

'Imelda. And don't take that flippant tone with me, young woman! That child is evil and I'll wait and speak to her father!'

'Then you'll have a long wait. He won't be home until this evening and I have my duties to attend to.'

'I'll wait. I'll pray for the poor man!'

'As you please. I'll have some lunch sent in to you later.'

She left closing the door quietly after her, unwilling to let the nun see that she was in any way disturbed. But she'd have to talk to Ellen. She'd have to get to the bottom of this once and for all. As she crossed the hall the doorbell rang again and she stopped dead. 'Oh, don't let it be him! Please, Holy Mother! Not before I've had time to talk to Ellen,' she prayed.

She opened the door again and was confronted by a young woman very smartly turned out in a silver grey two-piece, a fox fur around her shoulders and a small black velvet cloche hat covering carefully waved, light brown hair. She closely resembled her employer. 'Mrs Winskill?' Mary-Kate queried.

Lewis Vannin's elder daughter swept past her into the hall. 'Yes. Where's Mrs Rickard?'

'She's gone. I am the housekeeper now. I'm Miss O'Donnell.'

'Really. Is my father coming home for lunch?'

'I don't expect him.'

'Then who is in the front parlour?'

'One of the nuns from Ellen's school.'

'What does she want?'

'I'm afraid there has been some trouble.'

Mrs Winskill drew off her black kid gloves with obvious annoyance. 'Oh, not more! Where is the little wretch? What she needs is her backside tanning.'

Mary-Kate remembered Mrs Rickard's acid description of Elizabeth Winskill, née Vannin, and she felt even more protective towards Ellen. Was there no one who really cared about the poor child?

'I would think that is the last thing she needs. A little love and understanding wouldn't go amiss where Ellen's concerned.'

'Since you've only been here five minutes, I don't think you're in any position to comment at all, especially on things that don't concern you and which you know nothing about!'

'It doesn't take a fool to see that the child is desperately unhappy!'

'Where is she?' Elizabeth snapped, ignoring the implication.

'In her room.'

'And have you sent for Father?'

'No and I don't intend to until I've spoken to Ellen.'

'I think you're over-stepping your place, Miss O'Donnell. This is a family matter.'

'The more I see of families, the more I think I prefer strangers to relations!' Mary-Kate held the exercise book behind her, wondering if in fact she hadn't now gone too far.

Elizabeth Winskill glared at her. 'I'll go down to the office myself, this minute, and inform my father and I will tell Sister what's-her-name of my intentions.' And with that she turned on her heel and crossed to the parlour door, her heels tapping on the parquet floor.

Mary-Kate sighed. That hadn't been a very auspicious introduction and it boded ill for Ellen and for herself. She went up the stairs quickly and knocked on the bedroom door, then went in.

Ellen was sitting on the bed, still with her hat and coat on. Mary-Kate sat down beside her. Over the weeks she had tried to get closer to the child and had, to some extent, succeeded and that had lulled her into believing that Ellen's behaviour had improved.

'Ellen, why did you do such a terrible thing? You can't mean it, it's a wicked thing to have done and now your sister has gone for your Pa! What are we going to tell him?'

'I hate Lizzie and she hates me! Everyone hates me!'

'Don't be silly, of course they don't.'

Ellen took off her hat and threw it across the room.

'That's not going to do any good, is it? We're going to have to find some explanation, Ellen, because they'll be back soon.'

The light brown hair had slipped from its ribbons and

fell across the child's face like a curtain, hiding her expression, but her shoulders began to shake and Mary-Kate realized that she was crying. The sound tore at her heart.

'Oh, Ellen, what are we going to do with you?'

She began to sob harder and Mary-Kate took her in her arms, holding her close, tears welling in her own eyes as over and over again the little girl sobbed, 'I want my Ma! I want my Ma! Why did she go and leave me with them?'

Mary-Kate suddenly understood. The stealing, the defiance, the pent-up hatred, they were all cries for help that everyone had ignored. In his own grief, Ellen's father had obviously shut himself off from her. She had little love for her elder sister; that was evident and she suspected it was mutual. No one had seen or heard the cries of this child who so desperately needed to be loved and comforted. As Mary-Kate rocked her in her arms, all the love that was locked in her heart broke free and she vowed that even if it cost her her job, she wouldn't let them hurt Ellen any longer. Just quite what she would do, she didn't know, but somehow she would find a way. Ellen needed her and she wouldn't desert her. She wouldn't go down without putting up a fight.

Mary-Kate heard Elizabeth and her father return and go into the parlour. The child had at last sobbed herself quiet, but at the sounds from below she raised red, swollen eyes.

'You stay here and be quiet!'

'You won't let them send me away, Miss O'Donnell, will you?'

'Not if I can help it, Ellen. I'll do the best I can for you, I promise, and in return you'll have to promise me that you won't do anything bad in the future?'

The child clung to her. 'I won't! I promise I won't!'

Mary-Kate slowly and gently disentangled herself. 'I'll come back up as soon as I can.'

As she closed the door behind her she thought that tackling Bart and Maura had been simple compared with what she must now do. Within minutes she could well find herself without a job and out on the street!

As she opened the parlour door the voices ceased and three pairs of eyes turned towards her. For an instant she faltered, as the hostility of both Sister Imelda and Elizabeth was directed fully at her and she saw the grim set of the lips and the hard glint in the cold eyes of her employer.

'She's got the book, Father!'

'Thank you, Elizabeth, I can speak for myself! Do you have this book, Miss O'Donnell?'

'Yes. But could I have a word with you, sir, in private, please?'

'Whatever you've got to say can be said in front of us all. This is a family matter, as I've already pointed out to you.'

Mary-Kate ignored Elizabeth's outburst and continued to stare calmly but eloquently at Lewis Vannin.

'May I see this book?' he insisted.

She had no alternative but to hand it to him. Sister Imelda averted her eyes then raised them to the ceiling in silent invocation. Elizabeth glanced at the book and then looked away in disgust. Lewis Vannin stared at the caricature of himself for a long time before he closed the book.

'I will deal with my daughter appropriately, Sister Imelda.'

'That won't be sufficient, Mr Vannin. I must inform you that under no circumstances can we have her back at the convent. Seafield Convent cannot tolerate such a bad influence. Mother Superior made that quite clear to me! I think that you should take the child to the parish priest immediately.'

Mary-Kate couldn't help herself. 'So she can be exorcised, I presume?'

'Thank you, Miss O'Donnell and you Sister Imelda, I will deal with my daughter. I need no advice from either of you!' Mr Vannin snapped.

'So that's another school she's been expelled from! Oh, this will look fine won't it, when the word gets around.'

'I don't think we need discuss that now, Elizabeth.'

'We need to discuss what we're going to do with the little wretch!'

'Elizabeth!' The word was uttered like the snapping of a steel trap and his elder daughter fell silent and began to adjust the fur around her shoulders.

'Miss O'Donnell, will you see Sister Imelda out? I will write to Mother Superior.'

Mary-Kate moved forward to open the door and the nun rose and swept past her, her face like thunder. After she had closed the front door Mary-Kate passed her hand over her forehead. That was one less protagonist, which just left the other two, but they were far more formidable.

As she re-entered the room, Elizabeth was pacing up and down, urging all kinds of dire retribution. Her father stood staring at the book that he still held. Mary-Kate took her courage in both hands. She had to do her best for Ellen and it was now or never.

'May I have that word now, Mr Vannin, please?'

He looked up and nodded briefly, his expression vague and disturbed.

Elizabeth stopped pacing. 'Well, I can see that I'm not needed or wanted here!' she said venomously.

'I'm sorry, Mrs Winskill, I don't wish to appear rude or intrusive.'

'Whether you wish to or not, that is just what you are, Miss O'Donnell. As for you, Father, don't expect me to call again and don't come to me when that little madam gets into more trouble. I'm sure Miss O'Donnell will sort everything out for you!' And with that she snatched up her bag and gloves and stormed out.

It wasn't until the front door slammed that Mary-Kate spoke. 'Please forgive me, I had no wish to upset your daughter or cause a rift between you.'

'My daughter takes offence at the slightest thing. She spends most of her time being as objectionable as she can – except when she needs money.'

'I think it would be best if I took the book and burned it, sir. Ellen didn't mean it. I've talked to her . . .' She held out her hand.

He looked at the book again and then to her relief handed it to her. Leaning on the mantelshelf, he rested his head on one hand. 'What's got into the child. She's more trouble than she's worth!'

He appeared to be thinking aloud and Mary-Kate wondered if she should leave him alone and let him think on the matter. After all, she'd gone as far as she dared.

Then he turned to her, as if remembering her presence.

'What do you suggest I do with her? You seem ready enough with answers for other problems!'

She didn't miss the note of sarcasm but she ignored it. 'Ellen didn't mean it, she's only a child and a very unhappy one, too. Children often do and say the most hurtful things to hit back in the only way they know how.' She faltered. 'But I think Sister Imelda was taking things a bit far.'

'Ellen will have to be punished!'

'I agree. I, too, was shocked.'

'Miss O'Donnell, sit down, please.'

She sat on the edge of the chair Sister Imelda had recently vacated.

'You seem to know a great deal about children?'

'Not really. But you will remember that I have two younger sisters, one of whom has always been difficult to handle. That's all the experience I have.'

'If Ellen were your "difficult" younger sister, what would you do with her?'

She smiled ruefully. 'Ellen is an angel compared to Gina. In her worst tantrums Ma used to hold her head under the cold water pump.'

'Good God!'

'There are other schools you could try.'

'Who is going to take her after all this? And God knows what she'll do next!'

'She's promised me that she'll behave from now on.'

He looked at her with surprise. 'She's promised you?'

She nodded. 'She's only ten years old and she's desperately unhappy. She misses her mother and she thinks no one cares about her. She thinks you all hate her, that you want to be rid of her. That's why she's done all these terrible things.'

'She told you all this?'

'Yes.'

Vannin threw up his hands in despair. 'The times I've tried to talk to her!'

'Perhaps you didn't use the right words and . . . sometimes it's easier for a woman to talk to children, especially girls.'

He dropped his head in his hands and she felt sorry for him. She rose and walked across to his side. 'I know it's none of my business, Mrs Winskill was right about that, but for Sister Imelda to say Ellen was evil . . . I couldn't stand by and say nothing, even though she was a nun! Forgive me if I've interfered, but I was only thinking of Ellen.'

He turned slowly and looked directly into her eyes. 'You're a very determined and thoughtful young woman, Miss O'Donnell. In fact you seem to have wisdom beyond your years.'

Mary-Kate relaxed, feeling the worst was over and that she had at least managed to forestall any dire consequences for Ellen. 'So, will you try Ellen at another school? I don't think she'll cause any more trouble, but she must, of course, be punished.'

He nodded slowly. 'She'll stay in her room with only bread and water for three days. This evening I will write to Mother Superior and to the convent in Everton Valley.'

She was about to protest at the harshness of the punishment, but she kept quiet. She'd already said too much. 'I'll go and tell her.'

'No, send her down to me, please.'
'As you wish, sir.'

Gina was tired and utterly fed up. The euphoria that had enveloped her when she had first arrived in London had completely vanished. For a start, she didn't like Mrs Weston and her bossy, inquisitive ways.

Mrs Weston had been a theatrical landlady for years and knew every trick in the book, or so she had told Gina when she had shown her her bedroom, which she told her she expected to be kept tidy and clean. Nor did she want any damage done to the furniture with make-up or cigarettes.

'I don't smoke!' Gina had stated curtly.

Meals were taken in the dining room and with what she was paying she couldn't hope to expect roast beef every day. 'I serve plain, nourishing fare and I can't be doing with "faddy eaters",' had been the comment as Gina had studied the list of meal times, printed in large black lettering on a white card that was pinned to the back of the bedroom door. The room was dark and furnished with old-fashioned heavy pieces and cluttered with bric-a-brac.

'And I know every single piece, so don't go thinking I'd not miss anything. I know you lot – pawn the lock on the door if you could get away with it.'

'Mrs Weston, if you think I'd stoop so low as to steal, you're mistaken. Just what kind of a girl do you think I am? If that's what you think of me, I'm sure Mr Vinetti can find me somewhere else where I won't be insulted!'

'I doubt it. I'm just pointing out some of the things

some of my previous boarders have got up to. No need to fly off the handle.'

'Then I'll thank you not to pre-judge me and anyway, I don't intend to stay very long. I expect to have my own place soon.'

'I've heard that one before, too! Now, I'll show you the bathroom and don't think you can be coming in all hours of the night, either, and I'll have no men upstairs. Anyone who comes to see you, you can entertain in the parlour.'

As she followed Mrs Weston up another flight of stairs, Gina had thought it was worse than being at home.

Senora Scarlatti, the retired prima donna whom Edward had arranged to give her singing lessons was, in Gina's opinion, a veritable old witch, and there were times when their volatile natures erupted.

'From the stomach, Gina. You breathe from the stomach!' The Senora had prodded her in that part of her anatomy with the short cane she always carried.

'I'll choke!' Gina had cried with exasperation. 'How can I be expected to think about where I breathe from and sing these interminable scales at the same time? It's impossible!'

'You see, now, when you shout so loud, you fill your lungs with the air! You have breathed so deeply to take in the air to shout and you did not think about it. You shout! Always you shout! Sancta Maria, 'ow you shout. If you would only sing like that, Gina! But I will make you sing like that or I am not Gratziella Scarlatti,' her teacher had vowed.

She positively loathed Charlie Grayson who was teaching her to dance. He was a monster without a shred of pity, who worked her until every muscle ached and burned with pain and she was fit to drop. And worst of all, when she complained to Edward, which she did all the time, he just laughed and told her it was the price of fame.

When she thought about Edward at all, she felt confused. He had taken over her life, arranging everything, and when she had once bluntly asked him what he expected in return he had laughed and said, 'Money – eventually.'

'Don't you want anything else?' she'd probed, coyly.

'What else are you prepared to give me, Gina?'

'Nothing! I don't have time for things like . . . that!'

He had laughed again. 'It's a lonely world without love in it.'

'I hope you don't think that just because you've invested in me I'll go all silly and fall in love with you?'

His laughter had filled the room. 'My dear Gina. You're so naïve. How old are you, twenty-one? Yet you act like a child. You don't even know what love is, and I'm too busy and too old to start to teach you!'

She'd been infuriated. She'd always been in command of situations like this. All the boys she'd ever gone out with had been only too proud to be seen with her. While he, he was laughing at her and calling her a child. 'I wouldn't fall in love with you if you were the last man left alive! This is a business partnership, that's all and that's all it's ever going to be!' she had stormed back.

'That's all I ever intended it to be, and you're the one who started this conversation, Gina. But if I'd ever had any intentions of forming a "liaison", shall we say, I would never have brought you here. I never mix business with pleasure. I could have had my pleasure in Liverpool and left you there!'

She'd been speechless with fury and trembling at the insults. How dare he say such things to her, as if she were some cheap floosie! And he was so sure of himself! She'd slammed out and his quiet, mocking laughter had followed her. There were times when she hated Edward and the only thing that made it all bearable was her ambition and the sound of the applause in her ears at the end of her act.

She felt as though she was a truly seasoned performer now. Gone was the starry-eyed, impressionable girl. It was work, work and more work, dashing from one theatre to another, with lessons in between. But today had been the last straw and she was going to tell Edward that she wasn't ever going back to Charlie, not if she never danced another step as a result! Her blood boiled as she thought of his shouted insults – and in front of the whole class as well! He'd picked on her for the whole of the lesson, singling her out and making her repeat steps over and over again, but when he'd yelled, 'You've got two left feet, Gina, and you're about as light on them as a docker in army boots! Pick your feet up girl, you'll never make a dancer!' it had been the final straw. The fact that he yelled such insults to other members of his class was immaterial.

'And you're about as fit to teach as a bloody docker with or without boots!' she'd screamed back, before snatching up her things and storming out.

She had a matinee at the Hoxton Empire and although that wasn't for another two hours, she still wouldn't have time to go back to Bloomsbury. She decided to go to Edward's office instead.

All the way on the Underground she fumed. She was sick and tired of tatty, second-rate theatres! Where was the career Edward had promised her? And she didn't particularly like London either. It was such a vast, sprawling city. Oh, there were fine buildings, wonderful shops, hotels and parks, but it was impersonal and everyone was in a hurry to get somewhere. It would be different if you had money, she thought, then you would have the time to indulge in all the pleasures it offered and no doubt there would be time for friendships, too. But she didn't have the money. She didn't even have a friend. She barely made enough to live on, and as for her clothes . . . ! She had three dresses, including the pale green crêpe, and she was tired of wearing them and they were all beginning to look limp and faded.

By the time she arrived at Edward's office she was like a bubbling saucepan with the lid just about ready to blow off.

'Gina, what are you doing here?'

It was a warm day and Edward had his sleeves rolled up, his necktie was abandoned and his top button was undone, revealing a strong, muscled neck.

'I've had enough! Enough, Edward! I'm never going back there to that . . . that . . . eejit Charlie Grayson!'

He pulled a chair out and placed it in front of her. He was fully aware of the reasons why Charlie worked her so hard. Gina had a raw talent, Charlie had told him, but she needed to be worked hard. The rough edges of the diamond needed to be polished off.

'I can't sit down, I'm too angry!'

'When are you ever anything else? I presume he's been telling you a few home truths again? Gina, how many times do I have to tell you, I can't wave a magic wand, you have to work!'

'Work! I do nothing but work. I work until I'm fit to drop!'

'I warned you.'

'Oh, don't start that again. You sound like a cracked record. You said I had talent, a talent you didn't want to see ruined, well it is being ruined and in places like the Hoxton Empire! I won't do any more shows at second-rate music halls!'

'Then you won't work at all.' There was a cold edge to his voice. 'I didn't think you'd quit so easily.'

She glared at him. 'Where are the wonderful parts you promised me? Where are these wonderful Stage Musicals?'

'I promised you nothing!'

'And nothing is what you're going to get from me from now on!'

He'd seen her in a temper before, but never like this, and he wondered if he hadn't pushed her just that bit too hard. But he understood her and he knew that if you gave Gina sympathy she'd throw it right back in your face and only think the worse of you for being what she would call 'weak'. He walked to the door and opened it. 'Then if I'm getting nothing, there's the door. Find your own way to the top! It's not an easy road and there are a lot of pitfalls, but if that's the way you want it . . .' He swept his hand across the open space.

Gina hadn't expected this. Edward had called her bluff. His dark eyes seemed to be mocking her, daring

166

her . . . she jerked up her chin, she'd show him! Without a backward glance she walked through the door and out into the corridor.

'You'd better get over to Hoxton, the rent's due at the end of the week and Rose doesn't exist on charity!' he called after her. He closed the door. Had he gone too far? Then he smiled. She'd be back; sooner or later she'd be back. It usually didn't take long for her temper to cool down and then she'd return. Suddenly he frowned. What if she didn't? He felt some responsibility towards her – after all, he'd brought her here. But was it responsibility? His eyed darkened. Gina had only one thing on her mind and she'd use anyone to get to the top. If their feelings were hurt in the process she wouldn't care; he doubted she'd even notice.

By the time Gina got back to Bloomsbury after her matinee she had calmed down. She took off the light cotton coat that covered her 'stage' dress and threw it over the chair, then she sat down on the edge of the bed. Oh, what a mess today had been! She'd missed her timing on 'When I Grow Too Old To Dream' and the rest of the song had been a shambles, but a decent conductor would have sorted that out! She hated that song. She wanted to sing about happier things than old age. So what that it always went down well with the audience? Most of them were half way to old age anyway!

After the performance she'd taken an omnibus to the West End and had roamed up and down outside the theatres. It was on the stage of The Gaiety and The Palladium that she wanted to appear, not the Hoxton or Brixton Empires. The sight of the pinnacle of her desire had only depressed her and she'd come home.

Home. Gina glanced around the sparsely furnished room and, for the first time since she'd left Ireland, she felt home-sick. Home-sick and lonely. She reflected again on the fact that she didn't even have any friends, for she was too fiercely competitive to be liked by the other girls she came into contact with. She remained aloof, viewing them all with suspicion, always asking herself the same question. 'Is she better than me?'

She kicked off her shoes and massaged her aching feet with her thumbs. She'd have to decide what to do about her future.

'Are you there, Gina?'

Oh, Holy Saint Patrick, not her! Not now, I couldn't stand it! she thought as she heard Mrs Weston's voice. The rent was due, Edward hadn't needed to remind her, and she'd spent some of it on a length of turquoise taffeta that she intended to have made up to increase her wardrobe. Maybe if she kept very still and quiet her landlady would go away.

'Gina, there's two letters for you here.'

She kept quiet. Mrs Weston had used that excuse before to gain entry, her eyes darting about the room for any sign of anything she considered 'improper', and the 'letters' had proved only to be notes from Edward.

Gina heard the rustling of paper and watched as two envelopes were slid under the door, but only when the slow footsteps had died away did she get up and creep to the door. One was postmarked 'Liverpool' and the other 'Glasgow'. She ripped Bridget's letter open and took it over to the window. It wasn't quite dark and the street lamp provided ample light. Maybe Bridget had come to her senses and got herself a decent job. Maybe she'd stopped living with Bernie O'Hagan.

But she hadn't and her letter said that she was still working in that awful garment place. The way she went on about Bernie, Archie and this Eileen person and some boy called Andy, you'd think they were all one big family. Gina threw the letter on the bed and opened Mary-Kate's. It wasn't much better and full of trivia, nearly all of which Gina considered boring. She was still house-keeping for Lewis Vannin, still doing the books. Mary-Kate would never get herself a husband like that and to get married had been the sum of Mary-Kate's ambition.

'Oh, hell and damnation!' Gina cursed aloud. Why couldn't they write with something exciting; saying they were at least getting somewhere. She leaned her forehead against the window pane. And she'd walked out on Edward. Just where would that get her? Exactly nowhere, if she were to be brutally honest with herself. She needed him more than he needed her. Her damned temper again. Well, she wasn't going to let her dream slip away like the other two seemed to be doing. She'd go back to Edward. It would hurt. It would wound her pride terribly and she'd never forget the humiliation.

Her eyes narrowed, she could almost taste the bitter gall in her throat. Oh, she'd remember all the slights and insults, she'd store them all up until the day she could throw them back in the faces of the people who had thwarted her. But she couldn't allow herself that luxury until she was successful, until they needed her. Then she'd laugh in their faces and walk out! She'd show them she no longer needed or cared about them. Especially Charlie Grayson and Edward Vinetti!

Gina switched on the light – if Mrs Weston came back up, she'd pretend she'd been asleep. She opened the drawer of the chest and drew out the turquoise taffeta and held it against her. It was a lovely, glowing colour and suited her pale skin and flaming hair. She'd have it made up in the latest style with a dropped waist and an even shorter skirt than her other dresses, and, if she could afford it, she'd have a headband with plumes dyed to match, and if she couldn't . . . well, she'd cajole Edward into buying them for her. He was always saying she was his 'investment', he could invest in dressing her in a more stylish way! She smiled at her reflection, self-confidence restored, and all thoughts of home-sickness banished, along with the plight of both her sisters.

Chapter Nine

─◆◆◆─

THE SKY WAS LEADEN and a steely wind was blowing in from the Clyde, threatening rain. Bridget wrapped her scarf more tightly around her neck, then shifted the bundle she was carrying into a more comfortable position. Eileen kept silent pace beside her as they turned into Warwick Street.

It had become a Thursday night ritual, taking the washing down to the 'Steamy', a department of the public baths. It was a ritual Bridget hated, but it had to be done and true to her promise, after she'd watched Eileen struggle home with the washing, she'd offered to help.

The cavernous room was always filled with clouds of steam that rose from the rows of copper boilers; a twilight world where dim figures humped and heaved piles of wet washing from boiler to buckets to mangles. Eileen refused to hang it out in the court at the back of their tenement, even in summer, because of the soot-laden air, and so it was hung from a rack suspended from the kitchen ceiling, operated by a pulley system that

Archie had rigged up. Consequently, for the whole of the weekend the place smelled damp and fusty.

Despite the elements and the ritual, Bridget smiled to herself as she caught sight of a tall figure outlined under the sickly yellow glow of the street lamp. He was waiting for her.

The night Andy had taken her dancing at the Locarno had been the start of their relationship. After the first half hour she'd felt so at ease with him that she'd felt she'd known him all her life. He was amusing and attentive and made sure she'd danced every dance with him. But she'd seen the other side of his nature too, when a young man – obviously very much the worse for drink – had asked her to dance. He'd refused to take no for an answer and had become abusive. Andy hadn't argued, he'd simply lifted the drunk bodily off his feet by the collar of his jacket and frog-marched him to the two burly doormen, or 'bouncers' as he'd called them.

It had caused a minor incident that had embarrassed her until she'd overheard two girls wishing they had a man like that. After that she'd felt totally safe with him and on the way home, when he'd put his arm around her shoulder and kissed her gently on the forehead, she'd felt a strange sensation creeping over her. As she'd lain in bed that night, she realized with a feeling of detached amazement and pure happiness that she was in love. It had been a glorious summer.

They'd gone out to the 'country' at Newton Mearns where the villas of the rich were just beginning to encroach on the countryside. They'd often walked the vast, verdant acres of Glasgow Green, a huge park on the north bank of the river, and he'd even taken her to

Sauchiehall Street where she had to admit the shops were finer than those in Liverpool. They'd stood on the corner outside the windows of Copeland and Lye and had imagined what they would buy if they had all the money in the world to spend, and on the way back on the tram she'd nestled close to him and whispered that she'd sooner be broke with him, than be wildly rich and be without him.

He'd never met a girl like her before. She was warm and generous – still a little timid – not coarse or forward like most of the other girls he'd known. For the first time he'd had his sexual advances curtailed, but that had only made him want her more. At Newton Mearns they had wandered up Lang Byre Brig until the heat of the sun had forced them to seek shade. They'd sat in the long grass at the foot of a horse chestnut whose leaves rustled and whispered in the slight breeze, and he'd taken her in his arms and kissed her. Her arms had locked behind his head and she had clung to his lips, but when his hand had moved down her back, around her waist and across her thighs, she had stiffened and pulled away from him.

'I'm not a girl like that, Andy! I can't! It's wrong!'

'What's wrong with it, Bridget? You love me don't you?'

She had nodded emphatically but had refused to allow him to do any more than kiss her. He'd been moody and frustrated on the way back, but she had pretended not to notice and to his own surprise he found that he treated her far more protectively, and it had been that way ever since.

Bridget had found time to discover her adopted city as

she had been laid off from the factory in June. She'd managed to save some money whilst she was in work and so things hadn't been too bad, although she hadn't been able to find another job. Her presence at home had allowed Eileen to get to know her better and a friendship was growing between them. Then in August she'd been sent for by MacFarlane's again and was taken back as the orders for autumn stocks had rolled in. But all her earnings had been added to Eileen's and Bernie's to buy new sheets and blankets for the coming winter.

'Andy's waiting for you.' Eileen, too, had seen the shadowy figure. All her earlier suspicion and resentment had gone and she had become fond of Bridget. Bridget had quietly helped her with the household chores and had filled in the gaps in her elementary education. Eileen had been promoted to working behind the counter at the bakery because of it. 'Will you be going out tonight?'

'If it doesn't rain. Will you be all right with the washing?'

'Och, I did it all by myself before you came to live with us, I should be able to manage now, shouldn't I?'

Andy walked the last few steps to meet them and she reached up and kissed him lightly on the cheek. 'Will we go for a walk or do you think it'll rain?'

'It might hold off.'

'Come on up, I'll get my umbrella.'

Only when they were in the hallway did he take the heavy bundles from them both. That was something else she'd learned. Here the men were the bread-winners and that was all that was expected of them. They did nothing that could remotely be called 'women's work', and that included carrying shopping or bundles of washing, no matter how heavy they were.

After a few quick words to Bernie as she brushed her hair and jammed on her tam-o'-shanter and found her umbrella, they went back outside into the dark, windy street. Andy put his arm around her shoulder, drawing her close and she nestled into his side, drawing warmth from his body. They walked towards Glasgow Bridge, along Carlton Place, and the wind coming off the river cut through her coat and made her shiver.

'If it does rain you'll never keep that umbrella up.'

She smiled up at him. 'Then we'll have to find somewhere to shelter or get the tram back.' These few, precious hours she had alone with him were all she existed for. They made everything bearable and as the flying needle of her machine became only a blur, she would dispel the boredom by thinking of these moments.

'Will we go over the bridge on Saturday?' she asked.

'If you like.'

'I thought we'd look in the shops and then have something to eat in one of those nice Tea Rooms?'

He stopped walking and looked down at her. 'Tea Rooms? A right Jessie I'd look in one of those places! I'll take you for a drink.'

She was disappointed. The Tea Rooms looked so smart and so warm and inviting, but then she sighed. He'd never live it down if any of his friends saw him. That was a side of him she hated. The rough, cocky, devil-may-care attitude that he displayed when in the company of his cronies. Only she knew that he could be kind and gentle.

A figure was coming towards them, head bowed and shoulders hunched against the icy blasts, but as they drew near Bridget recognized Maggie Baird, one of the girls she worked with. A loud, blowsy piece with a none too savoury reputation. They couldn't avoid her and she had noticed them.

'Hello there, Andy, have yese nowhere warm to go the night, instead o' walkin' the streets?'

He laughed.

'I fancied some air, after being stuck in that room all day and then being half-choked in the 'Steamy',' Bridget said coldly.

'An did yese carry the washin' back for her then, Andy?'

'No, he did not! I do that myself.' But she didn't like Maggie or the way she was insinuating that she had some strange, demeaning power over Andy.

'And where are you off to, Maggie?' He had treated the insinuation with the contempt it deserved.

She grinned. 'I'm meetin' some friends in a nice, warm pub, we're havin' a few drams to keep oot the cold. An' I expect we'll be havin' a few laughs and do a bit o' blatherin'.' She smiled, invitingly.

Bridget pulled at his arm. 'We'd best be on our way, I think I felt a spot of rain.'

'Goodnight then, an' don't do anythin' I wouldn'a do!' Maggie laughed, pulling the collar of her coat up around her neck.

'She's a bold piece,' Bridget said as they walked on.

'She's not all that bad, she doesn't mean half of what she says.'

'Oh, you know her that well then?'

'I've known her all my life, she lives in our street. What's the matter with you tonight, Bridget?'

'Nothing, I'm just tired.' Somehow Maggie had disturbed her peace of mind. 'Will we go back now?'

They turned and began to retrace their steps, but after a few minutes the rain began to fall heavily. Cold, sheeting rain that hit the pavement and then bounced off. As Andy had predicted, the umbrella was useless, blowing inside out as soon as she put it up. They ran across the road and into the side doorway of a warehouse, just wide enough for them.

'We'll have to wait here until we hear a tram, then we'll make a dash for it.'

'Oh, I'm sorry I dragged you out on a night like this, I must be an eejit!'

He pulled her to him. 'I don't mind.'

His lips sought hers, kissing her gently at first, then with a stronger, more urgent desire. Whenever he kissed her like that she felt strangely dizzy and a feeling of warmth crept over her, despite the cold of the wind and the rain. She always felt safe and warm in his arms and she wished they could stay just like this forever. She felt so happy that it made her want to cry.

'Oh, Andy, hold me like this forever,' she whispered as his lips burned against her throat. She gently stroked the dark hair that curled low on the back of his neck. His mouth was on hers again, the tip of his tongue parting her lips. Then she felt his hand against her breast and it seemed to burn her flesh, despite the layers of clothing. She gasped as he clung to her mouth. She felt his fingers inside her coat, caressing her and the darkness swirled around her. Oh, she wanted him! She wanted him so much. It was a flame that was consuming her, willing him to go on . . .

'Bridie! Bridie! Oh, my own little Bridie!' he muttered.

Through the mists that clogged her mind the diminutive of her name rang clearly. Bridie! Little Bridie! Her Pa's name for her. She pushed him away, her face flushed. 'Andy, no! No more!'

'I want you, Bridget, I love you!'

'I can't! It's wrong! It's a sin! I love you, too, Andy, but . . . but I'm not like Maggie Baird!'

He held her away from him and looked down into her face. 'No, you're not like her. She doesn't lead a man on, tease him and then stiffen up and become all Holy!'

She was stung. 'I didn't lead you on and I wasn't teasing!'

'I'm only a man and I can't help my feelings or my needs.'

'I'm sorry! Oh, I'm truly sorry, but I just can't . . . not until I'm married.' She had been brought up too strictly, with the fear of eternal damnation, shame and disgrace, to throw those feelings to the winds now, even for him.

'Do you think I wouldn't marry you?'

'I don't want to trap you, I don't want that! I want you of your own free will.'

A distant expression came into his eyes and his grip on her relaxed. 'Come on, let's go back, it's eased off a bit.'

She felt utterly miserable. She did love him and she had wanted him, she still wanted him, but he made her feel guilty.

He took her hand and looked down at her again, then he sighed. 'Now you're crying. Oh, I'm sorry!'

She tried to brush away the tears with her free hand.

'No, it's me who's sorry, Andy. I've hurt you and I never meant to.'

He bent and kissed her cheek. 'Don't be an "eejit", you've not hurt me. Come on, I can hear a tram, if we run we'll get it.'

As she lay in bed beside Eileen and Bernie, both of whom were sleeping soundly, Bridget fidgeted in the narrow space, trying not to disturb them. Sleep had eluded her. Oh, if only he would ask her to marry him, to become engaged even, it would be different. She didn't want to lose him. She just couldn't imagine life without him. But to give in to him and to her own longings would make her little better than Maggie Baird. And if he did marry her, what then? Where would they live? How would they live? She pushed those questions to the back of her mind. Her love and longing for him carried her no further than the altar of St John's church. She lay staring at the dim shaft of moonlight that filtered in through the tiny, curtainless window and struggled with her conscience and her desires until she fell into a fitful sleep.

At lunchtime on Monday Bridget sat with Bernie and a few other girls on the low stone wall at the back of the factory, eating the meagre bits of food they had taken with them. The bulk of the factory shielded them from the wind and watery sunlight had tempted them from eating inside.

Andy had seemed his usual self over the weekend and had even taken her into the Waverley Hotel on Sauchiehall Street and had paid two shillings for a pot of tea and scones for her and a dram of the finest whisky for himself. That kind of money was too precious to be spent on such luxuries and she'd told him so, only to have him laugh and say, 'Och, I'll never understand women! One minute you want to have tea in those fancy Tea Rooms and then, when I bring you here and buy you tea, you say it's a waste of good money!'

She was in the middle of describing the interior of the Waverley Hotel to the group when Maggie Baird and two others came and sat beside them.

'Yese say he paid two shillin's for tea? Didn't I always say Big Andy MacDonald had his brains in his trewsers? I hope he got his money's worth!' Maggie laughed, coarsely.

Bernie turned towards her. 'It's a mind and a mouth like a sewer you've got!'

'Would yese listen t' her,' Maggie retorted, mockingly.

'I don't need to be bought, Maggie Baird, not like some people!' Bridget said coldly.

'Jesus! Listen t' her. Miss Prim an' Proper. I dinna see whit he sees in yese, Bridget O'Donnell. An' he'll get no comfort from yese, either! Och, I've met your type before.'

'And what type is that?' Bridget shot back.

Maggie pursed up her mouth and mimicked 'Yese'll no' be havin' me until yese wed me, Andy.'

'At least I don't have to resort to "having my card stamped" and I don't have to behave like a . . . a . . .'

'Hairey!' Bernie supplied, using the local name for a whore.

Maggie jumped to her feet. 'Who're yese callin' a hairey?'

'If the cap fits!' Bridget snapped.

The girl sitting next to Bernie started to snigger. Seeing she was outnumbered, Maggie just glared at Bridget. 'Yese think you've go' him, don't yese? Well, we'll be seein' aboot tha'! He's a man, isn't he, an' he'll no' go without for long. So, I'm givin' yese fair warning, I'll have him off yese in the end!'

'Yese'll have anyone in trewsers, Maggie Baird. Why don't yese move to the Saltmarket with the rest o' them?' one of Bridget's group sniggered.

Maggie's dark eyes narrowed as she glared at them all and then she turned and walked away.

'Take no notice of that one, Bridget, she's all mouth. Andy's your man and he wouldn't give the likes of that one a second look, that he wouldn't,' Bernie stated.

Bridget pulled off a piece of bread and ate it, but a nagging seed of doubt had been sown. It was as if Maggie's threat had brought all her fears to the surface again.

The cold wind, after the heat of the theatre, stung Gina's cheeks. She shivered and walked quickly up the narrow alley and out into the brightly lit street. Edward was waiting for her in his car, but on seeing her, he got out and opened the passenger door for her. She'd been working steadily and hard since the day she'd walked back into his office, ignoring the previous day's incident, and he had had the good grace to ignore it, too.

'And to what do I owe this honour? You don't usually pick me up and take me to supper?' She'd been surprised and intrigued ever since she'd been handed his note, just before she'd gone on stage.

'I think you deserve a little spoiling now and then, besides I think I've got a part for you.'

'A part! What in? Where?' She forgot how tired she was and how her feet ached.

'All in good time,' he laughed. He deliberately kept their social lives apart, for he had found himself thinking far too much about her lately. Now she looked like a pretty child on her birthday. Her eyes full of expectation and excitement as she anticipated the delights to come. It was strange how he always thought of her as being so young. Perhaps it came from the fact that he was much older, but then that really wasn't true; he was only thirty-one.

She clutched his arm. 'Oh, Edward, don't be so mean! Tell me now!'

'If you don't stop pulling my arm we'll end up wrapped around a lamp post and that would be the end of both of us!'

She let go and, delving into her handbag, pulled out a small mirror and studied her reflection. 'At least tell me where you're taking me?'

'To Stefano's.'

She was a little disappointed. She would have prefered somewhere much smarter, but at least it would be warm and comfortable and quiet and the food was good. She leaned back in her seat. Oh, was there really an end in sight to all the rushing about and the tatty theatres with their noisy and sometimes unappreciative audiences? Had her chance arrived at last?

The turquoise taffeta looked a little out of place amidst the sombre-suited customers in the quiet, little restaurant. Edward ordered a bottle of wine and handed her the menu.

'Oh, I'm too excited to eat! If you don't tell me all about it I'll . . . scream!'

'We'll be thrown out,' he joked, but seeing he could no longer keep her quiet, he decided to put her out of her misery. 'You've got an audition tomorrow for the London production of "Starlight and Syncopation" at the Gaiety in the Strand.' He filled her glass with wine and handed it to her.

Her eyes widened and her mouth formed an 'O' as she just stared at him, the glass half way to her lips.

'Say something, you look like a fish with your mouth open!'

She put the glass down with a rather shaky hand. 'Oh, Edward! It's going to be a roaring success, I know it. Oh, I don't know what to say . . .'

'Thank you would do for a start.'

She caught his hand and held it tightly. 'Oh, thank you! A million times! I just can't believe it. No more Charlie Grayson, no more tatty theatres.'

He felt a tremor of excitement pass from her hand to his own and he slowly pulled his hand away. Her face was transformed and he thought how beautiful she was; her pale skin glowing, her eyes sparkling, her lips parted in a smile. He had a sudden urge to lean over and kiss her. 'Don't get your hopes up too high. It's for the chorus and there will be others after a place, too!'

'I don't care. Oh, I know I'll get it! Is it singing and dancing? What shall I sing? Is there a "set" piece?'

'One thing at a time! Yes, it's singing and dancing. You can sing anything you like but I'd advise you to do something up to date, at least then they'll know you're really interested.'

'Interested! I'd kill to get the part.'

'I believe you would, too, Gina.'

She laughed. 'So, what shall I sing?'

'Do you know "Tea for Two"?'

She nodded as she sipped the wine. She felt exuberant and already intoxicated. Again she took his hand and began to sing softly,

'Tea for Two and Two for Tea,
And me for you and you for me,
Oh, can't you see how happy we would be . . .'

Again he drew his hand away and smiled. 'That's fine.' The words of the song brought on a surge of the strange desire again. 'Be there at half-past ten and tell them I sent you.'

Gina was there at ten o'clock, as were at least a dozen other girls, all with the same air of hopeful anticipation. Some were chatting and laughing nervously, others were quiet and preoccupied, some smoking. She scrutinized them all closely, her eyes hard and calculating as she tried to pick out their faults. There seemed to be only two who, in her opinion, posed any kind of threat. A tall, blonde girl and a girl with very dark hair, shingled closely into the back of her neck. She'd seen them before while working the halls.

She changed into her dancing shoes and began to do a few of the loosening up exercises Charlie had taught her. A few of the others followed her example, giving her the opportunity to gauge the competition. She shrugged to herself. As Charlie would put it, most of them seemed to have two left feet. Then to her surprise the blonde girl came over to her.

'I've seen you before, haven't I?'

'Yes, I've done most of the halls.'

'Me, too! Have one?' She offered Gina a cigarette from an engraved silver case.

Gina shook her head, thinking the case must have cost quite a bit. 'That's nice.'

'A friend of mine bought it for me.'

'Who?' Gina was always alert in the presence of anyone she thought of as opposition and the 'friend' obviously wasn't short of money. Perhaps it was the producer which would give the girl an advantage.

'Oh, I don't think you know him, Freddie Marshalsea?'

Again Gina shook her head; she'd never heard that name. At least it wasn't the producer.

'I'm Helen, by the way. Helen Mason.'

'Gina O'Donnell.'

Helen inhaled deeply and blew out the smoke. 'God, I'm nervous! I'm pinning everything on getting in this show. I'm sick and tired of the halls!'

'I know what you mean. I always feel positively ill before I go on. Do you know how many they need?'

'Six, so I've heard.' Helen looked around and then lowered her voice. 'Looking at this lot, I'd say we're in with a good chance, wouldn't you? Tell you what, if we both get in we'll go and celebrate? I won't feel like going back to my digs, the landlady's a harridan and her husband gives me the creeps!'

'I know the type. Do you come from London?'

'No, I'm from Manchester. I came down here for a

good time and to get on. There's not much life in Manchester. You're Irish, aren't you?'

'From County Tipperary.'

Helen laughed and began to hum 'It's a Long Way to Tipperary', but seeing the look on Gina's face she stopped. 'Sorry, I'm always putting my big foot in it. How did you end up in London?'

Briefly Gina told her.

Helen looked at her with admiration and some envy. 'Edward Vinetti! He's an absolute dish! Some people have all the luck.'

'I'd never thought of him like that. Most of the time I can't stand him and sometimes I absolutely hate him!'

'You're joking?'

'That I'm not! Sometimes he's so infuriating and insulting.'

'Oh, well, at least you're certain of a job here.'

'No more than you are. Just because he's my agent doesn't mean I'll get the job. If they don't think I can sing or dance well enough they won't take me on – Edward Vinetti or not! And I've just *got* to get this job! I'm *going* to get it!'

'Don't be so intense. It'll be a bloody miracle if I ever hit the big time, but I don't mind all that much.'

'Why?' Gina found it almost impossible to believe that everyone was not like herself.

'As long as it's not a bad job and I'm having some fun out of life, who cares? You're only young once and I intend to make the most of my youth! "You're going to the bad, Helen Mason!", that's what my folks told me. But I certainly don't want to end up like them. Working all hours, scrimping and saving, just to put on a respectable front for the benefit of the neighbours. All you get out of that is grey hairs and wrinkles. You'd think my mother was about sixty and she's not, but she's looked sixty for years. Well, I don't intend to end up like that!'

Gina smiled. Helen posed no threat if that's all the ambition she had.

'Even if they don't take me on, we can go and celebrate. You're sure to be all right. Unless you've got other plans?'

'No, I'd like that.'

Helen's name was called and she sucked in her breath. 'Keep your fingers crossed for me and I'll wait for you, either way!' she called back.

Helen had been called first and Gina remembered the girl who had won the talent contest. First was as bad as being last. But she hoped Helen would be successful, she liked her. She didn't have a friend and now that Helen had revealed the extent of her ambitions, she had warmed to her. Despite what she'd said about Edward, she realized he was her only friend. But she couldn't share confidences or gossip with him and that's where she'd missed her sisters. Yes, they'd go and celebrate afterwards, surely one of them would have something to be happy about? She was still nervous and she began to hum the tune of 'Tea for Two' over and over in her mind. Her hands felt sticky and it was very warm and clammy. The minutes dragged by and she began her exercises again.

Suddenly she was clasped in a tight hug. 'I got it! I got it! Oh, Gina, I'm so thrilled! Oh, won't it be just great if we're working together?'

'What did they say? When do you start? What was it

like?' Gina found herself caught up in Helen's excitement.

'Tomorrow! Oh, I was terrible! I was sure I'd made a right mess of it but when I'd finished they just said "Fine, be here tomorrow morning at ten". I'm down to my last few shillings but somehow we'll manage a bottle of wine!'

Gina's name was called. 'Oh, Holy Saint Patrick!' she cried, crossing herself.

Helen pressed something into her hand. 'Here, take this with you, it's my lucky silver threepenny bit. Go on. If you get it, we'll have two bottles of wine!'

It was now or never. Her throat felt raw and dry and her stomach was churning. 'Stop being such a fool! If they've taken her, they'll take you!' Gina muttered as she crossed the stage to where the pianist sat, waiting for her to tell him what she wished to sing.

She went through a short dance routine, choreographed by Charlie for just such occasions. It incorporated all the steps she knew and would need. Then she walked to the front of the stage. As usual, she could see no one but a voice from the void called to her to 'Carry on!' She nodded to the pianist and began the first verse, putting everything into it, but when she started to go into the second verse the voice from beyond interrupted her. 'Thank you, Miss O'Donnell, that's fine!'

The smile froze on her lips as she glared into the darkness. No one was going to rob her of this chance, too much depended on it! No one interrupted her.

'No one cuts me short! I'll carry on until I've finished,' she shouted back, nodding to the bemused pianist. He shrugged and started to play and she went into the second verse with spirit and vivacity, her nerves gone, quelled by anger.

At the back of the theatre, Edward Vinetti smiled to himself. That was typical of her and it was enough to ensure that she got the part. He'd watched her dance and he'd listened to her, knowing how much everything depended on this audition. He was almost certain that she'd got it, but when she'd shouted her defiance, he knew she wouldn't be overlooked or forgotten. His dark eyes became serious. He had invested in her and it would now pay off, for she had a talent that couldn't be hidden forever on the Halls, but as he listened to her and watched her, he wondered if he hadn't placed a cuckoo in the nest. He also told himself that any affection he had for her would have to be kept firmly in check. Gina was on her way and would no doubt break a few hearts, but his wasn't going to be one of them!

They could only afford one bottle of wine after all, but after half of it they'd exchanged life stories and by the time the bottle was empty they were both giggling like school friends who had known each other all their lives. Gina was far more tipsy than Helen, not being used to drinking.

'We'd better go, people are giving us funny looks,' Helen suggested.

'You're drunk, Helen Penel . . . Pen . . . Sure, why did they give you such a desperate name as Pen . . . el . . . ope?' Gina concentrated hard and sounded it out.

Helen giggled, then tried to look serious. 'They thought it was posh. Posh Penelope, isn't that funny? Where are we going now?'

'We can't go back to Rose's like this, she'll throw me out!'

'We can't go to Gertie's either, she'll kill me!'

'We can't stay here! P'raps we'd better go for a walk, we're quite tipsy you know, isn't that altogether desperate!'

'Oh, Gina, I love the way you talk. I know, we'll go to Freddie's.'

They got up, trying to appear completely sober, and arm in arm they walked out into the street and almost collided with Edward.

'I've been looking for you!'

'Edward! We're going to Freddie's.' Gina was having a little trouble with her words.

'You're not going anywhere like that, either of you!'

'This is my friend Helen. Helen Pen ... Helen Mason and we're going to Freddie's. He's her friend.'

'I know Helen and I know Freddie and neither of you are going to Freddie Marshalsea's!'

'Why not?' Gina demanded loudly.

'Because you're a disgrace, both of you, and Lord Marshalsea's butler would call the police! Now don't you start any of your tricks, Gina. Get in the car, both of you.'

At first Edward had been amused. It would do her good to relax for a change and he was glad she at last seemed to have found a friend – although Helen wasn't one he'd have chosen. She liked a good time and mixed with rather a 'fast' set, but his amusement had turned to annoyance. He hadn't realized Gina was quite so intoxicated and they were making a spectacle of themselves which wouldn't do any of them any good.

Thankfully Gina had decided not to pursue the matter and he bundled them both into the car.

'Where are we going now?' Gina asked.

'To my place where you can both sober up, and I hope it teaches you a lesson, Gina. You're going to have an almighty hangover.'

Chapter Ten

———◆———

THE NEWS FROM HOME was bad. With every letter she received and with nearly every newspaper she read, it got worse. Mary-Kate folded Sarah's latest letter and put it back in its envelope. Was there no end to it all? In August, Michael Collins who had been a prominent founder member of Ireland's fight for freedom and who was much loved and respected, had been murdered and in his own home County of Cork. Now it seemed that, with the Emergency Powers Act in force, it was open season – on both sides – for anyone caught carrying a gun. Sarah's letter had reported the first incident of real trouble in Clonmel. A group of Anti-Treaty Nationalists had attacked and burned down Feehey's butchers. Mr Feehey was the Mayor and very outspoken in his condemnation of the 'Irregulars' as they were now being called. The shock had caused Mrs Feehey to have a heart attack and she was very ill. Michael was being no help at all for he sided with the Irregulars, although he didn't actively participate in the outrage.

Sarah thanked God that Matty was too busy to be

much involved with either side. Everyone else was well, under the circumstances, and had she heard from Bridget lately? She'd had a letter from Gina, telling her how grand it was being in such a wildly popular show, and she was beginning to worry a little less about her daughter all alone in wicked London.

Mary-Kate sighed. Gina was doing just fine, but she hadn't heard from Bridget for over a month now, although she'd written four times. She looked at the kitchen clock. Ellen would be home soon and she'd better get started with preparations for supper. Ellen was doing well at school now and there had been no more trouble. She smiled, picking up a half-finished piece of embroidery. It was a tray cloth she had persuaded Ellen to make for Elizabeth for Christmas, as a peace offering.

Elizabeth still treated Mary-Kate coldly, but she had returned to visit her father, accompanied by her husband – a tall, thin young man with a perpetually harassed look on his face. It was obvious who wore the trousers in that house, she had thought the minute she'd set eyes on him. Ernest Winskill was no match for his wife's waspish tongue or overbearing manner. She wasn't sure exactly what he did for a living. 'Something in shipping' was how Elizabeth explained it, but she thought privately that it was Lewis Vannin who contributed most to that household. Elizabeth never wore the same outfit twice.

Annie came into the kitchen with a basket full of washing. 'It's as wet as it was when it first went out. There's no drying this weather and Ellen's coming up the path, you can hear her clattering that ruler all along the wall.'

'Put it all on the airer in front of the fire, Annie. Then we'd better start supper. Has Dick fixed that tap yet?'

'No, it needs a new washer. He's coming over to do it later on – so he said.'

Ellen came through the door and Mary-Kate eyed her with resignation, shaking her head. 'You look about as tidy as a tinker's horse! Have you lost your ribbons again? You cost your Pa a fortune in hair ribbons.'

'They always fall out because my hair is too fine. Why can't I have it cut?'

'Would you just listen to the bold piece, Annie. Wanting her hair cut at her age. Shame on you, Ellen Vannin!'

'I'm nearly grown up!'

'Oh, no you're not. I can't see what's the matter with it, you have lovely hair.' Mary-Kate took off the navy blue velour hat and pushed the soft, light brown hair back from the child's face. She and Ellen had become very close. 'Look at the state of your dress. Did you spill your dinner down it?' She looked down at the thin legs in the fawn-coloured lisle stockings. 'You've got another hole in the knee again, and will you stop rattling that ruler along the wall, you know how it irritates your Pa.'

'He's never home, so why does it irritate him?'

'People complain.'

Ellen ignored all this. 'Is that a letter from your Gina? Oh, wouldn't it be wonderful if we could go and see her?'

'Now don't start that again, Miss! Could you imagine your Pa's face if you said you wanted to be like Gina? And it's a letter from my Ma and it's not a nice one, either. It's desperate. So, go up and get changed, wash your hands and then do your piano practice before your Pa gets home, so you won't disturb him.'

Ellen grimaced but did as she was told.

Later, when the dishes had been cleared away and the tea tray laid, Mary-Kate and Ellen went into the small parlour that adjoined the library where Lewis Vannin was reading, Ellen with her homework, Mary-Kate with the ledgers and invoices. The door was open and Lewis Vannin often looked up from his newspaper and watched them.

He was content with his life now; Ellen had become much quieter and less trouble since Mary-Kate had come and he had to admit Mary-Kate O'Donnell was worth her weight in gold. She was very prudent and economical with his money and she ran his household far more efficiently and with less fuss than her predecessor had done. In fact, things had not gone so smoothly since before Molly died, he thought. Even Elizabeth wasn't so obnoxious. Mary-Kate seemed to have a calming effect on people, he deliberated, watching the two heads bent over their work.

Mary-Kate was considerably younger than him, but she had the qualities of a much more mature woman. It was as though she'd gradually taken over Molly's role. Occasionally he wondered what he would do if she ever got married and left him, but he hated disorganization, so he seldom dwelled on that subject. She seemed to spend her time off either with Ellen or shopping, and as far as he knew she'd only ever attended one Church Social, but she did go to Mass nearly every morning at six o'clock.

He returned to his newspaper. Ireland again. That

accursed country! Were they never to be free of it? Having fought the British Army for four years, they were now intent on massacring one another. The former rebels were now a recognized government and were seeking British aid in the way of arms with which to subdue their fellow countrymen. He would never understand them! A noise from the other room distracted him and he lowered his paper to see Ellen closing her books. Mary-Kate was Irish but she displayed none of the belligerence or deviousness that he associated with the race he read about. Maybe she was just different, or maybe it was only a handful of them that were so unruly and violent? He rose and walked to the sideboard and looked at the whisky decanter, then he went back to his chair. He took the odd drink now and then, but it was so easy to let it become a habit and he didn't approve of drinking, not to excess anyway.

Ellen had left the parlour and was about to barge into the kitchen as she usually did to tell Annie to boil the kettle for the late evening supper, but hearing raised voices she stopped. It was Annie and Dick and they were talking about Mary-Kate. She pressed her ear to the door.

'Well, it's the talk of the parish! Him in his fifties and her so young and unmarried and living under the same roof!'

'I thought you liked her, Annie?'

'I do, but that's not the point, is it? It's what people are saying about her and him that matters, and it's not very nice I can tell you, Dick Watson! She even sits beside him when they go to Mass on Sunday. You'd think that the child would at least sit between them! It's not proper at all and I'm not the only one who thinks so. It's the scandal of the neighbourhood!'

'I'd watch your tongue if you want to keep your job.'

'I'm only thinking of her! It's a wonder that sour-faced Elizabeth hasn't said something to him about it, but as soon as she hears about it she will, you mark my words.'

'And I suppose you'll be the one to tell her?'

'Not on your life! I'd not tell that one that people are saying her pa and Mary-Kate O'Donnell are . . . co-habiting. Aye, that's the word for it!'

Ellen drew away, her cheeks burning. She hated Annie! How could she say such terrible things about her pa and Mary-Kate? Then she went cold. What if someone did tell Lizzie and she came round in a temper and then . . . then Mary-Kate would have to go away! She wished she'd never listened. Mary-Kate said it was rude to eavesdrop on other people's conversations. She turned around to find Mary-Kate standing behind her.

'Ellen, what's the matter, you look terrified?'

'I . . . Oh, I hate that Annie Gillespie! Get Pa to get rid of her now, this minute.'

'Annie? Why?'

Ellen clung to her arm. 'She's been saying horrible things about you and . . . Pa . . . and if Lizzie hears about it . . .'

'What horrible things?'

Ellen looked up at her with tears in her eyes. All her old fears flooding back as she saw her world in danger of crashing about her ears again.

Mary-Kate shook her. 'What things, Ellen?'

'That you and Pa are ... co ... co-something! That you're living under the same roof and that it's a disgrace and that you even sit beside him at Mass and that I should sit between you and that if Lizzie hears them all gossiping she'll get mad and then you'll have to go away and I don't want you to go away! I hate Annie and I hate Lizzie!' It all came out in a rush, without even a pause for breath and she hid her face on Mary-Kate's chest and began to cry.

Mary-Kate stared hard at the closed door, a tremor of shock running through her. She'd never even thought about it like that! She worked for Lewis Vannin, that was all. She worked for him like Mrs Rickard had worked for him, didn't people understand that? It was so malicious and hurtful and so very, very untrue.

'Wipe your eyes and go on up to bed. I'll bring you up a drink. I have to speak to Annie.' She disentangled the child's arms from around her waist. 'Go on and don't fret yourself. I'll get to the bottom of this.'

Her mouth was set in a grim, determined line as she opened the kitchen door.

'I've put the kettle on, it won't be long,' Annie said brightly.

'I'm glad you have something to be so cheerful about, you've just upset Ellen terribly!'

'Ellen?'

'She overheard you telling Dick what a disgrace it is that I'm co-habiting with Mr Vannin! Fortunately she doesn't know what that means!'

Annie's face was bright red and her mouth dropped open. Then she began to splutter helplessly.

'Don't try to deny it, Annie. A child wouldn't make up

something like that! She's terrified that someone will tell Mrs Winskill of these vicious lies.'

'Oh, I didn't mean it – it's only what I've heard, what others have been saying!'

'What others?' Mary-Kate was trying to keep calm but her temper manifested itself in the pink tinge in her cheeks and the glow of anger in her eyes. 'What others?' she demanded.

'My friend, Emily, lives near your Aunt Maura and she said her Ma said . . .'

'So, that's it! That damned woman!' she exploded. So this was Maura's way of getting back at her. 'I want to hear no more about it from either of you and you can tell your friend Emily, and her Ma, to tell my dear aunt that she'd best look for somewhere else to live, because I swear to God that Mr Vannin will put her out on the street when he hears of this!'

Annie began to cry noisily. 'Oh, Miss O'Donnell, I didn't mean to repeat it. Honestly, I didn't. Oh, I'll get the sack and I'll not get another job like this and I don't want to leave!'

'You should have thought of that, shouldn't you? Before you passed on these vicious lies.'

'Oh, you won't tell Mr Vannin, will you? Oh, please, Miss O'Donnell!'

'I won't tell him tonight, but first thing in the morning I intend to go and see my aunt and put a stop to this. But if he decides to sack you when he does hear, Annie, you've only got yourself to blame!'

As she set the tea tray down on his desk Lewis Vannin noticed that Mary-Kate's hands were shaking.

'Is something wrong? You seem upset?'

'No, nothing! I . . . I had a letter from my mother today saying things at home are getting worse.'

'I know, the papers are full of it, but try not to worry about it as long as your mother and brother are well.'

'Oh, they are. If you don't mind, I think I'll retire early tonight. Goodnight.'

'Goodnight.'

Lewis Vannin drank his tea slowly. The only time he'd ever seen her so disturbed was the day Ellen had been expelled from Seafield Convent. It was more than events at home. Had Ellen been causing trouble again? he wondered. Or was it Elizabeth? Elizabeth would try the patience of the Virgin Mary.

He heard a scraping at the door and turned, watching the door handle move slowly. It was Ellen, in her nightdress, her feet bare, her hair falling over her shoulders. The sight of her startled him; she looked just the way Molly had when they'd first been married. 'Ellen, what's the matter?'

She shut the door quietly behind her and padded across to his chair. 'Pa, I . . . I don't want Mary-Kate to go away!'

'Go away? Is she thinking of leaving?' His tone was brusque. Was that why she'd been upset?

'If our Lizzie hears about what they're saying, she'll have to go away! Pa, you won't let her go, will you?'

He was irritated. What on earth was the child blabbering about? 'Who are "they" and what have they been saying that it should affect your sister and me?'

'Annie said . . .'

'Servants' gossip! What did the girl say? Come on, Ellen, out with it!'

Quite flatly she told him.

He looked away from the wan little face, shocked. No wonder she'd been upset. 'Go back to bed, Ellen.'

'But Pa . . .'

'Go to bed!'

She turned and padded silently out of the room.

He was numbed. He was a man of some standing in the community and to be talked about by all and sundry . . . like that! He rose and poured himself a large whisky and gulped it down. It was intolerable! Intolerable! That foul-mouthed little kitchen slut would get her cards tomorrow! He'd get to the bottom of this! And Dick Watson! The man wasn't exactly noted for his discretion! Were his workers already making lewd remarks behind his back? He refilled his glass. There was only one answer. Miss O'Donnell would have to go. No matter that his whole household would be thrown into utter chaos, he couldn't . . . wouldn't tolerate such scandalous rumours!

He sat down in the chair and placed the decanter beside him. What had he done to deserve this? He was a God-fearing man, fair and straight in all his dealings; a benefactor to the community and the Church. Hadn't he paid for the huge, circular, stained-glass window above the altar of the Church of the Blessed Sacrament? Why was God punishing him like this? First Molly's death, then Ellen's behaviour, and the constant thorn in his side that was Elizabeth and her spineless husband – and now this! But, he reflected morosely, these afflictions had started long before Molly's death. He had no sons into whose hands he could safely pass the business he was now successfully building, and that had been a bitter pill to swallow. Elizabeth and Ernest would fritter away everything and Ellen . . . Oh, Ellen was like him, but she was only a child and if anything should happen to him . . . Why couldn't Ellen have been a boy? He refilled his glass again and sank deeper and deeper into self-pity as the evening wore on.

Mary-Kate had tried to say her prayers, but her mind kept wandering and she lay awake, still seething with anger. Oh, Maura had done her work well. There was nothing else she could do now but leave. But what would happen to Ellen? She couldn't take her with her, she'd have no job and no home! She'd have to tell him herself, before Elizabeth heard.

She pounded and pumelled the pillow, wishing it were Maura's head. Then she sat up and hugged her knees. There must be another way around it. There had to be. She could have quite cheerfully strangled her aunt. Calm down, she told herself, this was getting her nowhere. She must think about it sensibly, logically. If she went she would have no job and no home and it would break Ellen's heart. If she stayed . . . that was out of the question. She wasn't having Madam Elizabeth calling her a Jezebel or any other such name and she was certain that Elizabeth would have a large vocabulary of adjectives that she wouldn't hesitate to use. She covered her face with her hands and uttered a hasty prayer to Saint Jude, the patron Saint of Impossible Causes, for if ever there was one, she was faced with it now.

She lay down again and pulled the quilt up to her chin and stared at the ceiling. She'd get precious little sleep tonight. She turned her head, thinking she heard the door open. Then she sat up.

'Ellen? Ellen, is that you?' She pushed back the bedclothes and reached for her dressing gown.

The child came in looking like a little ghost in her long, white nightgown and she could see she'd been crying. 'Oh, come here, you must be frozen! How long have you been standing out there on the landing?'

Ellen scrambled up on to the bed and cuddled into her, like a tiny nocturnal animal seeking warmth and comfort. 'I told Pa.'

'Oh, you didn't! Not everything Annie said?'

'I did. I don't want you to go away and I told him that, too!'

'What did he say?'

'He told me to go to bed.'

'Oh, Ellen, I wish you hadn't told him. I was going to tell him myself, tomorrow, after I'd been to see my aunt.'

'What do you want to see her for?'

'Because it was she who started these vicious lies.'

'Don't you hate her?'

'Yes!' Mary-Kate replied with venom.

Ellen drew away and looked up at her. 'Then it will be all right.'

'What will?'

'When Pa finds out it was her.'

'But the damage has been done, Ellen. Things can't be unsaid.'

Ellen's bottom lip began to tremble. 'Can't you still work here and sleep somewhere else? The nuns at the convent take a few lady boarders, you could go there.'

Oh, only a child could have seen it so clearly, Mary-Kate thought with astonishment. Why hadn't she thought of that solution?

'Maybe you're right, Ellen! Perhaps I could stay until after supper and then come back early in the morning, and if I stayed at the convent that would silence the wagging tongues.'

'So you won't be going away?'

'I don't know, it all depends on your Pa.'

Ellen struggled from her arms and prepared to jump from the bed. 'I'll go down and tell him now!'

Mary-Kate caught hold of her. 'Oh, no you won't! I think you've said and heard enough for one night. Now off to bed and get some sleep – and I mean straight to bed, your Pa won't be pleased to have another visit from you tonight.'

When the child had gone she sank back onto the pillows. She'd been in such a fury that she'd never thought of that simple solution. Oh, it was such a relief. But Maura wasn't going to get off, not by a long way!

Annie didn't turn up for work the following morning and so Mary-Kate had all the chores to do herself. Mr Vannin seemed to be in a particularly bad mood and this she put down to Ellen's revelations, until she saw that the whisky decanter was half empty.

Because of all the extra work she was later leaving the house than she had originally intended. She caught the tram at the bottom of Stalmine Road. It was only two stops, but this morning she didn't have either the time or the inclination to walk.

She got off just after Walton Hospital and walked the few yards up Rice Lane to Lancaster Street. The cinereous skies and the gusting wind, that blew the dead, brown leaves in small eddies around her feet, suited her mood entirely. As she walked up the street she noticed curtains twitching and realized that somehow the news of her intended visit had gone before her. Probably via Emily and her mother. She smiled grimly. It was no use Maura pretending to be out. She still had her key.

Mary-Kate stood for a moment on the step that hadn't seen donkey stone since the day she'd left, and looked up and down the street, deliberately. Then she opened her bag and drew out her key. That would give them all something to talk about. If they had imagined that she was going to stand on the step hammering vainly on the door, they were sadly mistaken. She opened the door quietly and stepped inside, wrinkling her nose at the familiar odours. She crept along the passage and opened the kitchen door.

The sight of both their faces afforded her grim satisfaction. Bart cringed as he caught sight of her, as though he'd been physically struck by the look on her face. Maura dropped the teapot and its contents spilled over the grubby tablecloth, turning it a uniform pale tan colour.

She tried to brazen it out. 'Jesus, Mary and Joseph! Sure, you could give a person a heart attack, Mary-Kate O'Donnell, creeping in like that.'

'What a pity I didn't Aunt! Although Uncle Bart looks as though he's about to have one. You weren't expecting me, were you? Or at least you thought I'd come knocking on the door and you'd be able to do your "party piece" of pretending not to be in. I still have my key!' She held it up. 'Well, you weren't content to leave things alone, were you? You had to get back at me, so you started rumours that I could take you to court for and so could Mr

Vannin. For slander! You could finish up around the corner in Walton Jail, Uncle Bart!'

His face turned ashen and his eyes bulged. Maura sat down suddenly on the chair, oblivious of the tea dripping from the soaked tablecloth on to her lap. 'God have mercy on us, you wouldn't do that, Mary-Kate?' she said hoarsely.

'I won't, but I can't speak for Mr Vannin. But you will both go to him and apologize, personally! Not that that will undo the damage you've done!'

'We were all right until you three came here, that we were. Damn our Sarah, she always was an interfering bitch!' Maura muttered.

Mary-Kate's temper snapped. 'That's it! That's it, Maura Milligan! Pack up and get out of this house by six o'clock tonight, do you hear me! Out!'

Maura jumped up and faced her. 'You can't do that! We've nowhere to go!'

'Oh, yes I can and I am. When I get back I will inform Mr Vannin that I've given you notice to quit, as from six o'clock, and he'll back me up, seeing as how you've besmirched and slandered his name and he carries a lot of weight in this neighbourhood, as well you know! So, I want you out!' She turned away, leaving them both gaping at her.

'Oh, Sweet Jesus! Where'll we go? Where'll we go?' Maura whined.

Mary-Kate turned. 'To hell, I hope, it's what you deserve, both of you!'

Mary-Kate called into Mr Vannin's office on her way back, something she had never done since the day she'd taken him the back rent. As she crossed the yard she felt that every pair of eyes was watching her, but she held her head high and walked slowly and with dignity.

Mr Johnson, Lewis Vannin's clerk, looked up with surprise. 'Oh, good day, Miss O'Donnell!'

'Is Mr Vannin in?'

'Yes, I'll tell him you're here.' He went into the other room for a few moments, then returned and held the door open for her. She thanked him.

Lewis Vannin was sitting at his desk, but on seeing her made to rise.

He still looked annoyed, Mary-Kate thought. 'There's no need to get up on my behalf. I've just been to see my despicable relatives and I have told them they are to get out of that house by six o'clock this evening.'

'Have you indeed. May I ask why?'

'Because it was my aunt who started the malicious lies.' She couldn't bring herself to look at him. 'So I told them to get out or be taken to court for slander.'

'And what was their reaction?'

'Exactly as I expected. Whining that they would have nowhere to go. Frankly I couldn't care less. They are spineless, vindictive parasites and I'm ashamed that the same blood runs in my veins!'

He leaned back in his chair. He'd never seen her like this before. He hadn't thought she was capable of such anger; she was shaking with rage. He wouldn't like to be on the receiving end of her tongue in this mood, he thought. 'So you have entirely washed your hands of them?'

'Yes!'

'Then I'll send a couple of men around later to see if

they've left and if not they'll "remove" them. I can easily let the house to tenants who will be an improvement.'

'Anyone would be an improvement on those two! Thank you for backing me up. I presume you will be home at the usual time for supper?'

'Yes.'

'There is something I wish to discuss with you, but this is neither the time nor the place. I will see you later on and thank you, again. You won't regret your action.'

It had started to rain as Mary-Kate left the yard, but that didn't deflect her from her purpose. She caught a tram to Walton Vale, crossed the road and went in through the iron gates of the church and into the porch, crossing herself with the holy water contained in the shell held by a large, plaster angel. She walked up the centre aisle, almost to the front, genuflected and then knelt, staring up at the large, circular stained-glass window above the altar. She'd heard that Lewis Vannin had paid for it and she wondered just how much it had cost. She dropped her head in her hands and prayed that he would accept the compromise that had been Ellen's idea, for if he demanded that she leave, she could see only one way left open to her. To return home to Clonmel.

It was cold, wet and windy when she came out and her spirits, which had risen in the church's atmosphere of tranquil hope, dropped abysmally. She stood at the tram stop, holding tightly to her umbrella, her back to the force of the downpour, until the tram arrived. By the time she got back she was soaked, and she had only just got changed when Ellen arrived home, soaking wet, her face pale, her eyes over-bright. Mary-Kate's heart sank.

Oh, she hadn't been in trouble again? That would just about put paid to any chance she had of trying to talk to Mr Vannin.

'Get your things off before you catch pneumonia!'

'I think I may already have it.'

She felt Ellen's forehead. She was burning up. 'Did they send you home on your own in this weather? Why didn't they get in touch with your pa, someone would have come for you?'

'I didn't want them to.'

Mary-Kate stripped off the wet garments and wrapped Ellen in a towel and then carried her upstairs herself. She dried her hair and pulled a warm, flannel nightgown over her head before tucking her into bed.

'I'll be up and light the fire in a minute and I'm sending Dick for the doctor. Now just you lie there!'

The doctor confirmed that it was just a very heavy cold and told her to give Ellen plenty of hot drinks and keep her warm, but if she were to get worse, then she must send for him again. 'And a drop of whisky in hot water with sugar and the juice of a lemon won't do any harm either!' he added as they reached the front door.

As she was showing him out, Lewis Vannin came up the front steps and Mary-Kate remembered that she hadn't even started supper. Her own head had begun to ache and her neck felt stiff with tension. He exchanged a few words with the doctor before seeing him to his car and then he came into the house.

'A heavy cold, she'll be all right,' Lewis Vannin said gruffly.

'Could I speak to you?' Mary-Kate couldn't wait any longer.

'You know you can speak to me at any time.'

She followed him into the library and then realized with a slight shock that the clock on the mantel said three forty-five. Why was he home so early? She'd had such a confusing day that it was no wonder she'd lost all track of time. He was pouring himself a drink from what remained in the decanter.

'Well?'

'I was very upset about the things Annie said last night, that's why I was so angry with those two today.' She paused, trying to frame her words carefully.

'Will you sit down, Mary-Kate, you're making me edgy!'

Her eyebrows shot up. It was the first time he'd ever called her by her Christian name. She sat. 'I realize that once things like that have been said, nothing can undo them, but if it would be acceptable to you, I will enquire at the convent about taking a room. I could come in during the day and stay there at night.' She folded her hands to stop herself from plucking nervously at her apron. 'I think that would be the best solution for . . . for everyone, including Ellen.' She waited with her head down, her heart racing, a silent prayer oh her lips. If he refused she would have to go home and that would mean leaving Ellen. She didn't care about what kind of reception she would receive in Clonmel.

Lewis Vannin cleared his throat. 'Last night I had a lot of time on my hands to think, after Ellen came down and told me what that little slut of a scullion had said, and I came to a decision.'

She looked up, her eyes entreating him not to dispense with her services. 'Yes?' she managed to utter.

'It is really the perfect solution to everything, including Ellen, to use your own words.'

'Oh, it is!' she interrupted, thinking he had agreed to her suggestion.

'Will you hear me out! I don't mean that you come in daily, although if you find my proposal too . . .' he searched for the right word '. . . unbearable . . .' That wasn't what he had intended to say at all and he finished the drink with some exasperation. Damn it, he'd never been good at this sort of thing! She was still staring at him with a slightly confused look in her hazel eyes. 'Well, what is your answer?'

'I'm sorry . . . but what proposal do you mean?'

'Marriage, Mary-Kate. I'm asking you to marry me!'

She was so shocked she couldn't utter a sound. She just sat staring at him as though she'd been turned to stone.

'It would silence all the malicious tongues. I'm not a poor man, you would have security and position. Ellen would have a mother and my house would have a mistress again. Of course, you could have your own room if you wish. I've no desire to force myself on you. You are a young woman compared to me. Far too young, some would say, but I've . . . become fond of you. You have brought a certain peace to my life. But if you don't feel that you can accept, then of course no more will be said on the matter. I will understand your reservations and your decision.'

Mary-Kate heard Gina's laughing voice through her torpor: '*Make sure your husband is rich, Mary-Kate, then sit back and be a Lady for the rest of your life!*' Oh, how cold and cynical it had sounded then. 'I . . . I don't know what to say,' she stammered.

'Will you at least think about it?'

She nodded and got shakily to her feet. 'I'll give you my answer . . . tomorrow.' Her voice sounded as though it belonged to someone else and she groped her way to the door. Supper, she must think of supper. He liked everything to be punctual. She clung to that shred of normality as he opened the door for her.

She stood in the hall still dazed, not knowing what to do or in which direction to go. It was as though she'd never been in this house before and didn't know what lay behind any of the doors or where the staircase led. The staircase! The staircase led to Ellen. Slowly she began to climb the stairs, feeling as though her shoes were filled with lead weights. On the landing she found Ellen curled up, clinging to the bannister rail. She bent and gathered her into her arms. 'What are you doing out of bed?'

'I'm sorry, I was listening, but I couldn't get back up the stairs. My legs went all wobbly. Are you going to be my new Ma, Mary-Kate?'

She looked down into the fevered little face. 'Yes, I think I am Ellen. I think I am!'

Chapter Eleven

BRIDGET OPENED THE LETTER and then let out a shriek.

'Holy Mother of God! What's the matter. Nothing's happened to your Matty has it? Or is it your Ma? Or have they gone and blown up the whole bloody town?' Bernie yelped with pain. 'Ouch! Haven't I gone and burnt my damned arm!' She banged the flat iron down on the hearth and began to blow on her fingers. 'And that's my best blouse ruined, too! What's the matter?'

'Mary-Kate's getting married!'

'Is that all! You mean to tell me I've burned my fingers and scorched my blouse just because your Mary-Kate's finally got herself a man?'

Bridget laughed. 'Go and run your fingers under the tap on the landing. You've not scorched it that much, it'll wash out and anyway, it's on the part that you tuck in.'

Eileen had looked up from the book she was struggling to read. 'Who's she marrying then?'

'The man she's been housekeeping for.'

'There's no fool like an old fool, me Ma used to say!'

Bernie said solemnly. 'She always was a smart one. Wasn't he your landlord as well? He can't be short of a few bob and didn't you say he had some kind of a business too?'

'Haulage.' Bridget re-read the letter but felt a stirring of distaste. Lewis Vannin was old enough to be their Pa and he had a married daughter. She knew Mary-Kate wouldn't be doing it just because he was well-off. Oh, she'd had her airs and graces, but she wouldn't marry someone as old as him just for his money. Still, she couldn't understand her sister. Fancy having him kiss you and sharing the same bed. She gave a little shudder. Now if it were someone like her Andy . . .

'Are you going then?'

'Where?'

'To the wedding of course, eejit! Or hasn't she invited you?'

'Of course she has and yes, I'm going.'

'You'll have to buy something new, seeing as how your new brother-in-law is so grand!'

She supposed Bernie was right. Her winter coat wasn't too bad, but she'd have to get a new hat and maybe a dress, if the money would run to it.

'We'll go over the bridge on Saturday.'

'I was supposed to be going with Andy.'

'Oh, what do men know about clothes at all? You wouldn't know a toque from a cloche, would you Archie?'

'What's a toque?' Archie muttered from behind his copy of *The Worker's Standard*.

'See! And Big Andy MacDonald's just as bad.'

'I wish you wouldn't call him that. It makes him sound like one of the "frighteners"!'

Everyone lived in fear and terror of the 'frighteners',

the henchmen of the money lenders, who were none too particular about how they got their money back, just as long as they got it.

'He could be one, if he wanted to, and he's the last person to be afraid of them! Didn't he take on that razor gang from Pollokshields nearly single-handed? They didn't come back in a hurry!'

Bridget cringed. If she were to live here for the rest of her life, she would never get used to the violence that surrounded her and from which Andy shielded her as best he could. She'd learned to ignore the drunken street fights and, when she was with him, the mere sight of him was enough to scatter the gangs who loitered on corners and in alleys. But she, like many respectable, peaceable citizens in the Gorbals, lived in terror of the notorious razor gangs who came marauding from other neighbourhoods, armed with knives, chains and their legendary caps, the peaks of which had razor blades, edges pointing to the fore, sewn into them. Blades that could slice through a man's cheek like a knife through butter. Andy had shown her one of these caps once and the scar that ran down his left arm that had been the result of the clash that Bernie spoke of. Bridget shuddered again.

'You don't know how lucky you are, Bridget O'Donnell, to have a man like that. But then "The Sisters O'Donnell" were always lucky.'

'I still haven't got a ring of any kind on this finger, have I?' Bridget said peevishly, holding up her left hand. Months it was now that they'd been 'walking out' and Mary-Kate's letter had only served to remind her that no matter how she hinted, Andy didn't seem to notice. Or was he just ignoring her? Lately, she'd had the odd twinge of doubt about him. Oh, it wasn't anything in his manner towards her, that hadn't changed and he still 'tried it on' as Bernie put it, and Bridget found it harder and harder to resist him. But it was just something about the way he looked at her sometimes. With resentment or was it reproach?

'Neither have I!' Bernie stated emphatically, staring pointedly at Archie, who didn't raise his eyes from his reading. Bernie wasn't one for hinting. She'd come straight out and asked him if he'd ever had any intentions of marrying her. He'd asked her if she wanted to start her married life living here and she'd said no, she certainly did not. Well then, they'd have to save up, had been his answer, to which she'd retorted that if he didn't spend so much of his money on drink and gambling it might get saved up quicker.

'Can I come with you?' Eileen asked, eagerly.

'No, you can't, you'll be working on Saturday,' Bernie shot back.

Eileen glared at her and then returned to her book.

Bridget rose. 'Id better go and see what I've got that's still decent.'

'You can borrow my white blouse, if you like,' Eileen offered generously. It was the first thing she'd had new in years. Bridget had bought the material and Mrs Lavinsky, the wife of the tailor, had made it up and Eileen had paid for that herself.

'And what would she want to be borrowing that thing for? Hasn't she got some grand things herself!' Bernie retorted scornfully.

Bernie always seemed to be putting the girl down,

Bridget thought. She smiled at Eileen. 'Thanks, it will look just fine.'

Bernie raised her eyes to the ceiling, but Eileen gave Bridget one of her rare smiles.

'It's from your sister in Liverpool,' Rose Weston informed Gina as she handed her the letter when she came in.

'Have you been holding it over the kettle?' Gina asked sharply.

'Starlight and Syncopation' was still running well although it was hard work, but she had been made second understudy. Anne Robins was first understudy, a part Gina had hoped and believed would have been hers by now. Delia Heysham was the star and she acted accordingly. Gina didn't like her much.

'I can read the postmark, can't I? Do you want waking up or not?'

'No, there's no matinee tomorrow, so I can have a lie-in and then Helen and I are going up West. I'm buying myself a decent pair of boots before my feet freeze.'

Gina and Helen had become friends and she had been to a couple of parties with her, although she'd never again drunk as much as she had on their night of celebration. She liked Helen's friends; they were fun to be with and she had even overcome her awe at the fact that Freddie Marshalsea was a Peer of the Realm. Edward didn't approve of them. 'Fast, frivolous and fickle' he called them. That had caused another row.

'I'll choose my own friends, thank you. You don't own me!'

'No, I don't, but just don't let your social life interfere with work.'

'Do you think I'm a complete fool?'

'Sometimes you act like one. They're no good, Gina.'

'And who are you to say that Lord Marshalsea is "no good"?'

'Don't be dazzled by titles, Gina.'

'I'm not. I'm not the simple country girl I once was.'

'Really?'

'No, I'm not. And I'll damned well please myself where I go and who with,' she'd yelled, incensed by his sarcastic tone.

'Then don't come running to me if your fine friends land you in trouble, because they will, if you're not careful. You're out of your depth, Gina.'

'I won't. And I'm not "out of my depth" as you put it. I can take care of myself,' she'd flung back at him before she'd stormed out to meet Helen.

Leaving Mrs Weston, Gina went up to her room and kept her coat on while she lit the gas fire, then she opened the letter. As she read it she began to smile. So Mary-Kate had found herself a husband, but what a husband! He might own half of Walton-on-the-Hill and have a thriving business, but he was so old. Still, if that was what Mary-Kate wanted. Gina grimaced. If she couldn't do better than Lewis Vannin, she wouldn't bother at all! But then she had no intention of getting married, not for years and years. Then she, too, remembered what she'd said to Mary-Kate on the deck of the *Connaught* and she laughed. She'd said make sure he's rich, she hadn't mentioned old!

She scanned the letter again. Next Friday at 3 pm. How was she going to manage that? She'd have to miss Friday night's performance and Friday was always a good night. And if you went sick you stood the chance of having someone else step in for you and sometimes they stayed! Perhaps she could get Edward to speak to George Christy, the Producer, with whom he seemed to be on very friendly terms. Edward had met Mary-Kate, of course, so perhaps he would go with her? She decided against that. He would tell them all that she was only in the chorus when she'd told them she was Miss Heysham's understudy. No, she'd have to go alone. She'd write Edward a note.

She rubbed her hands together, trying to warm them, then began to search for the writing pad. She couldn't miss her own sister's wedding, and probably Bridget would come from Glasgow and maybe Ma and Matty would come over. Suddenly, she realized just how much she'd missed them all. No, she couldn't miss this chance to meet up again and they'd all see how well she was doing, how well she looked, how smart her clothes were and wouldn't they all be so impressed that she now numbered a Lord and two 'Honourables' amongst her friends!

Rain as straight as stair rods had been falling from skies the colour of gunmetal all day and although a good fire burned in the hearth, Sarah felt that the dampness had seeped into the house. 'It's the stone walls,' she muttered to herself. Either that or she was getting old. Her joints ached these days, especially when it was damp and wet, and it seemed to be just that most days, now that autumn was on them.

She was glad they'd moved out of town. There had been other incidents to parallel the burning down of

Feehey's and now people eyed each other with suspicion. Bernie O'Hagan's eldest brother had been caught with a pistol under the arches of the old bridge. The Army had taken him and they'd heard later that he'd been shot. Without a trial. He'd always been a villain, she thought, but Dear God, even he had the right to a trial! They were getting as bad as the 'Tans' had been.

'Letter for you Ma, from Mary-Kate by the postmark.'

She hadn't heard Matty and her brother, Richard, come in, but she took the letter and laid it on the shelf above the range as the envelope was damp. Then she turned her attention to getting their sodden clothes off and placing a bowl of hot, boiled potatoes, another of carrots, and a baked ham on the table for them. 'Get that down you both, you'll need it to keep the cold out while you're milking.'

She watched them tuck in hungrily, and only then did she take the letter and open it.

Matty, chewing slowly on the ham, put down his fork. 'Ma, you're crying! What's the matter? Are those three all right?'

Sarah nodded emphatically and wiped her eyes on the corner of her apron. 'She's getting married! Mary-Kate's getting married to a fine, Catholic gentleman with his own house and business!'

'Who? Where did she meet this paragon?'

'Mr Vannin, the gentleman she's been keeping house for. We're all invited. She's sent us the fare and we're to stay with her. She's plenty of room for us all, she says. And Bridget will be down and Gina.' Sarah forestalled any remarks Matty might make about Lewis Vannin by chattering on. What did it matter at all if he was as old as herself? If he was good to Mary-Kate and she was fond of him, that was all that mattered. 'Oh, won't it be wonderful, the whole family together again!' she finished.

'And when is it to be then?'

'Next Friday at three o'clock. She says we can get the Thursday night boat and stay until Sunday or Monday even, and she says their crossing was so desperate that she'll not have us herded into the common Saloon. We're going to get a berth – whatever that is – so we can get some sleep.'

'Has she forgotten that it's a farm we're running and not a hotel? There's animals here that have to be fed and watered and milked.'

'Don't you want to go to your own sister's wedding?'

'Of course I do, but I don't see how we can all go.'

'You and Sarah go,' Richard put in. 'I'll stay here. I managed on my own for long enough, I can cope for a few days and besides, Sarah can't go alone, not with the way things are all over the country and especially in Dublin!'

Matty looked at his uncle with resignation, knowing there was no use arguing or trying to find excuses. He'd just have to grin and bear it and wear his best suit and collar and tie every day, now that Mary-Kate was going up in the world.

She'd almost got used to the idea. Almost, but not quite. Mary-Kate still didn't really understand herself why she'd accepted his proposal. They were virtually strangers, but dimly she realized that part of her had agreed to it for Ellen's sake and part for pride's sake and in the rare moments when she had time to think at all, she hoped she wouldn't regret it. 'Pride cometh before a fall' as Ma said. But he wasn't giving her time to think, to contemplate or reconsider. They were to be married in church, but by Special Licence, as it was to be a quiet wedding. That did away with the formality of having the banns called. And suddenly she'd found herself in a frenzy of activity. He'd stopped calling her Miss O'Donnell and was making every effort to please her.

They had a new girl in the kitchen, one she'd chosen herself, and Dick had been most formal towards her since the news had been leaked out by Ellen. Ellen had been almost delirious with joy, and as the child had recovered it had been as much as Mary-Kate could do to keep her quiet. But there was one person to whom the news was anathema and she had firmly declined Lewis's offer to tell his elder daughter himself. She told him that now she was to become his wife, she must try to find some common ground between herself and Elizabeth. They had wanted to tell Elizabeth first, it being only right and proper that they did so, but Ellen had already told half the street and so Elizabeth already knew, although she had not acknowledged the fact, which was why Mary-Kate had invited her over this afternoon.

She was nervous and glanced at her reflection in the gilt-framed mirror over the mantel in the front parlour. She still refused to have her hair cut, but she had adopted the new style of dress. She adjusted the long rope of pearls around her neck, they had been an engagement present from him, and smoothed the skirt of her dress. It was of a fine wool crêpe in a light, coffee colour, with a dropped waist and a softly pleated skirt that reached mid-calf. It had been purchased from Cripps in Bold Stret, as had her other two dresses. Her wedding dress, or rather the Ensemble, as it was called, consisted of a matching coat and dress in ivory, merino wool, edged with russet brown velvet ribbon. That had been bought from Gladys Drinkwater's, as had her ivory, wide-brimmed hat which sported a large cream silk gardenia. It had given her some satisfaction when Miss Drinkwater herself had fitted her, helped her choose the hat and gloves and asked 'Modom's name?' She had replied 'Miss O'Donnell. Miss Mary-Kate O'Donnell. I think you met my sister, Bridget?' Miss Drinkwater had looked blank. 'The one with "that accent". She came for a position with you and was turned away.' As recollection dawned, she had smiled at the woman's discomfort. There was nothing Miss Drinkwater could say; not at the price she was paying for the Ensemble!

Mary-Kate poked the fire, then plumped up the cushions on the sofa. She wished this were all over and done with, she certainly wasn't looking forward to it.

'Hasn't she come yet? She's going to be hateful, I know she is! Lizzie is always hateful!'

'Ellen, will you go away! If you hadn't blabbered everything to the whole neighbourhood, she wouldn't need to be "hateful" as you call it. You know your Pa is still cross with you and you're supposed to be recovering. Do you want to be going down with something else and be ill for the wedding?'

Undaunted, Ellen came into the room and peered through the lace curtains.

Mary-Kate pulled her away. 'Ellen, put that curtain down, don't you know how rude that is! Now go upstairs or I'll tell your pa!'

Ellen grimaced. 'When can I call you Ma?'

Mary-Kate laughed.

'Pa says I have to wait until after the wedding, that I've got to call you Miss O'Donnell until then, but he's so stuffy and old-fashioned!' Realizing what she'd said she clapped a hand over her mouth.

'Then you must do as you're told, but you can call me Ma when he's out.' They'd had a long discussion over just what Ellen would call her. She'd found out from Lewis that he'd always insisted on both girls calling their mother either Mama or Mother. She'd told Ellen that if she didn't feel as though she could call her Mother, then she must call her Step-Mother.

'Step-Mother!' Ellen had echoed. 'That always sounds so wicked, like in the fairy stories. I'll call you Ma.'

'Are you sure?'

For a reply, Ellen had hugged her and she had laughed. Ellen was a little precocious but she had a warm, affectionate demeanour and now that she felt secure and loved, she was a bright, pleasant child with an open, forthright manner and generous nature. Although she could be stubborn and wilful at times.

'Now will you go away! Oh, Lord! She's here and she's got Ernest with her!'

Ellen screwed up her nose as though smelling something unpleasant and then disappeared.

With a last pat to her hair, Mary-Kate went into the hall to greet them.

Elizabeth didn't acknowledge her greeting, but Ernest muttered something she took to be 'Good Afternoon'. It didn't help that Elizabeth, once she had thrown her fur-trimmed coat carelessly over a chair, was wearing a dress in the identical shade to her own. The fact that she wore pearls while Elizabeth wore three strands of dark brown beads, resembling small nuts, did not go unnoticed either.

'So, you've finally asked us here to tell us what we had to hear from strangers!'

'Surely not strangers, Elizabeth?'

'Outsiders then! We're not used to being treated like this, are we, Ernest? But I expect we'll have to get used to it. Obviously you have no conception of etiquette let alone common, ordinary manners!' The word 'common' was emphasized.

Mary-Kate ignored it. 'I'm truly sorry, but Ellen got quite carried away. You can be sure your father has spoken to her about how mistaken her behaviour was. She's very impetuous and I've also told her how hurtful her behaviour must be to you both.'

'That child will be nothing but trouble, you mark my words!'

'She's been as good as gold and her school report is excellent.'

'Where is my father?'

'At work.'

'Hasn't he got the nerve to face me himself?'

'Yes, but it was I who talked him out of it. I thought that just you and I should sit down and talk. I didn't know Ernest would be coming as well.'

'What is there to talk about? Seeing that Ellen has broadcast it from the rooftops, the whole neighbourhood already knows you're to be the second Mrs Vannin! It's a wonder you didn't put it in the *Liverpool Echo* and the *Walton Times*, and I don't see that there's anything to talk about, we have absolutely nothing in common!'

'We have your father and his welfare in common.' Mary-Kate had known it wouldn't be easy, but she could see that Elizabeth wasn't going to be placated.

'Not really. I have my own husband and my own household!'

'Don't you care about your father at all?'

For the first time Elizabeth looked discomforted. 'Of course I do. We both do, don't we Ernest? We only want what's best for him.'

'We do, dear, you're right.'

It was the first time she'd heard Ernest Winskill string more than two words together. 'And you don't think I'm what is *best* for him, do you? Please, let's be honest, at least then we'll both know where we stand.'

'No, I don't! We don't know where you come from, what kind of a family you have – except of course that awful pair that Father threw out!'

'That I threw out! I don't consider them family!' Mary-Kate stood up. She had intended to make an effort with Elizabeth but now she considered it futile. She didn't like her at all and the feeling was mutual. Elizabeth was a spoiled, selfish snob. 'I come from a decent family. My father had his own business and was a respected citizen of Clonmel, which is where I come from.'

'I thought as much. The daughter of a small-time merchant in some God-forsaken town in the sticks and in that dreadful country where they are always butchering someone!'

Although she had vowed to stay calm no matter what the provocation, she felt her temper beginning to rise. Just who did Elizabeth Winskill think she was? Her manners were appalling and she certainly couldn't be called Christian, not by a long stretch of the imagination. The fact that Elizabeth had had more money than she, certainly hadn't made her a better person. 'If you cared to read the papers, you would know that Ireland is in the middle of a civil war and that before that we suffered four years of war and destruction at the hands of people like you!'

Elizabeth wasn't a complete fool. She read the danger signs and realized that she was treading on unsafe ground and that she wasn't in possession of all the facts on the 'Irish Question' as her father always termed it. 'Well, that's as may be, but we haven't come here to discuss politics!'

'No, I asked you here to say that I hope we can at least be civil to each other, for your father's sake. We'll never be friends, I see that now, although I had hoped it would be different. But you resent me too much.'

What Elizabeth resented was not so much that Mary-Kate O'Donnell was becoming Mary-Kate Vannin, as the extent to which she depended on her father for her expenses. Expenses that Ernest's salary didn't stretch to and which she wouldn't give up without a fight. She'd never taken much notice of Mary-Kate when she'd only been housekeeper, but now she was seeing an astute young woman with a mind and a brain she suspected to be far more agile than her own.

'Elizabeth never expected her father to marry again. It's been a shock.'

'I'm sure it has, Ernest.' Mary-Kate smiled at him and he smiled back. He was pleasant enough, but totally dominated by his wife. 'And it takes time to get over such shocks but I . . . we hope that you'll continue to visit us, after all this is your home.'

She had the nerve to patronize her, Elizabeth thought. 'This has never been my home since the day I married, and especially after my mother, God rest her, died!'

Mary-Kate ignored the slight. 'You will be coming to the wedding?'

Elizabeth sniffed disdainfully and Ernest opened his mouth as if to reply and then thought better of it.

'It would look very strange if you were both missing. My mother and brother are coming over from Ireland, both my sisters will be here and Ellen is hoping her father will relent and allow her to be bridesmaid.'

'Bridesmaid! I've never heard anything so utterly . . . utterly . . . farcical! He's old enough to be your father and you want to turn it into an even worse spectacle by having that little wretch as bridesmaid! We'll be the laughing stock of the whole district.'

Mary-Kate bit back the words that sprang to her lips. 'That was the same argument both your father and I used. But we have promised she can carry a small posy and have a new dress. Ellen will get over it. Will you be coming?' she persisted, although she couldn't have cared less whether they came or not, in fact she could imagine how Gina would react to Elizabeth. They'd probably come to blows. 'Oh, I suppose so, but only so as not to let father down.'

'Good. I'll have Violet bring some tea in now that that's settled.'

'That won't be necessary, we have to go. Ernest has a very important meeting and I have a hair appointment.'

'As you wish. I'll see you both next Friday then. Three

o'clock at the Blessed Sacrament and then back here for a family meal.'

Elizabeth got up, smoothing down her skirt. 'My coat, Ernest.'

He dutifully helped her into it and followed her out.

Mary-Kate stood at the front door watching them as they descended the steps and Ernest solicitously helped his wife into the car. Well, if Madam Elizabeth thought she could come running up here every time she wanted money for some frippery or other, she was in for a shock. She'd soon find out that Mary-Kate wasn't one to lie down and be walked all over like Ernest Winskill!

Chapter Twelve

———◆———

THEY'D ALL GONE TO see Bridget off. Andy, Bernie, Archie and Eileen. Bernie had laughed and said anyone would think she were going off to Australia or somewhere instead of just Liverpool for a couple of days.

She settled back in her seat, thinking of the last time she'd made this journey. Oh, there was so much she had to tell the family and she was dying to see them and hear all their news and gossip.

She felt quite smart, thinking that the new hat she'd bought toned in quite nicely with her tweed coat. The hat was pale grey trimmed with a large black bow and she wore Eileen's white blouse and the new red skirt Bernie had persuaded her to buy. She wasn't at all sure about the skirt. Red was a colour she never wore as it clashed with her hair, but Bernie had said that with it being a skirt, not a dress, it would look just fine and that she was going to a wedding not a wake, and it did brighten up her outfit. She'd had to borrow some money from Andy and she hadn't liked that. She'd been laid off again at the factory for a few weeks. 'It's just a slack time right now. It'll pick up again soon enough,' Robbie Frazer had told her. But she was getting rather depressed; she wanted a permanent, steady job.

Andy had just laughed at her protestations that she'd pay him back next pay day, but she still felt badly about it, although he'd never bought her a present in all the time they'd been courting. Not even on her birthday. He'd taken her out to the Waverley Hotel instead, which Bernie insisted was far grander than some trinket from Woolworths. She had also said that it wasn't strange that he'd never bought her anything. For one thing there wasn't the money to spare and for another the men she knew didn't buy flowers and the like. Archie said men who bought flowers were 'Jessies'.

Bridget looked down at her feet. There hadn't been enough money for new shoes, so she'd polished up her old ones as best she could, but they looked scuffed and worn. She could only hope no one would notice. Gina was sure to be dressed to kill and anyway everyone would be looking at Mary-Kate. Besides, she wasn't earning a fortune and she wasn't marrying someone with money. That turned her thoughts to Andy. She wasn't marrying anyone. She began to think about her relationship with him, but finding it unproductive and depressing, she fell back on her usual method of blocking out her predicament, spinning a web of romantic daydreams as the train sped southwards towards the Border Country.

She was going to be late if she didn't hurry herself up. Gina looked at the clock. If she were going to catch the train from Euston, Edward should have been here by now. She glanced in the mirror. She would have loved to have gone in the beautiful sable coat that she'd seen in Harrods window, but then probably even Lewis Vannin's money wouldn't have run to the price they were asking for it. Her sage green, wool coat – the collar and cuffs trimmed with fur – would have to do. Underneath she wore a dress of a paler shade of green and over her short, shining hair she wore a cloche hat of pale green velour. She was quite satisfied with her appearance and was certain she'd outshine everyone else, except Mary-Kate. It wouldn't do to take Mary-Kate's glory away from her and if she knew her sister, she'd have chosen something extra-special for the occasion. Especially now that expense need not be spared.

'Gina! Gina!' Rose Weston's voice rang through the house.

Edward must have arrived. She snatched up her handbag and the small overnight bag she'd bought and ran down the stairs. 'Where have you been? If we don't hurry I'll miss my train.'

He wasn't smiling. In fact he looked ominously serious. 'Come out to the car.' He took her bag and her arm and led her to the car and settled her inside.

'What's the matter?'

He lit a cigarette. 'George phoned me. I've been with him. Anne Robins, Delia's understudy, has been hurt in an accident, and as you had the good luck to be made second understudy, tonight the stage is all yours – if you want it. Delia herself isn't feeling well.'

'If I want it! Oh, you know I do!' This was a chance in a million. Delia ill, too. Of course, Delia wasn't as young as she used to be and she was probably tired out.

'What about the wedding?'

'Oh, Damn!'

He looked into Gina's animated face. She'd not even asked how badly Anne was hurt or what was the matter with Delia, she'd even forgotten Mary-Kate's wedding. George had been frantic, he'd almost gone down on his knees to Delia, but she was having one of her tantrums and refused point blank to go on. She was exhausted, did he expect her to drop on stage? And what was that wretched girl doing riding pillion on a motorcycle anyway? He'd just have to manage with someone else. It was only for one night, what was the matter with him? And much more in the same vein. That was when he had telephoned Edward and he had suggested Gina. He had been unsure of his decision. He knew she would jump at the chance, knew that she could do it and do it well, probably even better than Delia Heysham, but he had thought she would have refused – at least hesitated. 'So, what are you going to do?'

She was torn between going to Liverpool to see her family and to see Mary-Kate married, and the longed-for opportunity of being the star of the show – even if it were for just one night. She felt annoyed. Oh, why couldn't Mary-Kate have got married on Saturday like most people did? But she couldn't afford to let this chance slip by. 'I'm not going. I'll send a telegram. You do understand, don't you? You of all people must understand what this means to me! What happened to Anne?'

He'd known her answer even before she'd opened her mouth. He had seen the determined set of her chin, the cold glitter in her eyes. 'I was wondering when you'd get around to asking. She was on the back of a motorcycle when it skidded and crashed. She's got a broken arm and a broken leg as well as cuts and bruises and she's badly shocked. Her boyfriend was killed outright. They collided with a lorry.'

'Oh, I'm sorry.'

He wondered if she really was. Anne's injuries would keep her away from the theatre for months and Gina was probably thinking just that. 'You won't have any regrets about not going to the wedding?'

'Of course I will! I was looking forward to seeing them all! It's not all fun here, I would have thought you'd understand.'

'Oh, I do Gina, I do! You are the most ambitious young woman I think I've ever met. I can think of a few who are just as hard and selfish, but not many!'

She turned on him. 'I'm not hard and selfish! You have to seize every opportunity and it's not my fault that Anne had an accident or that Mary-Kate picked a Friday to get married! I'm not selfish!'

He laughed and leaned forward and gave her a peck on the cheek. 'No, of course you're not! Go on, get unpacked and then try and stay calm for the rest of the morning. George is expecting you for this afternoon's rehearsal.' Edward got out and opened the door for her. 'Oh, and Gina, no temper tantrums, you can't afford them – yet!'

Sarah looked around her in awe, then she smiled. Oh, Mary-Kate had done very well for herself, that she had. This house was bigger and far more tastefully furnished than even Mrs Butler-Power's. They'd had quite an eventful journey, for the train had been boarded at Carlow by the Army and all the men, including Matty, had been searched before they had been allowed to resume their journey.

There were troops everywhere in Dublin and she had been shocked; she'd never seen the Free State Army in such numbers before, but they had boarded the ferry without any trouble, and, although the weather was a little rough, she had slept most of the way – thankful for the tiny cabin and narrow bunk. When they had arrived, her future son-in-law had sent his car for them and they had enjoyed their first sight of the city that Mary-Kate would now call home, in comfort and style.

Mary-Kate had hugged her mother and kissed her, exclaiming how much she'd missed her and Lewis Vannin had shaken her hand most cordially and called her 'mother-in-law', which had sounded very strange as he was as old as herself. Matty had said little, but had tucked into the breakfast set for them and had then sat in the kitchen talking to Violet. Lewis Vannin had retired to his library and she now sat on the bed in her room. Mary-Kate sat in a low chair facing her.

'How many bedrooms does the place have then?'

'Six.'

'Six! And just for the three of you! Wouldn't Mrs Butler-Power turn green with envy!' She fingered the rose pink eiderdown. 'And pink sateen in the spare bedroom, too! Now, what about you, Mary-Kate?'

'What about me?'

'You know what I mean! Are you happy, do you love him? It's all a bit sudden. It's not just all this that's influenced you, is it?'

'Oh, Ma! What a thing to say!'

'Are you happy?'

'Yes, I'm happy.'

'But?'

'And I'm fond of him, in my own way.'

'But you don't love him? Well, I'm old fashioned enough to believe that love comes after marriage. At least you're not some silly little thing, chasing after romantic daydreams. You always had your feet firmly on the ground. He seems to be a good man.'

'He is and I'm very fond of Ellen.'

'I can see that. She's a pert little piece but she idolizes you.'

'You have to wheedle Ellen around to your way of thinking. It's no use trying to force your will on her, I've found that out.'

'So, you've a ready-made family. I'm glad you're settled and comfortably off, too, I won't need to worry over you.'

Mary-Kate leaned over and took her mother's hand. 'Ma, you've never needed to worry about me, haven't I always been the "sensible one"?'

Sarah thought there was a note of sadness in her voice. 'Are you sure you're doing the right thing? There's still time to change your mind. It's a big step, Mary-Kate. It's forever! Until death do us part!'

'Ma I'm sure. I'm absolutely certain. I couldn't leave Ellen to be brought up by servants, strangers . . . Lewis is very busy. Now, there's an end to it. I thought I heard the door, it must be Gina or Bridget!'

So that was it, Sarah thought. It was the child. She was marrying him for the child's sake. She just hoped Ellen Vannin was worth it. Children caused you pain as well as joy, she'd found that out, but Mary-Kate seemed to be content enough on the surface. Oh, well, she'd made her decision, she'd have to stand by it now.

They met Ellen half-way up the stairs. Ma it's a telegram! Sorry Miss O'Donnell – it's a telegram for you!'

'Whatever are you calling her Miss O'Donnell for, child. In a few hours she'll be your new Ma?'

'Lewis is rather formal, Ma. It was his instruction.' Mary-Kate was opening the buff envelope.

He certainly has some very peculiar ways, Sarah thought. 'Who's it from?'

'Gina. She's not coming.' Mary-Kate couldn't keep the disappointment out of her voice.

'Oh, I wanted to see her! I wanted to ask her all about the theatre!'

'You, Miss, have too much to say for yourself!' Sarah scolded Ellen, taking the telegram from her daughter.

'*Something desperately important has come up. Sorry, but won't be able to make it. Congratulations and love to you both. Gina.*'

Sarah handed it back. What was so important that she would miss her own sister's wedding and the chance of seeing her family again?

'It must be something really important, no doubt she'll write and tell us what.'

'No doubt,' Sarah said coldly, making a mental note to write Gina a strongly-worded letter at the first opportunity.

'I'd better go and tell Lewis.'

'Yes, you do that. I want a word with this one here. Come on in here with me, Ellen Vannin, and if you mind what I say, you may call me Grandma!'

*

It was nearly two o'clock before Bridget arrived. The train had been late and she was hot and flustered. It was Matty who let her in and she gave a cry of joy and hugged him.

'Where is everyone?'

'All flapping around like chickens with their heads cut off – except our Mary-Kate.'

She looked around in amazement. Oh, what sheer luxury!

A child appeared on the staircase, dressed in a frock of pale blue layered tulle that was far too light for the time of year. 'Are you Bridget?' she asked.

Bridget nodded.

'That's Ellen. She seems to be everywhere at once! No wonder Himself's locked in his library! It's a madhouse, that it is!' Matty shook his head.

'Then Grandma says you're to come up straight away. She didn't think you were coming either and she's cross!'

Bridget was bemused but she followed Ellen up the carpeted stairs. 'Who else isn't coming?'

'Gina, she sent a telegram. Oh, I forgot, I have to call you Aunt Bridget and Aunt Gina now. Grandma is in here and Ma is getting ready and I have to help her.'

She left Bridget standing outside a door and disappeared through another one. What a strange child, Bridget thought. Who were Grandma and Ma? Then she remembered Mary-Kate's letters and she smiled. Ellen was obviously very proud and happy to have a new Ma and Grandma and two new aunts and an uncle.

'Bridget, where've you been, we'd almost given you up!'

She was clasped in a tight embrace and then released.

'Let me look at you! You're thinner and I'm not at all happy about you living up there in Scotland, but I'll speak to you about that later. You'd better hurry up and change!'

'I don't need to change.'

'You don't mean to tell me you're going in your old winter coat and those shoes?'

'I bought a new hat and skirt. I couldn't afford anything more, Ma. I don't earn a fortune!'

'Then tidy yourself up. You should have let me know you were short of money for some decent things and I'd have sent you some. I just hope no one notices those shoes. What's got into you, Bridget, you used to be so fussy?'

Bridget washed her face and was brushing her hair before replacing her hat. 'Ma, no one is going to notice me.'

'This Elizabeth person will if what the child's been telling me is right.'

'It's Mary-Kate's big day, everyone will be looking at her, not me.' Bridget tried to shrug aside her mother's comments, but she did feel dowdy. 'Isn't she his elder daughter?'

'Aye, and a holy terror by the sound of it or so Ellen says, but I think she might be exaggerating. She's spoilt is that one! She'll need a firm hand and I intend to tell Mary-Kate so, but I've had a good talk to her and I think she understands she must be good and quiet today. Now, are you ready?'

Bridget picked up her bag. Even beside her mother she felt impoverished. Sarah had a black wool coat over a grey wool dress, the collar of which was edged with dark grey bugle beads, and she wore a large-brimmed black hat, banded by a narrow grey ribbon. Obviously Mrs O'Leary had been busy.

They all met on the landing and tears came into both their eyes when they saw Mary-Kate. She looked beautiful, the cream wool making her skin glow translucently, the hat making her appear a little older but very elegant. Sarah held out her arms and hugged her.

'Oh, I wish your poor Pa could have been here to see you! You look beautiful, Mary-Kate, beautiful!'

'Oh, Ma, don't! You'll have me crying as well soon and I'm so nervous my hands are shaking, see!' She held out her gloved hands and Sarah held them tightly.

'God bless you. May you be as happy as your Pa and I were!'

Mary-Kate felt the tears pricking her eyes. She didn't want to think about the future; if she did she might change her mind. She just wished it were all over.

Bridget wiped her eyes. She felt happy for her sister and yet strangely depressed.

'Will you come down the lot of you, the taxi cab is here and Himself has been gone nearly ten minutes!' Matty called agitatedly from the hall below. He was giving his sister away, being her nearest male relative.

With a last dab to her eyes, taking Ellen's hand firmly in her own, Sarah followed her eldest daughter down the stairs, followed by Bridget.

It wasn't a full Nuptial Mass, just the Marriage Service, because it was a Special Licence, but there were quite a few people in the church.

Canon Ormond married them as befitted such a benefactor to the church as Lewis Vannin. Mary-Kate was surprised that her nervousness had vanished and she answered clearly and without hesitation. She took her vows to love, honour and obey, in sickness and in health, for better or for worse, for richer or poorer until death do us part, clearly and reverently. She never broke a promise and she was determined to fulfil those vows, come what may.

Behind her in the front pew on her left stood her family and on the right Ellen, Elizabeth and Ernest. Elizabeth was dressed to the nines in a short fur jacket over a dusky rose-pink dress and she positively glittered with jewels. Sarah glanced across at her and decided the child hadn't been exaggerating. She looked like a Christmas tree with all that jewellery on and had obviously set out to outshine her daughter, but she had only succeeded in making herself look over-dressed and fussy beside Mary-Kate's uncluttered, simple, elegant outfit. Now she was a little thankful Gina hadn't come, for putting those two together would be like putting a match to paraffin!

Elizabeth had glanced quickly over at her new stepmother's family and Bridget had happened to intercept that look. It was one of sheer disdain and it made her feel so small and plain and down-at-heel. The depression that had started on the staircase had grown as she contrasted her life, her home and surroundings with Mary-Kate's. And the look Elizabeth had given her had set the seal on it. For the first time in months she looked at her life without the aura of love that had blinkered her and she saw the dirt, the poverty and the squalor that she'd grown used to, and she was shocked. Of course, she didn't really envy Mary-Kate her husband, he was so old and looked very formidable and humourless, but nevertheless, when she got back there would be some changes. She'd get out of MacFarlane's, get a better job – as she had always intended – then she'd get out of the Gorbals. She'd somehow persuade Andy to marry her and they'd move away. She'd never get to Newton Mearns, but there were other places. She'd slipped down into the abysmal rut so gradually that she hadn't noticed and only seeing her sister and mother had forced her to face the reality of her life.

As the voices faded and the organ began to play 'Tantum Ergo' and the newly-weds went into the vestry to sign the civil forms before the Registrar, Bridget began to dream. They would be married at St John's and she would have a white dress and a long, white veil. Eileen and Bernie would be her bridesmaids and she'd have them in pale pink and then they'd go off to their new home. A nice little rented house or flat in a better area, away from all the filth and noise and violence.

Sarah touched her arm and brought her down to earth. Everyone was leaving. It was over. Mary-Kate was now Mrs Vannin.

There had been a decidedly strained atmosphere over the wedding supper caused mainly by Elizabeth's presence and her determination not to be anything other than cool towards everyone as a sign of her complete disapproval. But when Violet and her mother – who had been brought in to help – had cleared the table, things had relaxed a little. Soon after, they had all adjourned to the large, front parlour, where Lewis engaged Matty in a conversation about modern farming methods and trade and industry generally, staying clear of politics, while Ernest sat and listened.

Sarah sat between her two daughters on the long sofa, while Ellen sat on the floor at Mary-Kate's feet, quite overcome by the new family she had suddenly acquired and who were not in the least bit like her elder sister, as she had feared they might be. Elizabeth sat apart on a high-backed, winged chair, determined to remain aloof, but curious just the same.

'So, what is it that you do, Bridget?' she asked, seeing the girl's colour heighten as her eyes went straight to the old, shabby shoes.

'I work as a sewing machinist in one of Glasgow's biggest clothing manufacturing works.'

'How interesting.'

Bridget tried to smooth out the creases in the cheap, wool skirt, wishing Gina were here. She'd put that one in her place and smartish. But then she remembered Bernie's words. She couldn't rely on her sisters any more. 'Of course, I'm only using the time to learn. I intend to make a career in the business. I'll probably be a buyer in one of Glasgow's fashionable shops. You could say I'm learning the business from the bottom up!'

Elizabeth raised her eyebrows but said nothing.

Mary-Kate smiled. Good for Bridget. It looked as though she had learned to stand up for herself, although she looked pale and thin and her clothes were shabby. She must be finding it hard, she'd make sure she slipped her a few pounds before she left.

'Such a pity your other sister couldn't come, I was

looking forward to meeting her. It must be very glamorous being on the stage and in the West End, too!'

'I'm sorry, too, but it must have been something really important. You two would get on like a house on fire.'

More like an ammunition dump, Sarah thought grimly. 'And what does your husband do?'

'He's in shipping,' Elizabeth said vaguely.

'Doing exactly what?' Sarah persisted.

'I really don't know. I never ask about such boring things.'

'He's a clerk. I heard Pa say so!'

Elizabeth shot Ellen a look fit to kill.

'Haven't I told you, Miss, that little girls should be seen and not heard. You've far too much to say for yourself altogether!' Sarah scolded, but not harshly, noting Elizabeth's discomfort.

'Yes, Grandma.'

Elizabeth choked on her sherry. Grandma! The little monster was completely won over by them.

'And what do you do with yourself all day? Do you work?' Sarah continued.

Elizabeth looked at Sarah in horror. 'Work? I've never worked.'

'Really, you must get very bored.' Sarah, in other circumstances, would have told her straight that a day's work never hurt anyone and was to be recommended.

The conversation died, until Lewis joined them and said he hoped they would all be comfortable and it was a pleasure to have them to stay, but that it was time Ellen was in bed. She'd had enough excitement for one day.

Ellen was about to protest until she caught Mary-Kate's eye.

Elizabeth rose, glad to escape. 'We really must go, too, Ernest. Would you get my jacket?'

'No need, Ernest, Vi will fetch it,' Mary-Kate said.

Sarah looked at the clock; it was nearly eight. 'Come along, Ellen, we've both had a long day and I'm not as young as you. I think I'll go up myself.' She kissed Mary-Kate's cheek and clutched Ellen's hand. She wasn't quite sure what to do about her son-in-law.

He nodded. 'Goodnight, then.'

'I think it would be more sensible altogether if you called me Sarah, don't you?'

He smiled. 'Very well, goodnight, Sarah.'

She looked pointedly at Bridget. 'Don't you be staying up too late either, Bridget. I would like a word with you before you go to bed.'

There was a small flurry of activity as Elizabeth and Ernest left and Sarah and Ellen went upstairs, followed shortly by Bridget.

Lewis was about to refill Matty's glass.

'No, I've had enough, thanks. I'm not a drinking man and it's been a long day.' He paused, embarrassed. 'Would you mind if I borrowed a book from your fine library? I'm a great one for reading, but I don't get much time at home.'

'Help yourself, do, and if there's anything else you need, just ask.'

They shook hands and Matty left.

Mary-Kate got up and refilled Lewis's glass and handed it to him. 'Thank you, Lewis, for being so kind and generous to my family.'

'I couldn't do anything less.' He had been impressed by them, especially by Sarah, who seemed a fine, strong, sensible woman and it had surprised him. Nor was Mary-Kate's brother the philistine he had dreaded. Maybe he had been over-reacting. Had he really expected her brother to be an uncouth rebel.

Mary-Kate felt more nervous now than she had all day and she twisted the gold band on the finger of her left hand.

'Would you like another drink, my dear?'

She nodded, remaining silent while he filled her glass and handed it to her, then sat down beside her on the sofa. 'Elizabeth didn't behave too badly. I'd feared she would, although to wear every piece of jewellery she owns was in very bad taste, not to say downright common.'

'I'm quite relieved that she's gone, Lewis, I must be truthful. I did try to be friendly towards her but I'm afraid she will never accept me.'

'Does it matter so much?'

'No, not really. I'm also glad in a way that Gina couldn't come.'

'The "difficult one"?'

She smiled. 'That's an understatement. She's the worst temper of anyone I've ever met and well . . . I'm certain there would have been the divil of a row between those two.'

They both fell silent. She gazed into the fire. She'd told her Ma she was happy and she was. She was grateful to Lewis for he had been so generous and thoughtful, but she didn't love him and suddenly she was wondering if she could cope with that fact. She was his wife now and he had the right to expect that the marriage be consummated.

'Mary-Kate, do you find me unattractive?' he asked, quietly.

'No, I've told you, I'm fond of you.'

'Then . . . ?'

She looked at him, praying that her fear didn't show in her eyes.

'If it's distasteful to you, then I will sleep in the spare bedroom?'

For an instant she breathed a sigh of relief, but then how would that look to her Ma? If she refused to sleep with her husband on their wedding night, Sarah would take that as a sign that she had only married him out of a sense of gratitude and security, or even for his money. Sarah was possessed of a curious nature, she would be sure to go poking her nose into the bedrooms before Vi had time to do them all. 'No, No! That won't be necessary at all, Lewis.' Now that she'd said it, she wished with all her heart that she hadn't.

He finished his drink and then took her hand. 'Then I think it's time we retired as well.'

Mary-Kate managed a weak smile as he gently drew her to her feet. Oh, Holy Mother, what had she let herself in for?

Chapter Thirteen

———•◆•———

ALL THE WAY BACK on the train Bridget was miserable. Oh, they all had so much more than she had and what had she to look forward to? That poky, bare, drab little flat in that awful crumbling building with its shared water taps, shared lavatory, disgusting court and stinking ash-pit. And that boring job that was ruining her eyesight. The only bright thing in her life was Andy. She had to get away from everything before it was too late. Before she sank into the mire so deeply that she would never get out. Andy would be waiting for her at the station and she'd suggest that they go somewhere and have a quiet talk and tomorrow she would cross the Victoria Bridge and find herself a decent job.

At first she thought he wasn't there. She couldn't see him anywhere and that was unusual, for he towered head and shoulders over everyone else. Then she saw him leaning against the far wall, reading a newspaper. She waved to catch his attention and he looked up and smiled. Her spirits lifted. Her heart always beat faster when he smiled at her like that.

He held her close for a minute and kissed her. 'Did you have a good time, then?'

'Oh, wonderful! He's much older than her, but, oh, Andy, you should see the house! Polished wood floor in the hall, carpets everywhere and lovely ornaments and linen and the bathroom! I could have stayed in there for hours and hours!' She chattered non-stop as they crossed Bridge Street.

'You couldn't stay in the "bathroom" that long here. There'd be a line of people waiting that would stretch from here to the Necropolis!'

It was meant as a joke but she didn't laugh. It was just a reminder of the conditions they lived in. 'Andy, can we go somewhere?'

'Where would you like to go?'

'Somewhere quiet, I want to talk to you.'

'Where is there quiet around here? Only an alley or the back court of your place or mine.'

Privacy was another luxury that people didn't have in the Gorbals and Bridget frowned. An alley would be better than the back court with its stinking ash-pits where mangy dogs and cats scavenged and rats ran brazenly over your feet. She shuddered. 'The alley behind Feinstein's Bakery will do. At least the air doesn't stink there!'

They walked in silence through the dark, dirty streets until they turned into a narrow alleyway behind the bakery. Then Bridget slid her arms around Andy's neck. 'Have you missed me?'

'Of course I have!'

'Then show me how much.'

He kissed her passionately and slowly and she clung to his lips. He was the only man she ever wanted and she knew she couldn't hold him off for ever. She drew away from him. 'Andy, I'm going over the bridge tomorrow in search of a better job.'

'What's wrong with the one you've got?'

'Oh, don't you see? Look around you!'

'Oh, I see, your sister's fine house has turned your head.'

'No, but it made me look at my life. I've always wanted to work somewhere like Copeland and Lye and if I can get a job there, and with what you earn at Dixon's . . . we could move away from all this!'

He looked down into her earnest little face. 'Bridget, the likes of us don't move away from here and we don't get fancy jobs like that either. You're just dreaming, hen, you've always been a dreamer. Come here.' He pulled her to him and kissed her again. Again she pulled away, determined he wasn't going to evade the issue.

'They can and they do, Andy! Look at Rachel Lavinsky. She's working in the Mitchell Library now and she doesn't live at home anymore!'

'Aye, and she's worn out with working all day and studying all night. What kind of life is that?'

'It's got to be better than this. Oh, Andy, if you love me, at least say we'll try? If I can get a job, will you try?' she pleaded.

He didn't answer. He knew what she was asking in an indirect way.

She reached up and brushed his lips with hers, pressing her small firm breasts against his chest. 'Will you try, for me?'

He sighed. 'Aye, all right, I'll try. But you've got to get that job first.'

She kissed him fiercely. Oh, she'd known that if she tried hard enough he would see things her way! She'd get that job and then they could be married.

Bridget sat in Craig's Tea Shop a block down from Copeland and Lye's exclusive department store. The tears trickled down her cheeks and fell unheeded into the cup, mingling with the tea that was stone cold. How could she go back and tell him that despite all her requests and demands to see the staff manager, she had been politely but firmly turned away. It had been just like her excursion into Miss Drinkwater's all over again, only this time all she had to go back to was MacFarlane's and Warwick Street!

She became aware that the fierce-looking cashier sitting behind her till at the front of the shop was looking directly at her. She couldn't sit here any longer. She gulped down some of the cold tea, leaving the cup half full, gathered up her bag and rose. She'd been here an hour nearly, but she'd sooner walk the streets than go back home.

As she stepped into the aisle she collided with a waitress and the tray the girl was carrying went clattering to the floor, spilling hot tea down the front of her coat and scalding her hand. She cried out in pain, holding her hand. The girl was scrabbling on the floor amidst the broken crockery, spilt milk and sugar, looking for a napkin.

'Oh, miss, I'm so sorry! Here, let me wipe your coat for you! Oh, I'm so sorry!'

The harridan in the black dress had left her perch behind the till and stood before her. 'Is madam all right?

Oh, would you just look at the state of your good coat! And your hand! You,' she spat at the girl, 'get this mess cleared up this instant and then get your coat, I don't want to see you here when I come back!'

'Oh, please, don't dismiss her! It was partly my fault, I wasn't thinking!' Bridget cried.

'Nonsense! Now you come with me, madam, and we'll see to that hand and of course we'll have your coat cleaned for you. The fools they send you from the agencies, these days!'

Bridget was guided firmly towards the back of the shop where she was sat down and some cold fat was smoothed over the reddening patch on the back of her hand that had begun to smart, bringing tears to her eyes again. Now she'd been the cause of that poor girl losing her job! The woman was fussing over her coat. 'If I sponge it down I think most of it will come out, but we'll have it cleaned just the same.'

'Please, it's quite all right. It doesn't matter.'

'It most certainly does! I have the good name of my business to think of, madam. Now, we'll hear no more about it.'

Another waitress brought in a cup of strong tea.

'You drink that, madam, you've had a shock.'

Bridget wished she would stop calling her 'madam', it was grating on her already shredded nerves.

'I couldn't help noticing that you were a little upset? Is there anything I can do?'

'No, but thank you just the same. I . . . I'd been to Copeland and Lye for a job, but I . . . I didn't get it.'

The small black eyes bored into her. 'You are looking for work then?'

'Yes.'

The manageress smiled, seeing a way out of her present dilemma. 'Have you worked in this line before? With the public, I mean?'

Bridget nodded and drew Mrs O'Leary's letter from her bag and passed it over.

'This is a very good reference, perhaps we can help each other? I now find I have a vacancy for a waitress. Would you be interested? You seem just the kind of girl I need.'

'Me? I . . .' The way was open again. It wasn't what she had wanted, but Craig's was the most fashionable Tea Room on Sauchiehall Street. 'Yes! Yes, I'd be pleased to take up your offer. When would you like me to start?'

From out of the pocket of the black dress the manageress took a watch on a chain. 'It's nearly closing time, so you come back in the morning at seven-thirty sharp and we'll get you sorted out with your uniform, Miss O'Donnell.'

'Can I ask how much the wages are?'

'Not as much as you'd get along there on the corner, but fifteen shillings a week and your tips, of course, and a good girl can make quite a bit on her tips.'

'Oh, thank you, thank you, Miss . . . ?'

'Mrs Craig.'

She should have known.

On her way out she uttered a thankful prayer. What did it matter that it was freezing cold and that the wind promised sleet? At last she'd got a decent job and she might get to know some of the staff from other shops. Maybe one could be persuaded to speak for her – in time. Bridget pulled her damp coat closer to her. It was worth getting it ruined. Now Andy would have to stick to his part of the bargain.

The sleet had become heavier as Bridget got off the tram on the corner of Bedford Road and she hurried along, her head down against the full blast of the wind coming off the Clyde. She'd have something to eat and then she'd go round to Andy's place and tell him. Wait until she told Bernie! Excitement bubbled up and she hardly felt the stinging cold on her cheeks.

She ran up the stairs and found everyone out. Then she remembered that Eileen had gone to enrol in the library, now she had proved she could read well enough, and that Bernie and Archie were going for a drink straight after work to celebrate the fact that two of their friends were getting married, albeit under duress – Kirstie was pregnant. At least she wouldn't go up the aisle like that. She was glad now she'd held out. Andy could never say she'd trapped him. She made a sandwich of some fish paste and dry bread and brewed a cup of tea. Then she went and brushed her hair and put on the red skirt she'd worn for Mary-Kate's wedding. She was prepared to do battle against the elements again.

Andy lived in a tenement in Norfolk Street that faced the Gorbals Cross – a square, stone monument, a Doric column at each corner, curving inwards to form a sort of spire. On each side of the spire was a clock and above that a wrought-iron cross. Inside, it contained niches with plinths and a drinking fountain, supplied with water from Loch Katrine in the Trossachs. It was a favourite place for men to gather and talk and argue and discuss their troubles and grievances. But at this time and in such weather, it was abandoned.

Bridget crossed the road and walked quickly towards the blackened building and turned into the entrance. She was about to climb the staircase when she stopped, hearing voices from the space under the stairs.

'Och, come on, darlin', haven't I always wanted yese! Come on, I can't wait!'

It was Maggie Baird's voice. She was under the stairs with someone and Bridget knew what she was up to. The spaces under the stairs were always used for such purposes. She took another step.

'Come on, Andy, wit's wrong with yese? Yese weren't like this the other night. She'll no' find out. Yese know I canna get enough o' yese! I'm no' like her, all cold an' holy.'

She froze. Surely she'd been mistaken! The wind had distorted the words. Then she heard his voice, calling Maggie's name, over and over!

That slut! That whore! He was with her! Bridget ran blindly back out into the street, and heedless of the traffic ran up the steps of the Cross and slumped down inside on a stone plinth. No! He couldn't do it! He couldn't, not with Maggie! Not after what he'd said. He loved her! He was going to marry her. She had a job! Her tortured mind conjured up images of him with Maggie, images that shocked and revolted her, but that wouldn't go away. And it wasn't the first time! While she had been away he had been with Maggie!

How long she sat there she didn't know, but suddenly she knew she was freezing, that her teeth were chattering and that she had to get home. Somehow, she had to get back. She grasped the ice-cold stone and dragged herself to her feet. In that black void her heart had frozen, too. It had turned to flint as icy-cold as the stone walls of Gorbals Cross. She would never forget his voice or that fiendish kaleidoscope of images.

Eileen was in when she finally got back and at the sight of her grey, pinched face and bloodless lips, the girl shot up and ran to her.

'Bridget! Bridget, what's the matter?'

'Just get me a hot cup of tea, please.'

Eileen did as she was asked and Bridget drank it.

'Will I heat up the brick and wrap it in the old cloth and put it in the bed?'

Bridget nodded, but she'd never feel warm ever again and she'd never sleep peacefully again either. She lay down, not even bothering to take off her coat and Eileen, her expression timorous, left her alone.

Next day was clear and crisp, the pavements were slippery with frost and the crowds, hurrying along to work, were muffled up against it. Bridget didn't even feel the wind as she got off the tram and went into Craig's Tea Shop.

She was given the black dress, starched white cap and apron to put on and shown the kitchen and told her duties, all of which she digested solemnly, with hardly a word passing her lips. The work gave her something else to concentrate on and, as the day wore on, feeling began to seep back into her heart. But it was no longer a feeling of frosted sorrow. It was a slowly burning flame of anger. A fury with herself, with Andy, with them all!

Mrs Craig noticed the change in her. 'Are you feeling

quite well, Bridget, you look flushed and your eyes are very bright?'

'I'm fine, thank you, Mrs Craig. It's just a little warm in here.' She managed a smile. 'But I'll get used to it, don't worry.'

By the time the shop closed, the slow fuse of her anger was nearing its end. The sun was just a slither of fiery red on the skyline and the tattered clouds were shot through with orange and vermilion, when she reached the Gorbals Cross. As usual there were groups of men standing around it, and, as usual, Andy was amongst them, as was Archie. Bridget straightened her shoulders and jerked up her chin, her eyes blazing with fire as consuming as that of the setting sun.

'Bridget, how did the job go?' Archie asked goodnaturedly, then seeing her face he frowned.

She ignored Archie and pushed through the group and stopped in front of Andy.

'Bridget! Archie said you'd got the job. I'm right glad for you, hen.' He'd never seen her look like this before. He'd never seen her so angry.

She flung the money she owed him at his feet. 'That's what I owe you and I don't take the leavings of whores like Maggie Baird, Andy MacDonald!'

Everyone had fallen silent and was staring at them both, but she saw only him. 'And this is what I think of you!' And with that she drew back her arm and with all the strength she could muster, slapped him hard across the face. Then she turned and walked away. Oblivious of the outraged and affronted looks cast at her, she knew exactly what she'd done and it had been intentional. She'd humiliated him in front of everyone.

He, who was one of the hardest men in the Gorbals and feared by many. She'd hit him. A mere girl who just came up to his shoulder. Bridget O'Donnell had grown up.

Gina was trying to read Mary-Kate's letter amidst the hustle and noise in the dressing room. The sound of Delia Heysham's shrill voice carried clearly along the corridor, demanding her mint tea. The star's dresser had fallen and twisted her ankle and her first assistant was now taking the full weight of responsibility and she'd obviously upset her mistress. Gina had grown to hate Delia. She was an over-bearing tyrant who didn't spare anyone her tongue or her temper. Gina's one night of glory seemed years ago now. She'd been good that night. She'd known it. George and Edward had known it. The audience and the critics had known it, and so had Delia and that was why Gina had never been given another chance. But she'd had enough of hanging around, listening to Delia Heysham's tantrums and she'd tell Edward so. There were other shows, just as good. Helen was now in the chorus of another hit called 'Sunny'. If only she could find some way to get rid of Delia for a few days, even a week, then he would have to listen to her demands.

Jeannie, the assistant dresser, would quite obviously be flustered and muddled. If only she could just think of something to put Miss Heysham out of action for a while. Her eyes went over the rows of bottles and phials on the table in front of her. They were mostly make-up and perfume, but her gaze alighted on a bottle printed with the words 'Eyelash-Dye'. That was it! She looked down to hide the excitement in her eyes. Everyone knew the stuff was only made up of root dyes. It wouldn't kill you. She began to pretend she was searching for something amongst the cosmetics.

'Has anyone got a pair of eyelash curlers, my lashes look like stair rods?' she enquired loudly, her hand closing over the small, dark bottle.

'Try using Vaseline,' came one answer.

'I've tried that, it doesn't work.'

'I have, somewhere,' Laura Kent called back.

'Damn!' Gina muttered. 'Hurry up then, Laura, we've not got all night.'

Laura tipped the contents of her make-up purse on to the table and began rummaging amongst them. 'Sorry, can't seem to find them. I could have sworn I put them in.'

'Delia will have a pair,' someone else called.

'I'm not asking her,' Gina stated vehemently.

'Go and ask Jeannie for them. Judging by the hysterics along there I don't think she'll bother too much about a pair of eyelash curlers. I'm sure Delia's are waxed into that shape, like a moustache,' Laura laughed, pulling a face.

Gina grinned. 'I'll try, but if I come back covered in the famous mint tea, I'll hold you responsible, Laura Kent.'

Jeannie was harassed. 'What do you want?' she snapped on opening the door. 'You know Miss Heysham hates being disturbed.'

'Sorry. Could I borrow her eyelash curlers? I won't make a sound, I swear, please? I'll just creep in and out.' Gina lowered her voice and made a sympathetic *moue* with her lips. 'I know she's in one of her moods.'

'Jeannie, who's that and where *IS* my tea?'

'Tell her I've brought some Good Luck messages from her admirers. Tell her . . . anything, please?' Gina whispered, pushing Jeannie gently back into the room.

'It's only Gina. She's got some cards and messages.'

'I won't disturb you, Miss Heysham, I'll just pop them in here, then you can look at them later on, at your leisure.'

Delia glared at her, then to her relief, she told Jeannie to shut the door before she caught pneumonia and started to pull at the flowers adorning her headband. 'It's not on tightly. I'll lose it. It will fall down over one eye. Is that what you want? To make a fool of me? Fix it. If you'd done it properly in the first place you wouldn't have to do it again, so take that look off your face now!'

Delia was on form all right, Gina thought as she slipped quickly into the small adjoining room where extra costumes, make-up and wigs were kept, and where Jeannie had obviously been making the mint tea. Luck was with her tonight, that was certain. Gina poured the contents of the little bottle into the cup and stirred it. The colour darkened a little but with any luck, by the time Jeannie had finished fixing the headband, Delia would have to gulp it down and would hardly taste it. Then a thought struck her. It would be luke-warm by then and what if Delia refused to drink it? She wouldn't, for there wasn't time to make more, she told herself sternly. With a nod to Jeannie, Gina quickly slipped out of the room.

'Did you get them?' Laura asked.

'No. She's in a foul mood and so is Jeannie and I don't blame her. Oh, hell, I'm all behind now!'

'Hurry up then, I don't know why you made all that fuss just for curling your eyelashes. Hells Bells! What's going on now?'

The noise from the end of the corridor had risen considerably. Jeannie could be heard yelling and then she started to scream. There was instant pandemonium as they all tried to run into the corridor at once, but Gina got there first.

Jeannie was frantic. 'For God's sake get someone quickly, Gina! She's ill! She's really ill! Oh, Mr Christy.'

George elbowed his way through.

'She's collapsed. She was rolling in agony, Mr Christy, she was, on my life!'

For an instant Gina was guilt-stricken. Dear God, she'd never intended to kill her! She pushed her way forward after George and saw, over his shoulder, Delia lying on the floor, face down.

'Let her get some air! Move back! Move back! Joe, go and get an ambulance and be quick! The rest of you get back to your dressing rooms. The curtain goes up in fifteen minutes. Gina, you'll have to go on tonight and move yourself.'

Gina caught Jeannie by the wrist and pulled her into the tiny back room.

'You heard him. Pull yourself together and get my costume ready.'

She heard the raised voices in the other room and the clanging of the ambulance bell and, as she struggled into her costume, Delia was being carried out on a stretcher.

'George, what's the matter with her? What is it?' Gina called to him.

'They don't know for sure, but it could be appendix.

He

She's had a "grumbling" one for years. Now hurry up. I want you out there on time!'

Appendix! If that was true she needn't have gone to all that trouble. And she'd thought she'd poisoned Delia!

Edward got quite a start when he saw her. He knew she was not happy with her career, but then Gina would never be happy, she would always want more and more. He hadn't heard that Delia was ill, or indeed that anything was wrong with her at all, and he knew she would sooner die than let Gina take her place. The fading star doggedly refused to be outshone. So how had Gina managed it? He knew the show as well as she did, so he excused himself and went backstage to wait for her. It was there he heard of Delia's sudden collapse and removal to hospital and his suspicions deepened. He wouldn't put anything past Gina, and it had been known to happen before, although usually Epsom Salts were used, which was why leading ladies often refused point blank to drink anything fizzy, except champagne poured from a bottle they could see. Edward watched her from the wings. Gina had been overjoyed with the reviews she'd had the last time and now she was putting her soul into the show to make sure she got them again. If anything serious was wrong with Delia, he knew he had a new star on his hands. He rubbed his chin ruefully. She deserved it. She'd 'served her time'; it wasn't fair to hold her back any longer.

'Tell Miss O'Donnell I'll be waiting in the car for her, will you, Joe?' he called.

The lad nodded as he went out.

*

'So, tell me how you managed that? Did you poison her or beat her unconscious with your shoe?'

Gina laughed, her eyes sparkling. If only he knew how close he'd come to the truth. Appendix or not, she had intended to make Delia very ill. 'Appendicitis! Apparently she'd had something called a "grumbling" one for years.'

'Lucky you! Poor Delia! I'll send her some flowers because I know *you* won't.'

'Why should I? She's had her day, now it's my turn!'

'Oh, the arrogance of youth! Where would you like to go to celebrate?'

'The Ritz or the Café Royal!'

He laughed 'All right, the Café Royal.'

'You mean it? Oh, I'll have to go home and change. Turn around Edward!'

'Gina, we don't have time for you to prink and preen. Do you want to go or not?'

'Yes! Oh, who cares if its only my old dress! Soon I'll be able to buy them from all the best shops and when I go into restaurants people will recognize me! Oh, Edward, do you know what that means to me?'

'I've a fair idea! But don't go out and buy up Bond Street just yet!'

'But I *will* earn more, won't I?'

'Yes, less my ten per cent. I haven't taken it before because, my dear Gina, I felt sorry for you, struggling on that pittance.'

'You're teasing me?'

'I'm not! I intend to reap the benefit of my investment!'

'Ten per cent!'

'Gina, I didn't take you for a fool. You've known all along that that is the usual percentage.'

'Will I have enough left to get a nice place of my own?'

'Yes, but I wouldn't rush things, wait until you've some money in the bank first.'

I won't have much with you taking ten per cent of it, she thought, then she shrugged. Nothing was going to dim her happiness tonight. Even if she went right to the top, she'd never forget this night.

As they pulled up outside the restaurant and Edward got out to open the door for her, a young newspaper reporter dashed forward.

'Miss O'Donnell? I'd hoped to see you. I've just heard what a great success you were tonight! I'm hoping to get on in my field, journalism, could I have your exclusive story?'

'No press releases', Edward said firmly.

'Oh, Edward, don't be so mean! I haven't got a "story" as such,' she smiled.

'Then can you tell me how it feels to be an overnight success?'

The smile faded. 'Overnight success! There's no such thing! I've worked hard for months for this chance. No one just steps on to a stage and becomes an instant success! Excuse me.'

'You changed your tune?' Edward commented dryly.

'Are they all such fools?' Gina said waspishly.

'No, he was just young, inexperienced and looking for what they call a "scoop".'

Buoyant though her mood was, Gina couldn't help but be aware of the looks cast in her direction in the restaurant and she wished she'd worn something else. Well, the next time she came here things would be different.

Edward handed her the menu but as it was written entirely in French she stared over the rim of it at him.

'I'll order for both of us, if you like.'

She nodded. 'Can we have champagne?'

'If you like, but I don't want you to get drunk. You're half-way there already on success! And, if everything goes well . . .'

'What?'

'There's some talk of a London production of another Broadway success.'

'Oh, I'd give anything to star in a brand new musical! What's it called? What's it about? Is it modern?'

'It's not "modern" as you put it. It's set in America's Deep South and it's called "Steamboat". It is already a success, so those who get the four star parts – and there are four . . .' He spread his hands expressively.

'Edward, I want a part! I don't care how, but you've got to get me it! I'll give you fifty per cent of everything I earn if I get it.'

'My God! You mean it, don't you?'

'Of course I mean it! I've never been more serious in my life before.'

'I can't give you a signed and sealed guarantee, but I'll do my best and the rest is up to you. But don't think it will be easy! You're not the only one who can sing and dance!'

'But I do it better than any of them!'

'You're being arrogant again, Gina.'

'I'm not, I'm being honest.'

'Don't you ever think of anything else?'

'No, what else is there?'

To her astonishment Edward leaned over the table and kissed her full on the lips and when he drew away she gasped, confused.

'There's that!'

'Edward! What . . . ? Do you mean you . . . care?'

He laughed. 'No, I don't love you, if that's what you mean. That was just a sample, if you like, of some of the other pleasures in life that you're hell bent on missing out on!'

Gina tossed back her drink, her temper rising. How dare he! Here with everyone looking! She felt like slapping his handsome face with those sardonic, laughing eyes. Instead, she smiled and held out her glass to be refilled. It was just one more thing to add to her mental list. Her day would come.

Chapter Fourteen

———⬥———

BRIDGET ENJOYED WORKING FOR Mrs Craig. The work wasn't as hard or as boring as MacFarlane's, but it was tiring. She didn't mind that, for everything was different, the people she worked with were interesting and it didn't give her much time to dwell on the past.

The fury that had consumed her that never-to-be-forgotten day, had dwindled until it was just a dull ache and as the days and weeks passed, that, too, grew less. 'Time heals' was another of Mrs O'Hagan's adages that had been passed on by Bernie, and she had found it to be partly true. Some nights she slept well, worn out by the day's exertions. But there were others – fewer now – when sleep wouldn't come and she would get up and stand staring out of the window at the wall of the tenement next door. Those were the nights when she would re-live those hours and realize just how much they had changed her life – and her personality. She knew now that she had changed. She was harder, less naïve, in fact she'd grown up and faced the reality of the harshness of the world.

She was still living with Bernie and Archie for she'd quickly found, after a few enquiries, that she couldn't afford to move out of the Gorbals yet. But with her tips she had begun collecting things for the time when she would have her own place – even if it were only a broom-cupboard. Small items mainly linen, cushions, two lamps, a rug, some dishes and two pans and a kettle. She kept them all in boxes in the tiny bedroom. There were plenty of second-hand furniture shops where bigger items could be bought when needed.

In the first few days after her now almost legendary and humiliating attack on Andy's ego, Bridget had been shunned by all the men she came into contact with. They viewed her action as setting something of a precedent. Archie had followed her home in a highly agitated mood, but when he had started to lecture her she had turned to face him and the look in her eyes had silenced him abruptly. Bernie had had no such reservations. She had loudly applauded Bridget's actions and that fact had caused the first real row between them that Bridget had heard. And when the white-hot anger that had driven her for days had cooled, she noticed that many of the other women treated her with a new respect. As Bernie had remarked acidly, she had done what most of them had longed to do to their own menfolk for years, but hadn't the nerve or the guts.

Although she still lived in the same neighbourhood, but because she no longer worked at MacFarlane's and Andy no longer came to Warwick Street, Bridget had only seen him once, and that had been pure coincidence. She had been getting off the tram at the corner of Bedford Road on her way home from work and he had been waiting to get on. She had just stared at him until he had dropped his eyes and moved aside to let her pass. She had thought she would have felt sorrow, even longing, at the sight of him, but all she felt was cold contempt. She'd heard in the 'Steamy' that he and Maggie Baird were now 'courting' but strangely that hadn't hurt either. 'They deserve one another!' had been her vituperative comment to Eileen, uttered in a voice loud enough for everyone within earshot to hear.

Craig's was a firm favourite with the assistants of many of the larger shops and, as the lunchtime crowds found their way into the cafés, restaurants and tea rooms on Sauchiehall Street, Bridget, came out of her reverie and began to bustle about, laying places, taking orders, exchanging small-talk with the customers.

Mrs Craig, behind her desk, smiled benignly at her. Bridget was such an asset, she thought. She was efficient, tactful, honest, calm in an emergency and the regulars liked her. Mrs Craig had it in the back of her mind that one day, when the time came for her to retire, she might train Bridget to manage the shop.

'Four teas, four cheese and ham sandwiches, one pot of tea and a plate of "Specials", please, Kit!' Bridget called to the girl in the kitchen. Kit smiled back as she placed the order on Bridget's tray.

Weaving her way deftly between the tables, she went first to the young man who always sat alone in the corner, away from the window. He was a strange one, she thought. She judged him to be in his middle twenties, of medium height but slim build. He had a fair complexion and light brown hair that was always neatly cut. His clothes were impeccable. He seemed to wear a clean shirt every day and his ties and the handkerchief in the breast pocket of his suit jacket always matched. And he wore cufflinks. She'd taken special note of them because he appeared to have as many different pairs as he did neckties. He was always pleasant in his manner, his voice quiet, even when they were rushed off their feet and he had to wait. She'd never known him to be abrupt, never rude or impatient. He came in every day for lunch, and sometimes in the afternoon as well, and occasionally he would be joined by another young man and they would sit chatting earnestly. But he usually ate alone. Bridget had never seen him accompanied by a girl, but perhaps he was just shy.

'There you are, sir, a nice pot of fresh tea and your special sandwiches.' She smiled at him, as she placed the dishes down, adding a crisp, white napkin. 'Be careful, the pot is very hot!'

He smiled. 'Thank you, that's very considerate of you.'

Bridget served four other customers and exchanged a few pleasantries with them. Then she turned to a table where three girls, who worked in the Millinery Department of Copeland and Lye, were sitting. Ever since she'd found out they worked there, she'd cultivated her acquaintance with them. She'd always been ready with a sympathetic ear to listen to their complaints about their health, their customers, their bosses. Now she felt that the time was ripe to approach them about the possibility of getting a job there. After all the new season's stock would be in and they might need more help. She got her pad and pencil ready and smiled brightly.

'Have you been busy then this morning, ladies? I expect everyone is rushing out to buy their new hats?'

The oldest of the trio grimaced. 'They've been rushing out to buy everything, now the weather is changing!'

Another one joined in. 'And did you see the one I had? Every hat in the place she tried on and she looked *awful* in the one she finally chose. It looked like an upturned pudding basin squashed on her head!' The third girl laughed. 'I had one who insisted on having a veil added to a wide-brimmed straw. Can you imagine it? Mind you, if I had a face like that, I'd want it covered up, too.'

The older one nudged her. 'Keep your voice down, Kath, he's here again.'

Bridget smiled, although she didn't really approve of the way they made fun of their customers. After all, if there were no customers, none of them would have jobs. But she took a deep breath and under the pretext of brushing some imaginary crumbs from the spotless tablecloth, leaned closer. 'I hope you don't mind, but I was wondering if there are any vacancies – in any department?' she added hastily. 'You see, ever since I came to Glasgow I've always wanted to work at Copelands. It's such a smart shop.'

They all looked at each other with raised eyebrows and, although no one spoke, it seemed to Bridget that there was an invisible barrier between herself and them.

'You could try the Packing Department,' the elder one said with a trace of amusement in her voice.

'What's that?'

'It's where they pack up all the china and crystal and ornaments to be delivered.'

They were making fun of her and she bit her lip,

wishing she'd never spoken at all. Obviously, they thought that she was a cut lower than themselves. She was a mere waitress.

'I would have thought you would have been happy with the job you've got!' another said.

'I am! Are you ready to order?'

When she turned away, Mrs Craig gestured to her to come over and she prayed that she hadn't heard any of the conversation.

'Is there something wrong? A complaint?' Mrs Craig asked.

'No! No, nothing like that! I was just asking them if they would care to try a slice of your new cake, the "special" recipe one, but they weren't interested and I didn't press them.' Bridget leaned closer. 'You should hear what they say about their customers. It's not very nice at all, Mrs Craig!'

Mrs Craig frowned. 'Some of these young lassies have no respect at all, Bridget, not like you. You've always had an eye to the business but enough sense to know when not to be "pushy".'

But not enough to be considered for a position in a high-class store, she thought as she walked back towards the kitchen.

As she returned she saw them, heads together, smiling and whispering and as she set down their order she couldn't help but notice that there was a very pointed lack of conversation. Whatever they had been saying was about her, but she tried not to care.

The young gentleman across from them in the corner had finished and was preparing to leave. She went over to clear the table.

'I hope everything was to your satisfaction, sir?'

'Yes, thank you. It always is.'

He moved away and she gathered the dirty dishes, placing them on her tray. When she picked up the cup and saucer, underneath was a florin. He must have dropped it, left it by mistake. No one left two whole shillings as a tip, not even at Christmas. She left the tray on the table and went after him, reaching him as he was about to open the door.

'Excuse me, sir, but I think you dropped this.' Bridget held out the coin. 'The light isn't very good in that corner.'

He smiled. 'I didn't drop it, Miss O'Donnell.'

'How do you know my name?'

'Mrs Craig often calls to you and please, I want you to keep it. You work very hard and are very patient and pleasant and honest,' he added, indicating the coin in her hand with a nod of his head. 'Good day.'

She put the coin in her pocket, puzzled. Had he been testing her? Was he some sort of policeman or someone Mrs Craig knew? She went back to pick up her tray. The three girls were also leaving, but she studiously ignored them.

On the way home on the tram Bridget thought about the two incidents again. Two shillings; she hoped the young man wasn't using it as an excuse to 'buy' his way into asking her out. Two of the other waitresses frequently went out with customers, although Mrs Craig frowned on it. But he couldn't buy her friendship or anything else for that matter. She was finished with men. All she wanted from life now was a career and a nice place to live.

She looked out of the window as they crossed the Victoria Bridge thinking of the nice new home she had dreamed of with Andy. She hated the Gorbals. She loathed what it had done to her, although she had to admit that it had been instrumental in her 'growing up'. She hardly ever indulged in daydreams now. For one thing she had precious little time and for another there wasn't much to dream about. She was pinning all her hopes on getting a job at Copeland and Lye and of getting out of these slums. But her foray today in the former direction, had got her nowhere. Or had it? Why should she take any notice of them? They were no better than she. They worked in the Millinery Department. She'd sold hats and she'd trimmed hats for selling, she had more experience than they did! Why shouldn't she try again? She'd come a long way from the timid, gauche young girl who'd barged into Gladys Drinkwater's establishment and asked for a job. Tomorrow was her half-day off – why shouldn't she try again? The thought gave her renewed hope.

As she walked down Warwick Street, the familiar sights, sounds and, above all, the smells only strengthened her resolve. She *had* to get out of this place. She kicked the stinking, rotting remains of a cabbage stalk from the bottom of the stairs with the toe of her shoe. She'd been trying to save up, but she'd have to spend some of her precious hoard on a decent pair of shoes. She couldn't go asking for a job at Copeland's in scuffed shoes. She'd never forgotten her Ma's comments about her shoes at Mary-Kate's wedding.

Eileen was already in and so also, to Bridget's surprise, was Bernie. Eileen stood stirring a pan with a spoon in one hand, while in the other she held a book. Bernie was setting the table.

'Once she's got her head in a book you can't get any sense out of her at all. You can't even get a single word from her, sometimes I think she doesn't hear me.'

Bridget smiled. 'What are you doing home so early?'

'The drive belt broke, so we were all sent home. It was nearly time anyway. I hope they've damn well got it fixed by tomorrow! But I wanted to talk to you anyway.'

'What about?'

'Archie and me are getting married!'

Eileen stopped stirring and raised her eyes. Bridget thought she was about to make some comment, but she remained silent.

'That's wonderful! When?'

'Next month. We're going down to St John's tonight to arrange it all.'

Bridget hugged her. Bernie had been a good friend and she was happy for her. She'd never had much out of life. 'Will you be living here?'

'Where else can we go?'

Bridget sat down at the table. 'What's the matter?' she asked. Bernie looked uncomfortable, not at all like a girl who had just announced her heart's desire. Bridget sighed. It was inevitable, she supposed, living under the same roof. Bernie was probably pregnant.

'It's awkward you see.'

'You're not . . . ?'

'Indeed I'm not! Aren't I right proud of it that I'll go up that aisle of my own free will and so will Archie? I'm not pregnant!'

'Then what's the matter?'

'I wanted you to be my bridesmaid. Oh, no fancy clothes or anything, but Archie is insisting on having . . .'

'On having what? Come on, Bernie O'Hagan. You've never been bashful before.'

'Isn't he just insisting on having Andy MacDonald as his best man!'

'Oh!' It was uttered in a tense voice. 'I see what you mean.' Bridget stood up. 'Then you'll have to do as he wishes, Bernie, he's going to be your husband.'

'Sure, I don't know why he couldn't have had one of his other pals. He's just being bloody stubborn. Don't they all just stick together!'

'He wants him because he *is* his best friend. He was that long before I arrived. I don't mind, Bernie, really I don't! I would have liked to have been there, but never mind. You'll manage without me. Besides, it's only right that Eileen be your bridesmaid, she is Archie's only sister!' Bridget felt disappointed and awkward but there was no way on earth that she was going to be seen anywhere within a hundred miles of *him*. 'So just you tell Archie that everything is all right and if you don't, I will!'

'I can't afford a new frock,' Eileen said, sullenly.

'Archie will buy it for you and I'll help,' Bernie offered graciously, obviously greatly relieved that Bridget wasn't being awkward or upset. 'Mind, it will have to be practical, no taffetta or the like!'

Eileen returned to her book and Bridget went through into the bedroom and began to look through her boxes. She couldn't afford to buy Bernie anything really grand, but she had to give them something, they'd given her a home. Well, more a roof over her head, she thought. She took out the small lamp with the pink, frosted glass shade. It would look nice on the chest of drawers. She looked around. Archie and Bernie would have to have this room and Eileen would have to make do with the bed in the kitchen alcove. But where would she sleep? She sat back on her heels. Bernie's news had really settled the matter. Unless she wanted to sleep on the kitchen floor she had to find somewhere of her own and the only way she could do that was by getting a better job. Tomorrow afternoon she'd buy a new pair of shoes and then she'd go back to Copeland and Lye and try again.

After lunch the following day, Bridget bought a pair of black shoes in Tylers in Hope Street, just off Sauchiehall Street. She asked the assistant to put her old shoes in the box, she'd wear the new ones. That morning she'd gone to work in Eileen's white blouse, her red skirt and Bernie's new black jacket. She'd bemoaned the condition of her coat and explained the reason for wanting to look her best to Bernie, who generously offered to lend her the jacket. With the grey hat she'd bought for Mary-Kate's wedding, Mrs Craig had remarked how smart she looked and was she off somewhere special on her afternoon off? She'd replied that she was going shopping as her friend was getting married soon, which was partly the truth.

Copeland and Lye was only a few yards down the street, past Boots the Chemist and the La Scala Theatre. The doorman held the revolving doors for her and she smiled her thanks. Once inside, the opulence caused her self-confidence to waver, but she gripped her bag tightly and walked down the carpeted stairs. She had very little idea of the layout of the building. The first time she had come it had been such a humiliating experience that she'd tried to forget it.

She stopped at the first of many cosmetic counters and looked over the array of bottles and jars, picked up one labelled 'Mercurizing Wax'.

'Can I help you?' the assistant asked politely.

She put down the jar. 'No, thank you, I was just looking.'

She turned and crossed the floor and caught sight of the lift. The attendant was a girl about her own age, dressed in a tartan kilt, a white blouse with ruffles at the neck, and a short black velvet jacket. There were other people in the lift, most of them women. Bridget stepped inside.

'Which floor please?'

'Oh, which floor are dresses, please?'

'Inexpensive Gowns are on the third floor to the left, Exclusive Gowns are to the right.'

She stood in silence as the lift ascended. It looked as though all the passengers were going to the third floor, she thought, and they were all much better dressed than she.

As she stepped out she looked around, confused and nervous. Who should she ask for? Who in fact should she ask? She began to feel more and more apprehensive. Should she go back and ask the lift attendant?

'It's Miss O'Donnell, isn't it?'

She spun round. 'Oh, yes!' she stammered. It was the gentleman who always sat in the corner.

'Are you shopping or meeting someone?'

'Er, no . . . do you work here?'

'Yes.'

'Oh, I wonder could you help me then? Who do I ask for . . . for a position here?'

'What as? We have a restaurant on the top floor and a coffee lounge on the second floor.'

'No! No, I would like to work here.' She gestured towards the rows of dresses hanging on racks.

'Oh, I see.'

'I've always wanted to work somewhere like this. I have tried before.' She opened her bag and brought out Mrs O'Leary's letter, now rather creased and dog-eared, and handed it to him.

He read it carefully. 'I was about to go for tea, but perhaps I will have it here instead. Will you join me?'

She was at a loss for words. She didn't like to refuse the invitation, yet all she wanted was to speak to someone in the department. She wanted a job, not afternoon tea. But she nodded.

'We'll walk, it's often quicker than the lift.'

She followed him as they crossed the floor and descended a wide flight of stairs. He seemed far more confident in these surroundings, she thought. He nodded and exchanged a few words with other members of staff who passed by. At the bottom of the stairs was a large, circular area cordoned off from the staircase and furnished with small tables and fragile-looking chairs. Potted shrubs were tastefully arranged around the room and in one corner a small orchestra played soft chamber music. As he guided her towards a table, Bridget wondered why he came to Craig's when this was so much more luxurious.

When the waitress arrived, in a brown dress and cream cap and apron he ordered two cream teas.

'Thank you, Mr Duncan, sir,' the girl replied.

'Is she a friend of yours?' she ventured.

'No. I have a confession to make to you. I overheard you yesterday asking about a vacancy here.'

She blushed and looked away. If he'd heard that then he must have heard the reply.

'It wasn't very kind of them, was it, to suggest the Packing Department, but I'm afraid those three are not particularly nice girls.'

'I don't suppose they meant to be nasty.'

The teas arrived. A bone-china teapot, china cups with gold rims and the letters C & L intertwined in gold around the rims and a plate of scones, with fresh cream and jam in silver pots, were all placed deftly on the table.

'Don't you like working for Mrs Craig?' He asked, pouring the tea and studying her. Of course, he didn't know her that well, but she seemed a quiet, sincere girl and one of the few with whom he felt at ease. He'd heard her ask about a job and heard the reply and he'd felt sorry for her. She didn't deserve such treatment. Those three were the epitome of everything he disliked about most women. By nature he was quiet and rather retiring and he'd always shied away from anything violent, coarse or crude. Many of the girls he'd come in contact with fell into the latter categories. Their forward behaviour, the sly innuendoes, their malicious tongues filled him with repugnance and the fear that such characteristics would be used against him. Miss O'Donnell was different. He realized that she was speaking.

'I do like working for Mrs Craig, but I've already told

you why I want to leave and, after all, I do know quite a lot about clothing, the sewing and making-up, things like that.'

He made up his mind. 'I don't usually do this sort of thing, Miss O'Donnell, but I have watched you work and with your honesty and that reference, I'll do my best for you. Business is always brisk at this time of year. Would you like to wait and finish your tea?'

She stared hard at him. Who was he? 'May I ask your name?'

'Ian Duncan and I'm a departmental manager, here. Actually I'm the head of department for Gentlemen's Outfitting.'

Oh, surely someone in heaven was watching over her today, she thought as she watched him walk away. If he couldn't get her a job here then no one could! He had overheard her and he had probably deliberately given her that florin to test her. The reason why he nearly always sat alone became clear. Someone in his position wouldn't mix with ordinary sales assistants. She drank the tea without tasting it and the scones remained untouched.

It couldn't be this easy, it just couldn't! But then she'd often heard Archie say that the 'gaffers' always stuck together and helped each other and that it wasn't what you knew, but who you knew that counted. She'd never imagined that anyone like him would take an interest in her. Enough to help her anyway. Another thought struck her. He had to have a reason – what would he expect from her in return? Everyone knew that Jeannie MacBride, the supervisor at MacFarlane's, had got her position by 'carrying on' as Bernie put it, with Robbie

Frazer, the under manager. What if he expected her to reciprocate in a similar way?

She saw him coming back and stood up. She'd have to make it clear that anything like that was out of the question, even if it meant losing this chance.

'I've had a word with Miss Whyte, she's the manageress of the Inexpensive Gowns Department, and she'll see you.'

'Thank you, but . . .'

'But what?'

Bridget just didn't know how to say it without sounding terribly offensive and insensitive. 'Nothing . . . thank you.' As she followed him she felt despondent. She'd lost her chance to put the matter straight all because she was too afraid to come right out and say what she thought. Now she'd be in his debt.

Mr Duncan ushered her into a small room, not unlike Gladys Drinkwater's office, where a tall woman stood behind a desk. Bridget turned towards him apprehensively.

'I'll leave you in Miss Whyte's capable hands. Goodbye, Miss O'Donnell.'

'Goodbye and . . . thank you.'

The door closed and Miss Whyte sat down and motioned her to do the same. She sat on a straight-backed wooden chair facing the woman. She was about as old as Mrs Craig, she judged, and was of a similar build but there the similarity ended. Miss Whyte had a fresh complexion and piercing blue eyes. Her hair was a salt and pepper colour and was worn in an old-fashioned, no-nonsense style. But she was smiling. Bridget smiled back nervously.

'I believe you have a very good reference, Miss O'Donnell. May I see it?'

Again the letter was produced and carefully read.

'And what have you been doing since you left Ireland?'

'I'm employed as a waitress at Craig's Tea Rooms.'

'Have you worked there ever since you came to Glasgow?'

'No.' Bridget looked down at her hands. Miss Whyte would know all the clothing manufacturers and she would know that MacFarlane's was in the heart of the Gorbals. There was no point lying. She looked up. 'When I first came here I took the first job that was offered to me. I knew no one, except a girl I was at school with in Ireland. I worked as a machinist at MacFarlane's.'

She waited for the expression to change. For the smile to turn to a frown.

'Then you will know all about the manufacturing process, which is helpful. Can you sew by hand?'

'Yes, ma'am.'

'Good. We also do alterations here. Do you live in the Gorbals?'

Bridget's heart sank, but she nodded firmly. 'That is another reason why I want a good job. I hate it and I'm trying to get out.'

Miss Whyte's gaze was steady. 'It's very easy to condemn everyone who lives there as thieves and blackguards, but I know full well that there are decent people, forced by circumstances, to live there. My own parents spent their early life there.'

'I see.'

'So, Miss O'Donnell, I'm not prejudging you. It

doesn't matter to me where you live or where you come from or even what your religion is, just as long as you work well and have the good name of the firm at heart. This is a very prestigious store and our aim is to keep it that way. Our reputation is very precious to us – all of us. Nothing else matters.'

'I understand that, ma'am.'

'Good. Then I can start you as a sales assistant and alteration hand at a wage of eighteen shillings a week. We also provide you with a uniform, a brown skirt and cream blouse, which we expect you to keep neat and clean at all times. We do not allow jewellery, make-up, hair decorations, coloured shoes or fancy stockings.'

Bridget just stared at her in astonishment, unable to believe her ears.

'Will you need to give Mrs Craig notice?'

'Oh, yes! A week, I believe. Oh, thank you, ma'am. I can't tell you how much I appreciate this.'

'Actions speak louder than words, Miss O'Donnell. All you have to do to prove your appreciation is to work hard and give first-class service to the customer.'

'Oh, I will, ma'am, I will!'

'Then I will see you in a week's time. We open at nine sharp, but you will be expected to be here by eight-thirty to make sure your counters are dusted and tidied and stocked, but we'll talk more about that when you start.' Miss Whyte rose and extended her hand.

Bridget shook it. 'May I have a look round before I leave, just to see where things are?'

'Of course. For the moment you are a potential customer. You may browse to your heart's content.'

As she wandered through the department, noting the

types of dresses, the materials used and their prices, Bridget could not believe her luck. She would go straight over and tell Mrs Craig; that would only be fair. She wasn't looking forward to telling her, but she had to think of herself. Perhaps one day she would go to Craig's as a customer. It was a novel thought and one that made her want to dance down the carpeted staircase. Instead she restrained herself to a sedate descent. She'd done it! Oh, it was a wonderful feeling to know that you'd got what you'd always yearned for. Now she knew what Gina must feel. Wait until she told Bernie! Oh, she'd soon be able to get out of the Gorbals. Eighteen shillings a week. She would be able to rent somewhere clean and quiet for about nine or ten shillings. As soon as she got home she'd write to Mary-Kate and Ma and Gina!

Mrs Craig had been very upset. 'Oh, Bridget, how am I going to manage without you? I had such high hopes for you.'

'I'm sorry, Mrs Craig, you've been very good to me and I have enjoyed working here.' Bridget felt so guilty.

'What if I offered you another two shillings a week?'

That made her feel worse. 'I'm sorry, but it wouldn't make any difference to how I feel. You see, it's what I've always wanted. It's what I left Ireland for. The chance of a career in a shop like that.'

'I can see that you have made up your mind. Well, good luck to you, Bridget.'

'I'll work my week's notice, so that you can get a replacement. I wouldn't leave you short-handed.'

Mrs Craig sighed deeply. 'I suppose it's back to the

agency and a string of replacements until I find one that suits.'

Impulsively, Bridget had leaned over and kissed her on the cheek.

'You'll find someone soon, I know you will.' Then she'd had a bright idea. 'In fact, I know someone who would jump at the opportunity.'

'You do?'

'Yes. She has experience of working in a bakery, not serving unfortunately, but she would learn quickly and she's quiet and honest and trustworthy. She's younger than I am but maybe that would be better. You could train her and I'm certain she would stay with you for years.'

'Who is this paragon?'

'Eileen Dalrymple. She is the sister of my friend's fiancé. Shall I bring her with me tomorrow?'

'Yes, bring her along, and we will see.'

Bridget wanted to stop off at Feinstein's Bakery on her way home, but thought better of it. Just in case Mrs Craig found Eileen unsuitable, she didn't want her to lose the job she already had. Eileen deserved her chance, too, she thought. Oh, what a glorious day it had been.

As she opened the door she saw the envelope on the floor and picked it up. It was postmarked 'London'. It was the first letter she'd ever had from Gina. Of course, Mary-Kate kept her up to date with all Gina's news, but Gina wasn't exactly a prolific writer. Bridget tore it open. Inside was a brief note and a ticket.

Dear Bridget,

I've sent you a ticket for my opening night. You simply *must* come! It's going to be wonderful and

The Sisters O'Donnell

I've taken a box for you and Mary-Kate – the best
seats in the house, no less!
Love Gina

She looked at the ticket. It was for a box at the Theatre
Royal for the opening of 'Steamboat' for the fifteenth of
the month. She sighed heavily and frowned. That was the
day she started working at Copeland and Lye!

Chapter Fifteen

———◆———

MARY-KATE SMILED AS SHE opened the letter. It wasn't often Gina took the time and trouble to write. She read the brief, scrawled note and looked at the tickets and her smile faded. Lewis wouldn't go. He'd consider it a total waste of time and money. She looked up and caught sight of herself in the small mirror in the centre of the hallstand. Had marriage changed her? Or was it Lewis who had changed? All she'd ever wanted was to be a wife and mother and now she often wondered if the desire to achieve those objects had blinkered her vision, obscuring the reality of marriage.

She hadn't loved him, they had both known that, but somehow she'd thought that love would grow, but it hadn't. She'd finally admitted to herself that she was guilty of longing for a romantic fairy-tale love affair as Bridget was. It had all happened so fast and she had been in love with the idea of marriage. So much so that she had refused to even contemplate what it really entailed. She could never think about their wedding night without a tinge of colour creeping into her cheeks. It had been so repulsive and degrading and she had lain there, every muscle taut and rigid, biting back the cries of pain. Afterwards she had quietly cried herself to sleep and the following day they had both acted as if it had never happened at all. She had been so tempted to fling herself into her Ma's arms and beg her to take her home, but she couldn't do that. She had to appear the contented new wife, happy with her lot. But the day that Sarah had left she had hugged Mary-Kate and whispered, 'It takes time, Mary-Kate. Give it time,' and she'd known then that Sarah had seen beneath the veneer.

Lewis had been pleasant and courteous, he still was, and on the surface she appeared calm, but inside she seethed with a mass of conflicting emotions. In the end, with no one else to turn to, she'd gone to confession. Not to confess, but to ask advice, and even that had been an agony of embarrassment and it hadn't helped. Oh, Father Dean had been kind enough, but his advice all boiled down to one thing. She was his wife and she must accept everything that that word entailed.

The only thing that had kept her from packing up and leaving was Ellen. The child's face lit up each day when she woke her and the hug and the greeting, 'I like coming home to you, Ma!' almost made up for the torments of the marriage bed.

Mary-Kate peered at her reflection. A faint crease was appearing between her brows. She would have to stop frowning. She had got what she wanted. Far more than she had envisaged and there were times when she felt guilty and ungrateful. God had given her far more than she had ever prayed for and the least she could do was to be thankful. Time and again she told herself not to be such a fool, she would get used to it – in time, as Sarah had advised. But it didn't really help. She didn't blame Lewis, she blamed herself. Of course, she'd learned more about him since they'd been married. He was a man set in his ways and a young wife was not about to change those ways. She'd found that he could be stubborn and a little mean where money was concerned. Not that she was extravagant; she prided herself on being prudent and economical. It had been Ellen's birthday present that had caused the first real disagreement between them and had caused her to stand up for her beliefs.

Ellen wanted a bicycle and when Mary-Kate had first told Lewis this she had been taken aback by his reaction.

'A bicycle! Does she think I'm made of money?'

'Lewis it's her birthday! She's outgrown dolls and doll's houses.'

'I don't approve of young girls riding bicycles.'

'That's ridiculous! Lots of girls have them now.'

'Young ladies don't!'

'Young ladies most certainly do! Don't be so old-fashioned. Doctor Salmon's girls all have them, it's good exercise according to him, and Ellen's set her heart on it.'

'It's much too expensive! She had a small fortune spent on her at Christmas.'

'Lewis it's not Ellen's fault that her birthday falls so close to Christmas and besides, the things she got were small items. She didn't ask for a bicycle then, did she?'

'She knew she wouldn't get one!'

'Lewis, please . . . ?'

'She can twist you around her little finger, Mary-Kate. She's spoilt.'

'No more spoilt than her sister is,' she'd retorted, heatedly.

'What's that supposed to mean?'

'Only that it seems strange that you hand out money to Elizabeth for the least little thing, when she has a husband who is supposed to support her. Oh, I know she's only been once lately, but I don't know how often she used to come before we were married. You can't call that fair treatment, to deny Ellen her birthday present and give Elizabeth whatever she wants just to avoid one of her tantrums!'

It was the first time she'd ever mentioned that she knew what Elizabeth came for and Lewis had turned away from her, a cold look in his eyes, his mouth a tight, thin line. But Mary-Kate had been determined that now it was out in the open, she was going to let him know her views.

'I don't know what excuses she offers or what tales of woe she uses, but really, Lewis, she does have a good, hard-working husband. She shouldn't need to come to you for money. If she can't manage on Ernest's salary, she should get some kind of work. We are not a charitable institution.'

'She's never worked. Molly wouldn't hear of it and I . . . I indulged them both.'

'As it was your privilege to do, Lewis. But think how badly Ernest must feel? Would you be happy if your wife was running to her father for money? Of course you wouldn't! It's undermining his self-respect and it's demeaning.'

Lewis had nodded his agreement, reluctantly.

'I'm sorry if I have upset you by speaking out like this,

but it's so unfair to everyone, particularly to you, Lewis. You work very hard, you've always given her the best of everything, but she's Ernest's responsibility now.'

Thus appealed to, he was mollified. 'You're right, my dear,' he had agreed, and Ellen had got her bicycle.

Mary-Kate looked at the other letter. It was from her Ma and she hesitated before she opened it. Hatred and bitterness were the dominant feelings in Clonmel now. But perhaps there was some good news. She opened it and began to read. The crease between her brows deepening again as she frowned with consternation. The Feehey's had suffered yet another tragedy. This time the house had been burned down, totally gutted, and Michael had been hurt trying to defend his home and his parents, despite the fact that everyone thought he was in league with the Irregulars. Apparently his wound had been slight, but when the army had arrived he had disappeared and no one knew where he was and his poor father was distracted. A couple of men from Cahir had come to the farm asking pointed questions and Sarah had given them the rough side of her tongue. But they'd returned later when Matty and Uncle Richard were home and they had allowed them into the house, despite the fact that they were obviously Irregulars, and Mary-Kate knew how she felt about them. Only when Sarah had resorted to hurling everything from the flat iron, to her best soup tureen at them had they left and then she'd given both her brother and her son a piece of her mind. And now they were reduced to eating off chipped enamel dishes until she could replace smashed plates, all of which 'those two great eejits' could pay for!

At this news Mary-Kate went white. Oh, what right

did she have to be discontent with her lot when Ma and Matty and Uncle Richard lived in such danger! And what was wrong with Matty? Didn't he know that getting mixed up with *them* would only cause trouble? Look how it had torn the Feehey family apart and utterly ruined them. Oh, she'd write today and give Matty O'Donnell a piece of her mind, too!

When Lewis came home at lunchtime, which he sometimes did now, he noticed her preoccupation.

'Is something wrong? You look pale?'

'I had a letter from Ma this morning.' Mary-Kate set his meal down in front of him before handing him the letter.

He read it quickly. 'I would have thought Matty was sensible enough not to get mixed up with anyone from either side. Doesn't he realize he has responsibilities? Does he want to end up like this Feehey boy?'

'I intend to write to him and say just that.' She toyed with the food on her plate, her appetite gone. 'Lewis, I'm worried about Ma. Seriously worried.'

'Your mother is one of the most sensible and redoubtable women I've ever met, Mary-Kate. She saw them off smartish and I doubt they'll be back! She'll cope.'

'But what if things get worse?'

'I don't think they will. I believe there is talk of some sort of treaty and a Boundary Commission or something, that will let the counties of the north stay within the Empire. That should pacify everyone. And the government of the Free State seems to be rounding up and successfully stamping out these Irregulars. Was there any other post?'

Lewis had dismissed the subject, she thought. She had been going to ask him if Sarah could come and stay until things did get better. 'There was a note from Gina and two tickets for her opening night.'

'She wants us to go to London?'

'Yes. She's starring in a new musical play called "Steamboat".'

He pushed his empty plate away and tucked his thumbs into the pockets of his waistcoat. 'At our expense, I presume?'

'Yes, but the tickets are expensive ones. She's taken a box. She's invited Bridget, too. She doesn't say if she's asked Ma to come over.'

'When?'

'The fifteenth.'

'It's out of the question. It would mean at least two days in London, an hotel – and they don't come cheap – and I would have to leave Johnson in charge and I just can't afford to do that. I'm expecting the answer on a contract, a large contract, and I can't leave things to Johnson. I'm sorry.'

'It doesn't matter, Lewis.' She had known what his answer would be all along.

'Are you quite sure you are not ill? You've hardly touched your meal.'

'I'm fine, Lewis!'

'Ellen hasn't been in any trouble has she?'

'Ellen? No, why?'

'I've noticed that she's getting very boisterous lately.'

'She's growing up. She's at that stage when she's all arms and legs, like a young colt.' Mary-Kate paused a moment. 'Lewis, would you object if I took Ellen to

London? It would be such a treat for her and I would like to see Gina.'

He frowned. 'She could have come to our wedding if she'd wanted to!'

'You know why she didn't come.' Mary-Kate had been hurt when Gina had finally written with her explanation, but Gina had said that 'show business', as she called it, was such a cut-throat world that if you wanted to succeed you had to snatch every opportunity and that she knew Mary-Kate would understand. Oh, she'd understood, but she'd still felt hurt.

Lewis studied her closely. She looked different; thinner and paler and her face appeared to have a pinched look around the nose. In his way he did care for her. He was grateful to her for the ease with which his life now ran. He hadn't expected her to be a smouldering siren in bed, and he wouldn't have wanted that, but it was patently obvious that she disliked their love-making, although she did try to hide the fact. But he hadn't married her for that reason. He'd married her to stop the gossip, to run his home, to keep Ellen in check, but most of all to give him the son he desperately wanted. But as yet she showed no sign of becoming pregnant and it annoyed him. Perhaps if she were to have a short break it might help.

'All right, my dear, take Ellen with you. Go and see Gina's triumphant debut; it will do you good!'

'Oh, Lewis! Thank you!'

'But I don't want Ellen getting any foolish ideas about following in her aunt's footsteps.'

Mary-Kate rose and kissed him lightly on the cheek as she removed the empty dishes. 'She won't. And thank you again, Lewis. I'll write to Gina this evening.'

*

Ellen was speechless with delight, but only for a few minutes. Then a torrent of questions poured from her lips.

Mary-Kate put her hands over her ears in mock dismay. 'If you don't stop this minute, Ellen, you shan't go!'

Ellen pulled a face and clamped a hand over her mouth in a comic gesture. 'There, I'm quiet now,' she muttered through her fingers.

Mary-Kate laughed. 'I want you to go and thank your Pa, properly.'

'He'll be cross if I interrupt him.'

'No, he won't, not if you do it the right way.'

'Which way?'

'Don't just walk in and say, "Thank you, Pa, for letting me go to London." Sometimes I think you're two people, Ellen, you behave so differently towards him and me.'

'He's not like you. He always makes me feel as though I've done something wrong when I haven't.'

'That's a terrible thing to say! Now, go and say thank you and give him a kiss.'

Ellen looked startled. 'Kiss Pa?'

'Why not? I used to kiss my Pa if he went away, before I went to bed, or if he gave me a present.'

'I don't think Pa likes being kissed.'

'How do you know if you've never tried? Now go on!'

She watched Ellen cross the hall and knock on the dining room door and she made a shooing gesture with her hand to encourage the child to go in. She sighed, wondering if things had always been like this. There was no show of affection between any of the Vannins in public, and not much in private either, although Ellen was an affectionate child.

The doorbell rang and she called to Vi that she would answer it. It was Elizabeth.

'How nice to see you, Elizabeth! We haven't seen you for some weeks, is everything all right? How is Ernest?'

'We are fine, thank you. Is my father in?'

'Yes, he's in the dining room with Ellen. I'll tell them you're here.'

'Now what's she been up to? Has she been sent home from school again?'

Mary-Kate's expression hardened. 'It's half term and she hasn't been *up* to anything, quite the opposite!' She knocked on the dining room door and opened it. The sight that met her eyes was just what she had hoped for. Lewis had pushed his chair back and Ellen stood at his knee. Both heads were bent in mutual interest over something in the newspaper. Lewis's arm was around the child's shoulder. Mary-Kate smiled. Elizabeth's timing was perfect and by the look on her face Mary-Kate could see that she was decidedly put out. She wondered if Elizabeth's manner towards her sister was prompted by jealousy.

'Ma, look, there's something about Aunt Gina in the paper!' Then Ellen saw Elizabeth and her smile faded.

'If your Pa has finished with the paper, why don't you take it and read it in the kitchen. I'm sure Vi will be interested. Elizabeth's come to visit and you won't be interested in "grown up" talk, as you call it.'

'Off you go, Ellen, and take the paper with you. But don't get it muddled up.' Lewis smiled, giving the child a gentle push.

When she reached Mary-Kate, Ellen stopped. 'Aunt Gina's going to be famous. Will that make us famous, too, Ma?'

Mary-Kate laughed. 'No it won't.'

Ellen turned to her sister. 'Aunt Gina's going to be in a musical play called "Steamboat" in London and she's going to be famous and Ma and I are going to see her and we're going to stay in an hotel and we're having a box at the Royal Theatre!'

'The Theatre Royal,' Mary-Kate corrected. 'Now off you go, Miss Giddy-Gaddy!'

Elizabeth said nothing but Mary-Kate noticed the set of her chin. So that was it. She'd come for money!

'If you don't mind, I would like to speak to my father alone.'

'I do mind, as it happens.'

They both looked at her. Lewis with speculation and Elizabeth with amazement.

'What I have to say is private!'

'Your father is my husband!'

Lewis rose. So, the confrontation had come at last. 'Whatever you have to say can be said in front of Mary-Kate, Elizabeth.'

'Really, Father! You don't honestly expect me to . . . to . . .'

'To ask for pin money in front of me? Oh, come, Elizabeth, do you take me for a complete fool? I know the only reason you visit is for money to buy something that Ernest either can't or won't buy for you. What is it for this time?'

Elizabeth's cheeks flamed. 'How dare you!'

'No! How dare you, Elizabeth! You have a good

husband who provides for you as well as he can, it's about time you learned to curb your extravagances. Your father works too hard to have his money wasted!'

'Pa! Are you going to stand there and let her insult me like that!'

'Is it insulting to hear the truth?' he said quietly. Despite her words, Mary-Kate's voice had remained calm and, unintentionally, he took his cue from her. ·

'Oh, this is intolerable! Insufferable! You are quite prepared to spend a small fortune on a jaunt to London for her and that precocious little wretch, just so she can see some second-rate show that her sister has probably got a "bit" part in, and yet I can't even have a few pounds for . . .'

'Elizabeth, I suggest you leave before things are said that are best left alone,' Lewis interrupted. It had always galled him that his elder daughter took it for granted that she only had to mention the fact that her dead mother would turn in her grave if she knew how he was treating her, denying her the little luxuries she loved, and that Molly had always given her, and that he would provide the required amount. Mary-Kate was right and he should have put his foot down long ago, he knew that, it was emotional blackmail. But he had always given in. Mainly through the desire for peace but also because at the back of his mind he had the uneasy feeling that Molly would reproach him. But Mary-Kate had changed all that and made him see how foolish and superstitious he'd been.

Elizabeth was so furious that she was nearly in tears. How dare he take that woman's part! What was she? A jumped-up servant, nothing more! 'I don't know what you've said to turn him against me, but I know you for what you are, Mary-Kate O'Donnell! A grasping, scheming, conniving . . . bitch! You're not fit to live in my mother's house, let alone sleep in her bed! It's disgusting, that's what it is! Disgusting!'

'Elizabeth, get out of this house now!' Lewis thundered.

His voice fell on empty air. Elizabeth was half-way across the hall.

The slamming of the front door rattled all the windows and suddenly Mary-Kate felt sick and dizzy. She clutched the edge of the table.

'Oh, Lewis, I'm so sorry! I didn't mean to cause such a rift. Go after her.'

'Sit down, you're ill!' He pushed her gently down into a chair. 'You've nothing to apologize for and I'll be damned if I'm going after her. I should have sent her packing a long time ago. Let her manage on Ernest's salary. I can only apologize for the dreadful things she said.'

Her head was clearing. 'She was angry, Lewis. She probably didn't mean it.'

'Oh, yes she did! But don't let her upset you.'

'I hate to see your hard-earned money frittered away, Lewis. If I hadn't already promised Ellen we'd go, I'd write and tell Gina we can't make it.' Mary-Kate stood up, managing a wan smile. 'I'm all right now. I'll get Vi to bring in some tea.'

'You'll do no such thing. We both need a drink. When I think of the money I've lavished on her . . . the ungrateful . . .'

'Lewis, please! Everyone was upset I'm sure she'll calm down in time.'

He held out a glass of brandy and watched her sip it. 'I'm not going to stand for behaviour like that. You're my wife, Mary-Kate, and I'll not have her calling you names like that. Unless she apologizes – which she won't unless she is really in dire financial straits – she isn't welcome in my house.'

Mary-Kate took another sip and the liquid burned her throat. Oh, what a hornet's nest she had stirred up, but at least she'd put a stop to her step-daughter's parasitic habit, although she realized that she had made a serious enemy as a result.

Chapter Sixteen

'IT'S TOO TIGHT! CAN'T you do something with it?'
'Miss O'Donnell, unless you've put on weight overnight, it can't possibly be tight. You had your final fitting only yesterday. Now turn around and let me check that everything is just as it should be.'

Gina turned to face her dresser. Ellie was an old hand and completely disregarded all complaints and tantrums.

'I can hardly breathe, let alone sing!'

'You did just fine at rehearsal. It's nerves.'

It was nerves, she knew that, but she didn't need to be reminded that in ten minutes she would face the most daunting challenge of her career. The months of learning lines and songs and timing and endless rehearsals were all over and she felt sick.

'All I wanted to be was a singer – a famous singer! I never wanted to be an actress!' she had shouted at Edward after the first rehearsal had been a total disaster.

'You've known all along that it was a musical play and that you'd have to act as well. I seem to recall you begging me to move heaven and earth to get you the part. Now you've got it and, whether you like it or not, you're going to make a success of it,' he'd answered, coldly. So she had struggled on, despairing of ever being able to acquire the skill to act, and then, suddenly, it had clicked into place. If she imagined that she *was* Maybelle Leroy, immersed herself in the character, got into Maybelle's skin, as it were, then she found that all her stumbling self-consciousness was easily overcome. But it was the hardest lesson she'd ever had to learn.

Now she stood dressed in the pink and white flowered crinoline, frothing with frills and tightly nipped in at the waist, her own hair covered by a blonde wig styled in elaborate puffs and ringlets, ready for the biggest moment in her life. The thought terrified her.

'You'd best get along. You've got all those stairs to climb up and hitch that skirt up or you'll catch it on something and tear it or fall flat on your face!' Ellie instructed dryly.

'Are you sure I look just right? This wig feels as though it's slipping.'

'When I dress someone, nothing is left to chance! Now go on and mind you don't trip.'

The wide skirt was something of a nuisance and Gina found Ellie's advice sound as she made her way along the corridor to the wings. The stage had been transformed to look like the banks of the Mississippi River, complete with the steamboat, the *Magnolia Rose*, a replica in wood of a paddle steamer. Some of the cast, blacked up as negroes, were already on stage. She hitched up the cumbersome skirt higher, ready to ascend the concealed staircase that led to the upper deck.

'Gina I wouldn't have recognized you!'

'Oh, Edward! Fancy sneaking up on me like that. What are you doing here, you should be out the front.'

'I just wanted to say "Break a leg!" You certainly look the part.'

'I feel ill!'

He laughed. 'That's a good sign. No nerves, no performance! You'll be fine and we're all out there rooting for you, to use American parlance, which I think is quite apt in the circumstances.' Edward bent and kissed her on the cheek. 'Go on, you've got a packed house – if you don't make it tonight you never will! I'll have to go or I'll not get to my seat in time.'

He watched her go with a mixture of pride and affection. Oh, she was a handful at times, there was no doubt about that. But he admired her spirit and determination and she had an almost child-like belief that if she wanted something badly enough then she would surely get it. And beneath the tempestuous, often ruthless exterior, he sensed there was still a vulnerable young girl who could be hurt. Her very wilfulness and selfishness were weapons with which to combat disappointment, disillusionment and sensitivity, for no true artist could be totally without a core of sensitivity.

No staircase had ever looked so steep before. Gina's heart had never pounded as rapidly as before, either, and she was shaking. What if she forgot her lines, there were so many of them? What if she got dizzy up there on the platform that was the top deck? And, horror of horrors, what if she tripped on these damn skirts? Oh, she wished it were all over. The show had been a big hit on Broadway so there was no reason why it shouldn't be here. It just depended on – her! She swallowed hard. What would happen if when she got up there everything went completely blank, her mind frozen in sheer panic? The orchestra had finished tuning up and had begun to play the opening bars of 'Ole Man River'. She moved back, out of sight of the audience, for Maybelle Leroy didn't appear for ten more agonizing minutes.

Mary-Kate was reading the story to Ellen from the programme when Edward arrived.

'I'm sorry I'm so late, but I went to make sure Gina wasn't having hysterics. How are you, Mary-Kate?'

She smiled at him. He'd been kindness itself, making all the arrangements after she'd contacted him. He'd even arranged for someone to meet them at Euston Station and take them to the hotel to change and then a taxi cab had arrived to bring them to the theatre. 'I'm fine. *Is* Gina having hysterics?'

'Not quite, but she's as nervous as hell. Oh, I beg your pardon! This must be Ellen? How do you do, Ellen?' He extended his hand and smiled.

'How do you do, Mr Vinetti,' she replied, solemnly.

'Lewis is very busy,' Mary-Kate explained rather awkwardly. 'He's expecting to get an answer on a contract he's tendered for. If he gets it it will make a big difference to the business.'

'I'm glad he's busy, otherwise I couldn't have come!'

'Ellen!'

'She certainly doesn't mince her words, does she?' Edward laughed.

'Ma has read me the story, from the book, and it's so sad in parts, but isn't it romantic!'

'Now that's enough, Miss! I promised your Pa you wouldn't go getting any ideas about going on the stage.'

Edward grimaced. 'I should think one prima donna in the family is quite enough. Well, here we go, sit back and enjoy yourselves!'

As the curtain rose, Mary-Kate leaned forward, trying to pick out Gina, then she glanced at her programme and realized Gina wasn't due on just yet. She leaned back but handed the opera glasses to Ellen with the whispered instruction not to drop them.

The music was catchy, the set and costumes magnificent and when Gina at last appeared Mary-Kate gave a little gasp. Surely this wasn't the girl she'd waved goodbye to? Despite the blonde wig and the billowing crinoline that made her appear younger and very girlish, this was a young woman who oozed confidence and charm and, when she began to sing, Mary-Kate was amazed how much her voice had improved. Oh, how Gina had changed. There was an aura about her, a charisma that was electrifying. The young girl from the small Irish country town had gone. A woman with poise, vivacity and a talent to sing and act had taken her place. Now she knew what Edward had first seen in her. It was almost laughable that this young woman had failed to win a second-rate, provincial talent contest. Such was Gina's powerful portrayal of Maybelle that Mary-Kate soon forgot it was actually Gina and became as enthralled as Ellen.

Edward had at last relaxed. He had been almost as

tense as Gina, knowing that his own reputation, as well as hers, rested on her performance. He'd put his neck on the block for her. He'd cajoled, threatened and bribed to get her the part. After all, competition had been stiff and she was still a new name, an untried entity. They were all taking one hell of a risk. But now he knew he'd been right to trust his instincts. She was a true professional. He'd had serious qualms over her acting ability and there'd been so many rows and tantrums that he'd lost count, but tonight she was magnificent. Even the Southern drawl that she'd sworn that she would never master, sounded passable to everyone except anyone born in the South. There would be no holding her now and there was an irony in the words of her first song 'Only Make Believe, I Love You'. He hummed it to himself. Gina lived in a 'make believe' world. She wouldn't know reality if it hit her in the face, or rather she'd choose to ignore it.

Edward glanced at Mary-Kate, thinking how different she was from Gina. Oh, she was very elegant in a black, silk dress embroidered around the neck with beads and she wore a matching headband, but it was her serenity that impressed him. She obviously got on very well with the child, who was a pert little minx, but he wondered if she was happy with her elderly husband. With Mary-Kate you could never tell. Yet he knew from Gina that she was strong-minded when she chose to be and she also had a temper, although he could never imagine her indulging in the kind of screaming tantrums Gina threw.

When the curtain came down for the interval, amid resounding applause, Mary-Kate turned to him. 'Oh,

Edward wasn't she wonderful! I just can't believe it's really our Gina! She's changed so much and she's so talented. Now I know what you saw in her, she's going to be a big hit, isn't she?'

'Yes.'

She thought he didn't sound exactly overjoyed by this fact.

The door to the box opened and a waiter appeared bearing a bottle of champagne and glasses.

'It's always like a cattle stampede trying to get a drink, so I ordered in advance.'

'Oh, you shouldn't have, it must be so expensive!'

'In view of the fact that we couldn't make it to your wedding, I think it is the least I can do.'

Ellen was stage-struck and entranced by the beautiful girl who sang like an angel and who was actually her own aunt.

'Can Ellen have a drop, too?' Edward asked, coaxingly.'

'Oh, can I, Ma? Please? I won't tell Pa, I promise!'

'Oh, all right, but just a little! You're spoiling her Edward and she's already had her fair share of that!'

'I can see that,' he laughed as he poured a small amount into a glass and handed it to Ellen. 'To you and Lewis and to Gina!' He raised his glass.

'And to Gina and you!' Mary-Kate replied.

He smiled a little wryly. He was trying to keep his feelings for Gina under control.

'Will we see Aunt Gina when it's over?' Ellen asked excitedly.

'Of course. We're all going out to supper later.'

'Me, too?'

'You, too, although, like Cinderella, you must be in bed by midnight.'

'I'll do no good with her at all after this, Edward, you do realize that?' Mary-Kate laughed.

'A little excitement won't hurt either of you!'

Ellen handed back the glass. She hadn't really liked it much. 'It's starting again now! Ma, can I have the opera glasses? I want to see Aunt Gina more closely. You said her hair was red.'

'It is, that's a wig! Now hush!'

As the final curtain fell the applause was deafening and the cast received a standing ovation. Gina took four curtain calls! It was a success! She'd done it! She was a terrific hit! She was shaking, but now it was with emotion and tears trickled down her cheeks. If she were to drop down dead right now, she'd be a happy woman! The world was her oyster now. She could have a place of her own, dress in the height of fashion, frequent the Café Royal and the Ritz and everyone would recognize her and want her autograph! Her head was spinning as she dashed away the teardrops and hurried back to her dressing room, thrusting the bouquets into Ellie's arms.

'Did you hear them? Did you hear them, Ellie? Oh, I just can't believe its happening to me!'

'You were magnificent, Miss O'Donnell. Here, let me get you out of that dress, they'll all be hammering on the door in five minutes and you'll need a police escort to get out!'

Even as she began to unbutton Gina's dress, there was a loud knock on the door.

'Miss O'Donnell isn't seeing anyone for at least fifteen minutes!' Ellie shouted in an authoritarian voice. She was well used to Stage Door Johnnies and the like.

'Is she decent, Ellie? It's Edward Vinetti and I have Miss O'Donnell's sister with me!'

Gina was struggling into a pale blue crêpe-de-chine robe. 'Oh, let them in, Ellie!' she cried, snatching off the wig and running her fingers through her hair.

With a cry of delight, Gina launched herself at Mary-Kate and hugged her. 'Oh, I was so nervous and so petrified that I'd forget my lines!'

Mary-Kate held her away from her. 'Gina! Oh, how you've changed and I'm so proud of you! I only wish Ma could have been here but she won't leave Matty or Uncle Richard.'

Edward produced another bottle of champagne. 'I think we've all got something to celebrate. Come on, Ellie, you as well!'

Gina bent down. 'And you must be Ellen. Mary-Kate has written and told me about you, but she didn't tell me you were so pretty!'

'Gina, she'll be impossible after tonight! And before you ask, Ellen, no, you can't have any more champagne, your Pa would be furious!'

'Oh, Ma!' Even though she hadn't really liked it she wanted to join in.

Gina laughed. 'How odd that sounds!'

'I've booked a table at the Café Royal,' Edward broke in. 'So we'll finish this and leave you to change. I'll bring the car around, but I'm warning you, your friends are all probably flocking around the stage door.'

Gina laughed delightedly.

Twenty minutes later, as she walked to the car, Gina felt as though she was walking on air. Oh, if only those sceptics back home could see her now! Wouldn't that fool, Michael Feehey, just eat his words. She laughed aloud as Edward drove off.

'What are you thinking?' Mary-Kate asked.

'The Sisters O'Donnell! Do you remember Michael Feehey and Dinny MacGee?'

Her words had a sobering effect on Mary-Kate. Obviously Gina hadn't heard about the Feehey's latest tragedy. 'Yes, but I don't think Michael will be thinking about us three.'

'Why?'

Briefly Mary-Kate told her and Gina frowned. She'd been too busy to take any notice of the snatches she'd heard about the trouble in Ireland and she'd only read the bits of both her Ma's and Mary-Kate's letters that really interested her. And Clonmel certainly didn't interest her any more.

'I was disappointed that Bridget didn't come. I thought she would at least have made an effort.'

Edward glanced sideways at her. 'She found herself in much the same position you did when Mary-Kate got married, and she took the same decision – you of all people shouldn't blame her for that.'

'Oh, don't start lecturing me, Edward, not tonight. Nothing is going to spoil tonight. Absolutely nothing!'

As Edward helped them all out of the car, Gina stared around her with smug satisfaction. 'The last time he brought me here I looked awful. Everyone looked at me as though I was something the cat had dragged in.'

'They won't tonight!' Mary-Kate said, proudly. Gina looked radiant.

'I could drink champagne until morning! I don't really feel hungry, Edward.'

'You've had nothing to eat for hours and I don't intend to have a repeat performance of you and Helen Mason's "celebration" of "Starlight and Syncopation".'

'Oh, he's such a kill-joy, isn't he?' Gina laughed as they were shown to their table. This time the gazes centred on them were approving and congratulatory and she beamed at everyone. The taste of success was so sweet!

'And what are you going to do now?' Mary-Kate asked as they waited for Edward to order.

'I won't have much time to sit back and enjoy myself, if that's what you mean. If tonight is anything to go by, the show will run forever! But I'm going to find time to get a place of my own. I've had enough of Rose and her rules and regulations, and when it's finished I'm going to give a grand party and you *must* come! You and Lewis, and you, too, Ellen, Bridget and Ma and oh, everyone! Even that awful Elizabeth that you write about! Oh, she'll be green with envy, will that one!'

Edward nudged her and inclined his head in Ellen's direction.

Ellen was unperturbed. 'Lizzie wouldn't come. She hates it when people have nicer things than she does and she's not the centre of everyone's attention. And if she came, I wouldn't!' she added flatly.

'That's no way to talk about your sister, Ellen,' Mary-Kate reprimanded her. 'And you know what Grandma told you about little girls being seen and not heard?'

Edward was trying to hide his amusement while Gina looked a little puzzled.

'Grandma? Of course, you mean Ma! I just can't get used to it all.'

'And what is Bridget doing?' Edward asked, thinking a change of subject was called for.

'She has finally got the job she wanted. It's in a very exclusive shop in the centre of Glasgow and she has ambitions to get on. She's still living with Bernie O'Hagan who is getting married, by the way,' Mary-Kate said, turning to Gina.

'Not before time either. I don't know how Bridget can bear to live in the same house as that tinker.'

'Bernie's been a good friend to her,' Mary-Kate said quietly.

Gina frowned and ignored this statement, then her expression changed. 'Look, here's Helen and the crowd!' She waved to the group who had just arrived.

Edward looked slightly sour as Helen, followed by Freddie Marshalsea and Jimmie Masters detached themselves and came over to their table.

Helen hugged Gina. 'Gina! You were absolutely fantastic! You'll be all the rage tomorrow. I'm green with envy. Aren't you going to introduce us?' Helen enthused.

'This is my sister, Mary-Kate Vannin and her daughter, Ellen, and Edward you already know. This is my friend, Helen Mason, Mary-Kate, and this is Lord Frederick Marshalsea and The Honourable James Masters.'

'It's Freddie and Jimmie to friends, charmed to meet you, Mrs Vannin.' Freddie shook Mary-Kate's hand. 'Wasn't she just *perfect* tonight? You must be so proud of her?'

'I am – we all are.'

'I say, why don't we all sit down together? Have a bit of a party, what?' Freddie suggested.

Helen clapped her hands in delight and Gina was about to move her chair when Edward interrupted.

'Perhaps another night, this is really a family get-together. Gina hasn't seen her sister for so long and this supper is a treat for Ellen. I'm sure you understand?' He looked meaningfully at Ellen.

'Oh, yes, of course. See what you mean, old chap. Don't want to intrude on the family, do we? We'll make it another night, Gina. Have a good time, nice to meet you all.'

'I'll call you tomorrow, Gina,' Helen said, waving airily as they went to join the rest of their party.

Gina scowled at Edward. 'Why couldn't they have joined us, Mary-Kate wouldn't have minded, would you?'

'No, they seemed very nice.'

'But they're a little cosmopolitan for Ellen, don't you think, Gina?'

She knew what he meant and she supposed he was right, but she was still annoyed.

'What's "cosmopolitan"?' Ellen asked.

'It means you wouldn't have understood half of the conversation and you'd have been bored silly and we don't want that, do we?' Edward answered, smiling. In his opinion Helen and her friends were not fit company for Mary-Kate either.

'Aunt Gina, the girls in school will never believe me when I tell them about you! Could you write something special on my programme?'

Her good humour restored, Gina borrowed Edward's

pen and wrote, 'To my niece, Ellen Vannin, with lots of love, Gina O'Donnell.' She paused and then added. 'And I expect to see you at the party I'm going to give to celebrate the success of "Steamboat".'

'Oh, Gina, don't encourage her!'

'Why not? It's good for girls to have dreams. We all had dreams and we're all making them come true. You dream away, Ellen.'

Edward frowned again as he caught Mary-Kate's eye. Gina was so impetuous; she never thought before she spoke and Ellen was obviously identifying herself with Gina and that would only cause trouble for Mary-Kate later.

Mary-Kate was beginning to feel uncomfortable. What if, in a fit of her natural exuberance, Ellen told Lewis all about this evening. He would be horrified and he would blame her. Her head had begun to ache a little and she felt hot. If it wasn't for the fact that she would have upset Gina and seemed ungracious to Edward, she would have preferred to have gone back to the hotel. It had been a long day, a long journey and she was tired out.

'Are you going to see some of the sights while you're here?'

She realized Edward was speaking to her, but his voice was very muffled and with dawning horror she knew that she was going to faint. A mist swam before her eyes. It cleared and she saw his face and Ellen's, then it became a fog and the fog became total darkness.

When she came to, she was lying on a chaise longue in the restaurant vestibule and Edward, Gina and a strange man were bending over her. She struggled to rise.

'Oh, I'm sorry . . .' The mist threatened to envelope her again.

'Lie back, Mary-Kate. You fainted, you must rest for a few minutes before we take you back to the hotel.'

'Where's Ellen?'

'I'm here, Ma!'

She heard the sob in the child's voice and struggled to rise again. Once more Edward gently pushed her back and then Ellen was standing beside her. Mary-Kate took her hand. 'There's nothing to worry about, Ellen, I'm fine. It was just a bit too hot.'

Ellen suddenly burst into tears and clasped her arms around her neck. 'Oh, Ma! I'm frightened! I don't want you to get ill! I don't want you to die, too!'

Edward gently prised her away from Mary-Kate. 'Ellen, she's not going to die, get that right out of your head! She just fainted. It's probably all the travelling, the excitement, the champagne and the heat in here. Now be a good girl and stop crying, you're upsetting your Ma. I'm going to take you both back to the hotel, so she can rest, and this gentleman is a doctor and he's kindly agreed to come with us.'

Gina was far from pleased with a situation that was fast developing into something of a fiasco. Mary-Kate was absolutely ruining her evening and it just wasn't fair! 'Oh, I feel such a fool! Everyone is looking at us!' she hissed crossly.

'I thought that was what you wanted?' Edward snapped.

'Don't be facetious!' she snapped back.

The doctor was quietly talking to Mary-Kate in the background. Gina glared at Edward. It was probably all

316

his fault anyway. Mary-Kate wasn't used to drink and he'd probably been plying her with it half the evening!

'Are you feeling better now?' she asked her sister a little more graciously, stung by Edward's remark.

Mary-Kate nodded.

Gina turned to Edward. 'And just what am I supposed to do while you take them back?'

'I would have thought you'd have wanted to come with us? Of course you could join your friends, I'm sure they're far better company.' His tone was biting with sarcasm.

She glowered back. Indirectly he was calling her selfish. 'There won't be room for everyone in the car!' Couldn't he see what he was doing? This was *her* night and he knew how hard she'd worked for it! She deserved her night of glory.

Mary-Kate was getting up, assisted by the doctor. 'Gina, you stay, and so must you Edward. You've both worked so hard and Gina's done so well that she deserves to enjoy herself tonight, and I'm just spoiling it for her.'

'Mary-Kate, you can't go back to the hotel by yourself!' Edward insisted.

'I'll look after Ma! I'll take care of her!'

He smiled. 'You're a brave girl, Ellen, but I'm sure the doctor will agree with me that we can't let you take on such a responsibility.'

The colour was slowly coming back to Mary-Kate's cheeks.

'She's looking a lot better,' Gina pointed out. She'd only fainted, she wasn't on her death-bed, she thought. Although by the fuss they were all making you'd think she was! She couldn't see any reason why this doctor and

Ellen couldn't take Mary-Kate back to the hotel and she said so.

Edward caught her arm and pulled her a few paces away. 'You selfish bitch!' he hissed. 'She's your sister who you've not seen for ages, and you didn't even go to her wedding! But she came to see you and now, just because it's ruined your plans, you want her to go back to an hotel with just a stranger and a child! My God, Gina! If I wasn't a gentleman I swear I'd hit you. You don't deserve a sister like that.'

She jerked her arm free and her eyes narrowed with rage. 'Go to hell!' she spat back, before turning and smiling at her sister.

'Gina, I'm so sorry,' Mary-Kate said uncomfortably.

'Don't be silly!' Gina leaned forward and kissed Mary-Kate on the cheek. 'The good doctor and I will follow in a cab and once we've seen you safely back, then Edward and I will come back here, won't we Edward?' It was a statement, not a question.

He nodded. 'I'll get them to call a cab.'

'Now that's settled, we'd better get you back, Mrs Vannin. Ladies in your condition should take life a little slower, you know,' the doctor advised, in a gently admonishing voice.

The smile was wiped from Gina's face to be replaced with a look of dazed disbelief. Mary-Kate was pregnant! So that was the reason for all the fuss! Why hadn't she said so? She looked at Edward and to her rising chagrin, he was smiling in that sardonic way she hated.

He took her arm as the doctor and Ellen, who clung like a limpet to her step-mother, assisted by the maitre d', helped Mary-Kate towards the door.

'That's quite a surprise, isn't it? She's certainly "upstaged" you, hasn't she, my dear Gina?'

'One of these days you're going to regret every insult, Edward Vinetti! Just you mark my words!' she said furiously through gritted teeth. Oh, how she hated him. Right now she could have cheerfully scratched out those dark mocking eyes!

Chapter Seventeen

——◆——

THEY'D GOT A TAXI from the station and Mary-Kate had sworn Ellen to secrecy about the whole incident, promising to come to her later on before she went to bed.

Lewis was already home and came out to take her bag.

'Did you enjoy yourselves? If I'd known which train you were coming on I'd have come for you.'

'I told you we'd get a taxi, Lewis. Gina was wonderful! It's such a pity you couldn't come. Did you get the contract?'

'Yes. Now I can buy a motorized lorry and I'll have to hire a new man.'

'I'm so glad! Has Vi been looking after you properly?'

'Good Heavens, you've only been gone for thirty-six hours! Well Ellen, did you enjoy yourself and what do you think of your Aunt Gina?'

'She's very pretty, Pa.'

'You don't sound terribly enthusiastic.'

'She's tired, Lewis. We both are. Ellen, go and ask Vi if we could have a pot of tea in the parlour and then go and unpack and get washed. I want to speak to your Pa.'

Ellen did as she was told. Mary-Kate and Lewis went into the parlour and she sank down thankfully on the sofa. He came and sat beside her.

'I missed you. The house was strangely quiet, as though something was missing.'

'Ellen's chatter probably. She's a little upset, Lewis. After the show, we went for supper at the Café Royal and I'm afraid I fainted. The poor child was terrified that there was something really wrong with me, that I was going to die.'

'You fainted? Why didn't you contact me? I'd have come to the station for you myself!'

'Oh, it's nothing serious, Lewis. I believe most women faint when they are in the early stages of . . . of having a baby.'

She'd never seen such a change in a man. He sprang to his feet as agilely as a man half his age, then he sat down again and gathered her in his arms.

'Oh, Mary-Kate! My dear, Mary-Kate! Why didn't you tell me? I wouldn't have let you go all that way by yourself and with the added responsibility of Ellen.'

'I didn't know, Lewis. I've been feeling a bit washed out and tired, but I thought nothing of it. It was a doctor who happened to be at the restaurant and who kindly attended me, who told me. He said to go and see my own doctor when I got back.'

'I'd almost given up all hope! Oh, you don't realize how happy you've made me, my dear!'

'Lewis, I had no idea that you wanted more children. I thought you felt you had enough with Elizabeth and Ellen?'

'Of course I want more children, Mary-Kate, and I know you'll give me the one thing I've always longed for. A son!'

A cold shiver went down Mary-Kate's spine, like someone walking over her grave. She thought of his first wife and what Mrs Rickard had said. 'Three she bore him and three she buried!' Oh, dear God, please don't let that happen to me, she prayed. She disentangled herself from his embrace as Vi brought in the tea tray. Lewis shooed Vi away and insisted on pouring her tea himself.

'You'll have to take great care of yourself.'

'It's not an illness, Lewis. I still have a home to run.'

'We'll get another girl in.'

'That would just be a waste of money, maybe later on.'

'Whatever you wish.'

She finished the tea, but she couldn't help thinking that this man, who had begrudged spending money on Ellen's birthday present and watched every penny piece, would employ a household of servants as price for a son. 'I promised to go up and see Ellen. Of course I haven't told her yet and I don't think she understood what the doctor meant by "my condition", she was too upset.'

Lewis helped her to her feet. 'I think I'll have a drink to celebrate!' he said, beaming.

Ellen was sitting on her bed fingering the programme Gina had signed. All her clothes had been put away and her hair had been brushed out.

'Did you tell Pa about not being well?'

'Yes, I told him and I told him why, too.'

The grey eyes regarded her seriously. 'Why?'

'Because soon you're going to have either a baby brother or a baby sister.'

Ellen let out a deep breath. 'Oh, is that all!'

Mary-Kate laughed and took her hand. 'Is that all you've got to say. Your Pa is so delighted you'd think I'd given him the Crown Jewels! Aren't you happy?'

'I don't know. I'm happy you're not really ill. Will it cry all the time? Patricia Fearon in our class has a baby brother and she said he cries all the time and no one can get any sleep and it's just a nuisance.'

'I suppose they cry sometimes – even you do. But you'll be able to help me and take it for walks in the perambulator.'

Ellen brightened. 'I hope it is a boy. I had a baby brother but he died. Did Pa tell you?'

'Yes.'

'Lizzie won't be happy. She hates babies! She says they're noisy, messy things that just ruin your life and your figure.'

'If she had one of her own she wouldn't think like that. So now you can put your mind at rest and stop worrying about me and tomorrow you can write and thank Aunt Gina and Mr Vinetti for giving you such a grand time.'

Ellen wriggled down under the bedclothes. 'I will, I promise. And tonight I'll ask God to give me a baby brother. I don't want another sister. Our Lizzie's enough for anyone!'

Mary-Kate bent and kissed her. 'You ask God to forgive you for saying such things about Elizabeth, you little minx!'

Ellen hugged her. 'I love you, Ma.'

*

Mrs Craig had taken Eileen on in the tea rooms and the girl was delighted and Bridget was relieved. Archie had taken Bridget aside and thanked her and even Bernie seemed more amiable than usual, although this Bridget put down to the forthcoming nuptials.

Bernie couldn't afford the traditional long white dress and veil, but she was determined that she was going to be married with some style and so she had announced that she was going to buy her dress at Copeland and Lye and had arranged to come in and see Bridget.

There was only one thing that was worrying Bridget now, and that was accommodation. The nearer the wedding drew, the more anxious she became. She'd looked at numerous rooms in various parts of the city, but the only ones she had liked she just couldn't afford. Those she could afford were in districts that were almost as bad as the Gorbals. She hadn't set her heart on anything grandiose, she just wanted something clean with a few pieces of furniture – half-furnished they called them – in a decent neighbourhood. But so far she'd found nothing and she was beginning to despair.

She loved her job and she got on well with the girls she worked with, who were very different from the three from the Millinery Department, being older than both them and herself. Each morning the glass display cabinets had to be polished, the carpet around them brushed with a hand brush and dustpan and the stock replenished from the stockroom. All the mirrors had to be cleaned and the fitting rooms tidied. Bridget learned which customers had accounts and what the relevant procedure was for that, and at least some time in the day was spent in the sewing room where the alterations were done. Miss Whyte appeared pleased with her work and had told her so after her first week.

She had just finished fitting a customer. She carefully helped the woman out of the dress so as not to disturb the pins or scratch her, she folded the dress and as she emerged from the fitting room she saw Bernie looking through a rail of dresses. She passed the dress to Miss Whyte and walked over to Bernie.

'Can I help you, madam?' she asked, smiling.

Bernie turned, startled. Then she, too, smiled. 'Would you just listen to her! Haven't we gone all posh, then?'

'You're a customer and I have to speak to you like that. Now, have you seen anything you like?'

'I don't know. They're a bit expensive, aren't they? I thought you said they were "Inexpensive Gowns"?'

'They are. You should see the price of the Exclusive ones! How much do you want to pay, that way we won't waste time looking at things you can't afford?'

'About twenty-five shillings, but I suppose I could run to twenty-seven.'

'Right then, follow me, madam!'

They finally picked out four, after Bernie had deliberated on about a dozen, most of which Bridget had discarded as being too bright, too fussy or just plain unsuitable. 'You don't want to look as though you're going on a trip on a Clyde steamer, do you? It's something plain, but striking, you want. Something that will show off your best features which are your hair and your skin.'

'Who's going to see my hair, I'll be wearing a hat! I don't want to look "washed out", I want to be noticed on my wedding day!'

'Yes, but you don't want to look like Maggie Baird, do you?'

'Is everything all right, Miss O'Donnell?'

She hadn't seen or heard Miss Whyte come up behind her. 'Oh, yes. Madam is choosing a dress for a wedding. We've selected these four.'

The manageress nodded and walked away and she ushered Bernie into the dressing room.

Bernie grimaced. 'She looks desperate!'

'She's quite nice really, as long as you're doing your work well. Right, we'll start with this one.'

They finally decided on a pale cream muslin over a peach slub cotton. The muslin formed an overdress with a bloused top caught on the hip with a peach bow and the skirt had three wide bands of peach satin ribbon set into it around the hemline. As it was to be a Church wedding, the dress had long sleeves and a plain, round neck with small cream buttons as decoration.

Bernie studied herself. 'If Ma could see me now, sure, she'd never recognize me. Don't I look just grand?'

'No one would recognize you, Bernie. You look lovely! Now you need some shoes – cream, I think – gloves and a hat. I'd have a very light straw with a wide brim. Peach trimmed with cream, or cream trimmed with peach, but I'd steer clear of our Millinery Department. There's three of the worst little cats down there that I've ever met!'

Bernie was loath to take the dress off. 'How much did you say it was?'

'Twenty-six shillings.'

'Sure, there's not going to be a lot left over for all the rest and my bouquet, is there?'

'Go somewhere else for your accessories. There are plenty of good shops that are quite reasonable. I tell you what, I'll buy your hat as part of your wedding present.'

'Oh, Bridget!'

'You've been a good friend to me, Bernie, considering we really didn't know each other that well back home. Oh, Lord! We'll both be weeping and wailing in a minute! Come on, take it off and I'll pack it up for you. Why don't you and Archie have some photographs taken, you could send one to your Ma, she'd be ever so proud.'

'She would, wouldn't she? She always said I'd go to the Divil, but I've proved her wrong, haven't I?'

'You've proved a lot of people wrong, Bernie,' Bridget agreed, thinking of Gina. 'I'll go and wrap up your dress and put it in a box. They have the name of the shop on them so when you carry it home everyone will know where you got it!'

That made Bernie puff up with pride and Bridget left her to get dressed.

She packed the dress in tissue paper and then placed it in a large, stiff, card box. When Bernie had paid for it and she had handed the box over and watched her walk away, she felt a glow of satisfied achievement.

'She looks very pleased, Miss O'Donnell?' Miss Whyte had just finished explaining to the window dressers just how she wanted certain dresses displayed.

'She is. She looked lovely, too. That colour suits her, being so dark-haired.'

'She isn't the usual sort of customer we get. It was for a wedding, wasn't it?'

'It was for her own wedding. She wanted something special.'

'I thought you took a great deal of time helping her.'

'Sometimes people need advice. They haven't always got a lot of dress sense, shall we say, without being patronizing. I suggested the colours for her accessories, too, but I don't think she can afford to buy them here.'

'I have noticed that about you, Bridget. You have a very good eye for colour and style. I've a proposal to make to you.'

Bridget looked interested.

'It's our policy to have some of our gowns modelled, to show the customers just what they look like on. It helps sales. You are younger than the other assistants, you have a good figure and you are an attractive girl, I would like you to do it.'

'Me?' Bridget gasped.

'Wouldn't you like to try?'

'Oh, yes! It's just that I've never done anything like that before.'

'All you have to do is walk around the store. Go into the coffee lounge and the restaurant, smile and answer any questions on whatever you are wearing. Now, first things first. Go down to Ladies Footwear and tell Mrs Hamilton I sent you. Pick a pair of shoes – beige – that goes with everything, and then we'll select a dress for you. Off you go, now!'

The dress they'd chosen for Bridget to model had a pale apricot background, overlaid with a floral trellis of deep peach and pale green. 'It suits your colouring, Bridget, but I think we should have a hat, too. What colour do you think?'

'If I could match the pale green, in a light straw with

a medium brim turned up at the front, that would complement it.'

'Yes, I think you're right. Keep the dress and shoes on and go to Millinery, ask for Miss Tane. Now, have you got everything memorized? How much is the dress? What is it made of? What is it suitable for? And the shoes?'

'The dress is from our range of Inexpensive Gowns. It is printed cotton, suitable for afternoon wear and more informal occasions and costs twenty-three shillings. The shoes are leather and cost nine shillings and sixpence. They are the very finest imported leather. And I'll have to add the hat.'

'Very good. Now, off you go and remember to smile!'

The apprehension she felt disappeared when she walked into Millinery and discovered that Miss Tane was the oldest of the three girls she'd spoken to that day in Craig's.

'Miss Whyte sent me down to choose a hat. I'm modelling this dress.'

Miss Tane said nothing. She'd seen Bridget before in the store and wondered if she'd remembered all the cutting remarks she'd made about their customers. She'd obviously done well for herself to be chosen to model, she thought.

'I'm looking for a light straw, a pale apple green as near to this colour as possible. With a medium brim, but without a veil.' Bridget couldn't resist the barb, remembering how they'd all mocked the customer who had wanted a veil added to her hat.

Miss Tane looked abashed. 'I'll see what we've got. That's a nice dress.'

'Yes, isn't it? I chose it with Miss Whyte's help. She says I have good taste.'

Miss Tane's cheeks flushed as Bridget tried on and discarded two of the hats she'd brought. She settled for the third. 'This will do fine. How much is it?'

'You've got expensive tastes. It's twelve shillings.' Miss Tane lowered her voice. 'I'm sorry I was so unhelpful the other day. I didn't really mean to be nasty.'

'It doesn't matter now, I've got what I want. But perhaps you will think before you make fun of anyone again. We are all out working for the money, not because we enjoy it, so I don't see why we should look down our noses at others, do you?' And with that she walked towards the staircase.

After an hour the shoes were pinching and rubbing and her feet were hurting, but Bridget managed to keep smiling. Soon it would be lunchtime and she could change into her own, comfortable shoes. She was hungry and the smell coming from the restaurant was tantalizing. As she walked towards her own department she smiled to herself. It hadn't been that bad and quite a few people had taken a positive interest. She looked up and saw that Mr Duncan was coming up the staircase towards her. She'd seen him frequently since the day he'd arranged her interview with Miss Whyte, and he had always stopped and chatted for a few minutes. She was grateful to him, but she was always very polite. He'd walked back to the store with her one day, after she'd done some lunchtime shopping. They'd chatted about his work in the gentleman's wear department, the weather and family and he'd told her he lived with his mother who had been a widow for many years. He'd also asked her not to be so formal.

'I can't help it,' she'd replied, a little put out.

'It's not as if I'm the deputy manager and I'm not that much older than you.'

'I know, but you still have a very responsible job and I wouldn't want you or anyone else to think that I'm being . . . familiar.'

'There's a difference between being friendly and being familiar, Bridget. May I call you Bridget?'

She'd nodded.

'My name is Ian.'

'Oh, I couldn't call you that, Mr Duncan!'

He'd smiled. 'You would call that being familiar?'

'Yes.'

'I see. Can we at least be friends?'

She'd been instantly on her guard and had been glad that they'd reached the store and there hadn't been time for more conversation. She'd just smiled and nodded.

'Don't we look smart?' he said now. 'That colour really suits you. Have you sold many?' She'd really blossomed since she'd been working here, he thought.

'A couple, I think. But I must admit that I do feel a bit of a fool, just wandering around and smiling like a simpleton.'

'You look lovely and you must be doing well. Miss Whyte hasn't had anyone modelling gowns since Amy left to get married.'

'I'm not sure I like the modelling bit, but I like my job very much and I'll never be able to repay you.'

'It was just a word in the right ear and besides, you deserved a chance. You could "repay" me, as you put it, by having lunch with me?'

Bridget didn't quite know what to say. She fervently

hoped this wasn't going to be the start of something she didn't want. She did like him, you couldn't really dislike him, and to have him as just a platonic friend would suit her very much. Yet how could she refuse his offer? 'Thank you, I have to go and get changed first.'

'I'll meet you at the main entrance. We'll go to Craig's if you like?'

Bridget felt awkward as they entered the Tea Rooms, and after exchanging a few words with Mrs Craig, Ian Duncan guided her to the corner where he always sat.

'It feels odd sitting here. You do realize we'll get talked about?'

'So what? I don't much care, do you?'

She smiled and shrugged.

'Your usual, sir, and for you, madam? Bridget! It's you!' Eileen was looking down at her with a startled expression on her pale face.

She chuckled. 'Yes, it's me.'

'Oh, merciful heaven, I shouldn't have said that! What will madam have?'

Bridget laughed. 'I'll have the same as Mr Duncan and stop calling me "madam", it makes me feel a hundred! Mrs Craig can't hear you over here.'

Eileen scribbled down the order and hurried away.

'She's your replacement, isn't she? She's good, too. Very pleasant and efficient and obviously you know her well.'

'She's a good girl. She's the sister of my friend's fiancé.' Seeing Eileen had reminded Bridget about the approaching wedding and without realizing it she frowned and began to twist a strand of hair around her finger.

'What's the matter? Something's troubling you?'

'Oh, it's nothing, I'm fine, really.'

Eileen returned with the order and set it down neatly and efficiently along with the bill which she folded and slipped discreetly under the rim of a plate. Ian Duncan pocketed it.

'I hope you don't mind me asking, but is it money?'

'What?'

'Is it money that's troubling you?'

'No! Saint's above! I earn a good wage – thanks to you. I don't have any worries there.'

'Then what is it? I might just be able to help?'

She sipped her tea wondering if she should tell him. She didn't know him that well. He was really only an acquaintance, but he was such an open, friendly person . . . she sighed. 'Oh, all right. It was seeing Eileen – the waitress – that brought it to mind. In two weeks her brother is marrying my friend, Bernie. We all live in Warwick Street and up to now we three girls have shared the only bedroom, but after the wedding there just won't be room for me, too. Unless I sleep on the kitchen floor. Anyway I desperately want to get out of the Gorbals. I hate it! I was brought up in a small country town, my father had his own business and we never lived in conditions like that! I never thought such squalor was possible. I've looked everywhere for somewhere that's decent, in a quiet area, but it's hopeless. I simply don't know what to do and time is running out. But I'll have to sort myself out somehow. So you see, there's nothing you can do, but thank you just the same for being so thoughtful.'

Bridget ate a sandwich and Ian Duncan did the same.

Then he stirred his tea thoughtfully. She was the sort of girl his mother had been urging him to meet. He liked Bridget, but not in the way his mother intended. She was simply a nice girl who would make a good friend. Lately his mother seemed to be forever bringing up the fact that he was twenty-six and was showing no interest in finding someone to share his life. In fact she was always harping on that the Duncan name would die with him, unless he married, and that that would be a tragedy! It was useless to try to explain to her that he was quite content as he was. She never listened. She'd never really listened to him at all. Ever since his father's death she had constantly reminded him that she had to be strong, that she had to be mother and father to him. As he had grown older he thought the word 'domineering' was more apt than 'strong'. But for the sake of peace he usually agreed with her. Except on the matter of finding a 'nice girl'. In Bridget he'd found just that, and if she agreed to his proposal it would perhaps placate his mother – for a while. In fact it would suit them both.

'I hope you won't take this the wrong way, Bridget, but I think I can help you. As you know I live with my widowed mother in Cartland Drive, by the Northern Necropolis. It's a big house, far too big for just the two of us. I'm sure she wouldn't mind you having a couple of rooms, at a reasonable rate.'

She stared at him over the rim of her cup. That was a very select part of the city. But she couldn't accept! Just what did he think of her? What would other people think? 'It's very kind of you, Mr Duncan, but I couldn't!'

'Why not? Because of what people will think? No one at the store need know. You'll be a paying guest.'

'That's just a nice term for a lodger but it's not that, not entirely.'

'But if you're in such a desperate situation, I can't see any obstacles. I'll have to get Mother's approval, of course.'

She'd have to tell him this time. She just couldn't beat around the bush any longer. 'I hardly know you. You've been very kind, but this . . .'

'Oh, dear, you've taken it the wrong way!'

'It's just that all I want from life is my career and a respectable place to live. I . . . had a bad experience.'

'Concerning a man?' he asked quietly.

She nodded. 'We were going to get married but I caught him . . . Oh, you don't need to know all this.' She didn't know him well enough. 'Let's just say I've finished with men. I only want a career. I'm sorry I've had to be so blunt, you've been very kind to me, Mr Duncan.'

'I'm sorry, Bridget. I didn't mean to pry. I had nothing like that in mind, I assure you.' He was quite relieved by her confession. They could be 'just friends', there would be no complications. He looked at his neatly manicured nails. 'In fact, I don't find it easy to mix with girls, but you're different. I feel that we can be friends without . . . all that. I can talk to you and I feel almost as though I got to know you when you worked here at Craig's. I'm a bit of a loner really. I don't have many friends. In fact I really only have one. I don't drink, so I'm not "one of the lads" either.' He picked up the teaspoon and stirred his tea again. 'It probably comes of just having my mother to bring me up. I swear I had no ulterior motive. I am just trying to help!'

She was bereft of words. It was a very tempting offer.

'Think about it, please? I'll talk to Mother tonight and if she's agreeable, then perhaps you could let me know?'

She finished her tea. She just didn't know what to make of him at all. True, she'd never seen him with a girl and if he really meant what he said . . . 'I'll think about it tonight. Thank you.' With his mother present in the house, there wouldn't be any opportunity for 'ulterior motives' as he called it.

'Good. We'll have lunch again tomorrow, if you would like that?'

She smiled. 'I'd better get back now and get changed into my "finery".'

The day had been a success, she thought, as she got home. The Inexpensive Gowns Department had been quite busy. Although they only stocked two or three of each model, customers had been tempted to purchase other dresses which had been part of the original ploy. She also heard that the Millinery Department had been quite busy, too.

She was first in and so she put the kettle on and laid the table and was peeling the potatoes when Eileen came in, carrying a parcel.

'What have you been buying?'

'Material. I got it in my lunch break from that shop next to the La Scala. Who was that man you were with? He looked nice. He often comes into the tea rooms.'

'That was Mr Duncan, he's the manager of the Gentleman's Leisurewear Department!'

Eileen cocked her head on one side and smiled.

'You can take that look off your face, Eileen Dalrymple! There's nothing between him and me, but he got me my job. He "spoke" for me, just like I did for you.

336

He's a friend, nothing more! Now, what's this material for?'

'My dress for the wedding, of course! Mrs Lavinsky is going to make it.' Eileen undid the wrapping paper and revealed yards of pale blue taffeta. 'It cost me all my savings so Archie will have to pay for it to be made up. I thought I could wear it to go dancing in afterwards.'

Bridget's heart sank and her expression changed.

'Don't you like it?'

'Bernie is going to throw a fit!'

'But *I* paid for it!'

'It's not that! Oh, Eileen, you can't outshine a bride on her wedding day and Bernie's dress isn't going to look anything beside that!'

'I didn't intend to do it, Bridget! I knew she was going to your shop for her dress, so I thought I'd better get something special. They let me have it a bit cheaper because it was the end of the roll and it's a little marked, but they won't take it back. What am I going to do with it?'

'You'd better do something with it and quickly,' Bridget said, hearing Bernie's key in the door. But Eileen wasn't quick enough as Bernie staggered through the door laden with parcels.

'Oh, I'm fair worn out, that I am! I've spent hours trying on shoes and hats and looking for gloves.' She put the parcels down on the table and, kicking off her shoes, sank on to a chair. 'I got my shoes and gloves and a pair of earrings, but I couldn't make up my mind between two hats. You'll have to come with me Bridget, you're the one with all the style. Oh, and guess who I saw as I got off the tram? Maggie Baird! And you should have seen her face

337

when she saw the box with Copeland and Lye written all over it! It'll be round the whole neighbourhood in half an hour.'

Bridget smiled, Bernie had obviously been enjoying herself despite her exhaustion, but she knew any minute now things would change.

'What's that?' Bernie pointed to the blue taffeta.

'The material for my bridesmaid's dress,' Eileen muttered.

Bernie shot up off the chair but Bridget quickly stepped between her and Eileen. 'Bernie, before you start, she didn't do it on purpose! She knew you were going to really splash out on your dress and she thought she'd get something special, too. She got it cheap. She didn't mean to offend you!'

'She did that! Sure, she's always hated me! She never wanted me here! She's deliberately gone and got something much grander than mine. She just wants to ruin my day, she wants to look better than me. She wants people to look at her, not me! She's a nasty, sneaking, little . . . I'll swing for her, so help me, I will!' Bernie screamed.

Eileen burst into tears and Bridget grabbed Bernie's arms and thrust her back down onto the chair. 'Stop it! Stop it, both of you! Eileen, stop crying and make a cup of tea. Then we're going to sit down and sort this out, once and for all. I've found somewhere to live and I'm not going to leave you two ready to murder one another!'

They both stared at her and she realized what she'd said. Subconsciously, she'd made her decision.

'You've found somewhere?' Eileen echoed with a sob in her voice.

'Yes. You know I can't stay here unless I sleep on the kitchen floor, so I've got lodgings in Cartland Drive, that's what Mr Duncan and I were talking about today. I'm going to live with his widowed mother. Now, let's get this mess sorted out.'

After half an hour, when both Bernie's and Eileen's grievances against each other had been aired with Bridget as mediator, things were much calmer.

'You've both got to share the same house, so you'll both have to make the best of it. Eileen, you have to realize that Archie's first loyalty is to Bernie. She'll be his wife and it's not fair to put him in the position of having to take sides. You're young and soon you'll have your own life. And Bernie, you've got to remember that this is Eileen's home and has been for years. Now let's get this dress sorted out!'

'She's not wearing it and there's an end to it!' Bernie said dogmatically.

'They won't take the material back and it's too expensive to waste. How much did you buy, Eileen?'

'Seven and a half yards.'

'God, hasn't she gone and got enough to make two dresses!' Bernie snapped.

'That's it! Get Mrs Lavinsky to make you a skirt and a short, sleeveless jacket. You can wear a pretty blouse with it and you'll still have enough left for a fairly plain dress. It's a good thing skirts are shorter. Then you'll have two outfits. You see, if the two of you can just put your heads together, instead of banging them together, you'll get on fine. Will that suit?'

Eileen looked relieved and Bernie seemed mollified.

339

'It won't detract from your dress, Bernie, and Eileen will still look smart. You want her to look smart, don't you? You don't want people saying she looked dowdy, now do you?'

Eileen offered the olive branch. 'Archie'll be in soon. I'll get on with the tea since you're worn out, Bernie.'

Bernie managed a grim smile. 'You know you sounded just like your Mary-Kate then, Bridget!'

Bridget smiled at her. 'I take that as a compliment. Now, I can at least leave you knowing you won't be scratching each other's eyes out. Not for a while anyway!'

Chapter Eighteen

———•◆•———

CARTLAND DRIVE WAS A quiet street of Edwardian houses, all meticulously maintained and owned in the main by the more prosperous middle-class Glaswegians. Bridget had found out that Mr Duncan, Senior, had been a sea captain who had gone down with his ship in a gale while rounding the notorious Cape Horn. Ian had been eleven years old at the time. Mrs Duncan was a small woman with grey hair and pale blue, piercing eyes and was a good deal older than Bridget had imagined. Obviously she'd had her son late in life. She'd welcomed Bridget with a reserve that bordered on the formidable, and had imperiously dismissed her son to make some tea while she took Bridget around the house and had a 'wee talk' with her.

It was a big house. It had a wide hall with a cloak-room with leaded lights set into the door and a plate rack on which were displayed pieces of fine porcelain. The front parlour also had leaded panes in its window and a high, polished mahogany mantel at either end of which were two identical, oriental vases. There was something Mrs Duncan called a 'morning room' which was rather like a small sitting room cum informal dining room. Then there was the formal dining room, a kitchen and scullery and upstairs were four bedrooms and a bathroom.

'You see, it's quite a big house for just the two of us. Ian was right about that. Most persuasive in his argument really.'

'It's a lovely house, Mrs Duncan,' Bridget answered, thinking it was almost as grand as Mary-Kate's. And the furnishings, although rather old-fashioned, were good. 'How do you manage to keep everywhere so . . . nice?'

'I have a man who does the gardens, Dora who comes in a couple of mornings a week, and, of course, Ian is very tidy. Are you tidy, Miss O'Donnell?' she asked sharply.

'Yes, I am. I was brought up to be tidy and of course I will help with the chores, then perhaps you won't need your cleaning lady so often.'

Mrs Duncan ignored the suggestion. 'You know, I wasn't very enthusiastic about having a stranger in my home.'

'Oh, I can understand that,' Bridget replied, thinking of Eileen. 'But I won't be any trouble at all and it will be absolute heaven to have such peace and quiet. You don't know how much it means to have a good standard of living again.'

'Ah, yes. You live in Warwick Street.'

'Circumstances beyond my control, I'm afraid. But I wasn't brought up in a place like that. My father had his own business and both my parents were very well respected.'

The old lady scrutinized her. She seemed a decent young girl. Irish, but quiet, respectful and smartly dressed without being what she called 'flashy'. Not exactly what she would have liked for him, but then neither was the career he'd chosen. At least it was a start in the right direction that he'd at last found a quite suitable girl. Although she wasn't going to have any 'goings on' under her own roof. 'I'm an old lady and I speak my mind. Ian seems very taken with you, but I won't have anything "improper" going on in my house.'

Bridget stared back just as resolutely. 'Ian, Mr Duncan, got me my job and I'm very grateful. At present I am only interested in my career, Mrs Duncan, and I can assure you that nothing at all "improper" will ever occur. In fact, when he suggested this arrangement I wasn't at all sure about it. I don't want people talking and speculating.'

'Very wise of you. But unless you tell them, who is to know? I keep myself to myself. I don't like people poking their noses into my affairs. I never have. The neighbours think I'm a little eccentric, but I'm not interested in their views either. Ian likes his work, he's happy there. Of course, I would have preferred something more *professional* but . . .' she shrugged. 'When his father was alive we wanted him to join the Royal Navy, but after I was widowed I swore I would never risk losing another life to the sea! Mr Copeland – he's retired now of course – is my second cousin.'

So that was how Ian came to hold such a good

position at quite a youthful age. Obviously they were well-connected and didn't really need her as a paying guest.

'My mother is a widow,' Bridget explained. 'There were five of us but my eldest brother was killed, too, and after that my sisters and I left Ireland. My brother Matthew still lives at home with my mother.'

'Then you are no stranger to grief and loss, either?'

'No. Nor to fear, but at least I've now overcome my fear. The grief is always there though, isn't it? It never really goes away.'

'No, unfortunately it doesn't. It diminishes but it never fades entirely.'

Despite the sharp, aloof disposition, Bridget realized what a solitary life the old lady must have. It couldn't have been easy for her, despite the fact that she wasn't short of money, bringing up a son alone and that probably accounted for her rather domineering attitude. 'May I take it that you approve of me, Mrs Duncan, and are willing to take me?'

'Yes, you may. You've been honest with me and you don't appear to be flighty. I think we will get on. You can have the back bedroom and if you want some privacy we can turn the small bedroom under the gable into a sitting room for you. It's only ever been used as a storeroom and there's enough furniture here to furnish two houses. Now, I do hate discussing money but it must be sorted out. I own another house in Melville Street and I charge a rent of nine shillings for that. But I think seven shillings a week rent is fair for your rooms here, don't you?'

Seven shillings a week for all this! 'Oh, that's very fair

of you! Of course, I'll buy my own food and, as I said, I'll help out with the chores. I'm very practical and I can cook and sew.'

'Good. Well, that's all out of the way and done with. When would you like to move in?'

'Whenever it is convenient.'

'Shall we say next week, on your day off?'

'That would be just fine and thank you, again.' Oh, she was so relieved and astounded at her luck. She'd write to Ma, Mary-Kate and Gina as soon as she got back. Only five more days in Warwick Street! It was a miracle. No more overcrowding. No more dirt and smells. No more filthy, shared lavatories. No more having to go to Bedford Street for a bath and no more 'Steamy'. She'd have her very own bedroom and her very own sitting room! Just to sit in the evening in the stillness and to have a bed to herself again.

Ian brought in the tea tray.

'You will be pleased to know that I approve of Miss O'Donnell, Ian. And she is quite happy with the arrangements. She will be moving in next week.'

Ian smiled at Bridget as his mother handed her a cup of tea. Thank goodness for that. It would keep his mother from constantly carping about his single status and he hoped he had found a good friend in Bridget.

Archie and Bernie helped her to move her things and Bernie was completely overwhelmed by Bridget's good fortune.

'Trust you, Bridget O'Donnell! Haven't I always said that "The Sisters O'Donnell" were born lucky?'

'It's beautiful, isn't it? It's almost as grand as Mary-Kate's house. But you needn't be so envious, Bernie, you're getting married next week to a good man. Just you think about that!'

Bernie nodded. Yes, she was lucky in that. Archie was a good man and in many ways Warwick Street was far better than her old home in Clonmel. Here she commanded respect, which was far more than she'd ever had back home. There everyone had looked down their noses at her; she was an O'Hagan, a tinker's brat, something to be pitied or scorned.

Soon she'd be Mrs Archie Dalrymple with a decent job and not a bad home and one day they, too, might get out of the Gorbals. Bridget had proved that it wasn't impossible. True, Bridget might have a better job and a far nicer house to live in, but she didn't have a good man to love and look after her. Bridget had been so badly hurt by Andy MacDonald that Bernie doubted she'd ever trust another man and, in Bernie's opinion, that made her poorer than herself.

'I'll come over the night before the wedding, I promise, and you can put on your outfit for me – as long as you chase Archie out. It's bad luck if he sees it before the day. It's a shame I'm working, but I can't get a Saturday afternoon off, it's our busiest day.' Indeed she was glad of that fact; it was the perfect excuse, for although she would have dearly loved to have seen Bernie married, she wouldn't even contemplate sitting in a church with *him*!

'We'll have a drink, and you're not just having lemonade either – we've both got something to celebrate now.'

'Well, maybe I'll just have one very small drink, but no more! Not after you and your sherry on the *Connaught*, Bernie O'Hagan!'

Bernie hugged her, her eyes misting with tears. 'Oh, Bridget, we've come a long way since then, haven't we?'

After Warwick Street, Bridget's new home was palatial and she derived a great deal of pleasure arranging the furniture in her small sitting room under the gable. She hadn't used the room much since she'd arrived, though. Most evenings she spent in the parlour with Mrs Duncan and Ian, both of whom she got on well with. David McLeod, the young man she'd occasionally seen Ian with at Craig's, came a couple of times a week and they would discuss their hobby of ornithology. She couldn't for the life of her see just what was so fascinating about birds, but as Mrs Duncan remarked tartly, it was better than having him in some public house every night or wasting his money on other more harmful things. They were planning a week's holiday in the Western Isles later in the year and spent hours searching through books and magazines and studying maps.

Bridget still did some modelling at work, usually only one day a week for, as Miss Whyte said, she couldn't spare her for more than that as she was such a good little saleswoman. She had begun to acquire her own set of regular customers who sought her advice on accessories as well as dresses and who often confided their plans and worries to her.

'If I'm not careful, I'll have Millinery poaching you, Bridget!' Miss Whyte said one day, after Bridget had worn a small, white cloche hat trimmed with a large black satin bow. It had proved so popular that Miss Tane had had to send a rush order to the makers.

'No thank you, Miss Whyte! Wild horses wouldn't drag me down there.'

'Why not?'

'Let's just say I prefer my own department and the assistants here.'

She'd seen the twinkle in the manageress's eyes and knew she understood, although the 'three little cats', as some of the other girls called them, seemed to have sheathed their claws just lately and she wondered if they had been warned about their malicious tongues.

'Is David coming over tonight?' Bridget asked Ian as they walked from the tram stop on Armada Street towards Cartland Drive.

'Yes, he's had a letter from the hotel on Skye that we intend to make our base.'

'Won't you find it cold and wet and windy?'

'Oh, it shouldn't be too bad. We've been before. We take a boat out, if it's fine enough, to get close to some of the smaller islands, only don't for heaven's sake tell Mother. She hates anything to do with the sea and if she found out she'd insist on coming along as well!'

'I don't blame her! Do you really have to go looking at other islands? Isn't it dangerous?'

'Not really. We don't go out if the local fishermen say not to. Sometimes one of them even comes out with us.' Ian laughed. 'They think we're "tapped in the craig" to go looking at birds. "Craig" is head, by the way.'

'I know and I agree with them!'

'It's fun. You should come one day. It's really fascinating.'

'No, thanks.'

'You won't say anything to Mother, will you?'

'Of course not. Why should I worry her? Although I still think it's a bit thoughtless of you both, especially after what happened to your father.'

He shrugged and they walked the rest of the way in silence. They were quite at ease with each other now. Although during working hours no one would have guessed by her demeanour towards him that they lived in the same house. She insisted on calling him 'sir' even though he thought she was overdoing the formality. 'Mr Duncan, will do.'

'All right, Mr Duncan, sir,' she'd laughed.

The smell of lamb wafted to their nostrils as they opened the door. On Mondays Bridget bought the meat and on Tuesdays Dora made a casserole after she'd finished cleaning, so all Mrs Duncan had to do was to turn on the oven. Bridget took off her things and went and washed her hands and set the table. She always insisted on doing this and the washing up.

When the meal was on the table she frowned at the small portion Mrs Duncan took.

The old lady intercepted and interpreted the look. 'I don't need great, hearty meals, like you two. I'm an old woman and I don't spend my day dashing about, so I don't need as much food. It stands to reason.'

'But you should eat more than that,' Bridget urged.

'Bridget O'Donnell, I am the one that does the nagging in this house!'

349

Bridget smiled back, taking the reproof in generous spirit. Mrs Duncan's bark was far worse than her bite and she was becoming fond of her. 'David's coming over to discuss their holiday plans tonight.'

'Oh, those two! They clutter up my dining room with all their mess. Why can't we all have a few rubbers of whist, it's far more entertaining?'

Ian looked at Bridget, silently hoping to enlist her help.

'For you may be, but I always get in such a muddle,' she sighed. Mrs Duncan was trying to teach her the card game, but she found it rather daunting and always lost, much to Ian's amusement. 'Anyway, I've some letters to write this evening. Ma will think I've disappeared if I don't write soon. It's nearly a week since I got her letter.'

'Then you'd better get down to it! Don't put off until tomorrow what can be done today. And how is your sister in Liverpool?'

'Oh, she's fine. She says now that the morning sickness has passed, she feels bursting with health. Lewis wants to take on another girl in the house, but she won't hear of it, yet.'

'She should take notice of him. First babies can often be difficult. Ian was so difficult I never had another one.'

'I often wish you had. I found it lonely being an only child,' Ian said sadly.

'It wasn't the Almighty's will that I had any more, and in the light of the circumstances that followed, it was a blessing. Stop complaining.'

'I wouldn't have minded being an only child,' Bridget said in an effort to lighten the atmosphere. 'We were always squabbling and this is the first time in my life that I've had a bedroom to myself.'

'You see, Ian, be thankful!'

The doorbell interrupted the conversation.

'Good grief! Does that boy bolt his food or does he go without any? We haven't even cleared the table yet. You go and let him in, Ian, we'll clear up.'

When Bridget had written her letters she went down to the parlour. Besides whist, Mrs Duncan was teaching her to crochet and she was making a dressing-table set for Sarah. The old lady was working on a matinee coat for Mary-Kate's baby. They talked for a while about the day's events and the local news. Then they sat in the companionable silence that for Bridget was sheer bliss after Warwick Street and a hectic day at work, until the old lady looked at the carriage clock and put down her work.

'Just look at the time! We'll have our cup of tea now, I think. There won't be time for cards this evening. I'm sure these young men do it on purpose!'

Bridget went into the kitchen and made the tea and took it back on a tray into the parlour. 'I'll go and tell them to pack up their stuff.'

'I don't know what they find so interesting, I really don't! Go and tell them to come in for tea.'

Bridget opened the dining room door. 'You're not still poring over that map, are you? You must know it back to front by now! Your mother is pouring the tea so you'd better not keep her waiting.'

She smiled, looking at them. Their heads were close together as they scrutinized the map, and Bridget thought about Ian's earlier remarks about his lonely childhood. They were just like brothers, they were so close, she thought. In fact, closer than most brothers, for Fergal and Matty had always been scrapping and arguing and Dinny Magee had once thrown his younger brother, Dermot, into the Suir and had then had to go in after him, and they had both felt their Pa's belt across their backsides for that escapade. She'd never seen two friends who were so close. She shrugged. They were both a bit odd. Sure, anyone who spent their precious week's holiday watching birds in pouring rain, must be odd!

Between shows Gina had been trying to find a place of her own, now that she could at last afford one. She and Helen had seen countless rooms all over London, but the ones she liked were always far too expensive. She wanted something 'grand' she'd told Helen, but what she wanted and what she could afford were two totally different things.

It was Helen who hit on the suggestion of sharing.

'That way we can both afford something "grand" as you call it. I know I don't earn nearly as much as you, but it would help, wouldn't it? It would be that bit extra and we could share the expenses.'

Gina had really wanted a place that would be hers alone, but common sense told her that it was share with Helen or settle for something less elegant. So she'd agreed and they'd found some really lovely rooms on the ground floor of a large house not far from Mrs Weston's. It was still Bloomsbury, but the more 'select' end. They had both spent hours choosing furnishings and discussing colour schemes for both were determined that everything was going to be 'modern', Art Deco and Art Nouveau were all the rage. And when they were finally finished they were going to throw the party that Gina had promised.

She was enjoying life to the full. She was now successful and was well known in all the best places. People crowded around the theatre waiting to catch a glimpse of her and she loved it all. She revelled in every minute of it. It was wonderful to have enough money to buy nice clothes and she'd been given a few pieces of expensive jewellery by Jimmie Masters, who followed her around like a lap dog, as Edward had commented.

'You're jealous!' she'd replied.

'Of him! Good God, Gina, he's welcome to you. You won't catch me running around after you, waiting patiently for a pat on the head when you remember I'm there. I'm far too busy!' had been his reply. But he *was* jealous of Jimmie Masters. Despite himself, he knew his feelings for Gina were becoming more and more serious. He also knew that if he let her know that, she would treat him far worse than she treated poor Jimmie and he wasn't prepared to be mocked behind his back, as Mr Masters was. He had also been far from happy about Helen sharing Gina's flat.

'You don't like Helen, do you?' she'd said the day she'd shown him round and asked him if he liked it. 'Of course, it will look better when we've finished decorating and got rid of all this old stuff,' she'd added.

'You know my views on Helen Mason. She's a bad influence, but as long as your social life doesn't interfere with your work, you can do as you please.'

'I intend to. And she isn't a bad influence, she just

likes to have fun. What's wrong with that? You were always telling me to make friends, to broaden my outlook, and when I do you still complain. You're impossible, Edward!'

'I suppose I am, but that comes of being older and wiser, Gina.'

Everything was ready. The buffet was laid out in the small dining room and she'd hired waiters to serve the drinks. Gina checked her appearance in the full-length mirror in her bedroom. Helen had been right about the dress, she thought. The shades of purple, mauve, lilac and white suited her. She turned round and the chiffon skirt with the very latest handkerchief hemline swirled around her legs. The bodice was bloused and pleated into the deep purple satin sash that hugged her hips. The same colour was repeated in her satin headband which was adorned with one white and one mauve ostrich plume, both held by a diamond pin. She wore the drop earrings Jimmie had given her and the matching bracelet, through which she'd threaded a chiffon handkerchief. She'd discarded the long ropes of beads, thinking they ruined the effect, but Edward's corsage of lilac and white orchids was perfect. She touched the flowers again. It had been a thoughtful gesture, but quite out of character, and they must have cost him an arm and a leg. She smiled confidently at her reflection. She was certain that he really did hold some affection for her, in his own way, although he would never admit it. Well, if he ever did admit it she would enjoy seeing his face when she told him to 'Go to hell!' She'd enjoy watching him slink away with his tail between his legs.

Helen opened the door, dressed in sapphire shot taffeta that suited her complexion and made her eyes a darker blue. 'Gina, you look absolutely divine! I told you those colours were just right for you. Oh, by the way, Edward's arrived.'

'He's early.' Gina cast one last glance at herself in the mirror and then followed Helen into the lounge.

'Edward! Thank you for the orchids, they're divine!' Divine was their favourite adjective of the moment. 'How did you know what colour to get?'

'I guessed. Besides, there's not a great demand for them so they don't come in many colours. I had to go to Covent Garden for them. You look lovely, Gina.'

'Thank you. How do you like it now?' She swept her arm with its glittering bracelet and floating kerchief over the room. Helen had gone to get him a drink.

'It's . . . modern.'

She frowned irritably. 'You don't like it?'

'I didn't say that.'

'But you implied it. You didn't say it was tasteful or lovely or anything like that.'

Edward thought it looked rather flashy and a bit vulgar. He much preferred the pieces of furniture she'd got rid of, but to say so would have hurt her feelings and probably sparked off an argument. 'You said you wanted it very modern and it is. I can see you've both spent a great deal of time, effort and money on it. Everyone will be impressed.'

Gina smiled. 'Thank you. I'm so glad you're not going to be sarcastic and I'm not going to lose my temper tonight, no matter how you provoke me.'

'I don't provoke you, do I?'

'Sometimes you're infuriating! But I'm glad you've come, no one else has!'

Edward pulled a face of mock horror. 'You mean there's all that food and we're the only ones coming?'

'Don't be stupid, you know very well what I mean! None of the family is coming. You would have thought that at least one of them would have come. Mary-Kate promised Ellen.'

Edward took his drink from Helen, nodding his thanks. 'Gina, you can't expect Mary-Kate to come in her condition. I thought Lewis wrote and explained?'

'He did. They mustn't have told Ellen about it, otherwise she'd have got round Mary-Kate.'

'Even you can't be that blind, Gina! Do you honestly think your friends, especially after they've all had a drink, are fit company for a child of her age?'

She shrugged. 'Oh, I suppose you're right. But Bridget could have come, she's got a good job and a nice place that she pays buttons for, she would have enjoyed it. I begged Ma to come over but she said she couldn't. If our Matty and Uncle Richard can't take care of themselves by now, then they're even bigger eejits than I thought! They could have come too. I wanted everyone to come!'

'You've got lots of people coming.'

'But I wanted them all to see how well I've done. I wanted them to go back and tell everyone in Clonmel all about it.'

'Oh, I see! You didn't really want to see them, you just wanted them to go back and impress the whole town. Why didn't you invite the whole town?'

Edward was being hateful again and Gina glared at

him. 'I won't be baited. I refuse to let you ruin my evening.'

'Good, then we should both enjoy ourselves, shouldn't we? You'd better open the door, I think your first guests have arrived.'

Part II

Chapter Nineteen

———◆·◆·◆———

MARY-KATE SMILED AT THE antics of the baby boy playing on the kitchen floor with Ellen. James Patrick Vannin was everything both she and Lewis could have wished for in a son. Fearing that Ellen might feel just a little jealous of all the fuss made of the baby, Mary-Kate had encouraged Ellen to help her with him as much as possible. But, in fact, Ellen loved her little brother dearly.

It was hard to believe that the time had gone so quickly. Hard to believe that she'd forgotten the hours of pain that preceded the birth. But she'd never forgotten the sense of joy and contentment she'd felt, exhausted though she'd been, when Doctor Salmon had placed the baby in her arms. Lewis had been beside himself with happiness and pride and had even given all his workers a half crown extra in their wages, to 'Wet the baby's head', and for the first time in many, many years he had got gloriously, roisterously drunk.

They had both fretted and worried over the baby at first but it soon became evident that Jamie, as she called him, had a tenacious hold on life and had no intention of succumbing to the fate of his poor little half-brothers. When the baby had been a month old, Lewis had given her the deeds of the house as a gift. The business and all his property he intended to vest in his son, but Mary-Kate had protested.

'What about Elizabeth and Ellen?'

'What about them?'

'Surely you're not really going to leave them out?'

'Elizabeth deserves nothing!' Lewis had replied, curtly.

'She does, Lewis. She's still your daughter. Your eldest child.'

'Mary-Kate, I've never met a woman who is so tolerant or so forgiving.'

She'd just smiled. It was hard to forgive Elizabeth, but she did try. She prayed every day for the grace to think charitably about her step-daughter.

When Elizabeth had found out about her pregnancy there had been by far the worst scene ever. Despite knowing she was unwelcome in her father's house, she had burst in and screamed and raged at both of them until Lewis had lost his temper and slapped her hard across the face. He had forbidden her ever to come within a mile of his house and had shouted that she had forfeited any chance she'd had of ever inheriting anything. Mary-Kate had never forgotten that day.

Ellen, too, had borne the brunt of her sister's wrath, for as usual Ellen had been eavesdropping and when Elizabeth had flung open the door and found her outside, she lashed out at Ellen, hitting her viciously across the head. That more than anything had aroused Mary-Kate's anger. She could have forgiven Elizabeth almost anything, except that.

Ellen hadn't cried. She'd just stared after her sister's retreating back, her face white with shock, her eyes cold and hard as flint, exactly like her father's, and Mary-Kate had realized that Ellen really did hate Elizabeth.

Over the matter of the girls' inheritance, Lewis had finally relented.

'Elizabeth shall have the deeds to the house she lives in and Ellen shall have three houses in Rawcliffe Road. The rest goes to Jamie.'

And so the matter had been settled.

Mary-Kate's thoughts returned to the present as she heard Ellen ask, 'Shall I get Jamie ready and take him over to the park for an hour before he goes to bed, Ma? A little fresh air might make him sleep.'

'Would you? I've not even read Bridget's or Ma's letters yet and they came in the lunchtime post! You'd better wipe his face and hands first. What have you been giving him?'

'Chocolate.'

'Oh, Ellen, you spoil him worse than your Pa does! He'll be sick and look at his suit, you'll have to change him. You can't take him out like that.'

'That's all right, after all it's my fault he's so messy. Ugh! He's got it in my hair now.'

'Maybe that will teach you. You'll have to wash your hair.'

Mary-Kate smiled at Ellen who had picked up the child. He was endeavouring to wriggle free and was covering Ellen in a sticky mess in the process. She hadn't wanted a girl, not solely because Lewis desperately wanted a son, but because she had worried that Ellen would have seen a baby sister as a threat. And Ellen was very dear to her, she was the only daughter she ever wanted.

'I'll read these letters, then I'll help Vi prepare supper. I don't know where the time goes these days, there's so much to do.'

Ellen took Jamie to clean him up and Mary-Kate sat down. She did seem to spend a lot of time rushing about these days, but she didn't mind that. The business was doing very well and Lewis had acquired four more houses. She still did the books as well as running the household and she was grateful for Ellen's help when she wasn't at school. Vi's mother, who had helped out in the later days of pregnancy, no longer came, since she had a home of her own to run. She couldn't have been more contented, she thought. She had everything she wished for and she even found that she did care for Lewis, although she still wasn't at ease when he made love to her. That was the one cross she must bear, although after the arrival of Jamie and now that the business was taking so much of his time, his demands on her were less frequent.

Mary-Kate decided to take a few, quiet minutes to read her letters in the peace of the parlour. A rare treat for her. At last Ireland was at peace. The troubles were over and everyone was trying to pick up the pieces of their lives and forgive and forget, although for some the bitterness would always be there. Fortunately, Matty had managed to stay out of trouble and the farm was thriving. They were lucky. Others had been ruined, the Feeheys amongst them. With their home and business gone and no sign nor word of Michael, the worry had killed both his ailing mother and father. And there were others, even Mrs O'Hagan who had lost two sons. They were the tragedies of Clonmel. But things were returning to normal. When the photographs of Bernie's wedding had arrived, Mrs O'Hagan had livened herself up and done the rounds of the town, displaying them to everyone, starting with Father Maguire. The poor soul was so proud of Bernie that it was pitiful to see, Sarah had written. But Bernie had done well for herself, that she had, which was more than could be said for the rest of that family!

Mary-Kate scanned the lines. The weather was holding fair and Uncle Richard said the crops should do well this year, so well they might have to hire a few men to help with the harvest. However, all the money was to be spent on buying more land and wasn't that altogether just like Matty, when she wanted a new carpet for the front parlour as the old one was so shabby that she was ashamed to invite Father Maguire in when he called. More land meant more work and more wages to be paid out, and she'd told the pair of them that but, as usual, they wouldn't listen to her. She was writing to Gina as she hadn't heard from her for over a month and she was sure she was working herself into the ground with that musical and she wasn't at all sure she approved of this Helen person that Gina kept mentioning. Did Mary-Kate think the girl was leading Gina astray?

Mary-Kate smiled at that. No one 'led' Gina!

Mrs Butler-Power had asked after her but sure, she was only interested in how the business was doing and how much money Lewis had, she couldn't fool her!

There was talk of Mrs O'Leary marrying Mr Ryan, the solicitor, but that rumour had been going around since Bryan Boru was a boy and she'd believe it when she saw the ring on Mrs O'Leary's finger and the name over the shop changed. Would Mary-Kate kindly send her a photograph of her grandson, the one she had was nearly a year old now and anyway, when was she ever going to bring him to see his Grandma at all? It wasn't right that she hadn't even seen her only grandchild or been able to show him off to her friends. But she must close now or else she would miss the post, but having said that the good Lord above alone knew when Mary-Kate would receive the letter. The posts were a disgrace and if they didn't improve she was going to write to the Dáil about it. At least when the post had been the Royal Mail it had arrived on time!

Mary-Kate folded the letter and smiled. Ma never changed. She was an institution. War and death had swept over her but had never succeeded in breaking her. She had a photo of Jamie, Ellen and herself that she would send, but when she was ever going to find the time to take them to Ireland, she didn't know.

She turned Bridget's letter over in her hand. The quality of the paper was good and the address was printed on the top right-hand corner. It was a far cry from the small sheets of cheap, coarse paper Bridget had once used.

Bridget was well and she had been promoted. After years of being a confirmed spinster, Agnes Walker had announced she was getting married, to a man she had met on holiday of all things! Could Mary-Kate believe that? Miss Whyte had called her into the office and told her she was to replace Agnes as senior assistant. Of course, she'd been thrilled and the increase in salary would be more than welcome, but she'd also felt guilty and awkward about being promoted over the heads of the other two girls. But she would have to see how things progressed.

She was worried about Ian. Since he'd come back from his last holiday with David, he'd been strangely quieter and more moody than usual and David's visits had become less frequent. She'd asked him if they had had an argument but he'd assured her they hadn't. Yet it wasn't like him at all. Mrs Duncan was well, although she was becoming more frail and often irascible as she depended on Bridget quite a lot and that seemed to annoy her. But Bridget didn't mind, since she was fond of the old tartar, as Mary-Kate knew well. Eileen Dalrymple was being trained as manageress by Mrs Craig and Archie himself had called and thanked her for, as Mary-Kate knew, she had put the idea into her former employer's mind. Bernie was also fine but now she was worrying that she hadn't yet become pregnant and wasn't that just the most contrary thing? Most girls worried in case they were, but Bernie was getting very upset about it. She was even thinking of going to see some doctor who knew about these things, but Bridget had told her to save her money and not fret. It would happen, given time. She'd had a letter from Ma, full of gossip, and a brief, scrawled note from Gina, who seemed to be living the life of Riley in London. Her name was known in Glasgow now, thanks to the newspapers, and Bridget felt quite proud of the fact. One of these days she would go down and see Gina, when she had more time.

Mary-Kate sighed as she folded the letter. Time! When would there ever be enough time for any of them to do all the things they promised themselves they would do – one day?

When they returned from the park Ellen helped Mary-Kate to feed and bath Jamie and put him to bed and then they both went down to have supper with Lewis.

'Have you finished that maths homework yet, Ellen?' Lewis asked.

Ellen shook her head. 'Oh, I'll never be any good at algebra, Pa! I just don't understand it and I don't understand what use it is either, not for girls anyway. Most girls get married and have children when they grow up.'

'Is that what you want to do?'

'No!'

'Why not? I thought you loved children. You love Jamie,' Mary-Kate asked, surprised.

'Jamie's different, he's my brother.'

Mary-Kate looked at her step-daughter from beneath lowered lashes, praying she wasn't going to announce she wanted to follow Gina and go into the theatre.

'What do you want to do, then?' Lewis persisted.

Ellen shrugged. 'I don't really know.'

Mary-Kate laughed. 'Neither did I at your age, but persevere with your maths, it may come in useful one day, even if it's only to take over the books from me!'

'Will you help me, Pa, please?'

Lewis nodded.

Mary-Kate helped Vi to clear the dishes while Lewis took Ellen, with the much hated homework, into the library.

'That's it for tonight, Vi, thank you.'

'Are you sure you don't want me to put that washing in to soak before I go, Mrs Vannin? I don't mind.'

'No, you get off, Vi. You must be tired. I'll do it. Ellen can put her books away soon, too. She's got all week to finish her homework and she's been looking a little peaky lately.'

'Aye, she's growing up fast is Miss Ellen, if you follow my meaning!'

'Good Heavens, Vi! I never gave that a thought. I suppose I'll have to tell her about all that soon!'

Vi pulled a face. 'Oh, the "curse of womankind"!'

'Sometimes it is a "curse" but really it's a blessing, I suppose. Without it we'd have no children, would we?'

'I've never found anyone who can find some good in absolutely everything like you do, Mrs Vannin.'

Mary-Kate smiled. 'If you look hard enough you can, Vi. Now who on earth can that be?' She turned, startled. Someone was hammering on the front door and she could hear muffled shouts.

She got into the hall just as Lewis opened the door. One of the men from the yard stood there, panting, his face red, the sweat standing out on his forehead.

'My God! Davies! What's the matter?'

'The yard, Mr Vannin! Stables are on fire! Raised the alarm, then came straight here! Ran all the way!' he gasped.

Lewis snatched his jacket from the hallstand. 'Is anyone down there?'

'Only the lad. I told him to get the horses out.'

As they both ran out of the house, Mary-Kate turned and clutched Vi's arm. 'Vi, stay here with Ellen and Jamie, please!'

'Mrs Vannin, you're not going down there?' Vi cried.

'I've got to! I've got to see if there's anything I can do. Just stay, Vi, will you?'

She didn't even bother to get a coat or jacket, but ran down the steps following Lewis and Davies, who had already turned the corner. When she reached the bottom of the street Mary-Kate stopped momentarily. The glow of the flames illuminated the sky and she could smell the smoke on the night air. A fire engine hurtled past her, its bell clanging frantically, the men clinging on for dear life, still buttoning on their jackets. She broke into a run, trying to hurry her steps, but her breath was coming in short, stabbing gasps. Then she realized someone was running beside her and she looked down. It was Ellen. Her pale face strained, her hair loose and streaming out behind her.

'Go home! Go back, Ellen!'

'No, Ma! I'm coming with you!'

'Ellen, go home! Go back!' she screamed, but the child ran ahead of her and darted across the road. Fear gave her strength and quickened her steps. God alone knew what she was running into!

There was a large crowd on the corner of Parkinson Road and two fire engines were parked on the pavement. Mary-Kate pushed her way through until a policeman stopped her. Dimly, through the smoke and flames, she could see figures.

'You can't go any nearer, luv. It's too dangerous.'

'I'm Mrs Vannin, my husband is in there. Has a child run in? A young girl with long brown hair?'

'No, ma'am, not to my knowledge.'

She turned and the crowd seemed to converge

upon her. She was frantic and began to lash out wildly. 'Ellen! Ellen, where are you?' she screamed. There was no answer, no reassuring cry from Ellen. She plunged forward, shaking off the policeman's grip on her shoulder, hearing him shout behind her.

The heat hit her and after a few steps she was choking and half-blinded by the smoke, but she staggered on, trying to call to them both until the smoke burned her throat and silenced her. Dragging up her skirt, she tore a strip from her petticoat and pressed it over her nose and mouth. She could see very little but the rushing and roaring in her ears became louder and she knew she must be getting near the heart of the fire. As she turned her head slightly she caught a glimpse of a pale, terrified face. Ellen! She raised her free arm to try to shield her face from the intense heat as she relentlessly drove herself forward.

All around her, like shadows, figures darted in and out of the smoke and flames and the air was punctuated with the shouts of the fire-fighters and the terrified, high-pitched cries of the maddened horses. Again, silhouetted against the orange glow, she saw the small, thin figure. She looked upwards and lurched forward, a scream forced from her burning throat and hanging for an instant above the cacophony.

In that instant Ellen turned, the fear that had paralyzed her dispelled by the sound of Mary-Kate's voice. All she could see was a shadowy figure and then she was knocked sideways, all the horrors that surrounded her were blotted out as Mary-Kate threw herself bodily over the child and they both fell to the ground. The blazing beam missed them both by a few inches, sending a shower of sparks shooting into the air as it hit the ground.

Mary-Kate got to her feet pulling Ellen with her. She must try to think clearly! Where was she? How near to the stables? How far from the gates? Clutching Ellen closely, pressing the child's head against her chest to protect her face from the smoke and heat, she stumbled towards where she hoped the gate was. Suddenly she tripped and they both fell to their knees, but then hands were pulling her upwards and she realized it was the coils of the fire hoses she had fallen over. She shoved Ellen unceremoniously into the arms of a fireman and, before he could stop her, Mary-Kate had turned and plunged back into the inferno. Somewhere in there was Lewis. She had to find him.

Her eyes were smarting and watering so much that she could hardly see at all and her strength was failing. But she had to go on. She had to find him. Over the sheer pandemonium she heard the sound. The pounding of a gigantic hammer against an anvil, only much faster and more erratic and she knew she was near the stable block. The battering she could hear must be Lewis, desperately trying to force back bolts twisted by the heat and flames. The screams of terror – almost human in their intensity – echoed in her head. The charred panels of the heavy wooden door were splintering but she still couldn't see him. She tried to call him but the smoke defeated her. She groped blindly around her feet until her fingers closed on a thick wooden spar. If she could somehow beat back the bolt . . . she wouldn't think how ineffectual the attempt would be, nor that, if the bolt sheared, the crazed animal would trample her in its flight. She just couldn't stand by and let it be burnt to death!

She raised the spar and brought it down as hard as she could against the bolt, trying to knock it sideways. The effort caused a sharp pain in her chest, but she swung the spar upwards again, bringing it down in a wide arc. Had it moved or was it just her imagination? She struggled to raise it again but with a strangled scream she flung herself back against the wall as with an ear-splitting crash the heavy door fell outwards and downwards. An enormous black shape, eyes rolling white with terror, huge, white-feathered hooves thundering, black mane on fire, bore down on her. She threw up her arms in an attempt to protect herself and pressed herself closer to the wall. The horse passed so close that she felt the heat from its foam-flecked body and caught the odour of burning horsehair. Then a strong arm was around her waist, lifting her bodily off her feet and in the glare she saw the glint of the fireman's helmet. Exhausted though she was she tried to struggle, feebly battering her fists against his chest.

'My husband! My husband! Let me go! My husband's in there!'

'He's out, Mrs Vannin! He's out!'

She sagged against him like a rag doll.

'He helped my mate drag one of the wagons out and the last I saw of him, he was trying to hang on to the poor beast you got out. You could have been killed – the animal could have trampled you to death. If we don't get out now we'll both be blown sky high! There are drums of petrol for the lorry stored somewhere in here. They've sent for engines from Aintree and Anfield! Let's get you out of here.'

He half carried her to the gate and as Ellen saw the two figures she broke free of the police cordon that was trying to keep back the crowd that had rapidly swelled. Tears of relief poured down her face.

'Oh, Ma! Ma! We thought you'd gone!' she sobbed.

Mary-Kate held her tightly, tears creeping down her own cheeks and then Lewis was beside them both.

'Mary-Kate! Oh, you little fool! You could have been killed. Why did you do it?'

She fell into his arms, sobbing incoherently as he patted her shoulder. His hair and eyebrows were singed, his face blackened, his eyes red and burning from the smoke. 'Hush now, it's all right! I'm safe and it's under control, there are more engines on the way. You go home now, I'll come when I'm sure everything is . . .' He couldn't go on. Everything he'd worked for had gone up with the yard. His buildings were gutted. His two motorized lorries were burnt-out shells, most of his wagons were damaged and out of the ten horses he'd had, four of them had been roasted alive in their stables.

'Lewis, I couldn't stop her! I couldn't catch her, she was too quick for me. She knew you were in there.'

Ellen clung to her father. 'She saved me, Pa! A beam fell down and if Ma hadn't been there . . .'

'Oh, Mary-Kate!'

'I'd get them both home now, sir,' the fireman broke in. 'They've both been through it and are pretty shaken up. Mrs Vannin managed to loosen the stable bolt. She got the last horse out, but she could have been killed by it. Get them home, sir, we'll finish up here. You look done in yourself.'

Lewis nodded and bowed his head. Clasping his wife

with one arm and his daughter with the other, he pushed forward as the police moved the bystanders aside. 'We're all going home, Officer. Was a man ever so fortunate in having such a wife and such a daughter?'.

The officer nodded. 'There's not a lot you can do here, sir. We'll stay and secure the place, arrange for the horses to be stabled and get the . . . carcasses removed.'

As they reached the corner of Walton Park, a massive explosion shook the whole street and a sheet of flame shot high into the air. Ellen began to shake and Mary-Kate clutched Lewis's shoulder. He stared backwards. 'The petrol. They said it would go up. Well, it's all gone now. Let's go home.'

Vi was waiting on the doorstep and when she saw them she gave a cry and ran inside to put the kettle on. Despite the state of their clothes, Lewis led them into the parlour and they all sank on to the sofa.

'It's gone, Mary-Kate. Everything I've worked for!'

'It doesn't matter, Lewis. You have your life. You still have your property.'

He sighed heavily. 'You're right, my dear. And I have you two and Jamie, not that there's much left for him to inherit now!'

'Oh, Lewis, don't talk like that. You can build the business up again. He's only a baby yet.'

Vi brought in the tea but Mary-Kate rose and poured out a glass of whisky and gave it to Lewis. Her hands were shaking. 'This will do you more good.' She watched him drain the glass and then she turned to her step-daughter. 'Ellen, you were a very brave girl but you gave me a terrible fright!'

'I'm sorry, Ma! I was so frightened for Pa that I didn't

think, and then I couldn't find my way back and . . .' Shock caught up with her and she began to cry.

Mary-Kate bent and took her in her arms. 'Vi will run you a bath, now drink up your tea, there's my brave girl.'

Lewis rose and poured himself another glass of whisky.

Mary-Kate noticed he was limping. 'Lewis, you're hurt! What's the matter with your leg?'

'Oh, it's nothing! In its blind panic the horse kicked me. It's only bruised.'

'Let me see to it!'

'Later, my dear. Later. You go up and see to Jamie and Ellen and I'll be up shortly. Besides, you've not come through it unscathed yourself. Look at your hands.'

'Oh, cuts and scratches and a few blisters, that's all.' But Mary-Kate nodded and kissed him on the cheek. She was still shaking. She'd never been so frightened in all her life, not even during the worst of the troubles back home, but she must pull herself together for Lewis's sake and Ellen's.

He patted her cheek. 'We'll sort everything out in the morning. There'll be plenty to do, so we'd better get some rest.'

'I'll see to that leg before you go to bed. How did the fire start, did you find out?'

'No, don't worry about that. Not now. Just go on up, you're worn out.'

As Mary-Kate reached the bottom of the stairs she felt faint and she gripped the banister rail tightly, closing her eyes and fighting down the dizziness, then she fell to her knees as the enormity of the disaster and the dangers she had faced, overcame her.

The noise brought Lewis and Vi running into the hall.

'Mary-Kate! What's the matter, are you ill?' Lewis was helping her up and she clung to his arm.

'Vi, help me get her upstairs, it's all been too much for her.'

'I can manage, Lewis.' She felt a little calmer.

'I'll stay over, Mrs Vannin,' Vi stated firmly. 'You both need a good night's rest and just in case Jamie wakes, I'll be here to see to him.'

Mary-Kate nodded thankfully and clung tightly to Lewis's arm as they both went upstairs. She could only thank God that she still had all her family safe and sound.

There had been so much to do that Mary-Kate had hardly seen Lewis all next day and when he got home he was too tired to do more than eat and inform her that four wagons could be repaired and he'd arranged temporary stabling for his remaining horses with the Maypole Dairy. His men were clearing up the yard and re-building would start as soon as possible on new stables, but he'd have to sell some property to try to recover some of his losses.

'None of that matters, Lewis! We are all safe and we're not destitute,' Mary-Kate said.

'I know that, but I still have to pay my men – they have families to feed. In addition, it will take me years to recover the custom I'll lose and I want Jamie to have a thriving business when he grows up.'

'He will have, dear! Try to look on the bright side. Oh, Ernest called this afternoon, he said he was going over to see you. Did he call at the yard?'

'If he did, I didn't see him, but then I did have to go into town for a few hours. I suppose Elizabeth sent him?'

'Yes and I'm afraid I was rather sharp with him. I told him to tell her that she should have come herself, that you could have been killed or seriously hurt.'

'And what did he say to that?'

'That she'd heard you were safe and she didn't think we'd make her welcome.'

'I've more important things on my mind now than Elizabeth's injured pride.'

Mary-Kate shook her head. Would the rift ever heal?

He was still limping as they went upstairs. 'Lewis, will you let me have a look at that leg? I really think you should see Doctor Salmon.'

'Mary-Kate, I'm exhausted! Stop fussing over a scratch – I cleaned it and it's only bruised.'

'Sometimes, Lewis, you can be so stubborn,' she admonished.

For the next few days Mary-Kate hardly saw Lewis, except at breakfast and late in the evening when he came home exhausted and haggard and she began to worry about him. He would make himself ill, the way he was working, trying to fulfil as many contracts as he could. He was even employing freelance drivers who had their own carts. When the sale of one of the properties was through, he was going to buy another lorry, he told her, as they could do twice as many trips in an hour as a horse and cart would do.

'Lewis, you're driving yourself too hard! You don't look well.'

'Let's just get this week over, then we'll be back on the road to recovery. Just a few more days, my dear. They've started building temporary stabling and the wagons will be ready in two days. I'm managing to keep things going and I'm amazed that my customers have been so patient and understanding.'

'It's because you've always dealt fairly and honestly with them, Lewis. They respect your integrity and now you're reaping the benefit of it.' But as Mary-Kate smiled, she wondered whether anything was worth the price he was paying? She thought not.

Two days later Davies and Mr Johnson brought Lewis home.

'He just collapsed, ma'am. We brought him straight home, but you'd better get the doctor.'

'Oh, I told him he was working too hard. Mr Johnson, would you help me to get him upstairs? Mr Davies, I'll write a note and would you take it straight to Doctor Salmon? You know where his surgery is, Orrell Lane?'

The man nodded and stood, cap in hand, looking around the hall until she came back downstairs and handed him the note.

'Would you like me to stay with you, Mrs Vannin?' Mr Johnson asked.

'No, it's very kind of you, but you'd better get back. You know how Mr Vannin worries over the business. If he hadn't worried so much he wouldn't have made himself ill!'

She let them both out and then went back upstairs, a worried frown creasing her forehead. She should have been firm with him, insisted on him coming home earlier. Now, he'd have to rest. He wasn't a young man and no matter how much he disliked to be reminded of that fact, he would just have to get used to it now.

He was sitting on the edge of the bed and his face was ashen.

'Lewis! I told you to lie down. Doctor Salmon's on his way.'

'Everyone is fussing too much. I'm all right. Just tired, that's all.'

'I won't listen to you, Lewis. For the next week or so you're just going to have to do as you're told. Now, get undressed and get into that bed or the doctor won't be very pleased. Shall I help you?'

'No, I'm not an invalid! Where's Jamie?'

She smiled. 'Vi has taken him to the shops with her. He's fine, but he has missed his bedtime hug this week.'

Lewis smiled. 'He's a "grand" boy, as you would say, isn't he?'

'He is that! Now get into bed. I'll bring him up to see you when the doctor's gone. Vi should be back by then.'

Ellen arrived home from school as Vi returned.

'What's the matter, you look worried, Ma?'

'Your Pa's not well, Ellen. They brought him home from the yard. Doctor Salmon should be here any minute now. He's been over-working, that's all.'

'Can I go and see him?'

'No, wait until the doctor's been.'

'I think that's him now, Mrs Vannin,' Vi interrupted.

'Good. I'll go and let him in.'

Mary-Kate explained what had happened and Doctor Salmon shook his head. 'He's not a young man, Mary-Kate, and I've warned him about overdoing things, but he won't listen and having this fire hasn't helped. But let's have a look at him. Do you want to stay or shall we have a talk when I've finished?'

'We'll have a talk, Doctor. Lewis is a very private man in some respects and he'll tell you things he would never tell me, in case I worry. I'll get Vi to make some tea and we'll have it in the dining room. I'm afraid the sofa in the parlour is rather grubby.'

Twenty minutes later the doctor appeared at the dining room door. As soon as she saw his face Mary-Kate knew there was something very wrong and her stomach turned over with fear. 'What is it?'

'I'm afraid it's his leg.'

'His leg?'

'He said he was kicked as he was getting one of the horses out.'

'Yes, but he said he'd cleaned it and it was only bruised.'

'I'm afraid it's more than that. I'm going to have to send him to hospital.'

Her hand went to her throat and her eyes widened. 'Hospital! What for?'

'I can only hope we're not too late. I would say septicaemia has set in.'

'What's that?'

'Blood poisoning. At best they may have to amputate, at worst . . .'

She sat down and her hands were trembling. 'Amputate? Oh, dear God! No!'

'Has he not complained about it?'

'No. Oh, I begged him to let me look at it, but he's so stubborn.'

'Can you get some things together for him for the hospital?'

'Yes! Yes, of course! I'll go with him, Vi will stay with the children. Ellen is very sensible. Oh, dear Lord, Ellen!'

'Do you want me to tell her?'

'Would you, please? But don't tell her about . . . what they may have to do.'

'I won't. Now go on up to him. I've already told him the truth, he'll need you, Mary-Kate!'

Lewis was lying with his eyes closed and he seemed to have shrunk. He looked so old, so very different from the Lewis she knew. She touched his hand. 'Lewis, I'm coming with you. Everything is going to be just grand.'

He opened his eyes. 'I should have listened to you, Mary-Kate.'

'Oh, don't think like that, Lewis! The doctors will know what is best for you and you're a strong man and the good Lord will look after you. I'll just get a bag packed.'

She tried to sound calm and confident but inside she was so afraid. Afraid for him, for herself, for Ellen and for little Jamie. And she blamed herself. If only she'd insisted on tending his leg herself! But she couldn't think like that now. She must get things organized. She had to be her practical self.

As they were leaving for the hospital, she kissed Ellen and hugged Jamie and thanked Vi for being so good as to stay and look after them.

'Ma, is he going to . . . die?' Ellen whispered.

'Don't you even think like that, Ellen Vannin! You help Vi and I'll be home as soon as I can.' She bent and kissed her again, but Ellen's grey eyes were brimming with tears and she had difficulty fighting back her own.

She'd had to wait in the large, white-tiled waiting room in Walton Hospital. They wouldn't let her go into the ward with Lewis. The smell of carbolic soap and ether made her feel ill and she paced the room anxiously, occasionally peering along the corridor, wondering what was happening. What on earth were they doing? Why were they so long? It wasn't right that a wife should be kept away from her husband. She shuddered. There was an atmosphere of depression about the place and she remembered that Lewis had told her that in the old days it had been a workhouse. Oh, what were they doing?

At last Doctor Salmon appeared, accompanied by another doctor, and they spoke to the Sister. The woman nodded and then beckoned to Mary-Kate. She almost ran the few steps.

'Come in here, Mary-Kate.' Doctor Salmon led her into a small office. The other doctor followed and closed the door.

She looked from one to the other and swallowed hard. 'What?'

'Mary-Kate, if there was any other way we'd take it, but . . .'

Fear was creeping over her: it was oozing from the pores in her skin and she felt sick. 'But . . . what?'

'My dear, it's too late. If he'd come in a day or so ago . . . but there's nothing they can do now.'

'I'm so sorry, Mrs Vannin,' the other doctor concurred.

What were they telling her? Too late! Too late to save his leg?

'You can't save his leg?' she whispered.

Doctor Salmon took her hands in his. They were ice cold. He'd known Lewis Vannin for many years. He'd brought Ellen into the world and he'd ministered to Molly and her three tragic little sons. He'd brought Jamie into the world and now . . . 'It's too late to save his life, my dear. The poison is in the bloodstream. It's only a matter of time until the vital organs collapse and fail. A day, maybe less. A less fit man would have died before this. God knows how he's kept going.'

She couldn't take it in. It was absurd! It wasn't true! He'd been kicked by a horse, surely that couldn't cost him his life? 'Is there . . . nothing?' she heard herself ask.

'No. You can sit with him. They've put him in a side ward. Is there anything you want, my dear?'

Mary-Kate shook her head.

Doctor Salmon put his arm around her shoulder. 'Come along, I'll take you to him, unless you'd like a little time to compose yourself?'

'No. I want to see him now.'

Mary-Kate sat beside his bed, holding his hand, but Lewis had already slipped into a coma and didn't know she was there. As she looked at him she began to remember all the happy times they'd had together. But her thoughts were jumbled. She was back home, sitting beside her Pa, beside her brother. Oh, how she wished Sarah was with her. Lewis was going and leaving her alone. Sarah would understand how she felt. She would understand the fear and strange emptiness. She rubbed his hand, rough, workworn and scarred from the toil of the last few days.

A nurse brought her a cup of tea which she left to go cold, although she vaguely remembered thanking her and when the nurse returned she asked her to send for Canon Ormond. She sat, holding his hand, staring at him. His body was being poisoned and all because he'd tried to save a terrified animal. He'd tried to save something for Jamie and for her. She'd never felt so alone in her entire life.

Lewis had been given the last rites and because he was unconscious Mary-Kate had answered for him. The priest, who had been a friend of many years' standing, stayed with him, kneeling, praying silently, until at a quarter to four in the morning, Lewis Vannin slipped out of life. Mary-Kate knelt beside him, her cheek resting against his still warm hand and sobbed as Canon Ormond intoned the 'De Profundis' to speed the soul of his friend towards his Maker.

Chapter Twenty

———◆———

She'd got through it all far better than she had expected. She had had to be strong for Ellen's sake, for Ellen was taking it hard. She hadn't cried, not one tear. She'd just gone upstairs and locked herself in her father's dressing room and had refused to come out. Only when Mary-Kate had threatened to have the door broken down did she open it and although Mary-Kate had begged her to cry, to let loose all the grief she was bottling up inside, Ellen had just shaken her head, one of Lewis's gloves held tightly in her hand.

Mary-Kate was surprised at how kind people had been, too. She had never realized the extent to which Lewis had been respected, for cards and messages arrived from people she'd never heard of and the whole of his workforce, headed by Mr Johnson and Davies, had come to offer their condolences and had begged that four of them be allowed to carry the coffin. Doctor Salmon and Canon Ormond between them had taken care of all the formalities and arrangements. Vi and her mother had taken complete charge of the household and Ernest had sent telegrams to her mother, Bridget and Gina. Elizabeth was distraught, he'd informed her.

'Tell her . . . tell her to pray for him and thank you, Ernest, you've been so good.'

'It's nothing. Will your family be here for the funeral?'

'I don't know,' she answered, wishing with all her heart that she could just lay her head on Sarah's breast and cry out all her anguish.

Gina had sent a wreath, a large, expensive one, and a comforting note, deploring with all her heart that she wouldn't be able to come to the funeral, but that when it was all over, Mary-Kate must come down and bring the children. It would be good for them all. Edward, too, had sent her a note, asking if there was anything at all he could do? She'd been touched by his gesture, for she'd only met him a few times.

The postal service in the rural areas of the Free State was so bad that Sarah hadn't even received the telegram until the day of the funeral, but Bridget had come. And it had been Bridget who had found herself to be the strong one that day – she who had always been so timid, who had always shied away from situations like this. Oh, how she'd changed, she thought, as she held Mary-Kate's hand tightly throughout the Requiem Mass and the interment in Ford Cemetery. And it was to Bridget that Ellen finally sobbed out her pent up sorrow the night before her father's funeral. She had even had a few words of comfort for Elizabeth, who had sobbed noisily throughout the service. And she had sat up all night with Mary-Kate and listened with sorrow and shock to the events that had brought about Lewis's death.

'Oh, Mary-Kate, I wish I could stay longer. What are you going to do? Why don't you go down to Gina or back to Ma?'

'I can't. There are the children, the house, Vi, and . . . Oh, Bridget, such a short time, that's all I had with him. And I could have been a better wife to him!'

'Don't talk like that. You know it's not true.'

'It is! It's only now that I realize how much I loved him. He was good and kind and honourable. And I . . . I . . . dreaded him coming to my bed! What kind of a wife does that?'

'Stop it! Stop it, Mary-Kate!'

'I feel so guilty! I should have insisted on seeing to his leg. I should have thought . . .'

'Mary-Kate, tearing yourself apart like this won't do any good and you know it. You've got Ellen and Jamie to think of now.'

'I know. What can I do, Bridget? I relied on him so much.'

'You were always the sensible one, the practical one. You'll have to keep the family together. You'll have to run the business, for Jamie. You're no fool, Mary-Kate, you can do it.'

'But I know nothing about running a business!'

'Of course you do. You already do the books, don't you? Mr Johnson will keep the office going and I'm sure the men will help you out, they all turned out, didn't they? Why, they even carried . . . him, and they still need their jobs, don't they?'

'Oh, I don't know if I can face it!'

'You've got to. You've got to try, Mary-Kate. It's what Lewis would have wanted and expected of you, you know

388

I'm right!' Bridget fell silent. Was she really talking like this to Mary-Kate? Bridget, the one who had run like a scared rabbit from Lancaster Street from that weasel Bart. She'd changed. She'd grown to be more like her sister, like her mother.

Mary-Kate had known Bridget was right, but she was too tired, too bowed down with grief to think much about it now. She looked towards the window. It was dawn. 'You're going to be worn out, Bridget, you'll have had no sleep for two days. Do you have to go back this morning?'

'Yes, but Ma will be here soon. She'll take care of you until you're feeling better.'

'Oh, Bridget, I don't know what I'd have done without you.'

'You would have coped, Mary-Kate. You're stronger than you think. You always were.'

Mary-Kate looked at her sister, really looked at her for the first time since Bridget had arrived. 'You've changed, Bridget. You've grown up.'

'I had to. Life is hard, Mary-Kate and fate is unkind. We've both found that out to our cost, but perhaps it's all for a reason.'

As soon as Sarah arrived Mary-Kate felt as though a great weight had been lifted from her shoulders. Sarah took charge instantly and it was she who opened the door to Elizabeth and Ernest when Elizabeth at last came to the house she'd not set foot in for years.

Sarah showed them into the parlour where Mary-Kate and Ellen were trying to keep Jamie amused. All the pictures and the mirrors were draped in black and the room looked sombre despite the sunlight that came in through the window.

'I'm glad you've come Elizabeth. I wish you had come sooner,' Mary-Kate said with a catch in her voice. She wore a plain black dress with only a jet brooch at the neck and she looked very pale and thin.

Elizabeth also wore black, but the dress was embroidered with jet beads, and looked more like an evening dress than sombre mourning, Sarah thought.

'I . . . I couldn't bring myself to come. It was Ernest who persuaded me . . .' Elizabeth dabbed her eyes with a black-edged handkerchief. 'But at times . . . like this . . . we must be . . . practical.'

Sarah eyed her coldly. Elizabeth hated Mary-Kate and Sarah didn't think her views had been changed by her father's demise. So, the vultures were gathering. 'Practical' was it? Oh, she was hard and scheming to come here when Mary-Kate was so vulnerable. But Madam Elizabeth hadn't reckoned on her being here.

'Practical, now there's a fine word.'

Elizabeth ignored Sarah. 'It's so . . . so painful to me, Mary-Kate, to have to bring this up . . . but . . . did Father leave a will?'

Mary-Kate stared at her blankly for a second. 'A will?' she echoed. 'Oh, yes . . . I believe he did.'

'Elizabeth, don't you think we should leave this until later?' Ernest interrupted, looking uncomfortable.

'Ernest, it will have to be dealt with sooner or later. There's just no . . . suitable time.'

'It's all right, Ernest, I understand. Your father made provision for you, Elizabeth, despite . . . despite what he said.'

'In what way?'

'He left you the deeds to your house.'

'And?'

'Holy Mother of God! Your Pa's not cold in his grave and all you're interested in is how much money he's left you?' Sarah erupted.

'There isn't any money,' Mary-Kate said tiredly.

'What? I don't believe it!'

Mary-Kate pressed her fingers against her temples, wishing her step-daughter would just disappear. 'Mr Boreham, the solicitor, has the will. You may see him. But the business and the property, what's left, is for Jamie. Ellen has three houses and I have this house.'

'Mary-Kate, you've no need to tell her all this! She's a hard-hearted little madam, if ever I saw one! Would you kindly take your wife home, where she belongs, Ernest, and if I were you I'd go and see the solicitor. My daughter is not up to all this!'

Elizabeth turned on Sarah. 'I don't think any of this concerns you!'

'That's just where you're wrong! My daughter and my grandchildren concern me greatly. And as far as I can see, you came here to brow-beat her into agreeing to something. But you didn't expect me to be here, did you? Oh, I could see what your little game was right from the minute you walked through that door, dressed up as though you were going to the theatre and putting on such a fine display of grief. You'd make a good actress, Elizabeth, but it won't wear with me. I've already got one actress in the family and I learned her little tricks years ago!'

'And how is Mary-Kate going to run a business by herself?'

'As it's not your business, I don't see that it's any concern of yours, but at least now we've dropped all the pretence!'

'Ma, please?' Mary-Kate begged.

'Ellen, take Jamie upstairs. All this shouting is upsetting him and it's not helping you, either,' Sarah instructed.

Ellen picked up the little boy but, as she reached the door, she turned, her grey eyes blazing. 'You're hateful, Lizzie! You always have been and I hope you die tonight and go straight to Hell!'

When the door closed Sarah turned to Elizabeth. 'Are you satisfied now? Now that you've managed to upset everyone, even your little sister?'

'I didn't come here to upset anyone. She's always been a totally frightful child.'

'But she won't be a child for much longer. I'd look out for her – she hates you.'

Elizabeth was determined to hang on to her self-control and not be goaded. 'I came to put a proposition to you, Mary-Kate.'

'And just what kind of proposition would that be?' Sarah demanded.

Elizabeth kept her gaze on Mary-Kate. 'You will need someone to run the business and as Father saw fit to exclude me from his will . . .'

'No, he didn't. You've got your house.'

'*Ma!*' Mary-Kate's nerves were at snapping point.

'As I was saying, as everything is to go to his son, then Ernest will be quite willing to run the business for you until the boy is old enough to take over. He's very competent and quite trustworthy.'

He may be, but you're not, Sarah thought, and he dances to your tune. But she said nothing. It was Mary-Kate's decision.

'Ernest, what are your views?' Mary-Kate asked.

'I agree with my wife. It's too much for you, Mary-Kate. What with the shock, and the children to cope with, you need someone to take one worry off your shoulders.'

'I'll have to think about it, it's too soon yet . . .'

'Of course, we understand that. But Ernest is ready to take over just as soon as you are ready.'

'And that's an end to it, is it?'

'Yes!' Elizabeth snapped back at Sarah.

'Thank you both. Would you see them out Ma, please?'

'With the greatest of pleasure!'

When she came back, Sarah sat down facing her daughter. 'Mary-Kate I know it's been a terrible shock. After your Pa was killed I felt as though I didn't want to live either. I felt that the world was a dark and empty place. But I had to carry on because of you children and you'll have to do the same. You've got a treasure in Ellen, she's a good girl. You have your son and whatever you're feeling right now, Ernest does have a point. You can't run a business, about which you know little, and cope with all this! I hate to say it, but I think you should give the man a chance. He might just prove to be a godsend. He is honest and probably is efficient, but I'd watch that madam, I don't trust her an inch! Let Ernest take over the day to day affairs but you keep your eyes on the finances.'

'Oh, Ma, I'm so confused!'

'Of course you are, child.'

Mary-Kate reached out and Sarah took her hand. 'Ma, it was so quick. It was all so quick. I still can't believe he's gone. And I didn't have time to tell him how much I did love him. You'll never know just how much that hurts. He gave me everything. Everything!'

'And I suppose you gave him nothing? You gave him your affection, your trust, your loyalty and you gave him a son. Don't you think he knew you loved him? He did, Mary-Kate! It doesn't have to be spoken. In a marriage, actions speak just as loudly and clearly as words. Words can be empty. You've nothing to reproach yourself for. Now, I'll go up and see Ellen and persuade her to post this letter, although I'll probably be home weeks before it arrives. I'm going to write to the Dáil and complain, that I am! If they can't even get a telegram through on time, then God help the new Ireland! Oh, I wish I could stay longer than just a few weeks, but those two are less able to look after themselves than Ellen. They'd live on stale bread and cheese, left to themselves. The great eejits!'

Mary-Kate managed a weak smile. 'Men are worse than babies, aren't they?'

'They are! Of course, it's our fault, it's the way we bring them up! Now you rest, but think what I said about Ernest. At least he's an honest man, even if he is a doormat.'

'Days of Grace' had been running for a month. Everyone was raving over it and Gina had once again found herself being fêted by everyone. Her career had gone from strength to strength. Her life was a whirl of theatre suppers, parties, soirees and guest appearances. London society clamoured to entertain her and she was revelling in it.

Edward watched her with amusement. She was now making him quite a lot of money, but she hadn't really changed. Beneath the radiant smiles, the witty repartee, the glitter and glamour that she surrounded herself with, was an alert mind forever watching for advantageous opportunities. She was still searching, pushing forward, but for what he didn't know and he wondered if she really knew herself. She still used people and he was amazed that Helen Mason had lasted so long as her closest friend. But Helen was no threat to Gina. In fact, it suited Gina now to play 'Lady Bountiful' to Helen who was still only in the chorus. In return, Helen was grateful for the comforts of the flat in Bloomsbury and Gina's cast-off gowns which had been worn once or twice and then discarded. Edward still didn't like the friends Gina surrounded herself with, but he took some comfort from the fact that she was too devious and selfish to give her heart to any of the young men who were her constant companions. But he was worried about her health. Under the carefully made-up face and the shiny coiffured hair, she was looking tired. Too many late nights, too much champagne, snatched meals and constant work all were taking their toll and it was beginning to show. In private, her temper was very frayed. She was like an exquisite doll, he thought, beautifully dressed with a porcelain complexion and a fixed smile. But a doll that, when carelessly dropped, would shatter into brittle pieces. Gina lived on her nerves.

When the telegram had arrived informing her of Lewis Vannin's death, she had just got up. She'd called Edward and he'd gone over instantly. She'd looked pale and shocked, the white crêpe-de-chine robe with its high, ruffled neck enhancing her pallor.

'Gina, you look awful!'

'How else do you expect me to look? Glowing with health? I've had three hours' sleep and then . . .' She handed him the telegram and he noticed there were unshed tears in her eyes. 'Mary-Kate never said he was ill? In fact the last time she wrote she said everything was just fine.'

'I phoned before I came over. Apparently there was a fire at the yard. Lewis was kicked by one of his horses as he tried to get the beast out. The wound wasn't attended to and septicaemia set in. There was nothing anyone could do. The funeral is the day after tomorrow.'

'Oh, dear God! Poor Mary-Kate!' Gina reached for her cigarettes, another habit he disapproved of.

'Shall I make the arrangements?'

Gina had started pacing the floor, reminding him of a caged tiger he'd once seen in Regent's Park Zoo.

'What arrangements? Oh, I can't think straight! Poor Mary-Kate.'

'You *are* going?'

She sat down and stubbed out the cigarette. It was making her feel ill anyway and she knew he disapproved. 'I know this is going to sound desperately cruel, Edward, but how can I go? We're booked up for months, we've only been running a few weeks and people are paying to see me, not an understudy!'

He realized she was right, but surely this was one occasion when her heart should overrule her head. 'If you caught the sleeper straight after the show, you could be back in time for the performance next evening. You'd only miss the matinee.'

She ran her fingers through her hair and then pressed the tips of her fingers against her temples. 'Edward, look at me. I'm exhausted! I couldn't do that journey and then go on.'

'You seem to be able to find the energy to stay up half the night dancing when Freddie Marshalsea throws a party. Mary-Kate needs you! You didn't go to their wedding, the least you can do is go to his funeral.'

'Don't you think I know Mary-Kate needs me? Don't you think I want to be with her, comfort her? I know how she feels!'

'Do you, Gina?'

She jumped up and began pacing again and he couldn't see her face, but her voice was strangely quiet. 'Yes, I do. I saw my Pa buried and my brother and him only twenty-five years old. Oh, yes, I know how it feels.'

'Then isn't that even more of a reason why you should go?'

She shook her head violently. 'I can't, Edward! I just can't! Ma will come over and Bridget will go. I'll send a wreath – Mary-Kate will understand.'

Edward caught her by the shoulders, anger flooding his face. 'I just hope she does, Gina! And I hope that if you ever need her she'll forget how damned selfish you are! Knowing Mary-Kate, she will. Oh, go back to bed, Gina, you need your beauty sleep! You're beginning to look like Delia Heysham did before she retired.'

She twisted out of his grip, her face pale, her eyes haunted.

'You'll never understand, will you? Never! Oh, leave me alone! I don't need you to tell me how I look, I can see for myself in a mirror. Just leave me alone!'

Edward's anger had faded as for once she hadn't screamed the words at him. He'd reached out to take her hand but she'd moved away.

'Gina, what's the matter? What's driving you? You can't go on like this.'

Her eyes were still bright with unshed tears and for a moment he'd thought she was going to break down, but then she'd smiled.

'Leave me alone, Edward. If I told you, you wouldn't understand.'

'But something is driving you?' he'd persisted.

Again she'd smiled. 'Yes. Ambition. It's always been that and it always will be.'

He'd turned away. Exhaustion had obviously sapped her strength and weakened the volatility of her temper. And so he'd gone to arrange for a wreath to be sent from Gina to the brother-in-law she'd never known, and he wrote a letter to Mary-Kate.

He wondered why he loved Gina? Was it because she was so difficult, so selfish and so headstrong? These days she was like a highly-bred racehorse – skittish and edgy – which was why she needed a strong hand on the bridle. Yet he remembered her as she'd been the night he had first seen her in Liverpool. The fresh, young Irish girl with a voice and a face like an angel – and a temper that would make even Lucifer quake. He'd applauded her ambitions then; now he wondered if that ambition would destroy them both. He'd only himself to blame. He'd fuelled her dreams by bringing her to London. The theatre was his world, it always had been, yet there were times lately when he wished he could pack a bag and go away. As far away as possible and preferably where there were no theatres at all, but the only places like that were the African Bush or the outback of Australia.

At the end of the month the producer and the writer of the show were throwing a party and Edward and Gina had both been invited. Gina could hardly contain her excitement, thinking she'd at last been accepted into that exclusive, higher circle of theatrical society that she hovered on the fringe of. She'd talked about nothing else for a week wondering who she would meet, what she would wear, and praying she would be asked to sing.

The crowds had thinned as Edward parked the car and walked around to the stage door to collect Gina on the night of the party. Ellie opened the dressing room door to him and he knew by her expression that something was wrong.

'What's the matter, Ellie?' he whispered.

'She's not well, Mr Vinetti, but she won't admit it,' she whispered back as she ushered him in.

Gina was dressed in a stunning creation of white lace and silver-beaded fringe. A silver ribbon headband with two osprey feathers for decoration was fastened over her Titian hair. She was sitting applying rouge to her cheeks and, despite the artificial colour, she didn't look well.

'What's the matter?'

'There's nothing the matter! Ellie's fussing about nothing, as usual. Do you like my dress?'

'Beautiful, not to say stunning, but your tongue is a little sharp!'

'So would yours be if you felt like . . . Oh, pass me my wrap!'

Ellie handed her the short white fur cape and Gina pulled it around her shoulders and stood up. 'Are we ready?'

'You're not going. You're ill. I can tell just by looking at you!'

'Oh, don't start, Edward, please. I'm going to-night even if I have to crawl there. I'm going to enjoy myself.'

'That's what I think is the matter with you. You've been "enjoying" yourself too much!'

Gina's eyes narrowed. 'You can stay here if you want to, but I'm going! This is one of the biggest nights in my career – anyone who is anyone will be there. Ellie, get them to call me a cab.'

Ellie looked from Edward to Gina.

'Go on! Do as I tell you!'

'Miss O'Donnell, don't you think Mr Vinetti is right?'

Gina snatched up her bag and gloves and got as far as the door before she staggered and swayed.

Instantly they were both beside her.

She was fine, she told herself. It was just a dizzy spell. She'd had a few before, it would pass. But the light-headedness, the leaden feeling in her limbs didn't pass and she leaned her head against his shoulder.

He picked her up and carried her to the couch. 'Gina,

you're going home and I'm calling a doctor, although I don't think there's anything wrong with you that a few weeks rest won't cure.'

'I can't rest! What about the show?'

'To hell with the show! You're on the verge of collapse. You've had about two nights off since you went into rehearsal. You can't go on like that indefinitely, Gina. You'll end up in hospital and then your career will go right down the drain. I've seen it happen time and time again. In a few days, when you're a bit stronger, you're going home.'

She stared up at him, her expression dazed and puzzled. 'Home? I thought I was going home now?'

'I mean home to Ireland and I'm coming with you. I've had enough of London!'

The doctor diagnosed nervous exhaustion and recommended rest and a complete change of air and agreed that a trip home would be most beneficial. He gave Gina a sedative and she slept for two days and two nights, during which time Edward made all the arrangements. He had threatened Helen with instant and violent eviction if she disturbed Gina. He reminded her that Gina was now earning enough money to more than pay for the flat; she didn't need Helen's contributions.

He told Gina that they would have time to call and see Mary-Kate before they caught the overnight ferry to Dublin and, because she was so weak and depressed, she had begun to cry, blaming herself for neglecting her family so much.

'Pull yourself together, Gina, this isn't doing you any good! Mary-Kate has enough on her mind without you weeping and wailing and beating your breast with guilt. She will want to hear positive things, not a catalogue of your woes!'

So, three days later they boarded the train at Euston. Gina still looked pale and tired, but Edward was certain that a week in the quiet Irish countryside would work wonders.

It was supper time when they arrived at Mary-Kate's and it was Ellen who opened the door to them. Her eyes widened and her mouth formed an 'O'.

'Hello, Ellen, is your Ma at home?'

'Mr Vinetti! Aunt Gina!' She turned and ran back, yelling at the top of her voice for Mary-Kate. Edward smiled. She'd grown. She'd be a pretty young woman one day, when she'd filled out and lost her tomboyish ways.

Mary-Kate appeared from the kitchen, her black mourning dress making her look older and paler. She'd lost weight, Edward thought, but she hadn't lost that air of serenity.

Mary-Kate threw her arms wide and Gina ran to her. Edward put his arm around Ellen's shoulder as Mary-Kate and Gina embraced, tears in both their eyes.

Gina felt a wave of remorse sweep over her. Oh, how could she have been so selfish as not to have come when Mary-Kate needed her? As she clung to her sister, she remembered how they'd clung together in shock and disbelief when Matty had told them of their Pa's death. In her heart she knew that fear of a similar scene was the real reason why she hadn't come.

'Oh, Mary-Kate, I'm so sorry. I've been so selfish!'

'Gina, don't talk like that. You mustn't blame yourself. Oh, look at us, wailing like two banshees! Come on in. Why didn't you let me know you were coming? Where are you staying?'

'We can't stay long, I'm afraid. I'm taking her home for a complete rest. She's worn herself out and is under doctor's orders,' Edward answered. 'But we couldn't leave without seeing you.'

'You're going home to Clonmel?'

Gina nodded, wiping her eyes. 'I'm staying at Kilsheelan with Ma, and Edward is staying at Hearn's. Mary-Kate used to work at Hearn's Hotel, Edward.'

'I wish I were coming with you,' Mary-Kate said sadly.

'Why don't you? It would do you good.'

Mary-Kate smiled at Edward. 'I have too much to do here.' She led them into the parlour.

'How are things, Mary-Kate? We were both so terribly sorry about Lewis,' Edward asked gently.

She touched the gold locket she wore around her neck that held his picture and a lock of his hair. 'I'm managing. Ernest is looking after the business and he seems to be doing well, although he isn't terribly good with the men, so I hear. But life has to go on, and I have the children to think of. Ma told me that was the only thing that kept her going.'

'You were always the one who was so calm and rational. I wish I were like you,' Gina said quietly.

Edward laughed. 'I wish she were like you, too. Then I wouldn't have to drag her forcibly away from London to take a rest!'

'It will do you good, Gina, you've been working too

hard. Ma's been worried about you for a long time. What time does the boat leave?'

'Not until ten o'clock, so we'll have time to catch up on things, won't we?'

Ellen had insisted that she bath Jamie and put him to bed so Mary-Kate could spend the time with Gina. Edward volunteered to help.

'I didn't know you were interested in children?' Gina remarked in surprise.

'Oh, there are a lot of things you don't know about me, Gina! I'm a man of many surprises. Besides, I like children. It's only when they grow up they acquire the nasty habits of grown ups.' Edward laughed as he hoisted Jamie on to his shoulders and the little boy chuckled with delight.

'I'm glad he's going with you, Gina,' Mary-Kate said, as she watched the two of them leave the room. 'He'll take care of you. He's very fond of you.'

'Edward! He's only protecting his investment. You don't know him like I do.'

'You always were a bit of a fool, Gina, and I mean that in the nicest way. He loves you! Even I can see that. Why else would he put up with you? Knowing you, I don't suppose you've changed?'

'Now who's being a fool, Mary-Kate? Edward is much too cynical, too set in his ways, to love anyone. And there are times when I absolutely hate him.'

Mary-Kate smiled. 'They say love and hate are two sides of the one coin!'

'You're match-making! Well, it won't work! I don't intend to get married – ever!'

'You should, it can be a wonderful experience.'

'Oh, I'm sorry! I'm so thoughtless!'

'No, not thoughtless. Impetuous, you always were, but don't waste your life chasing dreams, Gina! Reality can be much more rewarding!'

As the *Pride of Erin* pulled away from the Princes Landing Stage, Gina stood and waved to Mary-Kate and Ellen who had insisted on going to see her off.

'She's a remarkable woman, your sister. I admire her very much.'

She thought about Mary-Kate's words and then dismissed them.

'She was always different from me and even Bridget. She's like Ma in many ways.'

'And who are you like, Gina, your father?'

She shook her head. 'No, not really. Oh, I get my determination from him, but I think I must be the "black sheep", every family has one I believe.'

'And are you looking forward to going home?'

She smiled. 'The last time I made this crossing, I vowed I'd travel First Class and that I'd need porters to carry my luggage and everyone on board would be thrilled to be travelling on the same boat as me!'

'Well, we are going First Class, you did need porters to get all your stuff on board, but I don't know about the passengers although I did see a few heads turn in your direction. Will that do?'

'Oh, I was boasting. I told everyone I'd come back rich and famous, the truth was I couldn't wait to leave!'

She watched the dim outline of the buildings of the Liverpool waterfront fade into the mist of the night. 'I wonder how much Clonmel has changed? I never took much notice of what was going on there, but I suppose it has changed. Nothing stays the same, does it?'

'No, Gina, nothing does, sadly.'

Chapter Twenty-One

———◆———

I T HADN'T CHANGED MUCH, Gina thought, at least not from this distance. The train was skirting the bottom of Sleivemanon and dropping down the gentle gradient of the hillside towards Prior Park Station.

'It's beautiful. So peaceful,' Edward remarked quietly as they looked down on the rich, rolling pastureland. The small town lay in a bowl as though cupped in a giant hand, circled by Slievenamon and the peaks of the Comeraghs in neighbouring Waterford County. The river was a silver ribbon, winding and twisting through it.

'"Cluain Meala" is its Irish name. It means "Honey Meadow",' Gina said with detachment. She was tired, for the journey had sapped what little strength she had.

'It's very apt. It must be the Irish blood in me, for it feels as though you're not the only one who is coming home.'

She looked at Edward with surprise. What a strange thing for him to say. But she didn't waste much time on exploring the reasoning behind his words. 'I hope Ma and Matty aren't late, I don't feel like waiting around.'

'Who knows, there may be a civic reception waiting for you!' he joked.

Gina brightened. 'Do you think so?'

'I was only joking. I told your mother you were to have complete rest, at least for a week.'

She looked disappointed.

'Oh, you'll have plenty of time to show yourself off and no doubt they won't let you leave without throwing some sort of a shindig!'

She smiled to herself, thinking of the day they'd all stood on the steps of St Mary's and announced that they were leaving. She was the first one to come back, but although that girlish boast had become reality, she couldn't take much satisfaction from it, she was too exhausted.

Matty and Sarah were both waiting behind the barrier and Sarah raised her hand to wave as she caught sight of them.

Gina smiled. Ma hadn't changed and neither had Matty, but as Sarah hugged her tightly she felt the tears sting her eyes and suddenly she realized just how much she'd missed her mother.

'Look at you! Skin and bone and worn to a shadow.' Sarah held her at arms' length.

'I'm just tired, Ma. But it's so good to be home.'

'It's plenty of rest you need and I'll make sure you get it. And is this the one who's been working you to death then?'

'Yes, this is Edward and he hasn't been working me to death at all!'

'I'm not guilty on that account. She's done all that by herself! Your daughter is one of the most stubborn women I've ever met, Mrs O'Donnell!' Edward smiled as he shook the hand Sarah extended to him.

'Sure, that's something I don't need reminding about. She hasn't changed then?'

Gina laughed. 'If anything, I've got worse I suppose, otherwise I wouldn't have ended up like this, would I?'

'Heaven preserve us! I didn't think you could get any worse. She needs a strong hand does this one.' Sarah looked meaningfully at Edward, but he just shrugged.

'Are we going to be standing here all day, then?' Matty interrupted.

'That we are not! Matty, load those cases into the trap, if you can get them all in and have enough room for us as well.' Sarah, her arm around Gina's waist, guided her towards the trap.

Matty with Edward's help took the luggage.

'Is it back you are to stay then? Sure, you look as though you've brought your entire wardrobe. We'll not get all this lot in!'

'Then leave some of it with Mr O'Brien and come back for it later, you great eejit! Himself won't mind, he'll keep an eye on it!' Sarah stated tersely as she helped Gina up, studying the pale face with a frown. She'd need more than a few days to get rid of that unhealthy pallor and put some weight on the gaunt frame. Gina looked ill. A mere shadow of her former self.

'If you've not come back for good, you'll have to stay at least two months so everyone can enjoy the fashion parade. You've enough here to wear at least two outfits a day,' Matty remarked in his dry fashion.

Edward roared with laughter at this and it was

obvious to both women that the two men had hit it off right away.

Everything was so much smaller than she remembered. The streets seemed narrower; the shops tiny and a little drab and the people who waved and called out to her were dressed in styles reminiscent of the previous decade. It all seemed a million miles away from London.

She'd forgotten, too, that there would be no bathroom, only an outside privy and that water still had to be carried in from the pump at the back of the house. How quickly she'd become accustomed to the hustle and bustle of city life, of wide streets congested with traffic, of elegant shops and houses all with the most modern conveniences. But she had also forgotten how tranquil it was and she began to relax as they meandered along the narrow lanes, where only the birdsong and the clip-clopping of the horse's hooves broke the silence.

Matty took the cases upstairs with instructions from Sarah not to bang them into every piece of furniture on the way, and after they'd had a light meal he offered to drive Edward back into town to the hotel and to collect the rest of the 'wardrobe', as he described it.

'And don't you be stopping there, Matty O'Donnell! There's things to be done.'

'Don't I know that well enough, Ma.'

'Aye, well, you tend to forget over a few jars of stout and I don't want you driving under the influence or the Garda bringing you home – again!'

Matty raised his eyes to the ceiling and grinned at Edward. 'Once! Last Christmas. You'd think it was a regular occurrence!'

'I'm saying nothing about the Tipperary Hunt and Declan O'Hagan and the fact that it took three of the Guards to separate you. That little episode I've forgotten!'

Matty grinned again at the open curiosity on Edward's face. 'She's forgotten it! Come on, I'll tell you about it on the way. Oh, it was a fine day, it was.'

When they'd gone, Sarah went upstairs and quietly opened the door to Gina's room. She stood watching her for a moment. She felt as though Gina were almost a stranger now. It was so long since she'd seen her and she had changed, but that didn't make her love her any the less.

'It's good to have you home, Gina. We've missed you and I haven't had to fill up that enamel jug for years. In fact, I think I threw it at those two renegades who came trying to get Matty to join them.'

Gina smiled. 'Oh, I've still got the divil of a temper, Ma, but I've missed you, too!'

Sarah sat on the end of the bed and studied her. 'Have you, Gina, truthfully? You were always the most independent, even when you were a little girl. You knew just what you wanted and how to get it. Are you happy now?'

'Yes, I suppose I am.'

'But once you're well enough, you'll go back to London and back to chasing your dreams again. Are they worth it, Gina?'

'To me they are, Ma.'

'And what will you be doing when you've got everything you've ever dreamed of? What will you do then?'

'I don't know. I still want to go to America. That's where the opportunities are now. I haven't given up that dream.'

'Oh, Gina, what are you trying to prove? You are a success and you've enough money and clothes to last a lifetime.'

Gina looked out of the window and watched the sunlight gleaming on the bronze feathers of the rooster that strutted around the yard, trying to find the right words. 'I don't know what I'm trying to prove, Ma. I just want to go on and on. It's all just like a dream – a lovely dream!'

'Don't waste your life chasing dreams, child! They have no substance. They're like bits of thistledown which, when you catch them in your hand, are limp and useless. It's only in the air that they float so beautifully.'

'I wanted to . . . to make Pa proud of me. To make the name O'Donnell one to be proud of, too.'

Sarah reached out and took her hand. 'He'd be right proud of you, Gina. Even if you hadn't gone to London and become such a success. And the name O'Donnell is famous enough, I'm thinking. Kings of Ulster, isn't that famous enough for you? You can't re-write history, Gina!'

She didn't answer. Her head was beginning to ache and lethargy was stealing over her. 'I think I'll lie down now, Ma.'

Sarah got up and gently stroked the short Titian hair. 'You do that, meanwhile I'll fend off the army of so-called "well-wishers" who will be beating their way to the door, led by Mrs Butler-Power no doubt! It's a wonder that woman's nose hasn't grown by a foot, for she's always poking it into everyone's business!'

Gina laughed. No, things hadn't changed much.

'It's good to hear you laughing again.'

The laughter bubbled up as though it had been suppressed, but to Sarah it had the ring of hysteria and then Gina began to cough. Sarah patted her on the back. 'Now see the state you've got yourself in!'

'Oh, I just breathed in at the wrong time,' Gina spluttered.

'And how long have you had that cough?'

Gina was taking deep breaths just as Signora Scarlatti had taught her.

'Did you hear me? How long have you had that cough?'

'It's not really a cough, Ma. I just get a bit short of breath sometimes. It's all to do with the breathing.'

'Is that so? Well, while you're here you can see Doctor Byrne. I don't like "coughs".'

'Ma, stop fussing! I saw the doctor in London and he said I was just exhausted and needed a rest.'

'And how long has he known you? You'll see Doctor Bryne. He's known you all your life – he brought you into the world – and there's an end to it. Now, get some rest.'

Gina sighed as she lay down. She was too tired to argue, but if it would keep Ma happy she would see old Doctor Byrne.

She went to see him two days later. She had insisted that there was nothing wrong with her that rest wouldn't cure, but Sarah was adamant. She did, however, put her foot down very firmly about her mother accompanying her. Edward would drive her there and back in the trap, she'd said determinedly, with the set of her chin that Sarah knew of old.

Doctor Byrne's house was in Queen Street and was the end one of a row of Georgian houses with ornamental ironwork railings and small balconies above the front doors. It hadn't changed and neither had he. He was a big, burly man with a ruddy complexion and for as long as she could remember he'd always worn tweed jackets that looked slightly shabby. In fact, he could be mistaken for a farmer not a doctor, Gina thought. His bushy hair was a little greyer, as were his eyebrows which seemed to sprout in all directions, but the blue eyes still twinkled and the smile still hovered on his lips. She'd always liked him.

'So, you've come home to see us at last!' He took her hand and shook it heartily. 'And just what have you been doing to yourself and what's all this about exhaustion and a cough?'

'It's Ma fussing as usual.' She smiled.

'Sit down and tell me all about it, then.'

She sat and told him of her collapse, of her hectic life-style and the diagnosis of the doctor in London.

'It's no wonder you dropped like a fly! Gina, the human body will only take so much punishment before it rebels. Do you sleep well at all? When you find the time, that is?'

She frowned. 'I've never really thought about it.'

'Think about it now.'

'I suppose so, although . . .'

'Go on.'

'Sometimes I wake up feeling . . . hot and sticky.'

'And this cough – how long have you had it?'

'It's not really a cough. I just sort of catch my breath wrong, if you know what I mean, then I cough and wheeze a bit, then I try to take deep breaths and it goes. So you see, it's not a proper cough.'

'How long have you had this cough that isn't a cough at all?'

'I don't know. I've not really taken much notice of it.' She was beginning to feel sorry she'd come.

'A few weeks, a month, a couple of months?' he persisted.

Gina was becoming irritated. 'Oh, I suppose a month, maybe.'

'And the tiredness, the exhaustion?'

'I'm always tired, I work very hard!' She couldn't keep the note of sharpness out of her voice.

'I think I'll just have a listen to your chest and then we'll see.'

She became alarmed. She'd only come to pacify Sarah. She started to protest and then, as if to confirm his doubts, she began to cough. He was instantly beside her, holding out a piece of white gauze.

'Spit it out Gina! Now! Don't swallow it!'

She shook her head.

'Do as you're told, girl! Spit it out!'

She pressed the cloth to her mouth and shuddered with disgust as she spat out the phlegm. Oh, how disgusting! How degrading! And why had it come on her now, of all times! She wished she'd never listened to Sarah. Dr Byrne was studying the gauze and she turned her head away.

'Now, I'll listen to that chest and I don't want any complaints!'

When he'd finished he sat on the edge of his desk looking down at her, the smile gone from his eyes. It was as he'd expected, but he'd hoped he was wrong. However, he'd seen too much of it not to recognize the symptoms and she was a classic case. Her working life was spent mingling with all kinds of people and in cramped dressing-rooms and corridors. She'd worked herself into the ground and left herself wide open to infection, but she was so young, so lovely and with such a wonderful career ahead. It was at a time like this that he hated his work. 'How long do you intend staying in Clonmel?'

'Only a couple of weeks, I can't spare any more time.' She was very apprehensive now.

'Gina, you need to stay for six months, maybe longer!'

She jumped up, fear in her eyes. 'What's wrong with me? What's wrong?'

The doctor caught her by the shoulders and gently eased her back into the chair and then took both her hands in his. 'I'll have to have it confirmed but, well, I've seen enough of this to be almost certain . . .'

'Enough of what? For God's sake tell me!'

'Oh, Gina, my child, it breaks my old heart, that it does, but : . . I'm sure it's . . . consumption.'

The dreaded word was out and he saw a whole gamut of emotions cross her face – shock, disbelief, horror, fear. She struggled to speak but he shook his head. 'If you have plenty of rest, good food, clear air, if we've found it in time . . .' He could tell she wasn't listening.

'How . . . how long?'

Again he shook his head. 'I don't know, child. Before God and the Holy Virgin, I don't know! Months, years . . . do you want me to tell your Ma?'

'No!' The word was clear, decisive.

'Why not?'

'I don't want anyone to know! No one!'

He thought he understood. The social stigma. You might just as well paint a black cross on the front door of the house, he thought. It was considered in much the same way as the plague; it made the entire family social outcasts. Oh, he understood.

She got up, shaking off his assistance.

'Gina, where are you going? There are some things I can give you to help.'

'I don't know! I just . . . want to be on my own!'

He opened the door for her. 'Come back and see me tomorrow and remember, this door is always open to you day or night!'

Edward came towards her, the concern evident in his eyes. 'Gina, you look awful. What's wrong?'

'Nothing! Just leave me alone. Take me . . . Oh, just drop me off by the river. I want to think! I want to be by myself! I'll walk home.'

'Your mother will skin me alive if I let you walk. Gina, something's wrong. What did the doctor say?'

She turned on him. 'Just leave me alone, Edward! Just go away!'

He shrugged. Obviously Doctor Byrne had said something to upset her. Perhaps he'd even advised a break in her career. 'All right, suit yourself. I'll drop you by Kilsheelan Bridge, it's not too far to walk from there.'

As soon as the sound of the horse's hooves had died away, Gina walked along the towpath until she was underneath the bridge. No one could see her here either from the road or from on top of the bridge. She leaned her back against the cold, damp stones of the arch. It couldn't be true! It couldn't! Only people like the

O'Hagans got consumption. Living in dirty, over-crowded hovels with not enough to eat. Not people like herself who had had the best of everything! He must be mistaken! He must! She felt cold and chilled and clutched her arms tightly around her. Oh, it was too monstrous, too horrible to even contemplate! There was no cure, she'd seen the slow, lingering decline. She'd heard of the awful, choking death. She began to shake. It wasn't going to happen to her! It wasn't! He was wrong. What did he know anyway? He was only a country doctor. But a tiny voice somewhere in her mind told her he was right. She began to cry. She wouldn't let it happen to her! She was too young, she still had so much to do, she wasn't going to die! Her mind refused to accept that. She'd fight it. She'd always been a fighter, she'd never been one to just give in. She'd fight with every ounce of strength and courage she had and no one, no one at all, would ever know! She could stand anything but pity and no one was going to pity her! But how long? How long before the cough got worse? Before she was unable to sing? She'd rest as much as she could, that's what she'd do. But how could she? People would notice and ask questions. Why wasn't she her usual vivacious self? No, she would have to go on. It would be the most daunting role that she'd ever had and she would give a fine performance. But at the end there'd be no applause. Just the flowers. Oh, there'd be the flowers – at the end.

Gina straightened up and wiped away the tears with the back of her hand. Not by a single word, a single gesture would she indicate to anyone that something was wrong. She'd cram as much as she possibly could into what time there was left. She'd glitter and sparkle and she'd go in a burst of glory. Somehow she'd find the strength and the courage. She looked around her. It was dank and the water looked dark and menacing and a terrible fear gripped her. She wanted to run to someone, to feel safe and protected. She fought it down. She wasn't afraid! She'd never been afraid of anything. She walked out into the sunlight, leaving the darkness and the fear behind and somehow the world looked brighter, the colours richer, the sounds sweeter, even the air clearer and fresher. She'd live every single moment of it to the full from now on.

Both Sarah and Edward had their work cut out keeping the curious at a distance, and only Father Maguire and Doctor Byrne had been allowed to enter the house. Doctor Byrne had pleaded with Gina to let him at least tell Sarah, but she had refused point blank, saying that she'd already caused her mother enough pain and she wasn't going to add to it. But, despite her promise to herself, when the parish priest sat with her in the parlour and with the wisdom that came from decades of listening to all the sorrows of mankind, asked her what was troubling her, she'd broken down and told him. He didn't try to console her with platitudes or make flowery speeches about the road to heaven being strewn with thorns. He took her hands and said, 'Just trust in the Good Lord, Gina. He'll give you the strength you need.'

After a week of peace, rest and good, plain food, Gina appeared to have recovered. The dark shadows had disappeared from beneath her eyes, the pinched look had gone from her face and Sarah swore she was putting on some weight. It was due, Gina told them, to the tonic Doctor Byrne had prescribed.

Edward had remarked on her apparent recovery.

'And why shouldn't she have made a wonderful recovery?' Sarah demanded. 'She's young and she's as stubborn as old man Heggartey's donkey, but don't think you'll get away with taking her back before she's made a public appearance! I can't keep Mrs Butler-Power away for ever, that one's got ideas above her station and always has had!'

'I suppose you're right, and I also suppose that it's only fair, but I'll make the arrangements.'

'What arrangements?' Gina enquired, coming into the kitchen.

'Never you mind, Miss! Edward has come to take you for a quiet walk and to do some fishing. Matty has informed him – in his infinite wisdom – that there's trout in the river, just past the bridge.'

It was a beautiful, late summer evening and they met no one as they drove the trap down the lane to the crossroads. Edward unhitched the horse and tied a long rope to its halter, allowing it to graze but not wander off.

'Who taught you to do that?' Gina laughed.

Whatever the good doctor had said to her that day had obviously had some effect, Edward thought. 'Matty. I've learned a lot of things since I've been here. I could get used to this kind of life. No one rushes. People have time to stop and talk to you, even if you've never set eyes on them before.'

'They're just curious and you'd be bored silly in a couple of months, especially in winter. It's not like this all the time. Sometimes it just rains and rains and rains and it's so miserable, even though it's a soft rain. And besides, nothing ever happens here.'

'How can you say that? Two wars, the emergence of a new nation and Clonmel's most famous daughter home at last. I wouldn't call that nothing!'

She sat down on the grass verge beside the towpath and watched him as he cast out his line towards the Gurteen bank, where the pines rose like dark sentinels. Just beyond them could be seen the neo-gothic turrets of Kilsheelan Castle. Gina pulled the head off a dandelion that had gone to seed. Dandelion clocks, they used to call them as children. She blew on it gently and watched the gossamer-like seeds drift off into the air and she remembered Sarah's words. She threw the remaining head and stalk into the slow-moving waters of the Suir and watched it float away.

She wondered if Edward really meant he was getting used to this kind of life. He'd changed since he'd been here. He'd lost that perpetually cynical look and they hadn't had one cross word. He had been made more than welcome by the town and he was quite at ease, dressed in an old pair of trousers and a shirt, wandering the lanes or leaning on the parapet down at the quays talking to the labourers and boatmen. This was a side of him she'd never seen before. She struggled to push back the black thoughts that usually only came with the dark hours of the night. Here, she could almost forget, almost . . . and when he was like this it weakened her resolve and more than once she had been tempted to tell him. The impulse passed, the fear receded.

She heard the 'plop' of a fish as it broke the surface and she heard him curse softly. She smiled. He might enjoy the quiet life but he was no fisherman. The smile faded as she remembered how Pa had often caught the brown-speckled trout by lying on his stomach and slowly and quietly immersing his hand and arm in the water, tickling the fish gently to lull it, then flipping it deftly on to the bank. Oh, how happy those days had been. Why couldn't time have stood still? She thought of the poem he'd taught them all about the Suir, but she could only remember a few lines now:

'When hauling horses and warbling sea-gulls
They join in chorus – melodious, pure –
Sure the trout and eels dance jigs and reels
By the lovely banks of the sweet river Suir'

'Don't look so miserable. I gave up – I must be using the wrong sort of bait.' Edward laid down the rod and stretched out on the grass beside her.

'Pa used to catch them with his hands.'

'Then he must have been a better man than I am, I can't even get them to take a fly! What's the matter? Why so glum?'

'Oh, I was just thinking.'

'What about? Going back?'

She shook her head. 'About this place.'

'It must be one of the most beautiful places on earth.'

'Not for me.' There was an edge to her voice.

'Oh, I can see you're better and itching to get back.'

'No, I was thinking about Pa and Fergal and . . . death.'

'Why so morbid?'

'You remember, when the telegram came about Lewis, I said I knew how Mary-Kate felt?'

He nodded, watching her closely, there was pain in her eyes.

'I told you you wouldn't understand.'

'But you didn't tell me what I wouldn't understand.'

'What drives me, what I'm trying to prove, as both you and Ma keep saying.'

'So what does, Gina?' Edward felt she was very close to opening her heart to him and he waited, hardly daring to breathe.

She looked up and pointed downriver. 'Down there you can just see the ruins of St Sillan's church. It's all overgrown now, but . . . that's where Fergal was killed. He was shot in an ambush. For me, after Pa died, it was the end. I hated everything about this place and everyone in it! After that I felt I would never find happiness here.' Oh, if only he knew how ironic those words were.

'Your father has something to do with all this, hasn't he?'

Gina picked another dandelion and twisted it between her fingers and nodded. 'The day I stood in St Mary's churchyard, when . . . they laid him to rest. I swore I'd make him proud of me. That I wouldn't stop until everyone knew who I was and that I was the best – that Patrick O'Donnell's daughter was the best!'

'You've done that now, Gina. Isn't it time you laid the ghost?'

She shivered. 'No, it's not time. I still have so much to do.'

He raised himself on one elbow and looked at her. 'When will it be time?'

'I want to go to America. I've always wanted to go. It was where I was determined to go when I left here.'

'So you can work yourself into the ground again? Oh, Gina, what am I going to do with you?' Edward laughed. 'Why not marry me and stay here? We could have a dozen little Ginas or Georges or Georginas!' he quipped. 'Who knows, it might be fun?'

Her heart turned cold. Even if she had wanted it, there could never be a marriage or children . . . not now. She sat up. 'Stop teasing me! You know I have no intention of marrying anyone and it's in very bad taste after what I've just told you. I thought you'd understand.'

He got up and picked up the rod and she couldn't see his face, but when he turned to help her up there was that familiar, amused look in his eyes, the cynical smile on his lips.

'It was a joke, Gina! I'm not the marrying kind either. You should know that by now!'

She'd been so certain he hadn't been joking. But strangely she was the one who felt hurt. She'd bared her soul to him and he'd joked. She would never, never confide in him again.

'Oh, by the way, before we leave I have promised that dreadful Butler-Power woman that you will sing a few songs from your wildly successful shows at some sort of soiree she's giving in your honour!'

'I thought I was supposed to be resting? How much are you charging her? You never miss an opportunity to make money do you, Edward?'

'That's how I make my living, in case you'd forgotten. But in fact I'm not charging anything this time. I think you can give your home town an hour of your time, free, don't you?'

He was hurt and disappointed. He'd almost found the deep-seated core of her ambition. He'd wanted to tell her that she had to give up her futile quest for her particular Holy Grail. It was only something that existed in her mind and heart. But yet again, he'd lost her.

Ian hadn't spoken a word the whole of the way home and Bridget could see something was troubling him, but knew it was useless to ask. David hadn't been over for almost a week and the last time he had come he'd only stayed half an hour. She decided to try another tack.

'Your mother's not well, although she refuses to admit it. Just the odd headache, she says.'

'Do you think she should see a doctor?'

'I don't know. What do you think, she's your mother?'

He shrugged.

'She's worrying over you. That's what's the matter with her.'

'She's imagining things. She's getting old, that's all.'

'You sound as though you don't care and that's not like you. You are one of the most caring people I know.'

He didn't answer.

'I don't imagine things, Ian. You've changed. You never laugh any more and you're moody. It's got something to do with David, hasn't it?'

'No! We've had all this out before, Bridget. I'm all right.'

She could see she was getting nowhere. 'Shall I suggest that your mother goes to see the doctor, or shall I just call him in? You know what she's like.'

'Has she complained of anything else other than headaches?'

'Only her rheumatics, but that's to be expected at her age.'

Ian kicked a small stone out of his path as they turned into Cartland Drive. 'Let's see how she goes.'

'And that's your answer to everything, isn't it? I don't know what's got into you lately, Ian Duncan! You don't seem to care about anything or anyone.'

'Will you just leave me alone, Bridget, please!'

It was her turn to shrug as they went in. He was worrying his mother silly, although with her usual indomitable spirit, Mrs Duncan wouldn't admit it or even deign to recognize the change in her son. But Bridget had made up her mind to go and see David and try and get some sense out of him.

She went into the parlour and saw that the old lady was sitting with a letter in her lap, her glasses on the cushion beside her.

'How are you? Any more headaches today?'

'Not the sort you mean!' came the sharp reply.

'Is there something wrong? I don't want to pry, but . . . ?'

'You're always prying, but you mean well.'

Bridget took no notice; she'd learned to ignore the forthright remarks.

'I had this at lunchtime, from Mrs Lennox. She's going to live with her daughter because she can't manage by herself any more. I can't say I blame her, but I just hope she won't regret giving up her home. If I remember rightly, that Alice of hers is a bossy piece, even as a wean she was too forward by half!'

Bridget sat down beside her. Mrs Lennox rented the small house Mrs Duncan owned in Melville Street in Pollokshields East. 'So, what will you do?'

'I'm too old to be bothered finding new tenants and getting someone to collect the rent and do the repairs. It's not worth the trouble. I'll sell it.'

'I know it's none of my business . . .'

'No, it's not, but you're going to say something anyway, so go on.'

'I know of someone who would jump at renting a house like that.'

'Half of Glasgow would "jump" at the chance!'

'I know that, but my friend Bernie would make an excellent tenant, she would!'

'The one who helped you move in here?'

'Yes. Archie is quite handy, he could fix anything that needs doing and Bernie will bring the rent here, or Eileen could give it to me. Won't you give them a chance, just as you gave me one?'

'You've the gift of the blarney, Bridget O'Donnell!'

'Then will you offer it to them?'

'Only if you do something for me in return.'

'What?'

'Find out why my son is moping around as if he had the cares of the whole world on his shoulders and can't speak a civil word to his own mother!'

Bridget sighed. 'I've tried. Believe me, time and again, I've tried.'

'This nonsense has gone on long enough!'

'I know. I'm going to see David to see if I can get to the bottom of it. They used to be so close, like brothers. I'm sure they've had a row.'

'Over some fast piece, no doubt! And not worth falling out over, I'd guess. I thought you and Ian had an "understanding"?'

'We're friends. I told you when I first came here that I was only interested in my career.'

'I had hoped . . . Och, never mind. Just do what you can.'

'I will, I promise. Will you let Bernie and Archie have the house?'

Mrs Duncan nodded. 'But if there is any rowdiness – out they go!'

'You won't regret it! Bernie's a good girl, she works hard and so does Archie. Can I go over after supper and tell them?'

'You may.'

'Oh, thank you! Ian isn't going out, so you won't be on your own.'

'For all the company he is these days, I just might as well be.'

'When is Mrs Lennox going?'

'At the end of the week, so your friends can move in whenever they like after that, but don't you forget your side of the bargain, Bridget.'

'I won't and thank you again!' Impulsively she leaned over and kissed the withered cheek.

'Oh, get off with you, girl! I'm not giving them the house, they'll be paying rent!'

As she got off the tram on the corner of Bedford Road she smiled to herself, anticipating the look on Bernie's face. On the rare occasions Bernie came to Cartland Drive she was always saying how lucky Bridget was, that she didn't know she was born and that one day she was determined to get out of Warwick Street herself.

The street hadn't changed, except that if anything it looked even more dilapidated. She wondered now how she had ever lived here, amidst all this filth. A woman was coming towards her, a grubby toddler clinging to her skirt, a very young baby wrapped tightly in the shawl that crossed over her bosom, a bundle of washing held on her hip. She smiled to herself, remembering the Thursday night rituals of the 'Steamy' and their constant battle against the soot and dirt.

As she drew closer there was something familiar about the woman and as she drew level she stopped and stared at her.

'Maggie Baird!' The exclamation was out before she realized it.

Maggie took in the crisp, pale blue cotton dress and jacket. The navy blue leather shoes and bag, the pale blue cloche hat trimmed with navy velvet ribbon. 'It's Maggie MacDonald now!'

So, he had married her, she thought, and judging by the age of the child, she'd had to resort to 'having her card stamped'. 'How are you, Maggie?'

'I'm managing. Things could be better but I see you've done all right for yourself?'

She could only feel pity for Maggie now. Condemned to a life of harsh, relentless, unrewarding drudgery in these squalid tenements and probably with an additional mouth to feed nearly every year. 'How is ... your husband?' She still wouldn't use his name.

'I told you, we're managing.' She wasn't going to tell Bridget O'Donnell that he spent nearly every night drinking away his wages while she sat at home cursing the day she'd married him. A spark of the old Maggie burst forth. 'You'd best be careful you don't get that fine dress dirty or spoil those expensive shoes.'

Bridget couldn't help herself. 'It doesn't matter if I do, I have plenty of others and enough money to buy more!' She knew it was cruel, that Maggie was hitting out in the only way she knew how, but Maggie had ruined her life. Or had she? No, she supposed she should be grateful to Maggie.

'And what brings you here?'

'I've come to see Bernie. I don't forget my friends and she'll be moving away from here, too, any day now.'

'Will she now, that's nice for her. It helps to have friends like you.'

'When Bernie was growing up, she had even less than you did, Maggie, but she didn't sit and moan about it. She got out and worked and she's done well for herself. A lot better than many in the same circumstances.'

'You all stick together, don't you? Bloody Irish parasites, taking our jobs, our houses!'

'And your men, too, I suppose! You're welcome to him, Maggie. You did me a big favour. And yes, we do stick together, for if we don't help each other, no one else will! Goodbye, Maggie. Tell Andy I was asking after him.'

Maggie stared after her. She was right. She'd done Bridget a favour. She should have left Andy alone. He would have married Bridget O'Donnell and then she wouldn't be dressed up to the nines, with her nose in the air. She would have been no better off than herself. 'Stop your blatherrin', Georgie MacDonald, an' wipe your nose!' She cuffed the child over the ear, hitched up the heavy bundle and went on her way.

The Sisters O'Donnell

*

Bernie caught her around the waist and danced her around the room, shrieking with delight. 'Oh, Bridget! Sure, you're not pulling my leg are you? You mean it? A house! A house to ourselves and for nine shillings a week and in East Pollokshields!'

Bridget laughed and disentangled herself and sat down, pretending to gasp for breath. Bernie collapsed on the old sofa beside her.

'I just can't believe it! Me, Bernie Dalrymple, with a house of my very own!'

'And you can move in at the end of the week if you like. Mrs Lennox will be gone by Friday.'

Eileen just sat staring at them both with tears trickling down her cheeks. A house! A whole room to herself! A place where she could go and shut herself in. Privacy, that luxury she'd never had in all her life. And a privy that would only be used by them.'

'Eileen, wipe your eyes and go down to the Workers' Circle and tell Archie to get home right away! I don't think my legs would carry me that far!' Bernie was laughing and crying at the same time.

'Can I tell him, Bernie? He'll want to know, he'll think something has happened to you?'

'Yes, yes, tell him! Go on! Tell them all! Tell everyone you meet on the street!'

Eileen was out of the room like a flash and Bernie jumped up again. 'Oh, I won't have nearly enough furniture! I'll have to go around to Mr Sonderheim and see what he's got. Oh, Bridget, what's it like? How many rooms are there? Has it got a parlour? Oh, I've always wanted a proper parlour!'

'I don't know, I didn't ask. But I should think it will have some kind of a parlour and haven't they got a little patch of garden at the back or is it the front?'

Bernie was transported into the realms of ecstasy. 'A garden! Oh, Archie will think he's died and gone to heaven, so he will! He's always wanted a garden.'

'Will you for heaven's sake sit down, you're making me dizzy! Aren't you even going to offer me a cup of tea?'

'Oh, I'm so excited I can't think straight! We'll move in on Saturday and we'll start packing tonight. I'll write to Ma and tell her!' Bernie continued to dance around the room.

'I can see I'll have to make my own tea for there's no doing any good with you, Bernadette Dalrymple!'

'Oh, Bridget, how can we ever thank you?'

'By shutting up and calming down. It's only a house!' she laughed.

'Holy Mother, would you just listen to her "only a house"!' Bernie flopped down on the sofa again.

'Guess who I met on my way here?' Bridget said as she put the kettle on.

'Who?'

'Maggie Baird. I hardly recognized her, she looked terrible.'

'So would you, too, if you'd married Andy! He spends every night getting drunk. I think he realizes he didn't get much of a bargain in Maggie and that he'd have been better off with you. You should be thankful she saved you from him, Bridget.'

'I am. I felt sorry for her. As I walked away I thought, "There but for the grace of God go I." I never thought I'd feel like that.'

'Did you tell her about the house?'

Bridget laughed. 'Not in so many words, but I did say you'd be moving out of here any day now.'

Bernie puffed up with pride. 'I'll make sure she knows, that everyone knows, that we're going up in the world!'

Bridget handed her a mug of tea. 'I saw a very nice china tea set, reduced in the sale. It would be lovely for your new parlour. I'll get it tomorrow as a house-warming present, as they call it up here.'

Bernie sipped her tea. 'Oh, me dream's out! Real china!' Then she became serious, her dark eyes melancholy.

'Now what's the matter?'

'If only I had a bairn, there would be nothing else in the whole world I would wish for. I'd have everything!'

'Are you still worrying over that! You'll need your wages to buy furniture and curtains and lino and besides, you know my Ma's old saying – which makes a change from one of your Ma's – "New house, new baby"!'

'Is that right?'

'How do I know? You've got years yet. Get yourself settled into your house and then think about bairns.'

Chapter Twenty-Two

———◆———

Bridget hunched her shoulders up against the
wind as she walked from the tram. The weather had
turned wild and the fierce, gusting wind ripped the leaves
from the trees prematurely. It could be the middle of
winter, she thought. She hoped Ian would be home
already.

She had gone to see David a couple of weeks ago, as
she had promised herself and Mrs Duncan she would, but
the visit hadn't done anything to calm her consternation,
for he had insisted that there was no bad feeling between
himself and Ian. He was just busier these days and
couldn't come over as often, that was all. She'd asked him
point blank if they had fallen out over some girl and he'd
laughed and said 'No' and that nothing could be further
from his mind.

The situation was far from resolved but just when
Bridget had determined to get them together and have it
out, once and for all, Ian's mood changed. He reverted
back to his usual, open, friendly self and David's visits
increased. Both she and Mrs Duncan had been totally

mystified, but as Mrs Duncan had said, they would never know what had been the cause of the rift unless Ian chose to tell them and that the whole thing was best left alone. What they didn't know they couldn't worry about! And to-morrow the two young men were going off on their usual holiday to Skye and David would be over after supper.

Bridget clamped a hand down firmly on her hat as a gust sought to tear it from her head. Thank goodness it was Tuesday and Dora would have left the casserole ready, for she was cold and tired. Miss Whyte had gone down with a very bad cold that had settled on her already weak chest, and Bridget had been running the department, which was why she was later getting home than usual.

She wasn't looking forward to the winter at all, for Mrs Duncan was gradually failing and her limbs were becoming stiffer and her joints more painfully inflamed with the cold and damp. The pain made her bad tempered and difficult to live with. Bridget got up earlier these mornings to make her her breakfast and take it up to her, something the old lady had at first resisted with the words, 'I'm not an invalid yet!' But as it took her nearly an hour to get herself up and dressed and down-stairs, she had become thankful for Bridget's foresight, although she wouldn't admit it. Neither would she admit that there were days when she felt like staying in bed all day, too exhausted, too pain-wracked to make the effort. Days when she just longed to drift in and out of sleep, but that would be 'giving up' she told herself and that was the one thing she, Louisa Duncan had never done and didn't intend to start now. Especially as Ian seemed to have overcome whatever trauma had held him in its grip, and Bridget was a good girl. If she could see those two married, she'd go gladly to her Maker. Oh, life was so wearisome now.

Bridget sniffed appreciatively as she opened the door. It smelled good. She was hungry as she'd only had an apple at lunchtime, they'd been so busy, and in the little time she had she'd had to get some shopping and call in and see Eileen for the rent. She smiled to herself. She'd been glad she'd gone, Eileen had some news for her. Bernie was at last pregnant – and the plans they had! Archie was going to paint the small front bedroom and they were going to turn it into a proper nursery, like rich people had! You'd think they were the only ones ever to have a bairn! Bernie was so proud of the little house that she kept it like a palace. Her tiny parlour was treated almost as a shrine, with the best of the second-hand furniture polished to death, as was the linoleum on the floor, and no one was even allowed to set a foot on the circular mat in the middle of the floor. On top of the sideboard, the china tea set was set out in all its floral glory and carefully dusted every week, along with the framed photo of Bernie and Archie on their wedding day. The tiny garden at the front was Archie's pride and joy and not a single weed was allowed to appear. He'd taken to borrowing books on gardening from the library which was a bit ridiculous, Eileen said, seeing as there was only room for the pocket-handkerchief lawn and a very narrow border of pansies. Bridget promised herself that she'd go and see Bernie later, after she'd got supper over.

'Oh, I'm ready for this! I'm starving and it's so cold out there,' she said, placing the round, brown-glazed dish on the cork mat in the middle of the table.

'I knew the weather was turning, my joints are very

stiff. I spent most of the night fighting with the bed,' Mrs Duncan said plaintively.

'Didn't you take the aspirin the doctor gave you?' Ian asked.

'It doesn't do any good at all. The man's a fool! Said there was nothing else he could do and advised me to go and live in a warmer climate. Warmer climate, at my age! I was born here and I'll die here, and I told him so.'

Bridget smiled to herself as she ate. She pitied the doctor.

'I hope you're taking plenty of woollens with you, Ian?' Mrs Duncan continued. 'All this nonsense of sitting for hours in the cold and damp and just to watch birds!'

'Oh, you know those two, a bit of wind and rain won't bother them.' Bridget smiled at Ian who gave her a wink as a sort of 'thank you'. 'I popped in to get the rent from Eileen at lunchtime and guess what?'

'What?' Mrs Duncan looked expectantly at her.

'Bernie is going to have a baby! You know how worried she's been, thinking there was something wrong. And Eileen said Archie is going to do up the small bedroom as a nursery, of all things!' Bridget laughed. 'Bernie O'Hagan with a nursery! That will give Clonmel something to talk about! If you don't mind I think I'll go over and see her later on.'

'Well, I'm very pleased for her. Just as long as she doesn't go on producing one a year, that's when the troubles start!'

'Oh, I don't think she'll do that. You could never tell how many actually lived in their house, there seemed to be so many of them. Bernie isn't as foolish as to repeat her Ma's mistakes.'

'How is your sister coping?'

'Gina or Mary-Kate?'

'Mary-Kate. Poor girl, I know what it's like to have to bring up a son alone.'

'I think she's coping quite well. She says she misses Lewis, that even now she listens for him coming up the steps. But she says Ellen is a great comfort to her and Ernest seems to be managing better than she expected with the business.'

'And Gina?'

'Oh, Gina! A few scrawled lines once a month, if I'm lucky. I get most of the news from Mary-Kate. She says Gina is still in "Days of Grace" and is still having a wonderful time, going to parties and the like. Mary-Kate hopes she won't go overdoing it again, but Gina was always stubborn.'

'And your mother?'

'Like you, she's complaining about her rheumatics. She swears the stone walls don't help because they're damp. Uncle Richard and Matty grumble that she is costing them a fortune in peat fires and that the house is like a conservatory. They could grow potatoes all year round in the kitchen it's so hot, Matty says, but she isn't taking any notice of them. And why should she at all when she has to feed extra mouths at lunchtime, now that they've taken on two men?'

'Why don't you leave the dishes. Go over and see Bernie before it gets late. You're looking tired and I don't like you being out too late. It's not safe to walk the streets these days.'

Bridget smiled. She wasn't going to remind Mrs Duncan that she'd lived in one of the most violent areas of the city. 'I'm hoping Miss Whyte will be back at work soon. I just didn't realize that there was so much to do running a department. I'm glad the stock is in, I don't know if I could cope with the buying side just yet.'

'You underestimate yourself, Bridget. You can do whatever you want, as long as you have enough faith in yourself.'

As Ian was immersed in a book about Arctic Terns, Bridget got up and began to clear the table. 'I'll just do these first. I hate coming down to dirty dishes in the morning. Are you going to stay in the parlour or shall I light the fire in your bedroom?'

'Ian can light the fire – if he can tear himself away from that book. I'm more comfortable in bed, if anything can be called *comfortable* these days. I'll try and read for a while.'

'You stay down here where it's warm until the bedroom heats up. I'll wash up,' Ian said.

He marked his place and closed the book and was halfway across the hall when David arrived.

'Come in and shut the door before we all freeze! I suppose I'll have to do the fire now.' Bridget smiled tiredly.

'No, you won't. I'll do it.'

'We'll both do it,' David offered, amicably.

'Sure, it doesn't take two of you to light a small fire. I'll do it and you two can wash up before you start cluttering up the place with all your stuff.' Bridget paused, one foot on the first stair, and beckoned to them both. 'Will you promise me something?' she whispered.

'Why are we whispering?' Ian asked.

'Because I don't want your mother to hear. Promise you'll be extra careful, especially in this weather?'

'Do you think we're totally mad, Bridget?'

'Hush!'

'No fisherman would take us out in weather like this.'

'Well I just wanted to make sure. If anything happened to you, how could I tell her I knew you went jaunting off in boats?'

'We don't "jaunt", we're not day trippers!' David whispered emphatically.

'All right. Go on and get those dishes done.'

'I'll probably have gone when you get back, Bridget. We're making an early start in the morning.'

'Have a good time and take care. Now go and clatter some pots or she'll be suspicious.'

Bridget closed the curtains, switched on the light and then made the fire, sitting back on her heels to watch it until she was sure it had caught. The aspirin, the jug of water – the top covered by a small, lace doily – and the glass were on the bedside table and the room looked cosy. She'd just fill the stone, hot-water bottle and put it in the bed.

She took it along to the bathroom and turned on the hot tap in the wash basin. The water was only tepid. She tutted loudly. Those two must have used all the hot water for the dishes. Now she'd have to go and boil the kettle. At this rate it would be nine o'clock before she got to Bernie's.

As she crossed the hall she noticed the crack of light from under the dining room door and from the kitchen, too. They'd left the light on and if Mrs Duncan saw that there would be a lecture on 'Waste not, Want not'. She pushed the kitchen door open gently and then stopped, her eyes widening. Her heart turned over and the colour drained from her face. She closed her eyes and sagged against the doorjamb. She was seeing things, she must be! She opened her eyes and was faced with the sickening truth. It wasn't an apparition. They had neither seen nor heard her. They were holding each other close, heads together, lips feverishly kissing lips, eyes, cheeks. She turned and ran, making no sound. She stumbled at the top of the stairs but recovered her balance, raced along the landing and into her own room, locking the door behind her with hands that shook.

Slowly she sat down on the bed in the darkness. It was utterly horrible! It revolted all her senses! It was against the laws of God and man! As she sat there shivering, the ghastly kalcidoscope that had hurtled through her mind the night she'd sat in the Gorbals Cross returned. But this time it wasn't images of Maggie and Andy, but Ian and David! Bridget felt the bile rise in her throat, but she forced it down. She couldn't be sick. Mrs Duncan would want to know what was the matter. Oh, so many things now took on new meanings. Their close friendship. The utter lack of interest in girls. Ian's fastidiousness about his appearance. She knew there were men 'like that', she'd heard the jokes about them – 'Jessies' as Archie called them – but Ian . . . she felt betrayed and sickened. And what about his mother? Oh, dear God, it would kill her!

She got up and began to pace the room. How could she stay here now, knowing this? Every time she looked at Ian she would see . . . She had to get out; she'd have to leave! But where could she go? What excuse could she give and how could she leave the old lady now? She couldn't go to see Bernie tonight. Bernie knew her too well and she'd drag the truth from her and oh, what could she tell them?

Bridget pressed her fingers against her temples. She'd have to go out, she couldn't stay in the house, not while they were here. Even if it meant she had to walk the streets! Thank God Ian and David were going away tomorrow. She wished they would never come back! She wished they would both just disappear off the face of the earth or that she'd never, ever gone into the kitchen. If only she could turn back the clock, just for an hour. If only she could have gone on innocently believing they were just friends. And Mrs Duncan had once thought that she and Ian . . . Oh, it was so awful!

She went down and put on her coat, hat and scarf and called a hasty 'Goodbye' as she closed the door behind her and began to walk down the street. For how long she walked or where she went she could never remember, but suddenly she found herself in Melville Street. She looked longingly at the neat little house, just a crack of light shining from the small gap in the drawn curtains. It looked so solid, so comfortingly secure. She opened the gate but then stopped. No, she couldn't. Suppose Archie insisted on going to the police; it was a crime, after all. Or worse, suppose he went up to Cartland Drive and confronted them, saying it was no fit place for Bridget to live? Suppose he did both? Her shoulders drooped as she turned away. There was nothing at all she could do, except go back.

As the wind howled and screamed around the house, rattling the window panes and driving the rain against them until it reminded her of the staccato rattle of a

Thompson gun, Bridget tossed and turned in bed. She tried pulling the covers over her head to shut out the sound that brought back older, darker feelings. In the end she got up and put on her dressing gown. She opened her bag and took out her rosary beads and knelt at the side of the bed and tried to pray, but that didn't work. Her mind refused to obey her, she couldn't concentrate on the words and after two decades she gave up.

She'd always been devout. She always attended Mass, even on Holy Days of Obligation when she had to get up at five o'clock in order to attend six o'clock Mass before she went to work. So why had God deserted her now, when she needed His help and guidance most? And how could He be so cruel as to allow such a thing to happen to an old lady who had lived a good, Christian life and had followed her own religious path with such devotion?

She got back into bed, keeping her dressing gown on, for she was half frozen with the cold. She clasped the beads between her numbed fingers and tried again to pray. But darkness was pressing in on her, cold hands were choking her and she fought for breath, her hands tearing at her throat. Then she woke up, coughing and gasping, realizing she must have fallen asleep with the rosary beads caught around her neck. She looked towards the window and saw the first fingers of the ragged, grey dawn creeping across the sky.

She got washed and dressed, not noticing how drawn she looked, not really caring that her blouse was creased. Normally she would have changed it. She went downstairs and forced herself to go into the kitchen. The room was cold for she'd forgotten to bank up the fire. She poked the embers and added more coal, pulling the damper down to draw it and make it burn more brightly. At least they had gone. Ian had left her a note, propped up against the kettle. *Didn't want to wake you. Will send a postcard. Take care. Ian.*

She dropped it into the flames and watched it turn to ash.

Bridget never knew just how she got through the next few days and nights. Gina would have been proud of the act she'd put on, she thought bitterly. But the cost was beginning to tell and only that morning Mrs Duncan had remarked that Ian was remiss in not sending her a postcard or letter.

'He's probably been too involved in watching some rare species or something,' Bridget had replied.

'It's so thoughtless! Can't even write a few lines to tell me he's all right. That's all the thanks you get, Bridget, for bending over backwards to bring up children. Take my advice and don't have any. They're selfish and ungrateful!'

In other circumstances Bridget would have defended him.

The high winds of the previous day had blown themselves out and milder weather had followed, but she hardly noticed, putting all her efforts and concentration into her work, knowing that soon he would be home and she would either have to confront him or somehow come to terms with her knowledge. It was late when she finally left the store, bidding 'Goodnight' to the doorman. She walked past Boots and looked longingly at Craig's. If only it were open she could have sat for a while with Eileen. She hated going home now. As she pulled up her coat collar a figure stepped out of the doorway of the Tea Rooms. It was Archie.

'Archie Dalrymple! You scared me half to death. Is Bernie all right?'

'Aye, she's fine, but she asked me to meet you.'

'What for?'

He held out a copy of the evening edition of the local newspaper.

She stared at him in mystification.

'Come on, Bridget. I'm no' standing here in the street reading this. We'll go for a drink.'

She let him take her arm and propel her into a pub where he sat her down at a table in the corner and went to the bar, returning with two glasses of Scotch. She looked at him in alarm.

'Go on, drink it up. I think you're going to need it.'

'What's the matter? Is it Eileen?'

Archie turned the paper over and pointed a stubby finger at a small paragraph at the bottom of the page.

She scanned the lines:

The fishing smack the *Bonny Kirstie* has been reported lost off the north coast of Skye. It is believed to have been caught in a freak squall. A fisherman who knew the owner of the *Bonny Kirstie* told our reporter that two Glasgow men, holidaying on Skye, had gone out in the boat but so far no bodies have been found, although a search of the area is now underway.

The lines of print merged together and she felt Archie's hand close over hers.

'It might not be them, Bridget. It could be someone else, but we thought we should warn you. Here, drink this up lassie, you've gone a terrible colour!'

It was all her fault! She'd wished it on him – on them both! She'd wished they would disappear off the face of the earth, that they'd never come back! Bridget just stared at Archie, her large hazel eyes wide with shock.

He hadn't expected this reaction. He held the glass to her lips, urging her to drink. She drank a few drops, coughed and spluttered and then started to cry.

'Och, hen, we'll go to the police station and see if there's any news yet. It might not be them at all.'

'It is Archie, I know it is. I wished it on them, I did. I killed them!'

'Bridget, don't be daft, you can't wish things like that! It's no' possible!'

Haltingly, between sobs and sips of whisky she told him, her face flushing scarlet at times, deathly white at others and when she'd finished Archie looked stunned.

'What about his mother? She's an old lady, I'm frightened for her,' Bridget suddenly thought.

Archie shook his head. 'Maybe, under the circumstances, it's for the best. If it ever got out . . . wouldn't that kill her? And they wouldn't have got away with their filthy . . . not forever, Bridget. There'd be a terrible scandal and Ian would have gone to jail. Even in Barlinnie Prison they'd have to keep him separate, he wouldn't be safe. Think about that.'

'I have . . . but this! I can't tell her that I knew they went out in boats, not after his father.'

'Then don't tell her. You're not going to tell her he was a . . . one of "those" are you? And Bridget, don't go blaming yourself. It was only natural for you to wish . . . well, they were the unnatural ones, weren't they?' Archie finished. As he'd listened to her he'd felt his skin crawl and the whisky tasted sour in his mouth. It was one thing to joke about 'them' but quite another to actually know one. Poor Bridget. He stood up. 'We'll go along to the police, then I'll take you home.'

It was true. The names had been confirmed, although no bodies had yet been found. Bridget broke down again, guilt sweeping over her.

'We'll get a car to take you home, Miss,' the Desk Sergeant said kindly.

She raised her head and looked up at Archie. 'How am I going to tell her? How?'

'One of the lads will go with you. We've more experience of dealing with these matters, unfortunately,' the Sergeant volunteered.

She nodded her thanks, but she wished with all her heart that she could stay in the safety of the police station.

Archie helped her to her feet and both he and the Sergeant assisted her into the car.

'Archie come with me, please? Bernie will understand.'

He got in beside her.

Bridget sat, still in her coat and hat, holding Mrs Duncan's hand long after they'd all gone. The curtains remained undrawn, the lamps unlit. Only the flames from the fire illuminated the room. Mrs Duncan hadn't screamed or fainted or become hysterical as Bridget had dreaded she might. She'd sat erect and listened until the policeman had finished. Then she had said just three words, quietly, but with an infinite depth of sorrow and hatred. 'The damned sea!' Since then she'd not uttered a word, nor had she cried. The hand in Bridget's was cold.

'Will I draw the curtains and make some tea?' she asked.

The grey head moved slightly and she took it to be a nod. Gently disentangling her hand she got up and pulled the heavy drapes, switched on a small table lamp and stirred up the fire. Then she went into the kitchen and took off her coat and hat and laid a tray while the kettle boiled, all the time wondering how she could do these mundane things at a time like this. If the old lady had broken down she would at least have been able to try and comfort her, but this strange silence, this bitter resignation, she didn't know how to cope with.

As Bridget poured the tea, Mrs Duncan spoke. 'Did you know about this boat trip?'

She couldn't look up. 'No. Do you think I would have kept something like that from you?' Silently she begged forgiveness for the lie.

'No.' Mrs Duncan sighed heavily. 'He was so like his father.'

Again Bridget couldn't look up. She wanted to cry out that he wasn't anything like his father. He was a pervert! She bit her tongue.

'Will you stay with me, Bridget? I know I'm a burden and it's no life for you, but I have no one else.' There wasn't a trace of self-pity in the voice.

'Of course I will! This won't make any difference. You've given me a home, a good home!'

The shrivelled, gnarled hand reached out and Bridget caught it and squeezed it gently.

'It's all yours now, Bridget. This house, the money, Melville Street.'

'Oh, don't! Don't talk like that, please. I don't want any of it if it means . . .' Everything caught up with her and with a choking cry she clung to the frail but indomitable old lady, the sobs wracking her shoulders.

The fact that Ian's body was never found added to his mother's anguish, but as the weeks went by she stopped searching the newspapers, and for this Bridget was thankful. To her surprise, Mrs Duncan had accepted the tragedy with more resignation than she had, for she could never forget that she had tempted fate, although Bernie told her not to be so superstitious.

As Miss Whyte's illness continued, it was with a mixture of pleasure and trepidation that she learned that she was to go to London to select the new stock, albeit under the guidance of Miss MacIver, the Head Buyer for Ladies Fashions. It would be a welcome break away from the sombre atmosphere in Cartland Drive. They were to travel down by train and stay overnight at a very select but quiet hotel for ladies only. Bridget was disappointed that there would be no time to see Gina, but as Miss MacIver remarked tartly, 'We are on a business trip, Miss O'Donnell, paid for by the company. It is not a social outing and if your sister were Queen Mary herself, you'd not have time to meet her!'

Because she would be away overnight, she was worried about Mrs Duncan.

'Bridget, will you stop fussing about me. Dora will come in and I'm not totally immobile!'

'I just don't like leaving you.'

'I'll hear no more about it. This is a wonderful opportunity for you and in this life you must seize every chance with both hands. You'll be Head of Department in no time at all.'

'If I choose the right things. What if I don't like anything? What if I like them all?' she agonized.

'Isn't that what Miss MacIver is there for? Guidance, advice? The woman has years of experience, just ask her – I'm sure they pay her enough! You'll learn. Look how quickly you've learned already. I expect you to be Head Buyer one day.'

'Oh, that will take years and years. Now, should I take a suitcase or just my tapestry bag?'

'The bag, unless you intend to stay for a week.'

Bridget laughed. 'I'll just have to try to stay calm and collected, but it won't be easy.'

'Well, you've quite worn me out with all this excitement and chatter. I think I'll have an early night and you should too. You've a long and tiring journey tomorrow. Such a pity you've no time to see your sister.'

'I know, but she'll probably be working, too.'

'No doubt too hard, again. You young girls are all the same, rushing here and there, no time for anything. Pass me my cane, there's a good girl.'

Bridget smiled as she passed her the cane with the carved ivory handle and helped her up. Mrs Duncan might be frail in body, but certainly not in spirit, she thought.

Next morning she awoke early feeling as though she had hardly slept at all for fear of oversleeping. She washed and dressed and fastened up her bag, then checked her appearance in the mirror. The beige knitted two-piece, trimmed with brown piping, looked simple but very smart. Her brown Harris tweed coat with the red fox collar made her feel much older and far superior in station than she actually was. The velvet toque would add to this illusion. She left her coat and bag in the hall and went into the kitchen to set the tray. She carried it upstairs and smiled as she opened the door. The fire was nearly out but the room was warm and she set the tray down on top of the dressing table while she drew the curtains back. The sun was struggling to shine between silver-grey folds of clouds that were still moving across the sky like huge ripples on a grey ocean.

'It's going to be a fine morning, I think, and it's about time, too. We've had that much rain I could almost believe I was back home. Do you like my suit?'

Bridget turned around, expecting to see Mrs Duncan gazing at her as she usually did, for she was always awake early. Her eyes were closed. Bridget sighed, wondering whether to wake her or leave her to rest. If she left her then her breakfast would be cold and she wouldn't have a hot drink until Dora arrived, unless she made it herself and her wrists were now so weak and painful that Bridget was afraid of her scalding herself. She touched her hand. 'I'm sorry to wake you, but I don't want to go and you not have had a hot breakfast.' She shook her gently, then with a cry she backed away, her hand covering her mouth. She was dead, she was sure of it! She picked up the thin hand. It was cold and limp, but she bent and held it to her cheek as tears trickled down her cheeks. London and Miss MacIver were forgotten. Although Mrs Duncan had appeared to overcome her loss, she knew that the old lady had secretly grieved for her son. It was always a bad thing to bottle up such emotions but the old lady's pride, rooted in her upbringing, had refused to allow her to grieve openly. But Bridget had known. And now it was all over for her and she would never know about the kind of man her son had been. She had been spared that. There was a merciful God after all.

The funeral had been very quiet. Just herself, Dora, Bernie and Archie and Eileen. She'd gone to see Mr Prebble, the family solicitor, at his request and he had been kindness itself. It was from him that she learned that she was indeed the sole heir to what he termed Mrs Duncan's Estate, which he detailed as £1,000 in stocks and shares, the house in Cartland Drive and the one in Melville Street.

'I know you are upset, Miss O'Donnell, but I must ask what you wish to do with the Estate after the six months probate required by law? The will leaves the matter entirely to you.'

'I don't know. What should I do?'

'Will you want to sell the stocks and shares?'

'Would that be best?' Bridget wasn't even quite sure what they were.

'If you need the money it would, if not I'd keep them. They are wisely invested and they bring in a yearly dividend of –' he glanced at the papers on his desk '– two hundred pounds.'

'Oh,' she replied weakly. 'Every year? For how long?'

He smiled kindly. 'Every year for as long as you keep them. Of course, if the value falls the dividend won't be as much and of course they can be sold at any time, all of them or just a few. But you have plenty of time to think about it.'

It was too complicated to take in all at once, especially as her mind was still so confused by the suddenness of Mrs Duncan's death. 'I don't know.'

'Let's go on to the property then. Will you want to sell it? The house in Cartland Drive is a big house, it would command a good price.'

'Where else would I go? It's my home. I won't be turned out, will I, because of this probate thing? I haven't got anywhere else to go.'

'No, of course not. But if after the prescribed period you decide to sell it, I will handle it for you.'

She was greatly relieved, thinking she'd have had to have gone to Bernie and ask to be put up for a while. A thought occurred to her after she'd thought of her friend. 'Could I have someone to live there with me now? Or would I have to wait for six months? I wouldn't be charging rent or anything like that.'

'I don't see why not. If you were to take in paying guests it would be different.'

'There is something you can do for me, Mr Prebble, please. If it's possible, that is.'

'Yes?'

'The house in Melville Street. After the six months are up, could you arrange for the deeds to be signed over to someone else, so that they own it?'

'You want to make it a gift to someone?'

'Yes.'

'Of course. What name would you wish to have on the deeds?'

'Two names please. Mr Archie Dalrymple and Mrs Bernadette Dalrymple.'

'It's most irregular for the wife's name to be included.'

'I would like their names – both of them – to be on it,' Bridget said firmly.

'Very well, Miss O'Donnell. I will set the wheels in motion, as they say.'

When she told them about the deeds, Bernie broke down and sobbed. 'Oh, Bridget! God Bless you!' she said fervently.

'It was nothing to do with me, Bernie,' Bridget lied. 'It was Mrs Duncan's wish, Mr Prebble said so.' She knew Archie was a proud man and she had no wish to humble that pride or cause a disagreement between them.

'We'll have a Mass said for her every year on the anniversary of her death for as long as we live, Bridget. I know she wasn't of our faith, but she was a good Christian woman,' Archie said quietly. There were very few men who had gone from a slum in the Gorbals to being the owner of their own house, and he was deeply moved by what he thought was the old lady's kindness.

'I wondered if Eileen would come and live with me?' Bridget said. 'It's such a big house and it feels so empty now. Mr Prebble said it would be all right as long as I don't charge rent or anything, which I wouldn't do anyway. I still can't take it in that I have so much money now, or will have in six months time.'

It was time for Eileen's eyes to brim with tears. She'd enjoyed living with Archie and Bernie, but now, to move into that house with Bridget . . . it was more than a dream come true. She gripped Bridget's hand tightly as Bernie turned to Archie.

'For the first time in our married life we'll be on our own, Archie.'

'Not for long. Don't forget the bairn.'

Bernie wiped her eyes and nodded. 'And if it's a girl we'll call her Louisa. That was Mrs Duncan's name wasn't it? It's only fitting.'

'She'd have liked that, I know she would, and it's such a pretty name,' Bridget agreed.

Chapter Twenty-Three

———◆———

M ARY-KATE HAD FIRST NOTICED the discrepancies a week ago when the month's statements had been prepared, ready for posting. Today she had decided to check over the books again. There were no entries for Dobson's, Hartley's, Plowden's or Burke's – four of their oldest and biggest customers. She checked over the 'Outgoings' again; there was nothing amiss there, everything was accounted for. So, if four of her biggest customers had not used their services over the past month, why were the figures for wages, fodder, bedding, petroleum and maintenance exactly the same as last month's? She looked up. Already it was getting dark, the nights were drawing in. Soon Ernest would be closing the yard for the night. She made up her mind to go down and see him. There were quite a lot of questions that she wanted answers to.

Things hadn't been easy for Mary-Kate since Lewis's death, although she had put a brave face on it. She was still unable to come to terms with her loss and, as she had told Bridget, she would often stop, listening for his footsteps. She would wake up in the mornings and be shocked all over again by his absence. It was the little things that hurt most: his shaving brush and mug, still in the bathroom; the photographs of herself and the children, still on his desk in the library; the black leather-bound pocket book also on the desk. She hated that room now, it reminded her so much of him and she still couldn't bring herself to spend time in there. It was Vi who kept it exactly as he'd left it, even to the box of fine Havana cigars, the silver cigar clipper and the heavy alabaster ashtray.

Then there was the picture in Jamie's bedroom entitled 'Mischief', that Lewis had seen and bought and hung himself, laughing as he'd hit his thumb, instead of the nail, with the head of the hammer. She could hear him now saying it was an appropriate picture for his son – 'Little Mischief'. Even the hammer itself brought back painful memories. For some strange reason the small tool, little bigger than a toffee hammer, was one of Jamie's favourite toys and, although the things he had 'mended' with it were consigned to the dustbin, she hadn't the heart to take it from him.

Mary-Kate had been having trouble with Elizabeth again, although only Ellen and Vi knew this. Elizabeth's visits had increased and she had begun to take a high-handed attitude and had started to try to interfere with the business, putting forward the most audacious and utterly unworkable ideas. The last time she had come, Mary-Kate had lost her temper and reminded her that this house now belonged solely to her and that if Elizabeth couldn't be civil then she need not come again.

She suspected that somehow Elizabeth had something

to do with the discrepancies. Ellen would be home from school in a few minutes, then she would go down to the yard. Vi would give Ellen her meal and see to Jamie.

Mary-Kate was putting on her hat when she heard the familiar rattling of a ruler being scraped against a wall. It was another of those 'little things'. It was a habit Ellen still hadn't outgrown and one that had always annoyed Lewis. Ellen would soon be of an age when most girls left school and started work, but she was determined to keep Ellen at school until she matriculated. After that Ellen could choose a career for herself if she didn't want to help with the business, which Mary-Kate didn't really want her to do. It was one thing for *her* to run a haulage business, quite another for a young girl straight from the school-room.

'I'm just nipping down to the yard to see Ernest,' Mary-Kate said as Ellen walked in. 'I won't be long. Vi will give you your tea and then you can see to Jamie, if you would, dear. He's been an absolute little divil today!'

'Oh, he hasn't been "mending" things again, has he? You'll have to take that little hammer off him, Ma, before he damages something really valuable!'

'I know. I'll have to hide it and hope he forgets about it.'

'We've already done that and he doesn't forget. He's like an elephant!'

'Well, I've more pressing matters to think of just now.'

'I think they were all going home when I passed on the tram.' Ellen had hung up her coat and scarf and had removed her hat. She pulled out the band that held her hair in its one, long plait and shook her head, freeing the tresses that fell below her shoulders.

'Who were?'

'The men at the yard. At least they were all standing around the gates.'

'At half-past four? What is Ernest thinking of?' Mary-Kate picked up her bag and the battered briefcase containing the ledgers. 'Tell Vi she can go at five-thirty, Ellen!' she called as she let herself out.

When she turned the corner and began to walk along Rice Lane towards the yard, she could see that Ellen hadn't been mistaken. Groups of men were standing around outside the gates. She hurried her steps as she crossed the road. What on earth was Ernest doing? She picked out Davies from the group and called to him. He detached himself and came over to her.

'Davies, what's going on? Why aren't the men working? Where's Mr Winskill?'

'We're not working, Mrs Vannin, because there's no work to do.'

'What do you mean, no work?'

'Just that and the men are sick of it! I'm sort of "speaking up" for them. Four contracts we've lost and two men laid off last week and another today. It's not right, Mrs Vannin, not right at all! I'm not a Union man, we never needed no Union when Mr Vannin was alive, but now I'm not so sure.'

She was astounded. 'Where is Mr Winskill?' Ernest had never been very good with the men, but she wanted no trouble with the Unions.

'He's gone home.'

'He's what! Who's in charge, Mr Johnson?'

'No, ma'am, he's gone home as well. Mrs Winskill is in the office.'

'Mrs Winskill?' Mary-Kate exploded. She might have known it! She pushed her way through the group. 'Can you all hear me?' she shouted.

'Aye!' they answered in a body.

'I have only just learned of the situation, but I intend to sort things out now! I think I may have been hasty in my decision to allow Mr Winskill to take over. From now on Mr Johnson and I will deal with everything.'

'And a good thing, too, Mrs Vannin!' someone shouted.

'Davies, the men who have been laid off, I want you to go and see them, tell them that they are to report to work tomorrow morning and that they will be paid what is owing to them.'

That brought a cheer.

'That is all I have to say for the time being, so you might as well all go home. Don't worry, you'll be paid for your full day. It's not your fault you've no work to do.'

She watched them disappear, going their separate ways.

'Do you want me to stay, ma'am?' Davies asked.

'No, but thank you. What I have to say to Mrs Winskill is not for your ears. Goodnight, Davies. I'll see you in the morning.'

'Goodnight, ma'am, and thanks, on behalf of the men. Maybe I shouldn't say this . . . but Mrs Winskill has got a vicious tongue for a lady.'

'It will be nothing compared to mine!' she answered grimly as she walked through the gates.

Elizabeth was sitting in the office, jotting down a column of figures. She looked startled to see Mary-Kate standing in the doorway watching her.

'Just what do you think you're doing, Elizabeth?'

'Trying to save money! Ernest is hopeless. These figures are a mess and he is utterly useless at dealing with that lazy, shiftless lot he calls "workmen"!'

Mary-Kate slammed the briefcase down on the desk and Elizabeth jumped. 'Don't try and fool me, Elizabeth! You haven't a head for figures either. You can't even manage your own household expenses! Just what do you mean by "saving money"?'

'We were employing far too many men to do the jobs we have, so I told Ernest to get rid of some.'

'And who gave you that right? Lewis left this business for Jamie, not you! And why have we lost four of our oldest and biggest customers?'

'They said the rates we were charging were too high and that they could get the work done far cheaper elsewhere, so I told Ernest to tell them to do just that!'

Mary-Kate was now shaking with anger. 'You increased our rates without consulting me? How dare you! Do you know how long your father had had contracts with all four? Ever since he started in business! And I see from the accounts that you have still been charging for the same amounts of fodder, bedding and wages. What have you done with the money you've defrauded? Bought yourself a new fur coat, I suppose! I'm only going to tell you this once, Elizabeth, so you'd better listen carefully. I want you and Ernest out of this office and this yard now, and in future I don't want either of you anywhere near me, my house, my children or my business!'

Elizabeth sprang up, knocking the chair over. 'I knew

it would come to this! I knew you'd turned Father against us, even before he died! You've never deceived me. I've always known you were after his money and you were lucky enough to have his son so that you could control everything! You deceitful, sly, conniving . . .' Her outburst ended in a scream as Mary-Kate slapped her hard across the face.

'Get out, Elizabeth! Get out and be thankful I don't bring charges of fraud against you. If it wasn't for dragging your father's name through the courts, I wouldn't hesitate! Both you and Ernest can go to hell from now on for all I care. Get out!'

Elizabeth edged away from her. She'd made a grave mistake in thinking that Mary-Kate had been so involved with her family and her grief that she wouldn't think to look too closely into the business. She reached the door and Mary-Kate picked up her bag from the desk and threw it at her.

'I've been more than patient with you. In fact, I've been far too charitable to you, but you underestimated me, didn't you? That was a fatal mistake!'

Elizabeth almost fell down the office steps, but she turned, pointing to a fully-loaded lorry standing in the middle of the yard.

'You'd better find someone to get that down to the docks tonight or else you'll lose the contract for Walker's as well. And seeing that you've sent every-one home, you're going to have to take it yourself!' she yelled before she turned and disappeared through the gates.

Mary-Kate stared after her. She was still shaking with rage. She should have known! She should have realized what Elizabeth was up to and just how much control she had over Ernest. But why hadn't Mr Johnson come and told her what was going on? Probably Elizabeth had threatened him with the sack if he did and he'd never get another job, not at his age. She picked up the chair and sank down on it. It was Lewis's chair and she covered her face with her hands. She would have to take over herself if there was to be any chance of a business for Jamie to inherit. Somehow she would have to win back the four major contracts Elizabeth and Ernest had lost, even if it meant going in person and begging! They were the most important customers of all! The four cornerstones of the entire business. Now Walker's was the only contract of any size they had left. Walker's! She jumped up and went to the door. There wasn't a soul in sight. What had Elizabeth said – the consignment had to get to the docks tonight? Had she been lying? Mary-Kate couldn't take that chance.

She went back into the office and picked up her bag and the briefcase, then she put out the light and locked the door and pocketed the key. She didn't have any idea how to drive, but she'd have to try. Even if she went after Davies, by the time he rounded up the driver and got back, it would be too late. A shadow fell across her path and she turned.

'Ellen! What are you doing here? You haven't left Jamie on his own have you?'

'No, Vi's with him. I came to see if you were all right, you were so long. I saw our Lizzie running down the road towards the tram stop. What's she been doing?'

'Trying to ruin us! A few more weeks and we'd all have been in the workhouse!'

'She looked furious.'

'She's every right to be – I slapped her. We won't be seeing those two again in a hurry!'

Ellen began to laugh. 'Oh, Ma, I wish I could have seen it. You should have done that months ago!'

'This time, Ellen, I agree with you. But she's left me with a problem. This lorry has to be at the docks tonight and there's no one to drive it, except me.'

'You can't drive!'

'I know that, but I'm going to have to try.' She yanked the door open and hitching up her skirt, climbed into the cab. Ellen jumped nimbly up beside her.

'I'm coming with you and don't argue. Vi will stay, you know she will.'

After a little while spent pushing buttons and pulling levers and pressing down on pedals, Mary-Kate knew it was no use. 'Damn!' she cried, banging her fists down on the wheel in frustration.

'I think there's some sort of handle you have to wind it up with first,' Ellen deliberated.

'Why didn't you say so?'

'I've only just remembered.'

They both got out and began to look for the crank handle, but when Mary-Kate finally found it her initial joy turned to desperation. 'We'll never be able to turn it, it's too heavy!' She was sorely tempted to vent her anger by kicking the iron-rimmed wheel, pretending it was Elizabeth's shinbone.

'Ma, there's a man watching us,' Ellen said in a loud whisper.

Mary-Kate turned. 'Where?'

'Over by the gates.'

'Perhaps it's Mr Davies.' She began to walk across the yard.

Ellen tugged sharply at her skirt. 'It's not. He'd have come over. Be careful, Ma.'

Mary-Kate stood still. The girl was right. It could be anyone and they were completely alone. 'Who's there? Come over here where I can see you clearly!' she called.

The figure walked hesitantly towards them, then stopped.

'I still can't see you. Who are you and what do you want?'

'Don't you recognize me, Mary-Kate O'Donnell?'

No one called her by her maiden name these days, but the voice was familiar. 'Should I?'

'Aye, you should.' He came closer.

Ellen shrank closer to her step-mother.

Mary-Kate's hand went to her throat. No. It couldn't be. Not after all these years. 'Dear God above! Is that you, Michael Feehey?'

'It is that.'

She began to laugh, overcome with relief and surprise. 'It's all right Ellen, he's a friend from home. How on earth did you find me?'

'I asked at the house.'

'But how did you find out where I lived?'

Ellen was tugging at her arm. 'Ma. The lorry. The lorry.'

All the questions fled from Mary-Kate's mind as she remembered their plight. 'You can drive can't you, Michael?'

'Yes.'

'Then get this thing started up and drive us to the

docks. We've got to get this load down there tonight. No arguments now, we can talk on the way.'

Without waiting for any further explanations both she and Ellen scrambled into the cab.

After a few turns of the crank handle the engine burst into life and Michael jumped in beside them and steered the vehicle towards the gates.

Once they were through, Ellen took two seconds to jump down and lock the gates before clambering back into the lorry.

Michael turned out on to Rice Lane.

'Do you know the way?' Mary-Kate asked.

'Yes. Along County Road, then Walton Road to the Rotunda. Down Boundary Road and Great Howard Street to Waterloo Road.'

She settled back and studied Michael. 'How on earth did you find me?'

'I heard about a young Irish woman who owned this business when I was working down at the docks. It's quite unusual you know. I've unloaded stuff from this lorry before, and so I asked the driver about you – what you looked like, what part of Ireland you came from and so on. It was just out of curiosity really, I never thought it would be you. But when he described you, I knew I had to see for myself. Besides, I couldn't stay working at the docks much longer. I got the address off the side of the lorry.'

'Why can't you work in the docks? What brought you here?'

'It's all a long story, Mary-Kate. Do you know which dock we're supposed to be going to?' Michael changed the subject.

She picked up a piece of paper from the dashboard. 'The Collingwood Dock. To be loaded on to the *City of Exeter*,' she read aloud.

They had negotiated the junction of Great Howard Street and Waterloo Road, commonly known as the Dock Road, and ahead was the twelve-foot high stone wall that bounded the docks.

'Oh, look out! Look out!' Ellen yelled suddenly and Michael dragged the wheel over, turning the vehicle into the middle of the road.

'What's the matter? What did you yell at me like that for?'

'I think we hit something,' Ellen cried.

Michael yanked on the brake as Ellen, followed by Mary-Kate, jumped down.

'Michael, stop the engine. We've hit a child!' Mary-Kate shouted.

He jumped down too. 'Oh, God. Is he hurt? I just didn't see him, I was thinking about . . . other things.' He was very agitated.

'Have you got a pain anywhere? Where does it hurt?' Mary-Kate asked the child.

The young boy, aged about six or seven and dressed in a ragged jumper and equally ragged trousers, just stared at them both with huge, dark eyes from under a shock of matted hair.

Michael touched Mary-Kate on the shoulder. 'Mary-Kate, I'll have to go. I can't face the police or all the fuss that will follow.'

'Michael, you've got to! You can't just run off. What will I do?'

'Please? Trust me? Tell them you were driving, tell

them anything! I'll drive you back home. I swear to God I will. I'll wait for you, just down the road.'

'But the boy? And I can't drive, Michael.'

'I'll explain everything Mary-Kate. I've got good reasons. I know it looks desperate but please, you've got to trust me. You've got to!'

She looked up helplessly as he ran off, quickly merging into the shadows, the sound of his footfalls growing fainter.

'He doesn't look hurt, Ma. He's not bleeding.' Ellen drew her attention back to her predicament. Gently, Mary-Kate felt the skinny arms and legs.

'Mind you, you wouldn't be able to see if he was bleeding or not, he's that dirty. What's your name? Where do you live?' Ellen asked.

The child just continued to stare up at them.

'He's too shocked to talk,' Mary-Kate said, biting her lip.

''E can't talk. What 'ave yer done ter 'im?'

They both looked up to see a girl of about Ellen's age staring at them. Like the boy, her legs and feet were bare and dirty. A thin cotton dress, torn and stained, was the only garment she seemed to have on, despite the coldness of the night.

'Is he your brother?' Mary-Kate asked.

The girl nodded.

'Well, you ask him if he's hurt. He ran straight out in front of us.'

The girl looked at her suspiciously. ''E couldn't 'ave, 'e can't run. 'E can't 'ardly walk, 'e's nearly a cripple.'

Mary-Kate felt terrible. 'Is he hurt?' she persisted.

'Are yer 'urt, our 'Arry?' the girl mouthed slowly.

The little boy pointed to his leg.

'It's 'is leg. 'Ere's the scuffer.'

They all turned as the Dock Policeman approached. Mary-Kate's heart sank. How was she going to get out of this mess? And, it was an almighty mess Michael had left her in. But she had to try.

'Officer, can you help us? I didn't see this child and I ran into him. I don't think he's badly hurt but I've got to get this load to the Collingwood Dock.'

The constable looked down at the little group. The lady was obviously very upset, in fact she looked near to tears, he thought.

'What's your Harry doing out at this time of night, Nell?'

The girl looked at him with resignation. 'Me Da's drunk again, an' yer know what 'e's like. Me Mam told me ter gerrout until 'e's gone ter sleep.'

The constable shook his head. 'Is he hurt?' He, too, bent down and felt the boys arms, legs and head, despite the fact that it was crawling with lice.

Unconsciously, Ellen began to scratch.

He gently picked the boy up and set him on his feet. 'He's all right, aren't you, Harry, lad? Go on, the pair of you. Sit in my hut until I get this lady sorted out.'

The girl put an arm around her brother and they both walked slowly across the road and disappeared into the hut at the dock gate.

'Don't worry about him, ma'am, he's had worse knocks than that before now. They both have, poor little sods. Beggin' your pardon, ma'am. Now, let's see what we can do about your predicament. What on earth is a lady like you doing driving that thing down here at this time of night?'

Mary-Kate told him, not exactly lying, just leaving out certain facts – the main one being that she hadn't been driving. 'Can you help me, please?' she finished.

'You'll need someone to unload it. There's a few men still loading up but you'll have to pay over the odds, it being short notice and so late.'

'Oh, I don't care, just as long as I can get the job done.'

'Nell! Nelly!' the constable yelled and the girl's head appeared. 'Do you want to earn a sixpence?'

She was beside them in a trice.

'Go and knock up anyone you can find to help unload this lorry. Tell them they'll get over the going rate.'

She was off like a bullet from a gun.

'I'll pay her the sixpence, ma'am. Don't you be worrying about that.'

'No, I can't let you do that. I don't mind, I'm just so grateful to you.'

'Does she live around here?' Ellen asked, incredulously.

'Aye. Now, if you stand aside I'll drive your vehicle through the gates and log it in.'

Mary-Kate watched with relief as he steered it adroitly through the dock gates and pulled up beside the hull of a ship, alongside which a few men were still working.

'Would you like to step inside my hut out of the weather until it's unloaded?' the constable offered.

Mary-Kate thanked him and went to stretch out her cold hands over the open brazier. The boy was sitting as close to the fire as he could.

The girl came back, panting. 'I'se gorra few of them, dey's cumin' down now. Can I 'ave me tanner?'

Mary-Kate opened her purse and gave her the sixpence.

She grinned. 'See, 'Arry! Stay 'ere with the scuffer an' the lady an' I'll go an gerrus some chips.' Nell darted off again as a group of men came through the gate and the constable directed them to the lorry with the instruction: 'Get your fingers out, lads, the lady's in a hurry to get home.'

'Sling yer hook, mate,' one called, jovially.

'I'll remember that, Mick Keegan, next time you're drunk and disorderly,' the constable called back good-naturedly.

'Ah, come off it, Paddy! Don't gerroff yer bike!' another called.

'Are you Irish?' Mary-Kate asked.

He laughed. 'No, Paddy Kelly's their nickname for all the Dock Police. They won't take long, ma'am. It's a job to get them started but once they make up their minds, there's no stopping them. They're the finest dockers in the country, when they want to be.'

'Where's Ellen? My daughter, where is she?' Mary-Kate asked with a worried frown.

'She was here just now. You stay there, I'll go and see if I can see her. Kids, they're nothing but trouble.'

Mary-Kate sat down on the wooden bench beside Harry, noticing how very thin he was. He looked as though he had never had a decent meal in his life. 'Your sister will be back soon,' she said, trying to sound cheerful. He stared up at her. He was so dirty, she thought. He reminded her of the O'Hagan boys. She forced herself to

471

reach out and stroke his head although she knew she stood the risk of catching the lice. Oh, she wished this were all over. And where was Ellen? She had no right wandering off, especially around here, particularly when she knew how upset Mary-Kate was. Why was everything taking so long? Vi would be worried sick and she hoped Jamie wouldn't be fretful. And why had Michael run off like that? What had he to hide? Would he come back?

The boy leaned against her, his eyes closing, the warmth making him drowsy. Instinctively, she started to draw away, then she checked herself. Poor little mite. God alone knew what kind of a home he had, what kind of a life he had.

Just then a man stuck his head around the door to say they were finished and the constable appeared with Ellen and the girl. In the girl's hand was a newspaper parcel, already stained with grease, and around her shoulders was Ellen's coat.

'Found the pair of them on their way back here. The men have finished now, so if you'll pay them, you can both get off home.'

The reprimand that had come to her lips for Ellen was forgotten as she went outside to thank the men and pay them.

'Will you be able to manage now? I can't leave here and none of this lot can drive and even if they could I wouldn't bank on seeing the lorry again!'

'I'll manage. I got here so I should be able to get home,' Mary-Kate said with a confidence she didn't feel. She'd kill Michael Feehey, that she would. What would she do if he'd disappeared? 'What about these children?' she asked.

'Best leave them here for a bit, let them eat and get warm, they'll be all right. They know their way. You take care, ma'am.'

'Thank you so much for your help, I just don't know what I would have done without you.'

'All part of the service.'

She managed a smile. 'Ellen, get your coat.'

'No, Ma. I told Nelly she could have it. She hasn't got one and I've got two more.'

Mary-Kate was too tired to argue and anyway the coat would only have to be thrown out, as the girl was probably as verminous as her brother.

She didn't know whether it was the fervent prayers she sent up, or just luck, or maybe both, but somehow she managed to keep the lorry going. The constable had kindly crank-started it and put it into gear for her.

'Takes a bit of getting used to, doesn't it, double-declutching?' he'd said.

'Oh, it does that,' she'd replied, not having the faintest idea what he was talking about and praying that Michael would keep his promise.

The engine was making a very peculiar noise but she didn't care. She just gripped the wheel tightly and kept her foot down on the pedals she'd seen the policeman use after he'd moved the gear lever around. All she wanted to do was get home but if Michael had disappeared then she knew the return journey would be a nightmare. All those junctions to contend with and the tram lines! Oh, Lord, what if the iron wheel rims got caught in the tram lines? They could end up anywhere.

Ellen was silent and preoccupied. She was still struggling with the shock of her first insight into the abject poverty of the slums of the Liverpool dock area. It was inconceivable that in such modern times there were people who had no money for food, for shoes or warm clothes and who were forced to live in dirty, overcrowded, crumbling houses in dark courts and alleys. She'd read about the 'bad old days' in her history books, when people lived ten and twelve in a room in damp cellars and cholera had raged through Liverpool, killing thousands. But she'd thought all that was in the past, that it was only history and that things had vastly improved. But they hadn't and it had shocked her and now she felt a sense of outrage and guilt. She would do something to help. As soon as she was old enough, she would find out what could be done and she would train in whatever profession necessary to help combat such conditions and such unfairness.

'Ma, do you remember Aunt Gina saying girls should have dreams?' she said quietly.

'Oh, Ellen, please. Not now. I'll have hysterics if he doesn't turn up!'

Ellen was not going to be put off that lightly, not now she'd found her vocation. 'I know what I want to do with my life. I want to help people like Nelly. I followed her. Her feet were bare, Ma, and mine were cold even in stockings and boots. She hasn't had anything to eat since yesterday! Why don't people help? Someone should do something to help them!'

'Ellen, there are a lot of people trying to help. There is always poverty, there always has been and there probably always will be,' Mary-Kate answered shortly. This was no time for a discussion on Social Reform.

'But it's not fair that some people should have so

much money and others have none. Look at the money Lizzie has wasted!'

'Don't talk to me about her! If it hadn't been for her we wouldn't be in this mess. Oh, where is that man!' She had a strong premonition that even if she got safely across all the road junctions, she wouldn't be able to get the lorry up Boundary Road; it was too steep.

Just as they reached the junction of Great Howard Street, Michael stepped out into the road, waving his cap.

'Oh, thank God!' Mary-Kate cried, and she meant it.

Chapter Twenty-Four

———◆———

'I'VE NEVER BEEN SO glad to see anyone in my entire life, that I haven't. Get in,' Mary-Kate instructed.

Michael squeezed his tall, lean frame into the cab. 'And I've never been more thankful to see a face from home as I am to see you, Mary-Kate.'

With a bit of manoeuvring, he got behind the wheel.

'Why did you run off like that and leave us?'

'I told you before it's a long story, Mary-Kate.' There was a deep sadness in Michael's voice, but also an edge of fear, and she noticed how he looked about him in a furtive way. And his clothes – they hung on him and were those of a labourer. They were none too clean either.

'Do you want me to drive you home?'

'No. Back to the yard, please.' Mary-Kate was beginning to relax.

'I'm sorry I ran off like that and scared you.'

'And so you should be! I had to blacken my soul with lies to shield you.'

'You've changed Mary-Kate. There was a time when nothing ruffled your feathers.'

She smiled at the memory of her younger self. 'Oh, this is my step-daughter, Ellen.' She suddenly remembered that in her panic to get to the docks in time, she hadn't introduced Ellen properly.

Ellen nodded. 'I heard from Ma about all your troubles in Ireland, Michael.'

His mouth twisted into a hard line. 'I don't want to talk about it, not now. It will keep until we get back.'

Mary-Kate remained silent for the rest of the journey, worn out by the events of the night. It was with relief that they arrived safely back at the yard.

Ellen jumped down to open the gates.

Michael switched off the engine and helped Mary-Kate down. She looked up at him in the dim light coming from the street lamps on the road outside. She had recognized him instantly, but now as she studied him closely, she realized that he had changed, too. Gone was the boy who had mocked her that day in St Mary's churchyard. This was a man, and a man who had seen trouble. Grief, fear and hardship had etched themselves into the lines of his face and the depths of his soul. They had even been transmitted to his gestures. The way he stood – round-shouldered, hands thrust inside his pockets, eyes darting past her looking for . . . what?

'Where do you live, Michael? How long have you been in Liverpool?'

'I've been here a couple of weeks, doing a bit of this and a bit of that. Usually down at the docks,' came the noncommittal and evasive reply.

'Will you see us home and stay and have something to eat?'

Michael nodded, following Mary-Kate towards the gates.

After locking up, the three of them walked the short distance in silence. As they turned into Walton Park, Michael looked around at the houses.

'You did the right thing leaving Ireland. I see you've done well for yourself. Just as you said you would. Rich and famous, wasn't it?' The ghost of his former smile flitted across his face.

'Never mind all that now. Come on in with you. You look as though you haven't had a decent meal inside a week, and I'm starving, too.'

Vi greeted them with a cry of relief. 'I was all for calling out the police when Ellen didn't come back! Where've you been, I've been half-demented?'

'Oh, Vi, I'm sorry you've been so worried and put to so much trouble. Is Jamie all right?' Mary-Kate's voice was full of concern.

'He hasn't stirred at all.'

'I had a row with Mrs Winskill and then I had to get a lorry down to the docks and there wasn't time to let you know,' Mary-Kate explained hurriedly. 'I'm sorry. Would you do me one last favour before you go? Make a pot of tea and find us something to eat? Oh, this is Mr Feehey. I knew him back home in Ireland and he drove the lorry for us.'

Vi bustled off into the kitchen as Michael looked around him. She'd really done herself proud had Mary-Kate. He'd also heard about Gina – the toast of London – and to think he'd once held out hopes of marrying her. He'd been so bloody cocksure of himself that he'd mocked the three of them and in front of half the town, too. Ah, well, that was all water under the bridge now. Too much had happened since those days. He followed Mary-Kate into a small room. It wasn't a dining room and it wasn't a parlour; it was something halfway between both. It reminded him of his mother's back kitchen. Ellen had disappeared but returned now.

'I've had a look in at Jamie, Ma, and he's fast asleep.'

'You're a good girl, Ellen. Now you'd better have a bite to eat and get to bed yourself. You won't be able to get up in the morning.'

'It's Saturday, had you forgotten?'

Mary-Kate had, but she smiled. 'Go on up just the same, but come here and give me a kiss before you go. I don't know what I would have done without you tonight.'

Ellen did as she was bid and then, as she turned to leave, she looked back. 'I meant what I said, Ma, about doing something to help people like Nelly.'

'I know you did and I'm sorry I was so sharp with you, but we'll talk about it tomorrow.' She remembered the two verminous children. 'Ellen, have a bath and wash your hair and leave your clothes out – they'll have to be burned.'

She would have to do the same herself, she thought, remembering the boy, but now she was tired.

Vi brought in a tray of tea and sandwiches and after she'd set it down, Mary-Kate told the girl to get off home.

She watched Michael bolt the food. She'd been right; he'd not had a meal for a while. She leaned back in her chair. 'Have you anywhere to stay, Michael?'

He looked uncomfortable. 'Sort of.'

'Is that yes or no? Come on, it's me you're talking to! We went to mixed infants together. You went fishing with Matty. We shared the terrors of the first Troubles together.'

'No. I've been sleeping rough.'

She'd guessed as much. 'Then you'll have a bed here and you can tell me what's been happening to you, right now!'

He looked down at his work-roughened hands, the nails split and dirty and he felt ashamed. 'Oh, I was a fool, Mary-Kate! A young, thoughtless eejit. Sure, the more Pa tried to talk sense into me, the more I opposed him. I thought we'd been betrayed by Collins and the rest. I couldn't see where it would lead, so I ran with the pack. Well, when they burned down the house, I knew the army and the Guards would be looking for me, so I ran.'

'Ma told me all that. Where did you go?'

'The Comeragh Mountains. "Refuge of Rebels" they used to call them. Some rebel I was. Afraid to show my face. Then I heard that both my parents were dead.' Michael dropped his head in his hands. 'It was all my fault.'

Mary-Kate leaned forward. 'Not all of it, Michael. You can't blame yourself for the acts of others.'

'It was my fault. I should never have got mixed up with them in the first place. Your Matty didn't. But I did try to stop them. I tried, but you can't reason with them and I was too late anyway. I worked my way up from Waterford to Dublin, but everywhere I went I was in fear of the army and the Guards, so I decided to come to England. But they followed me, said I'd been tried in my absence and sentenced to death as a traitor.'

'Who said so? The army? The Garda?'

He shook his head. 'No. *Them*. The Irregulars.'

'How can they make judgements like that? They're outlawed. They're the ones who will go on trial and face death if they're caught. Are they such fools then to think they still have any power at all?'

'Not fools, Mary-Kate. Desperate men. Fanatics. I saw two of them today, down at the docks. That's when I decided to try and find you. But when I hit that lad, I knew the police wouldn't look on me too kindly and then the word would get round and it would only be a matter of time before they caught up with me. I'm sorry, Mary-Kate, but I couldn't stay and be recognized.'

She clutched her throat. It was all over and done with, wasn't it? So why were there members of the now outlawed Irish Republican Army here in Liverpool?

'They are looking for me. You know the punishment for traitors.'

'You're no more a traitor than I am, Michael Feehey. You're safe here. They won't look for you in the suburbs. You can stay here.' An idea was forming in her mind. He was no fool, he was used to dealing with people, and he had been in business himself. 'And I have a job for you.'

'A job?'

'My late husband's business was a thriving one until his daughter, his elder daughter, encouraged me to put her husband in charge. But Ernest is a weak man and so she took over, unknown to me, and has managed to turn a profit into a loss. I have a son, Jamie, he's only young but my husband wanted him to inherit the business in due course. Obviously I can't do everything myself and there is property to manage as well. I need a good man to run the business for me, Michael. Will you do it? I'll pay you well.'

He looked down at his worn and dirty boots resting on her fine carpet. Once he'd had everything. A good home, loving parents, a thriving business, the respect of the community and the admiration of quite a few girls. Now he had nothing. No home. No job. No money. No country even. And here was Mary-Kate offering him everything. She, that he'd once mocked in his smug, safe little world. He was tempted, very tempted, but he also felt humiliated, although after what he'd done he had no cause to feel anything but grateful. He shook his head. 'I can't, Mary-Kate. I'm sorry. They'll find me and I don't want to involve you, not the way I did my Ma and Pa. In truth, I did hope you'd help me. I knew even that was wrong of me. I was clutching at straws. I never thought I'd come to this. I just want to get away.'

'Oh, Michael, why were you such a fool?'

'I've asked myself that over and over again. We thought we'd win. We were sure we had enough people on our side. People who wanted the whole of Ireland to be free.'

'They'd had enough. They wanted peace and an Irish Free State. They were content to let the people of Ulster stay within the Empire. Four years of war were enough, Michael. Stay here and work for me; it's the chance of a new beginning.'

He shook his head firmly. 'No, I can't. I'll have to leave Liverpool and soon!'

Mary-Kate could see he was determined. He was a frightened man. 'Where will you go? America?'

'God, no! There're too many of them fled there already! I'd be finished in a day or less. I don't know. London. France . . .' He shrugged.

She thought of Gina. Would Gina help him? He and Gina had once been quite close. She dismissed the thought. Gina wouldn't care what happened to him now. She wouldn't want him embarrassing her in front of her friends. But what about Bridget? 'Would you go to Glasgow?'

'Glasgow?' he echoed.

'To Bridget. She lives in Glasgow. She'd help you if I asked her.'

'I don't know, I hear the place is full of expatriot Irishmen as well.'

She leaned back. 'Michael, you can't run forever. There is nowhere in the world, except maybe India or Africa, where there are no Irish immigrants.'

He slumped in the chair. 'You're right, Mary-Kate. I'm sick of running and hiding and forever looking over my shoulder.'

'I'll write to Bridget tomorrow. Now, we're both exhausted. I suggest we get some sleep.' She rose. What a day it had been. Now she was faced with running the business herself, with the help of Mr Johnson and possibly with Davies as a sort of foreman. But somehow she'd manage. She'd always managed. Wasn't she the 'practical' one after all?

The letter had been written but before it could be posted, a letter arrived from Bridget, telling Mary-Kate of Mrs Duncan's death and her own good fortune. Eileen was living with her now, Bridget wrote, and she had had the deeds to the house in Melville Street signed over to Bernie and Archie, but they must never know that. Archie had his pride. Miss Whyte was still off ill and she was finding work exhausting but challenging. She hoped everything was going smoothly for Mary-Kate.

Mary-Kate could have laughed at this last line. Smoothly! Oh, life was anything but smooth. She decided to send the letter with Michael, instead of posting it, and so she gave him some money and told him to get some decent clothes and buy a ticket to Glasgow.

'I'll never forget you, Mary-Kate. God bless you!'

'Could I do less, Michael? Bridget will help you, too. God go with you.'

He smiled. 'Clonmel has reason to be proud of "The Sisters O'Donnell". I'm sorry I mocked you all – I was a young eejit then.'

'And now you're an older one. Get off with you, Michael Feehey, or you'll miss that train!'

It had been raining all day and Bridget sighed as she looked out at the dismal scene beyond the curtains. She was glad to go to work these days, for the house was too quiet and held too many memories. If it hadn't been for Eileen she felt as though she would have gone mad. She'd locked Ian's room and his mother's, after first covering the furniture with dust sheets. Her sitting room she'd turned into a bedroom for Eileen for there was no need for it now; she had a whole house to herself.

'Will I put the kettle on, Bridget, it's nearly tea time?' Eileen broke into her reverie.

'You might as well. What a miserable day and it's

going to be a miserable night and a long, miserable winter.'

'My but we're in a depressing mood,' Eileen said lightly.

Already dusk was falling, speeded by grey clouds and the mist-like rain. Before she let the curtain drop, Bridget noticed the figure of a man coming up the street, collar turned up, hat pulled low over his forehead. It wasn't a night to be out and about, she thought as she adjusted the heavy drapes to shut out the depressing scene. She heard the clattering in the kitchen as Eileen got the tea ready. Later on they'd have a game of cards or read and then get things ready for the beginning of the working week. She hoped Miss Whyte was better. She really did miss her and although Miss MacIver had done all the buying they were very busy with one person short in the department.

The doorbell echoed through the quiet house. Bridget went to answer it for Eileen was still busy, wondering who it could be at this time on a Sunday evening. Probably Archie and Bernie, although Bernie shouldn't be out in weather like this and she'd tell Archie so.

She didn't recognize him at first, but when he spoke her name, her hand went to her lips as though to force back the cry of surprise. He was soaking wet. He looked thinner and taller than she remembered. His dark brown hair was in need of a trim, his brown eyes and his prematurely lined face reminded her of a sad-eyed spaniel. 'Michael Feehey! Get inside with you. How on earth did you find me?'

Michael took off his hat and delved into the inside

pocket of his sodden jacket. The hat dripped water on to the polished floor. 'Mary-Kate said to give you this.'

Bridget took the damp and crumpled envelope from him as Eileen came through the kitchen door, a tray in her hands, her eyes widening in surprise.

'It's all right, Eileen. He's a friend from home. For heaven's sake take off that jacket, you'll catch pneumonia! Hang it on the hook over there, then come in by the fire and warm yourself.'

He followed them both into the parlour and after setting down the tray, Eileen took the jacket with the comment that she'd put it in front of the kitchen range to dry out.

Michael sat on the edge of a chair, facing Bridget as she read the letter. He'd have recognized her – just. She still had the same auburn hair and pale skin but she'd grown up so much. There was an air of self-confidence about her that had never been there before. She'd always been the shy and timid one, not like the other two on whom she'd depended a great deal. But now she looked as though she needed no one. He felt acutely uncomfortable. Mary-Kate had made him feel at ease. Bridget made him feel inferior. He watched the other girl as she poured him a cup of tea and wondered who she was and how Bridget had managed to acquire a home almost as grand as her elder sister's. That it was her home was quite obvious from her relaxed, confident attitude. He never thought he'd see the day when little Bridget O'Donnell could make him feel like a pauper.

Bridget folded the letter. Only because Mary-Kate had asked her to help him would she do so. His very presence stirred up old memories, old fears and she didn't approve of the things people said he'd done. 'You can stay here and I'll do my best to help you.' She looked at Eileen. 'Michael will be staying with us and I'll have to go and see Archie.'

'What for?'

'To see if he can find him work. I know we have no vacancies at all at the shop.'

'Who's Archie?' Michael asked. She must have a good job from the way she spoke.

'My brother,' Eileen answered.

'He is married to Bernie O'Hagan, that was. He works at the big iron foundry, Dixon's Blazes they call it. I'll have my tea, then I'll go and see him.'

'On a night like this, Bridget?' Eileen protested.

'I can't take time off work and besides, Archie will be at work himself during the day, too.'

'It could wait until tomorrow,' Eileen reasoned.

'I'll be tired out after a day's work.'

'Where will he sleep?'

Michael's uneasiness deepened. It was obvious that the younger girl disliked him, considering him an intruder, and Bridget, although her manner had been pleasant enough, had succeeded in making him feel that she was only helping him because her sister had asked her to.

'Air Ian's room for him.'

'Look, if I'm putting you out I'll find a hotel or something!'

'You'll do nothing of the sort, Michael Feehey, besides, it will be good to have a man about the house again. I know this is a quiet neighbourhood, but two women alone are always vulnerable, aren't they?'

Although the words were spoken to him, Bridget's gaze was directed upon Eileen, and her thoughts ran away with her as she wondered at Michael's appearance here. Mary-Kate had always been one for 'lame ducks', she'd help anyone. Bridget had never really taken much notice of Michael; he was older than her and had been chasing Gina. He'd always had plenty of money to spare, but to look at him now no one would ever have thought so. Still, he'd paid for his misguided loyalty and rashness and paid dearly, and after all, where would she have been if she hadn't had Bernie to run to?

By the time she got to Melville Street she was soaked through, despite the umbrella and galoshes. Archie's first question was, 'Is there anything wrong with Eileen?' as he'd pulled her into the narrow hallway.

'No, she's fine. I've come to see you about something.'

'It must be urgent for you to come out on a night like this?'

'It is.'

Bernie exclaimed over how wet she was and how much of an eejit she was to come out. She put down the knitting she was trying to master.

'I'll make a drink. Sure, I'll never learn how to knit in a million years! I'm dropping so many stitches it'll look like a lace pattern there's so many holes in it that were never intended to be there at all. I wish I'd taken more notice of Sister Marie-Juliana, at least she succeeded with you Bridget, but we weren't much on sewing and knitting in our house, as well you know.'

'Bernie, will you sit down!' Archie commanded.

'Do as you're told and besides, I think you're going to need to sit down,' Bridget added.

'Why?'

'Because Michael Feehey has just landed on my doorstep!'

'Holy Mother of God! Not him from the butcher's on the Main Guard?'

'Yes, except there's no butcher's now and no house and no Mr and Mrs Feehey either. Don't you remember, I told you all about it?'

Bernie nodded. 'What's he doing here? I thought you said he'd vanished off the face of the earth?'

'Mary-Kate sent him. He's looking for work and he's running from the IRA.'

'What's he running from them for? Aren't they outlawed? Aren't the army hunting them down and shooting them?'

'They are, but apparently those they haven't caught hold grudges against those who tried to thwart them and Michael did, over his parents' house.'

'And what right has he to come here with his troubles?'

'None, I suppose. But you know Mary-Kate, she'd help anyone. Besides, where would I have been without you to help me?'

'We owe you more than you owe us, Bridget,' Archie put in quietly. 'Eileen's job, this house . . . what can he do? Is he a skilled man?'

'Only in butchering and not only animals either!' Bernie interrupted. Michael Feehey had brought a dark shadow into her safe, comfortable little world and she'd never liked the Feeheys. Oh, Himself had been good enough, giving her Ma the bones and offal – stuff he couldn't sell – to help her feed her ever-hungry family. But only when Herself wasn't looking. Mrs Feehey had been right at the top of the list of those who'd looked down their noses at the O'Hagans. Nor had Bernie forgotten the taunts of Michael and his friends that she and her brothers and sisters had suffered. And she'd lost her elder brother, and she'd no time for anyone fool enough to go on fighting when everyone knew it was all over bar the shouting. 'Don't you go getting yourself into bother for him, Archie Dalrymple!'

'Nothing was ever proved against him, Bernie. He never took part in any of the raids and I don't think he could . . . harm anyone!'

'Nothing was ever proved against our Declan either, except that he had a pistol when they caught him. He never even got a trial! They shot him! Michael Feehey should think himself lucky.'

'Don't go upsetting yourself, Bernie. It's all in the past now, you've got to think of the bairn,' Archie soothed before he turned back to Bridget. 'I'll do my best, you know I will. But it will only be labouring. I'll ask a few of the lads who have brothers in the shipyards if there's anything going there.'

'And is he staying with you?' Bernie persisted.

'For now, he's nowhere else to go.'

'Then it's a good job Eileen's there, too, otherwise what would people think? And in such a neighbourhood, too.'

'She's got a point there, Bridget,' Archie agreed.

'I know. Mary-Kate knew about Eileen, otherwise I don't think she would have sent him.'

490

Archie opened the door of a cupboard set into the alcove beside the fireplace and brought out a bottle. 'You're not going back without a drop of this in your tea and it's no good protesting either. You must be chilled to the bone. Next thing you'll be down with a cold like Miss What's-her-name.'

'Just a very small one. I do hope Miss Whyte comes back soon. I've enough on my plate as it is.'

When Bridget got back home, Eileen relieved her of her wet clothes in the hall. 'What did our Archie say? What's he come here for? Who is he?'

'I'll explain it all in the morning on our way to work. It's late, so you get to bed now.'

Eileen's glance rested on the parlour door. 'There's a good fire in Ian's room and I've taken off all the dust sheets. I made up the bed and put a couple of hot water jars in it.'

Bridget nodded her thanks as Eileen went slowly upstairs.

Michael had sat for what seemed like hours after Bridget had gone. Upstairs he could hear the young girl moving around. At one stage he felt as though he should at least offer to help and he'd gone into the hall to find her carrying a brass scuttle full of coal.

'Will I carry that up for you?' he'd asked.

'No, I can manage. I've been carrying coal up and down stairs all my life,' had come the terse reply. So he'd gone back into the parlour, feeling even more uncomfortable.

The warmth of the fire, the muffled sounds from upstairs and the sheer peaceful feel of the house after his long journey, lulled him into a half-sleep until he was jerked into wakefulness by Bridget's return.

She noted the way his shoulders twitched nervously and his dark eyes moved rapidly over the room as she opened the door.

'You're back then. What did your friend say?'

Bridget sat down in the armchair facing Michael who sat on the edge of the sofa, his hands resting on his knees, giving him the appearance of someone with complete composure.

'He said he'd try and that he'd ask some of the men he knows in the shipyards, but it will only be labouring. You've not the skills for engineering.'

He gave a mirthless little laugh. 'No, I'm not much use at anything. Butchering was the only thing I knew about.'

She thought of Bernie's words. 'It wasn't easy for any of us, Michael. I don't think there was a family in Clonmel that didn't suffer one way or another.'

He looked into the fire. 'But I made my own family suffer. No one else did that, did they?'

'Seeing as we're being totally frank, no, they didn't. But you've got to put all that behind you now.'

'That's easy enough for you to say, Bridget.'

'Is it? There are a lot of things you don't know about me, Michael Feehey.'

'Oh, I know about your Pa and Fergal and I was as sorry as the rest of them.'

'We were all fighting on the same side then and besides, I didn't mean that.'

He looked at her speculatively for the first time. 'What did you mean?'

She leaned back wearily in the chair. 'I didn't leave Ireland to become rich or famous, not really. Oh, I dreamed that some day I'd have a job like the one I have now and maybe all this.' She gestured with her hand to encompass the comfortable parlour. 'But I left because I was terrified. Scared out of my wits of what would happen, so I ran at the first opportunity.'

'Why are you telling me all this?'

Bridget's hazel eyes held his gaze steadily. 'I don't know. To help you, I suppose. Did you do all the things they said you did?'

'No. I was just a loud-mouthed fool. But I realized that too late. I never killed anyone, Bridget. I never hurt anyone. I suppose some people will say I was guilty by association, but I only hung around on the fringes of the group. I thought I was the grand fellow all right then. We were going to take on the whole county and win. We were going to force the Dáil up in Dublin to take notice of us. We were having none of this Free State stuff. Grand speeches. Grand plans. But when it came to the action, I couldn't do it. So you see, didn't I just mess up the whole thing? Everyone on the Free State side thought I was in with the other lot, and the Nationalists thought I was a coward and a deserter and an informer. I was an outcast and so I ran and I hid until I was so sick of it all that I couldn't stand it any longer and I came here. And I'm still an outcast.'

Bridget gazed into the flames. She was remembering the sickening feeling of panic; how she'd been only too glad to run, too. 'I don't blame you for running.'

'It's different for you, Bridget. Everyone understands

if a woman is afraid, but I'd turned my back on everyone and everything.'

'So did I, in a way. I left Ma and Matty, even Mary-Kate and Gina.'

Michael covered his face with his hands. 'But you weren't responsible for the death of your parents.'

She remembered Mary-Kate's letter. 'Michael, it wasn't entirely your fault. You tried to stop them.'

'I didn't try hard enough. I could have gone to the army or the Guards.'

'Stop it! Stop feeling sorry for yourself. You're not the only person in the world who has suffered.'

He looked up at her. 'It's not self-pity, it's guilt.'

'Call it whatever you want, you can't go on tearing yourself to pieces. Guilt is destructive, self-pity is even worse and I know.' Bridget got up and put more coal on the fire, giving the embers a good stirring to hide her emotions. He'd brought back the memories of her early days in Glasgow when she'd felt an outcast. He'd also resurrected the ghost of Andrew MacDonald.

He watched her quick, decisive movements and he forgot about himself. She was almost a stranger, so why was he baring his soul to her? Because he had no choice or because he'd been remembering her the way she used to be? Shy and timid. What or who had made her into the confident young woman she now was? 'How did you come to end up in Glasgow?' he asked when she'd resumed her seat, her expression calm.

She told him and she told him of those days in Warwick Street while he listened, more at ease now. When she finally finished, Michael's estimation of her had grown considerably. He leaned forward, clasping his hands, knuckles downward, on his knees. 'And was there ever anyone . . . anyone special? No. No, forget I said that, it's none of my business.'

She looked down at her own hands. It was none of his business. Why should she tell him? She didn't look up. 'There was someone, but he belonged to the Gorbals and that part of my life. It . . . it was never meant to be.'

'I'm sorry.'

'There's no need to be. I wouldn't have the things I have now if . . .' She shrugged. 'So you see you have to put the past behind you and start again. I did.'

Michael was silent for a few minutes. He'd noticed the brief flash of pain in her eyes as she'd spoken about the obviously doomed love affair. He'd noticed the gleam of determination in them when she'd told him, unemotionally, about her life with Bernie O'Hagan and her fight to get out of the Gorbals. There must be some truth in her advice. He sighed heavily. 'You're right. I suppose the time comes when you have to stop running, take stock of your life, and your mistakes and try again. Try to do better. I don't want much from life, Bridget, not any more. I've no great dreams or ambitions now. I just want to belong somewhere! I want stability, I suppose.'

For the first time Bridget felt sorry for him. He'd had everything and now he just wanted to belong. It was such a simple thing. She smiled and, reaching out, she touched his hand. 'You belong here now, Michael, with us. Haven't we all come through the bad times? You, me, Eileen, Bernie.'

He looked at her with such relief in his dark eyes that

she felt the colour rising in her cheeks and a strange feeling of compassion and tenderness crept over her.

'You won't regret it, Bridget, I promise.'

She stood up. 'No, I don't think I will, Michael.'

Chapter Twenty-Five

B RIDGET DIDN'T REGRET IT and neither did Michael. Archie had managed to get him a job in the John Brown Yard and Bridget's initial fear that he might have been followed had been dispelled by Archie with the words, 'We take care of our own Bridget, you should know that by now, so dinna fret about it.' Eileen had dropped her suspicion of him after he'd redecorated her bedroom, which was sorely in need of fresh paint.

Michael had changed, Bridget thought as she watched him digging over the patch at the bottom of the garden that had run to weed since Mr Douglas, the man who kept the garden tidy, had injured his back. Gone was the cocky, blustering boy she'd known. He was quieter and more considerate and he'd always been generous. He worked hard and he got on well with Archie and the other men who frequented the Workers' Circle. Even Bernie had almost revised her opinion of him.

Watching him drive the spade into the hard earth and turn it and lift it, breaking it into clods, brought a smile to her lips. Back home, in the days when he'd had his mother waiting on him hand and foot, he wouldn't have known one end of a spade from the other. But it was he who had waved aside her intention to get someone to 'sort out that jungle at the bottom of the garden'. She'd take him a mug of tea. He'd been at it now for over two hours and it was a raw Sunday afternoon.

He leaned on the handle of the spade with one hand and took the mug with the other, after first wiping the beads of sweat from his forehead. 'God, wouldn't I make a fine fist of cutting peat from the bogs.'

She laughed. 'And shouldn't I have a camera and take a photograph of you to send to Ma. They wouldn't recognize you.'

He took a gulp of the scalding liquid. 'That they wouldn't. Wasn't I always turned out like a dandy and spent most of my time jaunting around in Pa's car and thinking I was "Jack the lad".'

She laughed again. He now found it easier to talk openly about his parents and his early life. It was something she'd encouraged him to do, feeling it was better than bottling it all up inside.

'And what grand plans have you for this piece of land when I've finally got it into some kind of shape and broken my back into the bargain?'

She studied the half dug patch with a small frown. 'Either roses or a rockery. It has a lot to do with how much sun and wind it gets. What do you think?'

'Sure, it's no use asking me, I'm not the expert. Archie's your man for that. Hasn't he always got some book about pruning or grafting and stuff like that?'

'I'll ask him.'

'Then be prepared for a long diatribe, because once

he gets going the only thing that will stop him mid-flow is if you ask him something about the Union. He's a great one for the Union, is Archie. They'll make him a shop steward one day.' Michael handed her back the empty mug and prepared to begin work again.

'Don't you think you've done enough for today? I don't want you ruining your back like Mr Douglas.'

'I've hardly got started, and why all the concern about my back?'

'Because I'm the one who will have to look after you if you do rick it or whatever Mr Douglas has done.'

He smiled slowly, a teasing light in his eyes. 'Is that so? It might not be such a bad thing altogether then?'

'Now just you stop that.'

His expression became serious. 'Stop what?'

'You know what.'

'I don't.'

'All these innuendos – you're always doing it.'

'Did you swallow the dictionary after lunch?'

Bridget laughed again. The relationship between them now was easy. Sometimes light-hearted and teasing, as now; at other times more serious. It was like getting to know a distant relation and finding you had so much in common, that there was a certain empathy between you, Bridget thought. 'Just say what you mean and don't be tormenting me with your teasing.'

'All right, no more innuendos as you call them. I wouldn't mind being looked after by you Bridget. Will that suit?'

'Don't we look after you now? Meals cooked, clothes washed and ironed. Isn't that being "looked after"?'

'I meant you, not you and Eileen, and you know full

well that that's what I meant; although I'd prefer to think that it was me that was looking after you.' He drove the spade hard into the ground. 'It's a man's place to look after a woman, not the other way around.'

'Oh, I see it hasn't taken you long to acquire the great Glaswegian attitude. Do I hear traces of indoctrination by one Archie Dalrymple here?' she quipped.

He turned and caught her hand. 'It's nothing like that Bridget, it's self-respect or pride, if you like.'

She understood. She gave his hand a quick squeeze. 'I was only joking, Michael. You know I wouldn't say anything to hurt you or your pride, not intentionally.'

The moment had passed. He smiled and she gave his hand another squeeze before going back indoors.

This year was going to be 'the best ever' Archie announced as the church bells pealed out, the ships on the River Clyde hooted noisily and the crowds on Sauchiehall Street and around the Gorbals Cross and other monuments cheered and kissed complete strangers and bellowed 'Auld Lang Syne' at the top of their voices as they celebrated Hogmanay in true style.

'This must be the first Hogmanay you've been sober since you were out of short trousers, Archie Dalrymple!' Bernie laughed as she kissed him and then took the traditional pieces of coal, bread and handful of salt from Michael who, being the darker of the two, had been their first-footer, letting the New Year in. Bernie's baby was nearly due now and she found movement difficult, calling herself 'a great lump of an elephant'.

'I wouldn't say he's entirely sober. We had a few drams on our way home, didn't we, Archie, man?'

'Michael Feehey, you swore you'd both come straight home!' Bridget berated him laughingly.

'Oh, I wish we could have gone dancing and then crowded out on to Sauchiehall Street with all the others.' Bernie was wistful, remembering other Hogmanays.

'A fine sight you'd look. You've to be kept quiet, so the doctor said, though he's a better man than I am if he can keep you quiet,' said Archie dryly.

'At least one of us will be "tripping the light fantastic" and having a wonderful time,' Bernie replied. Eileen had gone out accompanied by her 'young man', Lester Sinclair, a journeyman carpenter who had come to work at Craig's to do some alterations.

Bridget looked at her guests. Yes, this would be a good year for them all. Bernie would have her baby very soon. Archie had been elected a shop steward and Michael was content enough working at the John Brown yard. He'd lost that haunted look, put on weight and had begun to laugh again.

The biggest change had been in her own status. Miss Whyte had returned to work, rather pale after her long illness, which had been diagnosed as pleurisy, confiding in Bridget that she was going to retire. Her health wasn't up to it any more and she was going to live with her sister in the South of England where the climate would be more beneficial to her chest. She had also told Bridget that she had recommended that she take over as Head of Department and, when she had protested, she'd been reminded that she had coped and coped remarkably well in Miss Whyte's absence and that her efficiency and flair had not gone unnoticed.

Bridget sipped her sherry. She hadn't asked as much

from life as Gina, but she'd finally come within reach of the goal she'd set herself when she'd left Ireland. The Head of Department in the most exclusive shop in Glasgow. If she were really honest she knew that when she'd left home it had really only been a dream. She'd been fond of spinning daydreams in those days. But Glasgow had shaped her. Glasgow had made her grow up and had made her what she was now. She looked at Michael and smiled.

She'd asked Bernie and Archie over for the evening as they were the only 'family' she had in Glasgow. She rose and refilled everyone's glasses while Bernie watched her closely. With this new promotion, Bridget had everything except the one thing Bernie thought to be of paramount importance in life. She had no one to love her. She watched Bridget as she handed Michael his glass of whisky. Yes, she was in danger of becoming an old maid, in Bernie's opinion. Time had a way of creeping up on you. She had wondered about Michael and Bridget. These days he wasn't the snooty upstart he had been, for the tables were now turned. Bridget had a far better job and he was a guest in her home, a paying one, mind, but they'd make a fine couple, that they would. So far, all her attempts at match-making had failed. Bernie had to admit that she wasn't the most subtle of women – was that why she'd failed? Any suggestion to Bridget on her part had been met with derision or totally misunderstood, at least that's what Bridget would have her believe. She knew there was something between them, she wasn't that much of an eejit, but she wondered if the shadow of Andy MacDonald still haunted her friend. Oh, well, it was a new year and worth another try.

'I can see that the two of you are just bursting to get out and join the crowds. Go on with you, Archie'll stay here with me.'

Bridget was shocked. 'Bernie, I asked you over here, you're my guests. What kind of a hostess would I be if I upped and left you on your own?'

'Would you just listen to her. It's a "hostess" she is now, and I don't like being a "guest" thank you very much, it's altogether too stuffy. Just you leave Archie the bottle and we'll put our feet up like the two auld folks that we are. Go on, get off with you before everyone's gone home. You're getting too staid, Bridget O'Donnell, that you are, and I won't listen to any arguments, otherwise Archie and me will go home.'

'Just what are you up to, lassie?' Archie asked her as Michael and Bridget both disappeared into the hall.

'Nothing! What should I be "up to" at all?' she replied, with wide-eyed innocence.

It was a cold night, but it was crisp and clear as Michael and Bridget walked towards town. The nearer they drew to the centre of the city the more crowded it became. The whole of Glasgow looked to be out on the streets. Men, women and children, some mere babes in arms. They had countless bottles shoved at them with the command to 'Tak a wee drap!' and to refuse seemed churlish. By the time they reached Sauchiehall Street Michael was singing and she felt just a little tipsy as she clung tightly to his arm in case they got separated.

'I must be mad! I once swore I'd never have more than one glass and I've got to be in work in the morning!' she yelled above the noise.

'This morning! You've got to be in work this morning and so have I!' He laughed down at her.

They were caught up with a crowd of people who were attempting a fair imitation of a Highland Reel in a very crowded space and she found herself being whirled off her feet. She felt giddy and happy and bubbling with a freedom of spirit she'd not felt in a long time. But who could not help but catch the mood, and she had so much to be happy about. She was swung around by a stocky young man who uttered the most blood-curdling impression of a Clan battle cry she'd ever heard, and then she was caught in Michael's arms and held fast.

She laughed. 'I think we should go home while we can both stand.'

'Enjoy yourself, Bridget! You don't laugh often enough! You're a right bonnie lassie when you laugh. There's the rest of the year to be sober.' And bending his head he kissed her.

When she drew away she stared up at him. No one had kissed her like that since Andy, but she didn't feel angry or outraged or hurt. She felt happy, strangely happy. 'Michael Feehey, you're taking advantage of me!'

'And why not? It's a night to throw caution to the winds, Bridget!'

Should she throw caution to the winds, she thought, or would she regret tonight for the rest of her life? Before she had time to think, she was swept up and he was kissing her again and she was kissing him back, but there was none of the wild urgency she'd felt before, only a feeling of warmth, happiness and belonging.

*

Gina let herself in and frowned. She was getting fed up with Helen and the way she was always leaving things lying around, cluttering up the place. She herself was almost as untidy, but that wasn't the point, this was her place.

'Helen! Helen, are you in?' she called, walking into the lounge. There was no reply. She kicked off her shoes and sat down on the sofa. She'd refused the offer of supper with Jimmie Masters, she was just too tired.

So far she'd managed quite well. She rested as much as she could, she ate properly and with the aid of make-up she'd managed to hide her pallor. Stripped of the rouge and lipstick and the white powder to hide the dark circles beneath her eyes, her skin looked almost transparent. Fortunately, it was fashionable to be thin, although at times she knew she looked waif-like. But the cough was getting worse. The bouts had become more frequent and more exhausting, but even there she had been lucky for they were most prevalent during the night, except for the two awful evenings in succession when she'd succumbed just before she went on stage and her understudy had had to go on in her place. Even that she had passed off as a bad cold, forcing herself to croak hoarsely and take all the remedies everyone suggested.

But how much longer could she go on? When she was alone like this, the fear that bordered on panic engulfed her. It was hard, so very, very hard to be brave; to find the courage and inner strength needed to push back the dark thoughts. She shook herself. She wouldn't give in to them now. She'd go on until the end . . . just as she'd sworn to herself. But Helen had begun to notice the cough and urged her to see a doctor. How long before the others in their crowd noticed? She had to get away. Go somewhere where no one knew her too well. New York? She'd always wanted to go there. It had been her intention to go long before this. But could she go? Would her health hold up for so long? Of course it would. The crossing would be beneficial, with sea air, good food and plenty of rest.

Gina got up and stared into the fire. She must be mad, completely mad even to consider it. What if everything went wrong and she were to become seriously ill, if she were to . . . she wouldn't say *that* word. She should go home to Ireland and Sarah. The beads of sweat stood out on her forehead at the thought. The fear was back. But she'd fight it, she would! She just wouldn't think about any of that! She'd go to New York. She'd make new friends, she'd be a success and then when the time came, then she'd go home to Sarah.

She picked up the telephone and when the operator answered she asked for Edward's number and then waited until he answered.

'Gina? What's the matter? It's very late.'

'It's not that late. It's only half-past eleven. I want to talk to you, Edward.'

'About what?'

'Not over the phone.'

'You want me to come over now, at this time?'

'Yes. Oh, please, Edward. It's important.'

'Won't it wait until tomorrow?'

'Have you got someone with you?' She wasn't fool enough to think he was celibate, but the thought annoyed her just the same.

'No. You haven't been causing trouble have you? You

haven't gone and promised to marry Jimmie Masters or anything like that?'

'No, I haven't. You know I can't stand the man, he's a fool.'

'Ah, but a rich one, Gina. Or he will be one day.'

'Are you coming over or not?'

'Do I have a choice? I suppose if I don't come I'll have you hammering my door down?'

'Yes, you will.'

'I'll be over.'

She heard the click at the other end and replaced the receiver. She would tell him that this time she meant business. She'd mentioned it before, but he'd fobbed her off, saying she was still under contract, she needed more experience, that she just wasn't ready. Now she didn't have time for his excuses. He was her agent. It was his job to find her work, she paid him enough and this time she was determined. And she wouldn't lose her temper and yell at him, she'd learned that that only exhausted her and brought on the coughing. She would be cool and composed and absolutely adamant. She bundled up all Helen's belongings, opened the door to Helen's bedroom and threw them inside in a heap and shut the door.

Edward knew what was coming. He'd seen it simmering for months, but he'd managed to put her off. She still wasn't satisfied, she wanted Broadway. He knew that if she went he'd lose her entirely. He smiled to himself. Lose her? He'd never even come close to her. The nearest he'd ever come to her was the time they'd spent in Ireland, and as soon as she'd got back she'd thrown herself into the social whirl again.

If only he could take her away, somewhere quiet,

somewhere where she wouldn't need to *prove* herself. He hadn't been joking when he'd said 'Why not marry me?' that day in Kilsheelan. Like a fool, he'd meant it – and if she had said 'Yes' what would he have done? Rushed her off to the nearest priest before she could change her mind? Yes, he would have done just that. He loved her. He'd tried to stifle the feeling, and in the early days he'd succeeded, but no longer. When he saw her on the arm of another man he could quite cheerfully choke the life out of the man concerned. He loved her and he wanted her, but so far – except for that one slip – he'd hidden it successfully. But now? 'There's no fool like an old fool,' he muttered as he drove through the darkened streets towards Bloomsbury.

'So, what have you dragged me out for?' he asked as he eased his large frame down into a chair, crossing his legs and folding his arms.

'I want to go to New York.'

He looked pained. 'Oh, not that again! Gina, I've told you that you're not . . .'

'Ready,' she finished for him. 'I am ready. I've never been more ready in my life. I'm sick of London; I can do far better and I don't have time for your excuses.'

'You are a great success. No one I've ever handled has achieved so much in so short a time.'

'I'm not just anybody.'

'Don't you think you're getting a little too big for your boots, my dear? What will you do if the Americans don't want you? If they don't think you're quite the most wonderful thing in silk stockings? It could happen, have you thought of that?'

Gina resolutely refused to think about that. 'I am not going to lose my temper, Edward. This is not going to degenerate into a shouting match. I refuse to be provoked. But don't be so negative – you know I'll be a success. You just want to keep me here because you don't want me to get on.'

'Now why would I do that? I get ten per cent of all you earn.'

'You don't care all that much about money.'

'Don't I?'

He was being awkward. She could tell by the cool amusement in his dark eyes and the hint of a smile about his lips. He could be as difficult as he liked, she didn't need him now. 'So, you won't do anything to find me work there?'

'Not yet.'

'When?'

'When I feel you are ready and the right part comes along.'

'I don't need you, Edward. Not any more. I can make it on my own.'

He laughed. 'I seem to remember we've had this conversation before and you found you couldn't manage and came back. On that occasion I was a thorough gentleman and never mentioned it.' He got to his feet and faced her. 'This time, Gina, I don't intend to be a gentleman. I intend to be brutally frank. If you go, you go alone and you stand on your own, for I won't lift a finger to help you.'

She kept her composure with difficulty. 'Who asked you to?'

'You are to be congratulated, Gina. You're keeping

your temper very well, so far. You may yet make a fine actress.'

'I am one.' If only he knew just how true that statement was.

'And I suppose you intend to surround yourself with the American equivalent of Jimmie and Freddie and Helen and all the other parasites?'

'Jimmie and Freddie aren't parasites.'

'No, they have money of their own, I agree. But they are fast and fickle and frivolous. Never count on them when you really need them – they'll be gone. And when you've become a really great star, with all the trappings that go with it, then will you be satisfied? Will you have proved whatever it is you are so desperately seeking? No, you won't. Give it up, Gina. Be content with what you have.'

'I can't. I won't!'

He shrugged.

'Get out, Edward,' Gina said quietly as she turned away from him.

He looked down at her and it was as though someone were twisting a knife just under his ribs. He caught her by the shoulders and, turning her around, drew her to him and pressed his mouth down hard on hers, shutting off her cries of protest, holding her in a band of iron. He felt her struggles grow weaker and her lips move beneath his. Then he released her and she stood staring at him, the anger gone from her eyes, a glazed stunned look replacing it.

'Goodbye, Gina. Good luck.'

Minutes later, she was still staring at the door through which Edward's broad back had disappeared. She felt strangely dizzy, and it had nothing to do with her illness. He was letting her go – wasn't that what she wanted? But no one had ever kissed her like that before. Not Jimmie with his hesitant little pecks, not Charlie Lever who was squiring her around at the moment. But Edward had kissed her like that once before. She tried to remember when, but couldn't. She sank down on to the sofa, touching her lips with the tips of her fingers.

'What's the matter with Edward, he nearly knocked me over as I came up the steps? Have you two fallen out again?' Helen breezed in, throwing her coat, gloves and bag on to a chair.

Gina looked up. Lately Helen's laissez faire attitude to life annoyed her beyond endurance. 'Not really. I told him I don't need him any more. I told him to get out.' She was feeling more like her old self again.

'Do you know what I think'

'No, and I don't really want to hear your theories right now. I've got a headache and I'm exhausted.'

'I think you love him.'

'Well, you think wrong, Miss Know-it-All! I hate him. And, for your information, I won't be seeing him ever again because I'm going to America.'

Helen clapped her hands. 'You've got a film part? Oh, Gina, have you? Oh, isn't that just divine!'

'No I haven't – yet. But I'm going out first thing tomorrow morning to book my ticket for New York, and I'm going Luxury Class. And, in case you have any ideas about coming with me, you can forget them.'

'Why would I want to go with you? Who would look after this place for you? Will you get an American agent, or will you just try and make it on your own?'

'I'll get an agent. I'm not that much of an eejit to think I can just walk off the ship and take Broadway by storm.'

'We'll have the most wonderful farewell party imaginable. We'll invite absolutely everyone.' Helen's eyes sparkled at the thought.

That cheered Gina up. 'Yes. Yes, we'll have a really grand party.'

Edward drove at a furious speed, not caring for his own safety or that of others. He'd lost her. Just for a moment he'd thought that she . . . Oh, what the hell! What did it matter now? What did any of it matter now? He'd had enough. He wanted out. Out of everything. He was sick to death of it all. Sick of boosting flagging egos. Sick of calming down arrogant, spoilt, selfish women like Gina and Delia Heysham. Gina would end up another Delia, he thought with some satisfaction. One day she'd be knocked from her precarious pedestal by another younger, prettier girl and forced to retire back into the oblivion from which she'd come – from which he'd plucked her. Where would all her fine friends be then? They'd be off chasing the company of someone far more interesting. Off with the old, on with the new. He was sick of it all. She wanted to get out of London, did she? Well so did he. Tomorrow, after he'd drunk himself senseless tonight, he'd make his plans; plans to leave London, leave England, leave Gina. He'd pass his other clients to other agents who would be only too willing to take them. He'd book a passage on some tramp steamer; no luxury liner for him, they didn't sail to where he intended going. As far away as possible from everything that had been his world since as far back as he could remember. A clean break. He could never have her, so he'd go to hell. She'd told him to go there often enough.

Gina had written the invitations and she'd sent one to Mary-Kate and one to Bridget, enclosing a note explaining that she would write to Sarah herself. As she'd written them she'd prayed they would come. It might be the last time they would all be together.

But a few days later she'd received a long letter from Mary-Kate, asking her if she was doing the right thing. Without Edward to guide her, would she be able to cope? She'd laughed at that. Mary-Kate had also echoed Edward's words, wasn't she satisfied with what she'd already achieved? What right had Mary-Kate to preach to her? She didn't know the situation that faced her.

Mary-Kate's letter went on to explain that she couldn't come to the party. There was the business. Mr Johnson and Davies were doing their best, but it was hard work and she just couldn't leave them. Ellen had been terribly upset to miss the party for, as she knew, she idolized her Aunt Gina. But would she call to see them before she left? She would be sailing from Liverpool wouldn't she? Yes, she'd call and see them, Gina thought sadly, although it would break her heart.

She'd been delighted when Bridget's reply had arrived. Although she, too, was busy, she had asked for two days holiday and she and Michael would be very happy to attend her lavish party, although they would probably feel very out of place amongst her friends. But, Gina was not to worry, they wouldn't let her down. Bridget was going to buy the smartest evening dress from the Exclusive Gowns Department, and Glasgow was quite a fashionable place really. She hadn't seen Gina since she'd left Liverpool, and she just couldn't let her go all that way, halfway across the world, without saying goodbye.

There had been tears in Gina's eyes as she folded the letter. Bridget would seem like a stranger now. She wondered how she looked; had she changed? Very probably, and working in a place like that (although she didn't need to work according to Mary-Kate) she could probably afford to splash out on an Exclusive Gown. No, Bridget wouldn't let her down. But what about Michael? In her letters Bridget had said he'd changed, that she wouldn't recognize him as the same person who had chased after her in Clonmel. He was quieter, more serious and he worked in a shipyard. She hoped he wasn't going to announce that to everyone or regale them with tales of her girlhood in Clonmel. Would he notice the change in her and remark on it, drawing everyone's attention to how thin she was, how pale? He would remember her as she had looked years ago. The demons were back, but Gina shook her head, trying to drive them out and concentrate.

Bridget appeared to get on very well with Michael, in fact Gina had noticed in her last letters that her sister seemed to be fond of him. But Bridget was fond of that dreadful Bernie O'Hagan or whatever her name was now. She'd done well out of her friendship with Bridget had Bernie. Living in her own house, a respectable married woman with her first child. It was a far cry from that hovel on the road to Cahir, and yet she could almost envy Bernie now. Mary-Kate and Bridget were alike in the fact that they would help anyone, while she had only ever thought of herself. But she had had her driving ambition, her promise to her Pa. That was the reason she would give to Sarah when she wrote. But it would be hard to convince her Ma and she had put off writing the letter, knowing it would be so painful to both Sarah and herself. 'I just won't think about it! I won't!' she said aloud.

Chapter Twenty-Six

———◦◦◦———

THE ARRANGEMENTS FOR THE party had sapped Gina's strength and even though she had applied rouge and lipstick liberally and added a couple of drops of belladonna to her eyes to make them appear clear and sparkling, these embellishments did not entirely conceal the tired, drawn look she saw reflected in her mirror. In a way she was regretting her initial enthusiasm. She would have much preferred a quiet supper with Bridget and an early night. But she smiled at herself. The entire cast had given her a splendid send off and she had received a bouquet and a handwritten message from the producer. Nearly everything was ready. She was due to sail from Liverpool next week, after staying a few days with Mary-Kate. She was booked into an hotel in New York and she had an appointment with a highly recommended agent. She'd neither seen nor heard anything of Edward since the night of their final showdown.

Helen poked her head around the door. 'Gina, are you ready? Everyone's starting to arrive.'

She stood up. 'Almost. How do I look?'

'Wonderful, as usual.'

'You don't think I look tired? Do you think I need more rouge?'

'Stop fussing, you look divine!' Helen cocked her head thoughtfully to one side. 'I think I'd take a little of the lipstick off. That oxblood colour is too dark for you. It's probably that that's making you look pale. But don't take all night about it.'

The door closed and Gina reached for a cloth with which to remove some of the offending lipstick. As she bent forward she started to cough. Quickly grabbing a small, linen guest towel she pressed it to her mouth. Oh, why now? Now of all times! The last thing she needed was a bout of coughing that left her breathless and exhausted.

She sat at her dressing table almost bent double by the spasms, the towel pressed hard against her mouth in an attempt to mask the awful wheezing and gasping. It was passing and she began to straighten up, then slumped back in the chair. She wiped her mouth and stared in horror at the towel.

There had been dark stains on her handkerchiefs lately but nothing like this! This was bright, scarlet blood. She threw the towel across the room as though it had burned her fingers. It wasn't *that* bad yet! It just couldn't be. She still had so much to do!

'Gina, Bridget's here and everyone wants to know where you are? Come on!' Helen was impatient.

She pulled herself together. She couldn't let Bridget see her like this. The mask came down once more, but with such an effort. She was still acting. She was to all intents and appearances her old self. She got up, preparing to follow Helen, but then Bridget was standing in the doorway.

'Oh, Bridget, I've missed you! How you've changed. You've grown up!'

They hugged each other as Michael looked on.

'You're not on one of these new-fangled eating fads are you, Gina? You're so thin,' Bridget exclaimed.

'Don't be silly. I just work too hard, that's all.'

'And play too hard as well. But you look lovely. I'm so glad we came.'

Gina held her at arm's length. 'Let me look at you. It's so long since I've seen you I just wouldn't have recognized you.' She meant it. She was stunned by the realization that this wasn't the 'little' sister she'd left in Liverpool. Bridget was a beauty, and she'd done Gina proud, for the dress she wore matched anything in her own expensive wardrobe. It was of a deep turquoise satin, overlaid with chiffon of the same colour. The hemline was scalloped and edged with rows of seed pearls. It was sleeveless and the low-cut back was also pearl-edged. Decorating the right side of the bloused top was a large bow, the ends of which were left deliberately long, forming points that almost reached the ground. She wore satin evening pumps, dyed to match and her auburn hair had been cut in a close cap that enhanced her features and pale, flawless skin. In her ears were large, drop pearls and she wore two bracelets high above her left elbow. She carried it all with ease and confidence.

Gina turned to Michael. 'And I wouldn't have recognized you either, Michael.'

He laughed, a little embarrassed. The starched white

collar was uncomfortable and he'd had the divil's own job with the bow tie.

'I hope you're not going to regale everyone with tales from home?' Gina teased.

He laughed again, but she didn't hear the note of bitterness. 'Now would I do that to you, Gina? Besides, I'm sure most of your friends wouldn't be in the least bit interested in Ireland.'

She was feeling much better now. The lethargy had passed. She was going to enjoy herself tonight and so was Bridget. Tomorrow could take care of itself. 'Come on, I'll introduce you to everyone,' she laughed, leading Bridget out into a lounge already full of people.

Gina's appearance brought cries of delight and feigned annoyance and soon she was surrounded by a crowd as she helplessly endeavoured to introduce her sister. Michael tactfully drew Bridget out of the group.

'She's changed, Michael.'

'What did you expect?'

'She's still beautiful, still so exuberant and full of confidence, but there's something hard about her now. She's not the same person. It's as though she's put up a barrier between herself – her real self – and everyone else.'

'Maybe when you're in the theatre you have to. Maybe you have to keep up that "make believe" world.'

'Perhaps you're right. Gina always knew what she wanted and how to get it. Facing reality was never her strong point. I don't think she would ever even admit the possibility of not being a success.'

'She's done very well. There are some very distinguished people here.'

'And you're an expert on the upper classes now are you?' Bridget teased. Then her smile faded. 'She's changed and I don't think I like what she's become – and all that make-up. It makes her look . . . well, a little cheap. I hate to have to say it, but it does and she doesn't need it.'

'Then I'm very glad I stopped chasing her.' Michael squeezed her hand.

'Well, I suppose, as we're here and I paid a small fortune for this dress, we might as well enjoy ourselves. Shall we dance, Mr Feehey?'

'You're a bold piece, Bridget O'Donnell! That's my prerogative.'

'We're in London now and it's not bold, it's modern!'

'Call it what you like, but I'll do the asking.' And he led her into the middle of the room to join the others. The party was in full swing.

Gina took the proferred glass of champagne from Jimmie and then disentangled herself from his embrace. He was becoming a moribund nuisance. He'd begged her not to go. He'd asked her to marry him, albeit when he came into his inheritance, and she'd been touched by his devotion. But that hadn't changed her opinion of him. She still thought him a fool and she didn't suffer fools gladly. Besides she couldn't contemplate marriage to anyone now.

'You didn't say you had such a gorgeous sister.'

'You didn't ask. Are you deserting me, Jimmie?' she asked, flippantly.

'Oh, Gina, you know I wouldn't do that. Besides, she looks very happy with the chap she's with.'

'I think she is, they've known each other for years. But

she has grown to be a real beauty, I'll have to be careful, won't I?' she quipped before moving deftly away towards another group.

Bridget had been asked to dance with four other men before Michael put his foot down very firmly and had led her to a small sofa that had been pushed back against one wall.

'Don't tell me you're jealous?' she laughed.

'Of course I am.'

She smiled. 'That's all right then. In fact I've come to the conclusion that I don't like her friends much at all. Lords and Honourables they may be but they're shallow. They say things they don't mean and some are downright eejits. And as for that one over there, the tall thin one, he said "I was chasing about your country a few years ago, rounding up some rebels." How tactless and insensitive! Chasing around, as though he were on some sort of picnic!'

The smile on Michael's face vanished to be replaced by a grim, brooding scowl.

'Oh, I shouldn't have mentioned it. Forget it, he's just a blustering fool. They've all had too much to drink already. I thought the Scots could drink, but this lot take some beating. At least in Glasgow they can hold their liquor.'

Helen came towards them dragging a girl with her. The girl looked ghastly and her hand was clamped over her mouth.

'Oh, God! I just hope she makes it to the bathroom. Gina will go absolutely mad if she throws up all over the carpet!' Helen opened a door and shoved the girl inside, then pushed her way back through the throng.

'How disgusting! Not even a woman in the Gorbals would get herself into that state! I'm glad Mary-Kate didn't come, she would have been horrified, and Gina certainly knew what she was doing when she didn't invite Ma. She would have given her the "rounds of the kitchen" and in front of all her fine friends,' Bridget said grimly.

'I've got to admit that it's turning out to be a far from entertaining evening,' Michael agreed.

'What time is it?'

'A quarter past eleven.'

'Do you think we can make our escape at midnight, like Cinderella? I can't see that we'll get much time to talk to her. This lot probably won't go home until the early hours, if they get home at all. It would have been much better if we'd just gone out for supper, the three of us. It's rather a waste of time, isn't it? A few minutes alone with her, after all this time.' Bridget was disappointed.

'To say nothing of the expense or the fact that I feel as though I'm being half strangled by this collar and look a right eejit got up like a penguin in Phoenix Park Zoo!'

Bridget started to laugh. 'Never having seen a penguin, except in books of course, I can't give a verdict on that!'

Someone put a record on Gina's gramophone and Helen's voice shrilled over the clamour. 'Gina! Gina, where are you? We've simply *got* to dance to this. It's our *pièce de résistance*.'

Helen had jumped up on to the top of a table and Gina felt hands reaching out and lifting her up too. Then she was looking over a room full of smiling, encouraging faces. She laughed and clapped her hands delightedly.

Why not? It wouldn't hurt; she could rest tomorrow. Tonight she was enjoying herself.

She and Helen executed as spirited an exhibition of the charleston as their small stage would allow. The long ropes of beads around Gina's neck clicked like castanets as they swung. The layers of long, silver fringing on her dress swirled jauntily, revealing slim legs in sheer silk stockings that were held up, just above the hemline, by white lace garters decorated with tiny satin bows. Her feet in their white satin pumps were 'shimmying' fast and furiously. Everyone was clapping and cheering their encouragement. Oh, it was so exhilarating. She was a 'star'. She'd always be a 'star' wherever she went.

Her eyes were bright and her cheeks were naturally flushed after her exertions as the music finished and she was caught around the waist and swung down and set on her feet. Charlie Lever put a glass of champagne in her hand and as she smiled at him, she caught sight of Bridget making her way towards her.

'Wasn't that a hoot!' Gina laughed, a little breathlessly.

'Is that what you call it?'

Gina stared at Bridget in amazement. 'Oh, for heaven's sake, Bridget, it was only a bit of a lark!'

Bridget had been embarrassed and disgusted by Gina's behaviour. Michael had studiously examined his empty glass, but she'd noticed that most of the other men present had been far less polite. Some had even nudged one another and smirked. It was her sister they were ogling, not some cheap little, good-time girl! But it was her sister who was making a fool of herself. She was belittling herself and acting cheap and Bridget felt as though Gina's degrading behaviour reflected on her, casting her in the same mould in the eyes of these people that Gina called her friends.

'I don't think Ma would call kicking your legs up and showing everyone your garters, not to mention other things, a "bit of a lark". I'm sorry, Gina, but we're leaving. We've a long journey back tomorrow.' Bridget bent forward and kissed her sister on the cheek before she could speak. 'Take care of yourself and good luck. Now, I don't want any arguments, we're not going to part on bad terms. You have your friends and your own lifestyle and I have mine. You just write and let me know how well you're doing. Promise?' She caught Gina's hands in her own and squeezed them tightly.

Gina was so shocked she just nodded.

'Say "I promise".'

'I promise,' Gina said, a little shakily, as she watched Michael clear a way through to the door from where they both turned to wave to her. Bridget had censored her. Told her that she disapproved of her. Why, she'd turned into a prude! She might look and dress in the modern vogue, but she still had that small town attitude. Gina was hurt and annoyed. Her own sister had taken her to task in front of everyone and she'd walked out of her farewell party!

'What's the matter? Has there been a falling out?' Charlie Lever was beside her. She smiled brightly. 'Heavens no! They've got a frightfully long journey tomorrow and have to be up at the crack of dawn.' She dismissed the annoyance and the hurt, taking a sip from his glass. 'I feel just like these bubbles tonight. As though I could simply float away.'

'We're going to miss you so much, Gina. You're such fun to be with and so delightful.'

'Thank you, Charlie.' She waved her hand in front of her face, imitating the movements of a fan. 'It's so hot in here, especially after all my exertions.'

He took her hand.

'Where are you taking me?' She laughed as he led her through the groups of dancing, carousing people.

'For a bit of fresh air.'

'Not the verandah. We'll freeze out there.'

He pushed open the French doors that led out on to a small verandah overlooking the back garden. After the stifling heat inside it was refreshingly cool. The stars were bright and the moon was ringed by a pale, translucent circle. Already the glitter of frost could be seen on the grass.

'It's a beautiful night,' she sighed.

'Not as beautiful as you, Gina.'

'Oh, Charlie, you and your flattery. That's the oldest cliché there is.'

'But I mean it.' He pulled her towards him and kissed her.

She responded. She didn't mind a kiss and a cuddle and she quite liked Charlie. At least he didn't slobber all over her like Jimmie. As she pulled away she looked up at him. 'That's my farewell kiss, just for you.'

He drew her close again. 'Is that all I'm going to get to remember you by?'

Before she could make a witty reply she felt the bubbling sensation that preceded an attack. Oh, no! Please God, not now! Not now, she prayed. She shouldn't have come out here. Rapid changes in temperature always affected her. The first spasm made her cling tightly to Charlie for support. She snatched the flimsy wisp of lawn that passed for a handkerchief from the bracelet around her wrist.

'Gina, what's the matter? Are you ill?'

She couldn't answer him, she was fighting for her breath.

'Good God Almighty! You are ill. We'll get a doctor.'

She tried to shake her head but couldn't. She felt so weak and yet so afraid. The scrap of a handkerchief was bright red, and still she coughed and fought for her breath as the blood gurgled and bubbled into her mouth.

Charlie picked her up and pushed his way back inside. Immediately, a sea of faces swam before her eyes. Helen, Jimmie, Freddie, Adele, Bertie. All sober now, their eyes shifting from her to Charlie. She turned her head and realized that there was blood all over the front of Charlie's shirt.

'Get a doctor, for Christ's sake!' he yelled.

Freddie's face disappeared and the voices were becoming fainter.

'Get her to bed, Helen. Just show me which is her room.'

She felt herself being lowered on to the bed and Helen propping pillows up behind her. Doctor Byrnes had warned her this would happen eventually. She remembered the word he had used. Haemorrhage. Dimly she realized she'd brought it on herself. The dancing, the wine, the heat. Helen and Adele Dunhill were talking in low voices.

'I'll be all right now, Helen,' she whispered.

'Just lie back, the doctor is on his way.'

Why couldn't she have just got through tonight? But she was too exhausted to even think clearly any more.

By the time the doctor arrived she was feeling a little better and only those in her closest circle of friends remained, sitting quietly talking and smoking in the lounge. Helen sat at the foot of the bed.

'Do you want me to stay, Gina?' she asked, as the doctor took out his stethoscope.

Gina nodded.

The doctor examined her, then stood looking down at her. 'You know, I presume, that you have pulmonary tuberculosis?'

She nodded again.

'How long have you known?'

'Quite a long time,' she whispered.

He looked startled. 'And you've continued to work and tax your already weakened state? Young lady, you have been extremely foolish! You've shortened your life, do you realize that, and you have probably passed on the condition. Were you not warned about that?'

She couldn't remember. 'I . . . I wanted to enjoy what time I had and I didn't want anyone's pity. I'm going to New York next week . . .'

'Miss O'Donnell, don't waste your breath and my time and don't go on deceiving yourself. You are definitely not going to New York. You are not fit to undertake such a journey, nor would the United States Immigration Authority allow you into the country. There is little you can do now except rest and conserve your strength.'

Gina had closed her eyes, but the tears trickled from beneath her lashes. 'How . . . how long, now, Doctor?'

'A matter of months. Weeks if you don't heed my instructions. I will give you something to help you sleep and I'll call again tomorrow. You are best propped up with pillows. You must keep warm but a little fresh air won't do any harm.' As he reached into his bag he signalled to Helen to open the window a little. It was a very pale and subdued Helen who pulled up the sash window and shivered as the cold night air crept into the room. Gina looked so pale and haggard that she seemed to be at death's door. Why hadn't she told anyone? And if what the doctor said was true . . . Oh, God, she could have caught it!

'Doctor, could I have a private word, when you've finished, of course?' Helen asked quietly.

Chapter Twenty-Seven

———◆———

DESPITE THE SEDATIVE, GINA spent a restless night and awoke heavy-eyed and feeling completely drained. Her head felt as though it were filled with cotton wool. Slowly she got out of bed and pulled on a robe and went into the lounge. It was still strewn with the debris of the party. She called Helen but there was no answer and she realized she must have gone out. The clock on the mantel said half-past eleven.

She felt terrible. She could no longer push it from her mind now. It was all over. She had to face the terrible finality of it. The wonderful career and the still unfulfilled ambitions had turned to dust. But at least she had her friends, they would help her through the long, dark days ahead. She picked up the phone and asked for Charlie's number. When she was put through she was informed by a polite but firm voice that Lord Charles Lever had left town, early this morning. She was stunned and asked to know when he would be back. The voice replied he was sorry, but His Lordship had not informed him of that fact.

She tried Jimmie next. He'd gone, too, but he had left her a message. It was most inconvenient, but his father had called him home. It was 'Duty' and something to do with his inheritance, so he'd had to go, but she wasn't to think that he wasn't thinking of her. He was.

She tried Freddie and Bertie, then Adele Dunhill and even Sally Chatterton, whom she didn't really like, only to receive similar messages. They were out. Not available. Gone to the country.

They'd all disappeared and she was alone! They didn't want anything more to do with her! Consumption carried with it social stigma and fear. It was almost as bad as having leprosy. She was now 'unclean'. She'd known that. It was one of the reasons whey she'd told no one. But friends were different, weren't they? They should care.

Then she thought of Bridget. She didn't care now what Bridget would think or say. She wanted Bridget to come over and comfort her. Bridget wouldn't desert her. Bridget was her sister.

The number rang and a clipped female voice answered.

'May I speak to either Miss Bridget O'Donnell or Mr Michael Feehey, please?'

'Just one moment, please.'

Gina's relief was visible.

'I'm sorry, but both parties have checked out. They left at eight o'clock this morning.'

She didn't even speak. She simply replaced the receiver and then pressed her fingers against her throbbing temples.

She heard the front door open and Helen came in,

dressed in her best coat and hat and carrying, a suitcase. 'Oh, I thought you'd still be in bed. How are you feeling?'

'Awful. Everyone's gone, Helen. I've tried them all.'

Helen looked uncomfortable.

'What's that for?'

Helen hastily pushed the case behind an easy chair and sat down. 'I thought I'd go and visit my aunt in Wales for a while.'

Gina stared at her stupidly, then a spark of her old spirit burst forth. 'So you're going too? You were going to sneak off without telling me. I thought you were a true friend and true friends stand by you in times of trouble. When I think of all I've done for you, Helen Mason! I've let you share this flat, virtually for free. I've given you clothes, money, food, anything you asked for. I even got you your present job and now . . .'

'Gina, stop it! You'll bring on another attack. The doctor said you mustn't get upset.'

'Upset? I'm furious.'

'I wasn't sneaking off. Really I wasn't! I had a word with the doctor myself last night. He said I could have caught it. He recommended that I get away to the country if possible.'

'And what about me?'

'He thinks you should go into a sanatorium. There are some very good ones now.'

Gina felt as though all the breath had been knocked out of her. A sanatorium. They just wanted to put her away, out of sight. She was an embarrassment to all her friends. They didn't care about her. 'Get out Helen! GO! NOW! Go before I contaminate you further.'

'Gina, please, I'm only being sensible about this.'

'Edward was right when he called you a parasite!' Her fingers closed over a small cut-glass posy bowl and she hurled it at Helen. It missed and shattered into a thousand shards against the wall. 'Get out, you pathetic, ungrateful bitch!'

Helen had gone and she was alone. Gina leaned back against the cushions on the sofa and closed her eyes. She couldn't pretend any longer. She couldn't ignore it. She was very ill. She was going to die and she was riddled with fear. All her life she'd been brought up to believe that death was just the result of the soul leaving the body to go on to the glories of heaven, and that to doubt that was a sin against hope. To doubt was the sin of despair. But she'd also been brought up to fear death. The lines of a hymn sung long ago in childhood went through her mind:

> Through life's long day
> And death's dark night
> O, gentle Jesus, be our light

But it was the words 'death's dark night' that stuck in her mind and brought on the clawing panic. She couldn't face it alone! Not in a sanatorium, with strangers. She wanted to go home. She wanted her Ma. She wanted Sarah's arms around her, chasing away the fears of 'death's dark night'. She wanted Sarah's hand to hold on to before she took that long journey. She'd go home. She didn't care what any doctor said about her not being fit to travel. She'd go home.

The doorbell interrupted her train of thought. It would be the doctor. She would tell him now about her plans.

When she opened the door Edward was standing on the step.

'Oh, it's you,' she said weakly.

'Is that all you're going to say, Gina?' She looked as though she'd been crying, he thought. In fact she looked dreadful.

'I thought you were someone else. Come in.'

'Not if I'm intruding.'

'You're not.' In a strange way she was glad to see him.

He followed her into the lounge. 'I called to say goodbye.'

'Goodbye,' she echoed. Had the news gone round so quickly?

'Yes. I've had a bellyful of London and the theatre and everyone connected with it. You've told me often enough to "go to hell", so I'm taking your advice, my dear. I'm going to South America, to a green hell. Brazil, to be exact. I have booked a passage on the *S.S. Hildebrand*. One thousand miles up the River Amazon to Manâos, deep in the heart of the jungle. Not your usual luxury cruise, I'll admit. Not a fancy liner to New York, like you.'

'I'm not going,' she said flatly.

He masked his surprise with a smile. 'Why not?'

'Because I'm going home instead.'

'Why?'

'For a rest. I've been over-doing it again.' She managed a smile as he looked around the still untidy room.

'So I see.' He stood up and crossed to where she sat. She looked worn out. 'Then at least I don't have to worry about you. You seem to have learned some sense.'

But too late. Too late, her heart cried. 'Yes, I've learned sense so you can go off to your green hell without worrying about me.'

'Thank you.' He didn't remind her that she was the reason for his going. He bent and kissed her cheek gently. 'Goodbye, Gina.'

'Goodbye, Edward.' Quite suddenly it struck her that she would never see him again and she felt the room grow darker. A few minutes ago she'd thought she'd sunk to the very depths of despair, but now she realized that she hadn't. Edward was going and she wanted him to stay. She realized just how much she'd depended on him and how much she needed him. The blinkers had been torn away by the realization that he was actually going out of her life forever. The twin illusions – fame and fortune – had blinded her. She'd gone on grasping at rainbows, the reality deliberately ignored. She loved him. She'd loved him for years, but she'd been blinded by her relentless ambition. And now she must do the hardest thing of all. She must let him go and go without knowing. It would be the first totally unselfish thing she'd ever done.

'I'll send a postcard, if they have such things there. Give my regards to your Ma and Matty and Richard.'

She couldn't trust herself to speak, so she just nodded.

'I'll see myself out.' He heard himself say the words calmly and wondered how he had kept his voice steady. He shouldn't have come. He was a fool. He'd hoped . . . Hell! What did it matter? What did any of it matter now?

As he turned to close the front door, he caught sight of a middle-aged man standing in the hallway.

'You have been visiting Miss O'Donnell?'

'That's my business.'

The man was unperturbed. 'And how is she this morning?'

Edward stared at him with open hostility. He was old enough to be her father. 'She seems well enough. I'm glad my departure was so timely. I wouldn't wish to intrude, although you don't appear to be her usual type.'

'I beg your pardon, sir!'

Edward noticed the black leather bag in the man's hand. 'Who are you?'

'Doctor Chapman-Aldis. And who are you, sir?'

Edward groaned inwardly. 'I'm sorry, Doctor. I didn't realize – she didn't tell me. I'm Edward Vinetti, Miss O'Donnell's agent. Ex agent.'

'So you're the one who has been working her into her grave. By God! Money, that's all your kind care about, no matter the cost to health or sanity.'

Edward caught him by the arm. 'What do you mean, working her into her grave? What cost to her health? I'm the one who's tried to stop her making herself ill. Tried to stop her working herself to a standstill. I took her to Ireland the last time she collapsed. Is that what has happened again?'

The older man stared hard and long into the dark eyes and finally decided he'd been wrong. He lowered his voice. 'She didn't tell you? You don't know?'

'Know what?'

'She's dying, Mr Vinetti. Tuberculosis. I was called last night when she haemorrhaged. I want her to go into a very good sanatorium.' He winced visibly as Edward's grip on his arm tightened.

'Tell me you're mistaken! Tell me it's something else . . . anything!'

'Mr Vinetti, please keep your voice down. I'm sorry, there's no mistake.'

'She's not going to any institution, do you hear me! I'll take care of her.'

He wanted to beat the man's face with his fists until he retracted his words. But he knew there was nothing he could do to alter the stark truth. But Gina. No, not Gina! So full of life and vitality and ambition. Not his Gina. His beautiful, stubborn, wilful, selfish Gina. No, not selfish, not any more. She'd said nothing. She was battling on alone. She was letting him go without even hinting; trying to make it easier by saying she was going home, that she'd learned sense.

'Look, come inside with me. You've had a shock.'

Edward realized the doctor was speaking to him. 'No. No, not yet. I'll . . . I'll sit in my car and try to calm down. I'll see her when you've gone. Don't tell her you've told me. Don't tell her you've even seen me, please? I need time to think.'

Minutes later, Edward sank heavily into the driving seat of his car. Why had Gina kept it from him? But, of course, he should have guessed. The first collapse. The visits to Doctor Byrne. My God, how she must have suffered, for he was certain that not even Sarah knew. She'd carried on alone. His dear, brave darling. The fear, the pain, the torment, all of it she'd borne alone and yet kept up such a dazzling façade. Too proud to invite pity. Too stubborn to ask for help – even now. He didn't care any more whether she loved him or not. He loved her and there wasn't much time left. She'd have the best of everything. He'd look after her. He'd stay with her. They'd go to Switzerland; there were special clinics there and the mountain air was reported to work miracles. He'd marry her. She'd be entirely his – for as long as they had. He threw open the car door and swung his feet on to the pavement.

The doctor had gone. He'd been very persuasive but Gina had remained resolute. She was going home. He'd pointed out all the dangers of the journey, but she'd refused to listen. She would visit Mary-Kate for a few days to recover from the train journey and build up her strength for the ferry crossing and the journey to Clonmel. She would have to write to both Sarah and Mary-Kate and that would be so hard, so very hard. She couldn't leave them in ignorance as she'd left Edward. Tears started in her eyes at the thought of him, but there was no time now for regrets or for wishing things had been different. He didn't love her. Oh, he was fond of her and Mary-Kate had mistaken that affection for love. But it wasn't love. She sighed. She'd write now. She couldn't put off things until another day as she'd always done in the past.

She'd made two attempts to explain to Sarah and had consigned them both to the paperbasket. She'd started the third when the doorbell rang. For a brief, fleeting moment she hoped he'd come back. But why should he? Wearily she made her way to the door. She didn't really care who it was. Even if Helen had decided to come back, she didn't care now.

A young lad, dressed in a dark blue uniform that was too big for him stood on the step. 'Miss Gina O'Donnell?'

She nodded and he handed her a buff-coloured envelope, then jumped on his bike and pedalled off, whistling.

She walked slowly back into the lounge, turning the envelope over in her hand. A telegram. Perhaps it was from Jimmie, to cheer her up. Poor Jimmie. She'd been so cruel to him. But this was just the sort of thing he'd do. None of the others would think of such a gesture. She was a social leper, an outcast to them now. Even Jimmie had left town, but hadn't he said he was thinking about her?

She ripped it open. The short message danced before her eyes and she crumpled it up in her hand. She felt as though she'd been clubbed over the head. No! It couldn't be true. Not that, not now! She sank down on the sofa and pressed her cheek against the cushions and broke down. The years had rolled back and she was standing beside a yawning hole in St Mary's churchyard and her heart was breaking all over again. 'Oh, Pa! Pa! Why did you have to die? None of this would have happened if you'd lived. I wouldn't have caught consumption if I'd stayed at home, but I wanted to make you proud of me and I went on and on, trying to grasp more and more and now there's nothing left. Nothing that I really care about. There's no one who cares about me,' she sobbed. She looked around the room with dull hatred. Its glaring, brash vulgarity was the epitome of what she had become. She struggled to her feet and, turning, saw Edward standing in the doorway.

'The door was open, Gina. I saw the doctor, he . . . he told me. I had to come back.'

She held out her arms and within seconds he was holding her in his embrace.

'Oh, Edward, I've been such a fool. I love you! I love you, but I had to let you go!'

'Hush. Hush now. I'm back and I won't leave you.'

'Take me to Ireland, Edward. Please?'

'Gina. My brave, sweet darling! Of course I'll take you back. We'll be married there and I'll take care of you. You'll have the very best of everything.'

'It's no use, it's too late!'

'No, it's never too late.'

She turned her wan, tear-streaked face upwards. 'You're wrong Edward, it is too late.'

He saw the paper clutched tightly in her hand. Gently he pried open her fingers and took it and read it. It was from Matty. A few words. But a few words that would change so many lives.

Gina. Ma died last night. Heart Attack. Come
Home Immediately.
Matty.

He led her to the sofa and gently sat her down, drawing her close to him. 'Gina, I'm sorry. So very sorry. She was a wonderful woman and I admired her greatly.'

'Why now? Why now when I need her so much?'

He stroked her hair. 'I can't give you an answer to that, my darling. But Gina, why didn't you tell me? Why didn't you tell anyone?'

'Because I just couldn't stand being an object of pity.'

'You wouldn't have been. Not to me. I know how brave you are. You've never lacked guts. My God, it's taken a hell of a lot of courage to keep going all this time alone. Thank God I came back. I could have gone and never known, never even guessed.' He held her tightly. The thought made cold shivers run down his spine. He could have gone and then he would have read in some newspaper somewhere that she'd died and he would never have forgiven himself.

She dabbed her eyes with her handkerchief. 'When can we go? I don't want to stay here now. I hate this place.'

'Don't worry about that. I'll make all the arrangements. Just tell me you'll marry me, Gina, and then we'll go to Switzerland.'

She sighed. Oh, it was so hard but she had to do it. She could no longer go on being so totally self-centred. 'I don't want to go to Switzerland, Edward. I just want to go home. I . . . I can't marry you.'

He held her away from him and looked down into her eyes. 'Why? You said . . .'

She pressed her fingertips against his lips to silence him. 'It's not fair. It's not right. No, listen to me, Edward, please. For years I've thought only of myself – of my career and my ambitions, but now everything has changed. I'm thinking of you. It just wouldn't be fair to you. I can't give you children, I can't even make plans for next year. Marriage is a commitment and I don't want you to feel bound by anything like that. I don't want you to think of it all as a duty. It's just not fair on you, my love.'

'But Gina, it's a commitment I want to make. For

God's sake, I love you. It has nothing to do with duty. I want to be with you. I want to take care of you. We've wasted so much time, please don't let us squander what we have left. Marry me, Gina?'

Her heart felt as though it were bursting. She didn't deserve him, not after the way she'd treated him.

He cupped her chin in his hand, forcing her to look up into his face. 'Marry me?'

Slowly she nodded and then he kissed her gently on the lips.

'But I still don't feel as though I'm being fair.'

'All's fair in love and war, Gina, and as you and I are no longer at war, I'm the one who will decide if it's fair, and I've made up my mind that you will be Mrs Edward Vinetti.'

She smiled. 'But what will you do? The theatre is your life.'

'Not any more. I was leaving anyway, remember, and besides how could I go back to that? It would all seem so empty and useless.'

She was a little more composed now. Calmness and, in a strange way, relief and contentment filled her. 'What will you do?' she persisted. 'I don't want you to feel bound to play nursemaid.'

He leaned back against the cushions, drawing her head against his chest. 'I'd not thought. It's all happened so fast.' He fell silent and she lay in the crook of his arm, listening to the steady beat of his heart.

'What kind of a farmer do you think I'd make?' he asked.

A smile crossed her face. 'Are you serious?'

'Of course. I think I'd enjoy it and they say hard

labour is good for the soul. It could be my salvation.'

'Oh, Edward, you can't even ride a horse.' There wasn't a trace of mockery in her voice.

'I could learn.'

'You mean buy a farm of our own?'

'I was thinking more along the lines of throwing in my lot with Matty and Richard, if they'll have me. I could suggest that I buy my way into some sort of partnership.'

Edward was doing this for her sake, she knew, and she tightened her arms around his chest. 'I'm not the ideal person for a farmer's wife, am I? I could give the occasional performance. Sing in the choir or at a wedding or two.'

'You could, so long as it doesn't tire you, but there's no need.'

'I'd like to.'

'So, do you think they'd have me?'

'I think they'd be delighted. They'll be able to expand and buy more land and machinery. They'll hire more men and before you know where you are you'll be three "Gentleman Farmers" owning half the county. They may even have you out with the Tipperary Hunt.' She fought to keep her tone light.

'Then it's settled. I know it may sound insensitive of me to ask this right now, but what about the wedding?'

'It can't be right away, not with Ma . . .' The tears brimmed up again and the lump in her throat choked off her words.

'I know that, but I'm sure the priest will understand when we explain and arrange a dispensation or whatever is necessary.' He kissed the tip of her nose. 'And I'll have to go to confession for the first time in decades and hope they haven't excommunicated me by now. Oh, Gina O'Donnell, the tortures you're putting me through.' He wiped away the tears from her cheek with the tip of his finger and smiled in his old, half-cynical way.

She caught his hand and held it against her cheek. She was so lucky to have him. Despite the sorrow, she felt as though some of her old spirit had returned. 'I'm not giving in to it, Edward, I'm not going to become an invalid overnight!'

He laughed. 'That sounds more like you. I've a feeling that you are going to make a very unsatisfactory patient, but I'll let Doctor Byrne worry about that!'

Chapter Twenty-Eight

———◆———

EILEEN AND LESTER SINCLAIR had announced their engagement and Bridget had put on a small family party for them. She'd invited his parents and two sisters, Archie and Bernie and two of the girls from Craig's that Eileen was very friendly with.

The Sinclairs were nice people and everyone liked Lester. Bridget was glad, for Eileen deserved a good man. Bridget had promised to bear the full cost of a splendid traditional wedding and had given the couple a good deposit for a home of their own. So as not to injure Archie's pride, she had agreed when he insisted on paying for the drink, a far from small contribution since all of Craig's and most of Dixon's Blazes appeared to have been invited. They had all laughed when Bernie had said what a pity it was that baby Louisa Bernadette Dalrymple couldn't be bridesmaid, and she hoped that all Archie's cronies would behave themselves, otherwise the whole thing would end up a right stramash altogether, and she wasn't having Eileen's day ruined, and Bridget's money wasted, by a crowd of Scots-Irish drunks.

'Michael, will you see that Mr Sinclair has his glass refilled before you make your speech,' Bridget whispered, keeping an eagle-eye on her guests' comfort.

'Do I have to make a speech? It's really Archie's place, not mine. She's his sister.'

'Oh, you know Archie. He's grand on speeches about workers' rights, but when it comes to something like this he gets all embarrassed and tongue-tied. And anyway, you promised.'

'Oh, very well. You know you're getting to be a very domineering woman, Bridget O'Donnell,' he laughed.

'It's probably got something to do with my job,' she teased. They were so at ease with one another now, she thought. There was an understanding between them, although no words, no promises and no questions had been uttered. 'Is everyone here?'

'Everyone except Alizon from Craig's.'

Bridget's gaze swept the room. She nodded. 'She should be here any minute now. She's always late. Eileen says she will be late for her own funeral. We'll have to wait for her.'

'Not any longer,' he answered, as the doorbell rang.

'Don't you be thinking you're escaping! I'll go.'

Bridget pulled open the front door. 'Alizon MacLean, we're all waiting on you. Oh . . .' Her voice trailed off as she saw the boy on the bicycle.

'Miss O'Donnell?'

She nodded and he handed her the envelope. She went cold; telegrams were always such harbingers of bad news. She slipped into the morning room to open it.

She was still standing there, staring into space, her face white, when Michael came looking for her.

'Bridget?' He saw the piece of paper in her hand and took it from her. Then he took her in his arms.

'Why can't I cry, Michael? Why can't I cry?' she said in a strangled voice.

'It's the shock. The tears will come later.'

She looked up at him. Theirs was a love that had needed no words; words could be false and empty. Nor did they need constantly to reassure each other. There was no need to shout their feelings from the rooftops; they were kindred spirits. 'Will we go home, Michael?' was all she said.

He nodded slowly. He loved her deeply with a love that had matured and developed ever since that first night when they'd sat up and talked. That night she had set in motion the healing process that was gradually obliterating the deep scars of guilt. She'd offered him peace and stability and for the first time in years, happiness.

'Home for good, Bridget?'

'Yes.'

'What about all this? Your job – you've worked so hard?'

'None of that matters now, Michael. I've proved to myself that I could realize my dreams. I wish she could have come here, to have seen everything I've done. Oh, Michael, I do love you.' She leaned her cheek against his shoulder.

'Then we'll go home and we'll be married.' It was a statement made in a firm, quiet voice. It was time – time to put his feelings of trepidation aside, and time to think of Bridget and of building a new life together. For her he'd be prepared to face his fears. Fears that would probably always be with him. His love for her would help him. She was worth it.

Mary-Kate dropped her head in her hands. Oh, Ma! Why hadn't Matty said she was ill? Why hadn't he sent for her sooner? She'd planned to take Ellen and Jamie home this summer, but Sarah would never see her grandson now. The pain in her heart grew unbearable. Oh, there were so many things that had remained unsaid. Of them all, she had been closest to Sarah, but she had put off the visit and for what? Business, money, contracts. What were they beside the loss she now felt? Nothing. They didn't matter at all. They should never have mattered. Sarah had come to her when Lewis had died. She'd comforted her, but Mary-Kate hadn't been there to hold Sarah's hand at the end. Life had been good to her. God had been good to her, despite the loss of Lewis. But now the world was a bleak and bitter place and she had been left without the one person who understood her most. Left to cope with her grief, her loss and her guilt.

She felt a hand on her shoulder and lifted her head.

Ellen was standing beside her. 'Why are you crying, Ma?'

'It's my . . . your Grandma, Ellen. She died last night.'

Ellen stared directly at her. She had seen so much of death in her short life. Her mother, her baby brother, her Pa and now the grandmother she had grown to love and to whom she had written every week. Why was it that as soon as you learned to love someone, God snatched them away from you? She reached out for Mary-Kate's hand. 'Will you be going home, Ma?'

Mary-Kate nodded. 'Yes, Ellen, we're all going home.'

There had been no traditional wake. Mary-Kate and Bridget had vehemently over-ruled Matty and Uncle Richard on that, because of Gina's condition. Bridget, nerves taut with grief, had stormed that she didn't care if everyone from here to Waterford talked about them, there would be no wake. So Sarah had been buried on the 21st February, on a damp, grey depressing morning. But the weather had not deterred half the town from turning out and the family had all been deeply touched by the gesture. The hard, frozen earth had been freshly dug. The grave-diggers had leaned on their shovels, caps respectfully in their hands, while Father Maguire had committed Sarah's body to the ground. On the white marble headstone that bore the names of their father and their elder brother, another name had already been added.

> 'Sarah Margaret O'Donnell
> Wife of Patrick and
> mother of Fergal
> God Rest her Soul'

Mary-Kate, with Ellen at her side and her son in her arms, had watched with the calm composure that was so characteristic of her. Her time of weeping for Sarah was over, but the pain would always remain. Her mother's death had allowed her to come and find a brief period of happiness 'across the water' in Ireland. So near yet so far. But she had her son and Ellen and her memories, together with the promise she'd made, that for the rest of her life she would try to be as good a mother to them as Sarah had been to her. And Mary-Kate never broke a promise.

Gina's head had rested against Edward's shoulder, his arm firmly around her waist. It had taken her own illness and her mother's death to make her realize just what were the most precious things in life. Not fame or money. Not adulation or power. But there hadn't been time to tell Sarah that. Gina had accepted her fate now, thankful that she had been given the gifts of love and happiness – for a little while.

She had glanced at her younger sister. Bridget had got what she wanted from life, but she'd suffered and changed during the process and Gina's mind had gone back to that day – that April day so long ago – when they'd all stood here and Michael Feehey and his cronies had taunted them. He'd changed, too, she'd thought. His own parents were buried in that churchyard.

Edward had remembered that fine, sunny day when he'd first seen Clonmel. The few weeks he had spent here had been the happiest in his life, except for the bitter-sweet time that he and Gina had left. He grieved for Sarah but he knew she would have approved of their forthcoming marriage. Just how he would cope in the days that lay ahead he didn't know, but he'd make Gina happy and he'd pray for the courage to keep going. Silently he had thanked Sarah for the priceless legacy she'd left him.

Bridget had remembered her mother as she had been

the last time she'd seen her, at Mary-Kate's wedding, and she'd wished that she hadn't rushed straight back to Glasgow after Lewis Vannin had died, thereby missing seeing Sarah. She'd remembered how at the wedding she had been so ashamed of her shabby clothes and her poor job, and she wished that Sarah could have lived to see how she had put all that behind her and to have given her blessing to her marriage to Michael. Bridget had squeezed his hand, knowing that he, too, would be remembering.

He had, but not with a sorrow that was born only of love and loss. His sorrow was born of guilt and remorse. He hadn't even been there when they had buried his parents. He'd been hiding; skulking in the wild bog and bracken of the Comeraghs. He thought that time had healed those scars, but standing there in the churchyard had re-opened the wounds. The tightening of Bridget's hand in his reminded him that no amount of torturing himself would bring them back, or remove the fear of his former comrades' fanatical threats against him.

Matty's heart had been heavy. He hadn't been able to take it in that Sarah had gone. That she'd never again be waiting when he came in tired and cold from the fields, a hot meal on the table, a welcoming fire in the range and the unfailing admonition, 'Get those clumping great boots off my clean floor, Matty O'Donnell. This is my kitchen, not a shebeen.' Now it would be Gina's kitchen, but he was still struggling with the fact that his beautiful, talented sister would probably never see the red and gold leaves of the trees that bordered the churchyard flutter to the ground in autumn.

*

The following day could have been a day in April, so different was it from the day before. Winters in the south-east of Ireland were often damp and mild, with occasional days that were almost like spring. The sky was pale blue with not a cloud in sight and the sun was warm on their faces as they sat in a corner of the yard, where for the past four years Sarah had planted geraniums, marigolds and sweet, night-scented stock.

It was so mild that everyone had agreed it would benefit Gina to be out in the fresh air and she sat, with rugs tucked around her, between her two sisters. Of the men there was no sign. They had all gone off to look at some land that was up for sale out towards Ballyboe, after having stayed up half the night listening to Edward's proposal that he buy his way into a partnership with them and turn his hand to farming.

'So, Edward is to become a farmer then?' Mary-Kate sounded faintly amused.

'He's going to try,' Gina answered.

'Those two were quick enough to accept his offer, so they must have some faith in him or his money. But why Michael has gone as well I don't know.' Bridget sounded a little put out.

'Perhaps it was to give us some time alone, or maybe he feels a little unsure of himself and other people's attitude to him,' Mary-Kate suggested.

'You may be right but he shouldn't be unsure now. He never committed a crime, no matter what some people will think and besides, everyone is trying to forget. Trying to build a new life out of the ruins of the old.'

Mary-Kate sighed. 'There are some who will neither forgive nor forget.'

'I know, but Matty said they've nearly all gone – either fled or imprisoned – and we've nothing to fear from them now.' Bridget paused. 'I'm going to instruct Mr Prebble to sell all my stocks and shares and the house in Cartland Drive. Eileen is staying with Bernie until the wedding.'

'So, you've come home for good, too?' Mary-Kate sounded wistful.

'Yes, we talked about it on the journey. We're going to open a shop in Clonmel, a very small department store and we're going to be married.' She reached out and took Gina's hand. For Gina's sake, too, they had come home to stay. She wanted to spend all the time she could – all the time there was left – with Gina. And she wanted to make that time as happy as was humanly possible. 'But I won't steal your glory, Gina. You must be married first. I'll never forgive myself for walking out of your party. Never.'

'Oh, Bridget, don't be an eejit. It was a terrible party and I was acting disgracefully and besides, how were you to know that I was ill?'

At the mention of her condition, it was as though a small cloud had crossed the face of the sun, until Gina smiled again. 'There will be no more talk of "stealing anyone's glory". We'll be married on the same day at a double wedding – here at Kilsheelan, where Ma and Pa were married. It will be the first double wedding at St Mary's and I won't hear a single word of objection, not at all! Haven't we always been different from everyone else? Haven't we always done things in style? Haven't we all achieved what we set out to do? What was it I said to Michael?'

'Rich and famous or both,' Bridget reminded her laughingly.

'And between us all we managed it, one way or another,' Mary-Kate reflected.

'So it will be a double wedding,' Gina persisted.

'If that's what you want.'

'I do, so that's settled.'

'And when will it be?' Mary-Kate asked.

'Just as soon as we can get a dispensation and get things arranged. You will stay on, won't you?'

Mary-Kate smiled at Gina. 'Of course I will. The business will survive without me for a while and besides, I couldn't miss the event of the year now could I? Sure, they'll come from miles around, you see if they don't. The famous Miss Gina O'Donnell and the wealthy Miss Bridget O'Donnell. You'll be the talk of the place for months.'

Mary-Kate glanced out of the bedroom window. 'I don't think it's going to rain after all, there's a patch of bright sky over towards the river.'

The room was in complete disorder with clothes and boxes, small parcels and tissue paper on every available surface. Bridget and Gina were to be married at ten o'clock that morning and everyone, except Gina, had been up for hours. Mary-Kate turned around and surveyed the scene, shaking her head. It was just like the old days in Anne Street, before they had left Ireland. She herself was ready, dressed in a silver grey, long sleeved two-piece. The skirt was plain and almost straight as was the jacket, which ended just on the hipline. The top was fastened down the left side with black velvet frogging and the cuffs were trimmed with black. On the bed, grouped neatly together, were the silver-grey toque hat with its cluster of black feathers and her bag and gloves. Her expression softened as she watched Gina, seated before the dressing table, carefully applying just the slightest touch of rouge to her pale cheeks, while Bridget searched amongst the discarded boxes and tissue on the bed for her shoes.

She found one. 'Oh, just look at this mess. Where has the other one gone? I could have sworn I'd kept them in the box.'

'It's beside Gina's hat and you're right, this is a nice mess. The only consolation is that probably Matty's and Uncle Richard's rooms are in the same state.'

'Has Matty gone yet? He was supposed to be at Hearn's Hotel at a quarter past nine,' Gina said, hair brush halted in mid-stroke. As there was no one in Clonmel that Edward knew well enough, Matty was to be his best man. Uncle Richard was giving them both away.

'Stop fretting, he's gone.'

'Oh, I just hope Michael hasn't a hangover. Dinny MacGee isn't exactly a person who thinks in terms of moderation,' Bridget muttered.

'I hope none of them are feeling under the weather. I don't know what time it was when Matty and Uncle Richard got home last night, but they made enough noise trying to be quiet and Uncle Richard looked a bit sheepish early this morning,' Mary-Kate remarked.

All the male members of the wedding party had gone to Mulcahy's Bar the previous evening at the suggestion of Dinny MacGee, who was to be Michael's best man. He and Michael had quickly resumed their old friendship and Dinny was now a married man himself although, as Bridget remarked, Mary Kennedy didn't seem to have had much of a restraining influence on him.

'How do you feel?' Mary-Kate asked, taking the hairbrush from Gina and giving the shiny Titian waves a last brush, before placing the small, lilac cloche hat over them. As they were still in mourning, their choice of colours had been very limited. Bridget and Ellen had accompanied Mary-Kate to Dublin to buy all their outfits, including Gina's, and Mrs O'Leary had been most helpful with alterations and trimmings. Lilac suited Gina. She'd insisted that white would make her look ghastly, and she had been delighted with Bridget's idea of the cape.

Her dress was of crêpe de chine with a bias cut skirt and long sleeves. A small bunch of white artificial flowers -- supplied by Mrs O'Leary – had been added at the high neckline. But the material was too flimsy to be worn in early March and so Bridget had bought yards of lilac wool crepon in the same shade and Mrs O'Leary had run up the cape to Bridget's design. Mary-Kate had unpicked the rows of pearl beading from one of Gina's evening gowns and had sewn this around the border. It had been a labour of love on her part and the loose, flowing garment that resembled an evening cloak, now lay on the bed.

'I feel nervous, that's how I feel. Not sickly nervous, just excitedly nervous,' Gina replied, smiling at Mary-Kate in the mirror. 'I haven't over done the rouge, have I?'

'No, you look beautiful. You both look beautiful.'

'I knew I should have let Celia Delaney trim my

hair, this hat just won't sit right!' Bridget was struggling with the small-brimmed white straw with its large white satin bow. 'Oh, I'm so nervous, I'm all fingers and thumbs.'

'Sit down and let me try.' Mary-Kate moved calmly from Gina to her youngest sister and began to smooth down the thick, auburn hair before placing the hat at just the right angle and securing it with a pearl-topped hat pin. 'You'll freeze in that dress, Bridget. Oh, I know you fell in love with it straight away and it's not needed to have a single alteration, but I did warn you that it was more suitable for summer. You're shivering already.'

'But not with cold.' Bridget smoothed down the white lace skirt. She'd chosen lace over heavy white satin, but the sleeves were unlined and her arms were covered only by the flimsy lace.

Ellen poked her head around the door. 'Ma, there's a woman downstairs asking to see Aunt Bridget.'

'Oh, not Mrs Butler-Power again! Ellen, tell her I can't see her, tell her anything,' Bridget cried.

Just as Mary-Kate had predicted, word of their weddings had soon got around and they had all been surprised by the gifts and tokens they had received. Mrs O'Leary – who was finally to become the second Mrs Ryan in May – had been most helpful, for Bridget and Michael were to buy her shop and the grocery next door. They were going to live above the premises, but until Mrs O'Leary had moved out they were renting a small house she had found for them down near the Quays. This arrangement had almost caused open warfare to break out between Mrs O'Leary and Mrs Butler-Power, who had no intention of being left out of the event which was becoming the talk of half the county. She had been 'dropping in' with increasing regularity in an attempt to become involved and therefore to gain first-hand information about what was going on. This was mainly to spite Mrs O'Leary, whom she considered to be a social upstart and quite unworthy of being the wife of a solicitor altogether.

'It's not her. I know *her* well enough by now,' Ellen replied.

'Who is it then?'

'She said to tell Aunt Bridget that she's Mrs Dalrymple's mother.'

Mary-Kate's eyebrows rose.

'Mrs O'Hagan? Bernie's Ma is downstairs?' Bridget sounded stunned.

Ellen nodded. 'Shall I tell her you're not dressed?'

'No. I'll come down.'

'Ellen, is Jamie all right?' Mary-Kate asked.

'Of course he is Ma and he's not even a little bit grubby.'

'I knew I could rely on you, dear, but just make sure you don't get any marks on your dress.'

Ellen raised her eyes to the ceiling and grinned, but secretly she was pleased. She was to be a bridesmaid and Mary-Kate was matron of honour. The plain russet taffeta dress with its dropped waist and softly pleated skirt was the first 'grown up' dress she'd had and, with her hair swept up and circled by a headband of matching material, she felt very much a young lady.

When Bridget entered the kitchen the small, thin woman in the drab dark brown coat looked as though she'd seen a vision. She bit her lip and nervously fiddled with the one button that held the coat fastened. 'Oh, don't you look just like an angel,' she stammered.

'Thank you, Mrs O'Hagan. It was nice of you to call.'

As Bridget extended her hand, she seemed to shrink further into the folds of the old, shabby garment. Awkwardly she rubbed her right hand on the side of the coat before giving Bridget a limp handshake. Then she looked around timorously. 'Sure, I don't think I should have come up here at all.'

'Why not?'

'Well, it's only folk like Mrs O'Leary, grand folk, who should come calling. But I wanted to thank you for my Bernie.' She bit her lip again. 'I wish I had something to give you ... a Mass Card even, but ...' She shuffled her feet. 'I just came to wish you good luck and God's Blessing on you. I'll be going now.' She turned away, her eyes fixed on the door as though she expected the Taoiseach himself to come through it at any minute.

'Mrs O'Hagan, don't go yet, please.'

She turned. 'Oh, I wouldn't want to be here when anyone else comes or to be holding up the "dressing up".'

Bridget smiled at this description of the morning's activities. 'We're all ready, and thank you for coming. I do mean that. Bernie is my closest friend and she was very good to me when I needed help.'

Some of the uneasiness left the older woman's face and her shoulders became less rounded. 'She's a fine, grand girl my Bernie, isn't she?' Before Bridget could reply, Mrs O'Hagan looked around and lowered her voice as though they were about to be overheard. 'She wants me to go to see her and stay with her. She said she'll send me the money. Father Maguire reads her letters to me.'

'So when are you going?'

'Oh, I'm not. Himself wouldn't stand for that. Not for me going off on my own all that way and leaving him with no one to see to him.'

Bridget nodded. What Mrs O'Hagan hadn't said was that her idle, useless husband would take any money Bernie sent and drink himself and his tinker friends under the table with it. 'Why don't I ask Bernie to have a photograph taken of herself and baby Louisa Bernadette in the nursery. She could send it to you.'

'Oh, would you do that? Would you really? Oh, isn't it a great thing altogether that a baby can have a room all to itself?'

Mrs O'Hagan was so proud that the expression on her face tugged at Bridget's heart. 'It is and she'll probably come home to see you all one day.'

Mary-Kate came into the room carrying her bag and gloves. 'Mrs O'Hagan, how good of you to call.'

'I just wanted to wish you all well. 'Tis little enough.' The timid, uncomfortable look was back and after waving her hands once in a gesture of nervous agitation she sidled towards the door. 'Well, I won't be keeping you now . . .'

Mary-Kate glanced at Bridget, then she smiled. 'Could you do me a great favour, Mrs O'Hagan?'

'Me? What can I be doing?'

'As Ellen is to be bridesmaid she won't be able to look after my son all the time. Would you look after him in church and see he doesn't start a riot?'

Mrs O'Hagan looked dumbfounded and Bridget looked at her sister as though she'd gone raving mad.

'Oh, I couldn't do that. Not me! Not with everyone from miles around there watchin'. I was just going to try to slip in at the back if there was room.'

'Of course you can do it. Haven't you a wealth of experience with small, unruly children?'

'But . . . but what will people say? We've never been . . . like you.'

'Haven't you the right to be up with the best of them? That house in Glasgow doesn't belong solely to Archie you know. It's half Bernie's too, Bridget tells me. Bernie's a woman of some standing now – a woman of property – and she's your daughter.'

A look of wonderment crept slowly over the pale, pinched face. 'She is that, too. I'd not thought of it like that.'

'Good, then Ellen will hand Jamie over to you. Usually he's not much trouble and then when we come out of church you can pass him back to me.'

'Right then. I'd best be getting down there, hadn't I?'

When she'd gone Bridget turned to Mary-Kate. 'Honestly, you'd find goodness in all the imps of Hell, Mary-Kate.'

'Lewis said something like that once, but God above, she's had such a desperate life, poor soul, that I felt sorry for her.'

'The tongues will be wagging all the way to Cahir and Mrs Butler-Power will be ready to commit murder!'

'Ah, let them talk. The only good thing Mrs O'Hagan has to cling to in her miserable life is the way her Bernie has turned out, and everyone should have something to be proud of. And I really did need someone to look after Jamie,' Mary-Kate added.

Ellen came back into the room. 'Uncle Richard is in the parlour having "a hair of the dog" and Aunt Gina's ready. She's on her way down. Where did you put the flowers, Ma?'

'They're out in the wash house. I hope they haven't wilted. Will you get them Ellen?'

Ellen disappeared and returned almost simultaneously with Gina. She handed the two bouquets of white Madonna lilies that Edward had had sent down from Dublin to Gina and Bridget. There was a spray of roses for Mary-Kate. Her own small posy she placed on the dresser.

'They're beautiful. It was so good of him and they must have cost a small fortune at this time of the year,' Mary-Kate said as Ellen helped her to pin the spray to her dress. 'I think Ma would have approved and she'd have been so proud of you both.'

Bridget swallowed hard. 'I thought it was very thoughtful of you to have chosen her favourite hymns. Sure, Gina can't sing at her own wedding and anyone else would have just murdered *Ave Maria*.' She tried to lift the air of sadness that had descended.

'Yes, everyone can join in with hymns they know well. Ma always said *Hail Queen of Heaven* reminded her of us and our wanderings and that *Sweet Saviour Bless Us* was guaranteed to give you hope and strength,' Mary-Kate said with a tender smile.

As she touched the soft petals of the lilies, Gina remembered the whole of the hymn whose few lines had filled her with fear and despair not so long ago. She sang them softly to herself.

> 'Sweet Saviour Bless us e're we go
> Thy love into our minds instil
> And make our lukewarm hearts to glow
> With thine own love and perfect peace
> Through life's long day
> And death's dark night
> O Gentle Jesus be our light'

Ellen broke the silent reverie by pouring four small glasses of sherry and suggesting that they all cheer up. Her smile crumpled as Mary-Kate pointed out that as they were all going to Holy Communion they couldn't break their fast.

'But Uncle Richard has!' Ellen was stricken.

'That's his affair! If he wants everyone to talk about him, it's on his own head,' Gina replied with some spirit.

Mary-Kate had been thinking of her own wedding day. Of her mother and Lewis and of the fact that Gina hadn't been there that day. But now at last the three of them were together. She smiled at Ellen while stroking the head of her son who was clinging to her skirt. Despite her smile and the love and joy in her heart for her sisters, she felt the tears prick her eyes. For Ellen and Jamie, Liverpool was home and for their sakes it would become home for her, too. And when her time came they would bury her body in Ford Cemetery with Lewis, but her heart and her spirit would always be here in Cluain Meala – the Honey Meadow.

Bridget picked up a glass. 'Never mind Ellen, it was a

lovely thought and we could still have a toast by just putting our glasses together.' She handed a glass to each of her sisters. 'To us all!'

With a laugh that reminded them of the healthy, vivacious girl who had enchanted the guests at the castle across the river with her pure, young voice, Gina touched her glass first to Mary-Kate's then to Bridget's.

'A toast then. To "The Sisters O'Donnell"!'

Author's Note

Many people have contributed and assisted me during the researching and writing of this book, but I would particularly like to express my gratitude to my friend, Mrs Brenda Whelan, for advice on the world of the Theatre Musical. For her wealth of knowledge and experience of both Glasgow and the Department Store, Copeland and Lye, which she so willingly and unstintingly shared with me, my friend and colleague, Mrs Kathleen Baird. And last but by no means least, all my friends at Marks & Spencer's Southport Store, for their unflagging interest and encouragement.

My Great-Grandmother, Mary O'Donnell, came to Liverpool from Clonmel, Co. Tipperary, in the latter part of the last century and this is, in part, her story. Therefore, I would like to dedicate this book to her memory. I never knew you but I owe you so much Mary-Kate.

Lyn Andrews

Every Mother's Son

Lyn Andrews

Molly Keegan and Bernie O'Sullivan have been friends forever. As young girls they left Ireland seeking exciting new beginnings in Liverpool. And now, as young women, they are marrying their sweethearts and looking forward to enjoying the lives they've worked so hard to build. But as the Liverpool Blitz begins, it seems as if their dreams are about to be destroyed.

Night after night, horrific bombing tears the city apart. Every day Molly and Bernie struggle to keep their families safe. As wives and mothers, both know that they could face great tragedy. But they also know that their friendship, and their love for their husbands and sons, will give them the strength to find the happiness they deserve . . .

Praise for Lyn Andrews' unforgettable novels

'Gutsy . . . a vivid picture of a hard-up, hard-working community . . . will keep the pages turning' *Daily Express*

'Lyn Andrews presents her readers with more than just another saga of romance and family strife. She has a realism that is almost tangible' *Liverpool Echo*

978 0 7553 0842 2

headline

From This Day Forth

Lyn Andrews

Next-door neighbours Celia and Lizzie are the best of friends. But their families, the Miltons and the Slatterys, are the worst of enemies, divided by religion and by their men's status at the Cammell Laird's shipyard. Lizzie and Celia must keep their friendship a secret – for if Celia's violent father Charlie ever found out about it the consequences would be appalling.

But one day the unthinkable happens. Joe Slattery, Lizzie's brother, does a good turn for the Milton family. From that day forth, Celia Milton just can't get the dark-eyed Joe out of her mind. And, despite himself, Joe Slattery finds that he is increasingly drawn to the girl next door and to a love that seems doomed to heart-break – unless they can find a way around the prejudice of generations and the terrifying bigotry of Charlie Milton.

Praise for Lyn Andrews' unforgettable novels

'A compelling read' *Woman's Own*

'Gutsy . . . A vivid picture of a hard-up, hard-working community . . . will keep the pages turning' *Daily Express*

'The Catherine Cookson of Liverpool' *Northern Echo*

978 0 7472 5177 4

headline

Friends Forever

Lyn Andrews

In 1928 Bernie O'Sullivan and Molly Keegan catch their first glimpse of the bustling city they're about to call home. Both seventeen, and best friends since childhood, the girls have left Ireland behind to seek work and an exciting new life in Liverpool.

The girls are dismayed to discover that the relatives they are to stay with have barely two pennies to rub together; the promised grand house is a run-down building in one of Liverpool's worst slum areas. Desperate to escape the filthy streets, Bernie secures a position as a domestic servant, while Molly is taken on as a shop assistant. Soon they have settled in new rooms and find themselves in love with local men. For both, though, love holds surprises and the danger of ruin in an unforgiving world.

Bernie and Molly have tough times to face but the bond of their lifelong friendship gives them the strength to rise to every challenge and to hold on to their dreams.

Praise for Lyn Andrews' unforgettable novels

'A compelling read' *Woman's Own*

'Gutsy . . . A vivid picture of a hard-up, hard-working community . . . will keep the pages turning' *Daily Express*

978 0 7553 0840 8

headline

Now you can buy any of these other bestselling books by **Lyn Andrews** from your bookshop or *direct from the publisher*.

FREE P&P AND UK DELIVERY
(Overseas and Ireland £3.50 per book)

Far From Home	£6.99
Every Mother's Son	£6.99
Friends Forever	£6.99
A Mother's Love	£6.99
Across a Summer Sea	£6.99
When Daylight Comes	£5.99
A Wing and a Prayer	£6.99
Love and a Promise	£6.99
The House on Lonely Street	£6.99
My Sister's Child	£6.99
Take These Broken Wings	£6.99
The Ties That Bind	£6.99
Angels of Mercy	£6.99
When Tomorrow Dawns	£6.99
From This Day Forth	£6.99
Where the Mersey Flows	£6.99
Liverpool Songbird	£6.99

TO ORDER SIMPLY CALL THIS NUMBER

01235 400 414

or visit our website: www.headline.co.uk

Prices and availability subject to change without notice.